THE
RELUCTANT
MATADOR

A Hugo Marston Novel

THE
RELUCTANT
MATADOR

MARK PRYOR

SEVENTH STREET BOOKS®
AN IMPRINT OF PROMETHEUS BOOKS
59 JOHN GLENN DRIVE • AMHERST, NY 14228
www.seventhstreetbooks.com

Published 2015 by Seventh Street Books®, an imprint of Prometheus Books

Cover image © Bigstock
Cover design by Grace M. Conti-Zilsberger
Taurus ornament courtesy of Stefan Stenudd

This is a work of fiction. Characters, organizations, products, locales, and events portrayed in this novel either are products of the author's imagination or are used fictitiously.

Inquiries should be addressed to
Seventh Street Books
59 John Glenn Drive
Amherst, New York 14228
VOICE: 716–691–0133
FAX: 716–691–0137
WWW.SEVENTHSTREETBOOKS.COM

19 18 17 16 15   5 4 3 2 1

Library of Congress Cataloging-in-Publication Data

Pryor, Mark, 1967-
     The reluctant matador : a Hugo Marston novel / by Mark Pryor.
          pages ; cm
     ISBN 978-1-63388-002-3 (pbk.) — ISBN 978-1-63388-003-0 (e-book)
     I. Title.

PS3616.R976R45 2015
813'.6—dc23

                                                                2015003738

Printed in the United States of America

To Henry, my cuddle-bug, my giggling partner, my tough-tackling toad. Best of all, my son. Be all that you can be, but remain all that you are— sweet, thoughtful, funny, a light of my life.

AUTHOR'S NOTE

As much as I love Paris and Barcelona, I have been forced to take occasional liberties with their history and geography. Events have been created and streets invented to suit my own selfish needs. All errors and misrepresentations intentional and otherwise, are mine and mine alone.

CHAPTER ONE

A gentle breeze greeted Hugo Marston as he stepped out of his apartment building onto an empty Rue Jacob. At seven a.m. on a Sunday, the tourists and working people of Paris were still sleeping, though Hugo knew the calm and quiet wouldn't last much more than an hour.

He felt a rumble in his stomach, already picturing the treat he'd planned: pancakes, maple syrup, bacon, sausages. . . . He did this once or twice a year—the Texan in him yearning for a ranch-sized breakfast to start an otherwise empty weekend. He tucked his hands in his pockets and started to stroll toward the River Seine, the early-morning air clean and invigorating.

It didn't take long, though, for a sliver of impatience to tug at him as he walked. This breakfast wasn't just for himself; it was a chance to check in with the young lady who was the closest thing he had to a daughter. A young lady who was a stranger to Paris and, unless he'd read her tone wrong, a young lady in some measure of trouble.

Amy was in Paris for the same reason any nineteen-year-old American girl might be—to see the sights and make her fortune. She was the daughter of Hugo's friend and former colleague, Bart Denum. Stepdaughter, to be precise. Her last name was Dreiss, not Denum, but in every way other than legal, she was Denum's baby girl. Hugo had come to know her as a result of an accident that had savaged his life and theirs—Hugo's first wife, Ellie, had been a passenger in the car Amy's mother was driving when they were hit by a pickup truck. The old man driving it hadn't seen the stop light, or perhaps had ignored it. Police said that the man was sober, just old, and that was no crime.

Old or not, crime or not, Hugo had lost the love of his life that evening, and Amy had lost her mother. It was a shared tragedy that brought Bart and Hugo closer and Amy deeper into Hugo's world. She was the sweet, pretty girl flitting in and out of his life whenever he and Denum hung out on weekends and holidays, the teenager who never became surly, just hugged a little less. She wasn't just Denum's little angel, she was his entire world, and Hugo adored her, too.

Hugo had spent a few minutes with Amy the week she'd come to Paris. It was the first time he'd seen her in more than three years, and he was startled by how much she'd changed, how she'd blossomed from a spidery, awkward teenager into a beautiful young woman. They'd had coffee in Montmartre, sitting outside a café that sprawled onto a cobbled street, one of the narrow, winding roads that snaked up toward Sacré-Coeur Basilica. She'd been as bubbly as he remembered, but he also had the sense she was there to explore on her own, and that Hugo was the surrogate father she didn't need watching over her shoulder. After half an hour, Hugo gave her his business card, scribbled his cell number and home address on the back.

"Go have fun, Amy," he said. "I'll get the coffee. You can get the next one when you get a job."

She took the card. "Thanks, Hugo."

"Call if you need anything. Anything at all. Or just show up; I'm always home."

"Not much of a party animal, huh?"

"No, but that reminds me. If you show up, you might meet Tom."

"Boyfriend?" She winked.

"Feels like it sometimes. He's an old friend from my FBI days. Your dad knows him, I think. Anyway, let's just say he's the wild one. Don't lend him money or buy him a drink."

"He sounds like fun."

"Tom is . . . fun." Hugo laughed. "But things never end up where you think they will. You can trust him with your life, no doubt, but if you go out partying with him, you usually end up having to."

Her laughter tinkled and several men nearby eyed her with undisguised interest. She reached over and kissed his cheek. "I'll call if I need anything, I promise."

♉

She had called, five days ago. She wouldn't tell him why or what she wanted, only that she needed to talk to him about something that she couldn't tell her dad, not yet. Hugo hadn't been comfortable with that but had suggested that they meet at a restaurant appropriately named Breakfast in America. She agreed but made him promise not to tell Bart anything, not until they'd spoken.

He'd almost broken that promise. Two texts and one phone call to confirm their meeting had gone unanswered. But then, yesterday, she sent one brief e-mail saying she'd be there, so he decided to wait and talk to her at breakfast. No need to panic Bart if she'd just lost her phone. He just hoped she'd show.

As he got close to the river, Hugo noticed a crowd gathered at the end of the Pont de l'Alma, their shouts quickening his step as he approached the bridge. He scanned the area to spot the problem but saw only the panicked faces of the crowd. He saw some people reaching for cell phones while others pointed down to the water. Two men broke from the group and started for the steps that led down to the river, and instinctively Hugo broke into a run. The three reached the bottom of the steps at the same time and one of them shouted at Hugo in French, telling him what he'd already guessed.

"There's someone in the water."

"Alive?" Hugo asked.

Neither man responded, and in seconds they were at the edge of the walkway, leaning over the metal railing as all three peered down into the murky water of the Seine. At first Hugo saw nothing, heard only the people on the bridge above shouting and the panting of the two men beside him. The water gave off a brackish, stale odor, and he wrinkled his nose.

Then he saw it—a shadow beneath the surface, barely three feet from the walkway. One of the other men, a young, black man in jeans and a brown leather jacket, saw it, too. The man hopped over the railing and crouched on the lip of concrete beside the water, one hand on a vertical rail and the other reaching out toward the object.

"I thought I saw movement, before we came down," the second man said. He was white and in his fifties, gray-haired but trim, wearing a blue suit with no tie. Expensive leather gloves poked out of his jacket pocket.

"From the bridge?" Hugo asked.

"*Oui.*"

"I can't reach," the black man said, "grab my wrist so I can lean farther out."

The water was unusually high thanks to a wet summer in Burgundy, where the Seine began its journey. Here, in Paris, the river lapped at its artificial banks, threatening to spill over, and yet it seemed to Hugo the waters wanted to hang on to their human prize, taunting the rescuers by keeping the black shape out of their reach.

"I have a better idea," Hugo said. He slipped off his belt and ran the end through the buckle to make a short lasso. His eyes scanned the water, hoping to see a splash, a wriggle, any movement at all. Nothing. He handed the belt over anyway.

The young man leaned out and flicked the loop of the belt toward the form in the water, but they all recoiled as the body suddenly rolled over.

"*Vite!*" the older man said. "He's still alive!"

On his third attempt, the younger man splashed the water and grabbed an arm, pulling the unmoving figure to the bank. The three of them groaned and strained to pull the limp body up over the railing and lay it down on the concrete walkway.

"*Merde*, it's a woman," the young man said.

A naked woman, with dark-brown skin that had grayed with cold and exposure to the water. Hugo reached down and put his fingers on her throat, concentrating on feeling a pulse. His companions remained kneeling beside her body, staring. Staring not because the girl was naked, Hugo knew, but because the scene was surreal. Like him, they'd probably been out walking before the city woke, enjoying the cool October morning and savoring the gentle breeze playing up from the Seine. And now they were looking at a still, lifeless, young woman, battered and drowned by the river that until now had been an object of beauty to them.

"She's dead?" the older man whispered.

"*Oui*," Hugo said. He suspected she'd been dead for some time, her body cold and not just from the water. That claylike cold that all corpses possessed, the human body returning to its natural state, to the earth. Of the earth.

"Are you sure?" asked the younger man. "She moved in the water, we saw her. We should try CPR."

"No, it won't help," Hugo said. "She's gone. The movement was the current or maybe gas escaping from her body. A fish bumping her even, but she's dead for sure. And in case this isn't an accident, it's best we touch her as little as possible."

Hugo heard the distant wail of sirens, the cavalry arriving much too late on this occasion. He leaned over the body, careful not to touch any part of her, his FBI instincts kicking in, the policeman in him wanting to get a start on finding out how this young woman died. Maybe an accident, maybe suicide. Or possibly murder, his own field of expertise. He'd left that world behind when he joined the State Department to head up security at the US Embassies in London and now Paris. Or so he thought. Several times he'd been drawn back to his former life, been forced to use the skills he'd learned at the behavioral-sciences unit in Quantico to track down a killer. He had no great desire to do it again and would be happy to turn things over to the Brigade Criminelle, Paris's force responsible for handling kidnappings, arson, and murder. Hugo checked himself as he always did: *If this is murder*.

To that end, he couldn't help but look more closely. The girl appeared to be twenty years old, at most. With the drawn-down nature of death, it was hard to be sure, but Hugo thought she showed signs of malnutrition. He looked at the older man next to him.

"Can I borrow your gloves?" Hugo asked.

"My gloves? Why?"

"I'm a cop. I want to check something."

The man handed them over, eyeing Hugo uncertainly. "Shouldn't you wait for them?" He jerked his head toward the swelling sound of the sirens.

"Probably," Hugo muttered, taking the gloves. He pulled them on and picked up the girl's left arm, studying it carefully. He did the same with the right, then rolled her onto her side.

"*Monsieur, s'il vous plaît*, leave her alone!" The voice came from behind him and was a command, not a request. Hugo turned to see two uniformed *flics* approaching. He and the two other men moved away from the body.

"What happened here?" The cop in charge looked to be in his fifties, with a physique that suggested he exercised every day of his life. His head was bald and his eyes were suspicious. His colleague was half his age, slight and pale, and couldn't keep his eyes off the dead form on the riverwalk. *A rookie*, Hugo thought.

"They saw the body in the water, we just pulled her out," Hugo said.

"You're certain she's dead?"

"*Oui, absolutement.*"

The cop knelt beside the body to check for himself. "Then why were you touching her?"

Hugo reached into his pocket and pulled out his embassy credentials. "I didn't mean to interfere, *monsieur*, I'm a policeman at heart and saw a few things that concerned me. I used gloves and didn't contaminate the body, I assure you."

"You better hope not." The senior cop frowned and plucked Hugo's credentials from his hand. He scrutinized them for a moment, then looked up. "*Attendez*, you're Hugo Marston?"

"Yes."

The *flic* broke into a grin and offered his hand. "I'm Jules Agard. I'm a friend of Camille Lerens; she's told me all about you."

Hugo shook the man's hand and said, "Nice to meet you, Jules."

"Likewise. She seems to think you're some kind of crime-solving superhero."

Hugo laughed. "Then she doesn't know me very well, but thanks. How is she? I've not seen her for a couple of weeks and we're overdue a coffee, or something stronger."

He'd met Lieutenant Lerens during a murder investigation the previous year. She was, without doubt, one of the brightest and toughest *flics* in Paris. She had to be because, as far as Hugo knew, she was the only transgender cop in the city. Hugo knew that she still had problems with some older policemen, but her immediate superiors had quickly realized that her abilities and her dedication to her job were in no way related to her gender, and the institutional prejudice that initially blocked her career path eventually crumbled and let her progress up the ranks. Her wicked sense of humor did her no harm, either.

"You should call her," Agard said. "She spent last night in hospital after being assaulted by a drunk."

"*Vraiment?* Is she okay?"

"A few bumps and bruises. The *mec* has a few himself, as well as a serious charge to face."

"Good," said Hugo. "It wasn't to do with her . . ."

"*Non*," Agard said. "Some drunk English tourist. So, what do we have here?" He turned to his colleague. "Don't just stare, Bellard, get out your notebook and take some statements."

"*Oui, monsieur.*"

"Fresh out of the academy," Agard said under his breath. "*Alors*, you said you saw something that concerned you."

"Yes. I'm guessing this is murder."

"I'm listening."

"She's been in the water a while, a day maybe. The current has pulled her clothes off, but she wasn't wearing much to begin with."

"How do you know?"

"Because the current's not strong enough to pull off pants. Also, because of the marks on her body."

Agard glanced over at the girl. "Explain."

"She looks malnourished—you can almost see her hip bones. I think the medical examiner will also find antemortem bruising, though I can't be sure because of her skin color and the time in the water."

"You mean she was beaten?"

"I do."

"Which indicates murder."

"Right," Hugo said. "Although her face isn't marked and she has no defensive wounds on her hands or forearms. But there's something else, have a look." Both men crouched beside the body. "You have proper gloves?" Hugo asked.

"*Oui.*" Agard reached into a back pocket and pulled on pale-blue surgical gloves.

"Good. Roll her onto her side."

With a grunt, Agard tipped the girl's body to reveal her back. "What am I looking at? Those circles?"

"Yes. Cigarette burns would be my guess."

"*Merde*, domestic abuse. That makes me so angry, and look how many there are. She was basically tortured before being killed, poor girl."

"Yes, I'm afraid she was."

"*Merci*, Hugo. I'll make a note of all this. We'll find the husband or boyfriend who did this, I promise."

They shook hands, and Hugo resumed his walk, trying to shake off the image of the young woman. But as he crossed the bridge, the river beneath him looked gray and slick, cold and lethal, utterly devoid of mercy for even a poor, tortured girl. He shivered as a breeze caressed his neck, and he quickened his stride.

As he turned onto Rue de Rivoli, Hugo's phone vibrated in his pocket. He checked the display, and immediately his spirits lifted. It was Claudia, the only woman he'd felt anything for since his divorce.

Claudia, the bright-eyed reporter, daughter of French nobility, classy, sexy, and, Hugo suspected, not quite as interested in him as he was in her.

"Claudia, *bonjour*."

"Hugo, how are you?"

"Fine. On my way to breakfast but I got waylaid."

"Breakfast by yourself?"

"No. The daughter of an old friend is over here looking for work; I'm meeting her at the restaurant."

"Oh, that's nice. What kind of work?"

"Modeling."

"Runway or commercial?"

"No clue. They're different career paths?"

Her laughter was soft and made him long to see her. "Oh Hugo, you're so cute. I do miss you."

"Then join us."

"Where are you going?"

"I'm having my biannual craving, so we're meeting at Breakfast in America."

"I wish I could, but I have plans. Although, the most handsome man in Paris, off to breakfast with a model. I should probably interfere for my own interests."

"Didn't know you still had an interest," Hugo said, suddenly feeling like a needy teenager. "Sorry, that came out wrong."

Claudia laughed again. "Silly. That's why I was calling. I'd like to see you. Have drinks then dinner, spend some time together."

"I would like that, very much."

"Tonight?" she asked.

"Tonight is perfect."

"I'll come by your apartment at seven, we can take a stroll and choose somewhere along the way."

They rang off, Hugo's mood immediately improved, and he began to enjoy his walk along Rue de Rivoli, the city opening up around him. He slowed as he passed a crepe vendor, the man's hot plate filling the air with the alluring aroma of his paper-thin pancakes. A pair of grateful businessmen took hot cups of coffee from the vendor, lips pursed in unison as they blew steam from the cups. Hugo walked on and allowed his mind to linger on Claudia, the socialite and professional woman who could chill politicians with a look, and who could also giggle like a schoolgirl and dance in her underwear to make Hugo laugh. Well, laugh for a little while because Claudia's underwear tended to provoke other reactions in Hugo, reactions that brought out more of Claudia's talents.

He was smiling as he turned onto Rue Malher, replacing the delights of Claudia with the prospect of a gigantic breakfast. He checked his watch: not quite eight, which made him a few minutes early.

He loitered outside the restaurant, waiting for Amy, trying to suppress the rising worry that she wouldn't show. He distracted himself by watching the other people on the street, several passers-by, tourists, and dog walkers, all with their own missions, and of marginal interest to Hugo. One man caught his eye, though, a man who lingered across the street, walking in little circles, his head down. Hugo surveyed him, wondering what he might see, what he might be able to deduce about him. The man was tall but slightly built and maybe Hispanic. He wore jeans, a white shirt, and a blue blazer, and the clothes fit him the way a wealthy man's clothes always fit. A gold watch caught occasional flashes of the sun as the man ran his hands through his hair every thirty seconds or so, and a matching necklace told Hugo the man made good money, and liked to spend it. As Hugo started to lose interest, the man glanced over and seemed to hold Hugo's eye for a second too long. It was nothing Hugo could identify, and certainly nothing he could ever explain rationally, but in his time as an FBI agent he'd learned that people have a sixth sense, a tingle in the back of the neck, for a reason. He'd trusted his sense in the past, and never regretted it. The man looked away, and Hugo studied him more closely. As if to block Hugo's gaze, the man turned his back, fished in a pocket for his cigarettes, and lit one up.

Hugo stared at the man for a full minute, enough time to conclude that he was up to no good, a simple trick he'd used many times: a normal person would resent being stared at, would either move away or confront the person doing the staring. This guy, on the other hand, was pretending a little too hard not to notice. Drug dealer? Shaking down a local store? *Nothing to do with Amy, surely. How could he be?*

Hugo took a deep breath and smiled at his own raging imagination. Being so close to crime for so many years, he often had to check himself, recognize that a man leaning against a wall might just be waiting for a lover, that two people on a park bench might just be resting and not spying. Like the poor drowned girl, this man had nothing to do with him, and Hugo had no reason to clutter his own world with imagined crimes. Sure, being head of security at the US Embassy could be tedious, more meetings than action, but peace and a lack of stress was good for the soul.

Hugo's stomach growled and he checked his watch. Ten minutes gone, so time to get a table, to wait with a cup of coffee in his hand. Inside, the place was busy—it always was—but owner Craig Carlson spotted him above the heads of the other customers and waved him to a free table. When Hugo got there, they shook hands.

"Long time, no see," Craig said. "Flying solo today?"

"Good to see you," Hugo said. "No, a young lady is meeting me."

Carlson raised an eyebrow. "Oh, yes?"

"Nothing like that. A friend's daughter, over here for a few months. I'm just checking in with her."

"Checking in, or checking up?"

Hugo smiled. *Good question.*

Carlson moved off as a waitress arrived with a mug of coffee, and Hugo sat back to wait. Maybe it was the coffee, it was always strong and good here, but Hugo didn't like the way his heart rate had picked up, nor the way he caught himself checking his watch every thirty seconds. He looked out of the window and saw that the man was still there, lighting another cigarette. Hugo shrugged and focused on his coffee, tried to ignore the worry that touched at the back of his neck, the merest brush of cold, teasing fingers. Amy was fine, just late. Like all teenagers, she had a million more important things to do than meet her dad's middle-aged friend for breakfast. Things like sleep. That she was late should have been no surprise, Hugo told himself. He should have expected it.

Thirty minutes later, Hugo called Amy's cell phone but wasn't even able to leave a message. A metallic voice let him know her mail box was full. He shook his head, stood, and dropped cash on the table to pay for his coffee. He waved to Carlson and stepped out into the street, far from happy about the call he now had to make to his friend across the Atlantic. He took the phone out of his pocket and glanced around, looking for the man in the white shirt and blazer. He was gone.

Hugo dialed Bart Denum in Florida. When his friend didn't answer, Hugo left a brief message, no details just a request for a call back. Before he could put his phone away, it rang and, to Hugo's surprise, it was Claudia again.

"Hello," he said. "Don't tell me you want a rain check already."

"Not at all. Are you with your friend? I'm sorry to interrupt."

"She didn't show up. Everything OK?"

"With me, yes. But I just got a call from Tom."

"At this time of day?" Tom Green, as Hugo had started to explain to Amy, was Hugo's best friend, had been since their days at the FBI Academy. What he'd not told her, and couldn't, was that in recent years Tom had been freelancing for the CIA or, as he put it, was "a semi-retired spook." He lived in Hugo's spare room, at least when he was in the country. Tom never talked about his work, even though Hugo knew his friend battled many demons from what he'd seen and done. Tom's weapons in that fight were his brash, uncouth, and reckless personality, his bluster hiding a deeply troubled psyche. His biggest and most potent weapon had been the bottle. For years, Tom had binged on everything he could, acknowledging his problem only when it almost cost him his life. In recent months, though, he'd been dry, kicking his whisky habit to the curb while maintaining his unreliable and foul-mouthed temperament. And his love for sleeping until noon.

"Yes, at this time of day," Claudia said. "I know, I thought maybe someone had stolen his phone and called me by accident."

"I bet. He went out around eight last night and I didn't see him come in. I assumed he was sleeping when I left the apartment, he usually is."

"Well, I'm afraid he needs your help."

"Can't find the coffee grinder?" Hugo snorted. "Why call you and not me, the big idiot?"

"Because he's embarrassed."

"Embarrassed? That doesn't sound like Tom."

"This is a first, even for him. The big idiot pissed off some traffic cops and landed himself in jail. Go bail him out, will you?"

CHAPTER TWO

Hugo sat by himself in the small waiting room, trying not to squirm on his plastic chair while a surly, mustached police officer read and reread Tom's paperwork. Finally, the man left his station behind the counter and disappeared into the back of the police station. Hugo knew that about the only stroke of luck in this whole episode was that Tom had been snagged in a suburb in the north west of the city, a part of Paris where the streets were normally quiet and the jails usually empty.

Ten minutes later, Tom trudged out behind the *flic*, head down and eyes glued to the floor. He was pale and his clothes were rumpled, like he'd tossed and turned in them all night. Which he probably had. He smoothed his hair down with one hand as the officer handed him a brown paper bag. Tom peered inside it, still avoiding looking at Hugo, and then took out his belt, laces, and a wallet. He finally glanced over at Hugo.

"You'd probably prefer that I hung myself in there, eh?"

"No, Tom, not really."

Tom stuffed his laces and wallet into his pants pockets, put on his belt, and then handed the bag back to the officer.

"Sign here, please, *monsieur*," the *flic* said.

Tom put both hands on the counter either side of the clipboard, as if signing his name was a task to contemplate before doing. He drew a long breath and then signed. He nodded to the *flic* and then turned and walked to the front door of the station. Hugo stood and followed him out.

In the parking lot, Tom stopped. "You drive up here?"

"This doesn't count as official business. We'll have to take the metro, sorry."

"Hugo." Tom didn't move, just dug his hands into his pockets and stared at the cobbled ground.

"It's okay, Tom."

"You're like my fucking dad, you know. You say, 'It's okay' and I hear, 'You're a loser.'" Tom held up a hand. "I know you're not saying that. And you're not my dad."

It was a long time into their friendship before Tom had opened up about his father, Vincent. He'd died when Tom was fifteen, and Hugo could tell from the way he talked about his old man that Tom never forgave him for dying, and never forgave himself for being mad at the man he'd loved more than any other.

"Tom. You're right, I'm not your dad. And it really is okay. You think I never tied one on, got picked up for driving when I shouldn't?"

"Seriously, you? Get arrested?"

"Well, no, but not because I'm an angel."

Tom shook his head, trying to suppress a smile. "Stop trying to make me feel better."

"I'm your friend, that's my job."

"I'm supposed to be sober, Hugo. You know how fucking hard it is to be sober when you're a drunk?"

Hugo stepped closer, lowered his voice. "You're not a drunk, Tom. Not anymore. You slipped one time. That's all." Hugo put a hand on his friend's arm. "I don't know one single person who's given up booze and not fallen off the wagon. Not one. It happens. It's all part of being—"

"A drunk?"

"Sober, you asshole," Hugo grinned. He checked his watch. "You hungry?"

"Yeah, what did you have in mind?"

"I was just at Breakfast in America. An aborted attempt to eat pancakes and bacon."

"Aborted thanks to me?" Tom asked sheepishly.

"No, actually. Let's get over there and I'll tell you about it."

"Pancakes and bacon? Fuck yes. You mind if we swing by the apartment first so I can change?"

"I was going to insist on it, you smell like a brewery."

They walked in silence to the metro stop, Tom wincing at the screeching of the trains that echoed through the tunnels. Underground, they passed a tramp begging on some dirty stairs, and Hugo thought about making a joke, comparing the odors of the man and Tom, but his friend looked so forlorn, Hugo decided to leave him alone. On the ride home, Tom sat back with his arms crossed and closed his eyes. When they reached their stop at Saint-Germain-des-Prés, Hugo stood and nudged Tom with his foot.

"Wake up, old man, we're here."

They trudged up the steps into the fresh air, which seemed to revive Tom a little. "Helluva day."

"Hence my early-morning walk toward pancakes," Hugo said.

"Yeah. So was that true, you've never been arrested?"

"Yes, it's true."

"Shame. Still, you'd think the food in a French jail would be good, right? Especially in the burbs."

"Can't say I'd thought about it."

"Yeah, well, it was awful. A sad day when the French can't serve a decent piece of bread, even in a jail. Sad day."

Hugo smiled. "Hey, can I ask you a question?"

"One question, or is this where the third degree starts?"

"I'm not going to grill you, Tom, I told you I'm not upset you fell off the wagon. It happens."

"Thanks, Dad."

"If you didn't want to call me, which is fine, I'm wondering why you didn't call the embassy. You'd have been out of there in about fifteen minutes." Hugo snapped his fingers as the realization hit. "Ah yes, never mind. Forget I asked."

"Why?"

"Because it strikes me that even if *you* didn't call the embassy, the police should have. The fact that they didn't means you never told them who you are."

"Too drunk. Couldn't remember my own name."

"No, that doesn't add up either. A quick look at your wallet . . ."

"Do you need me for this conversation?"

They turned the corner onto Rue Jacob. A warm breeze picked up and a cluster of yellow leaves scuttled ahead of them. As they neared the door to the apartment building, Hugo saw a figure sitting on the steps. She was in a jogging suit, but the corn-row hair and dark-skinned profile were unmistakable. Camille Lerens.

"Look who it is, maybe she has a fun case for us. Plus, she was attacked last night, probably in worse shape than you."

"I doubt it." Tom lowered his head and trailed behind Hugo, like he didn't want to be seen or heard. When they got to the steps, Lerens stood and Hugo was pleased to see she looked uninjured. One slightly blackened eye but no slings, casts, or facial cuts. They exchanged *bisous*, Hugo careful to lightly brush her cheek with his in case there was unseen damage.

"Camille, *comment ça va?*" I heard you got into some trouble last night. Are you OK?"

"Yes, I'm fine, thanks." She looked past Hugo at Tom. "And how is our little drunk this morning?"

"Hungover," Hugo said. "But be nice, everyone makes mistakes now and again."

"Oh, isn't that the truth," Lerens said, her eyes still on Tom. "*Alors*, Tom, you want to tell your protective friend here what my mistake was last night?"

Hugo looked back and forth between them. "I don't . . . *Your* mistake?"

Lerens nodded. "*Oui*, it was a big one, wouldn't you say, Tom?"

The realization swept over Hugo like a wave, and he turned to face Tom. "You. Claudia said the traffic cops picked you up, so I assumed you were driving drunk, but you did that—you're the one who assaulted Camille."

Tom still stared at the ground, but he raised a hand in protest. "Hold up, cowboy, that's not what happened."

"It better not be," Hugo said.

"Or what?" Tom growled.

"Ease up, both of you," Lerens said. "I'm the one who got pummeled."

"'Pummeled' is a little strong," Tom said, morose again.

"I think I should be the judge of that," Lerens said.

"So what the hell happened?" Hugo demanded.

"Yesterday afternoon," Lerens began, "Tom called me to see if I wanted to go out."

Hugo raised an eyebrow. "Like on a date?"

"No!" Lerens and Tom said in unison.

"Sorry, couldn't resist. Go on."

"He suggested some bar in the suburbs, I said I'd meet him there. Then I got caught at work, couldn't make it. I was doing paperwork, listening to the police scanner, and I heard about a drunk foreigner picking fights outside that bar. I headed over there as fast as I could and arrived just in time to see Tom squaring up to a couple of motorcycle *flics*. I tried to get between them, make everyone calm down and see some sense, but then Mohammed Ali here started swinging."

"Oh lordy," Hugo muttered.

"We got him under control pretty quickly, but he landed a couple on me before we did. Lucky for him, he didn't connect with the other two *flics*."

Hugo thought for a moment. "And that's why no one at the embassy was notified."

"What do you mean?" Tom said, looking up.

"Am I right?" Hugo looked at Lerens.

She nodded. "I'm not pressing charges, but I thought it appropriate he spend a night in the tank. Give me a little satisfaction, and him some consequences."

"Thanks for not pressing charges," Tom said. "And I'm fine with you leaving me in jail overnight, too. I'd have left me in there longer."

"I tried to," Lerens said, "but at shift change this morning, the commander got all antsy about you being a US citizen, and him getting in trouble."

"If it makes us even, you can punch me in the junk, if you want," Tom said. A twinkle had returned to his eyes, but Hugo knew his friend was genuinely sorry.

"I might," Lerens said, trying not to smile. "But if I do, it'll be when you're not expecting it. Come to think of it, you might enjoy that, so forget it."

"Why don't you come upstairs?" Hugo said to Lerens. "Tom's getting changed and then he's buying me breakfast. American pancakes. I'm sure he'd be delighted to buy some for you, too."

"You know," Lerens said, "this may be hard to believe, but I've never had your pancakes. Never seen America as the origin of culinary delights, but I'd love to try them."

They started up the steps, and Hugo held the door for both of them, nodding to Dimitrios the Cretan concierge. As they entered the elevator, Tom was educating Lerens about American food. "No one does steak like a Texan. Hot dogs are the best sports food ever. And a good hamburger is the most satisfying meal in the world."

"I'll agree on the steak, maybe," Lerens said. "But hot dogs? I don't like to eat food when I can't recognize which part of the animal it came from. Or which animal, for that matter."

Tom punched the button for the top floor. "You prefer the recognizable but almost meat-free leg of a frog, then?"

"Correct. Bigger's not always better." Lerens gave a little snort of laughter. "And having been on both sides of the fence, I should know."

"Wait, you told us you only liked girls," Tom said.

"Don't change the subject," Lerens smirked. "And I didn't say 'only,' I just said I liked girls."

"Man, you really are playing every side of this game, aren't you?" Tom muttered.

"Don't get your hopes up," Lerens muttered back.

Hugo let them into the apartment, relived the tension was gone. Relieved, too, that Lerens knew just how to handle Tom. As a transgender cop, she no doubt caught flak from her colleagues, and clearly she'd figured out that humor was a powerful weapon in combating prejudice. Anyone who could out-banter Tom had a gift indeed.

As soon as they were inside, Hugo's phone rang. It was Bart Denum.

"Hi, Bart, thanks for calling back."

"Of course, what's up?"

"I just wondered if you'd heard from Amy lately. We were supposed to have breakfast this morning, only she didn't show."

A slight pause on the line, then Denum said, "Oh, Jesus, I knew something was wrong."

"What do you mean?"

"I was going to call you, Hugo, have you check up on her."

"Why?"

"She's not returning my calls, for the last three days. That doesn't sound like a long time, but it was my birthday yesterday and we'd arranged to talk. I got one e-mail, real brief, but we've talked on my birthday, and hers, every year since the accident. It's like . . . our thing." Denum sighed. "But she's nineteen now and in Paris, I didn't want to crowd her. Figured she'd get to it, but now . . ."

"Yeah, seems a little odd. I wondered if she'd just lost her phone."

"Could be, but she'd have said so and she knows how to get hold of me if she really wants to. And now she stood you up, too?"

"Yes."

"Why were you meeting?"

"She called last week. Said she wanted to talk about something." Hugo left out the part about keeping her dad in the dark.

"And you tried calling her?"

"And texting. I didn't hear from her, waited at the restaurant for over thirty minutes. I'm sure something else came up."

"First thing on a Sunday morning?"

There was a moment's silence, and Hugo knew that Bart was trying to stay calm, think of rational reasons his daughter had missed the meeting. "Well, damn. That worries me, Hugo. I'm really starting to wonder if something's going on."

"I know you're worried, and I don't blame you. But remember that she's a teenager, and I'm sure she's enjoying the long leash she's on. It shouldn't be a surprise that she'd resist when you or I give that leash a tug."

"But you know what she's like. She's not the rebel type; she's thoughtful and responsible. And to not show up at all? To not even call you? That's not her, Hugo, and you know it."

A vision of the man lurking outside the restaurant appeared in Hugo's mind, but he dismissed it. The man had nothing to do with Amy; he was just a visible symbol of something not right, someone out of place. And Bart had a point. It wasn't like Amy to not show up, not even call.

"Text me her address, I'll go by and see her."

"OK." Denum paused. "Hugo, I'm thinking about coming over there."

"Paris is lovely this time of year, but there's no need yet. I'm sure she's fine."

"I don't know what makes you so damn sure . . ." Denum softened his tone. "I'm sorry Hugo, I'm really worried. It's just me and her, and if something happens to her . . ."

He didn't finish the sentence because he didn't need to. Hugo had survived Ellie's death by throwing himself at danger, distracting himself with the least safe assignments he could claim. Africa, the Middle East. Bart didn't have that option, he had Amy to take care of, and Hugo suspected his friend had been forced to subsume his grief to hers, to be the strong one, and as a result had never really recovered. And that made him fragile where Amy was concerned—the merest hint of losing her was enough to make the strong man crack.

And he'd cracked once before, in London. Hugo and Denum were stationed at the US Embassy there, and one July morning a jihadist in a trench coat had shown up in front of the embassy at the same moment Denum had arrived for work. A cool summer morning on a leafy street, a normal day at the office turned upside down by a man with a death wish, for himself and others.

After the incident, Hugo had watched the security-camera footage over and over. He watched as the two men stood just feet from each other, almost as if both were frozen in fear and indecision. For a few seconds they stared at each other, then the man opened his coat and let Denum know they were both about to die. A US Marine shot the bomber in the shoulder before he could detonate, a gunshot that triggered something in Denum, caused him to pull out his own gun and unload it into the falling body of the terrorist. Denum had been shuffled out of the service immediately, free of criminal charges on the theory that the bomber was as good as dead anyway, but Denum was put under the watch of some specialized mental-health experts for six months. Hugo had helped him get a desk job with the TSA in Washington, and he'd done well there, made friends, and moved up.

Now, years later, his breakdown was a thing of the past, a moment of horror not spoken about, but Hugo often wondered if the dark hands that had gripped his friend that day had entirely let go, or whether they trailed their oily fingers through his mind, waiting for another chance to operate him like a puppet.

Hugo hoped not, because of all the things likely to push him back into the fog, a missing Amy would top the list.

"I'll go over to her place," Hugo assured him. "I'll find her, and if she's not there, I'll talk to her neighbors. Let me check it out before you dash over here, OK?"

"You'll go today?"

"Yes, I will." Hugo saw that plate of pancakes disappear for a second time. "I'll go right now, I promise. This is what I do, Bart, you know that. I look for people who've gone missing, and I find them."

Denum's voice was quiet when he spoke. "That's what worries me."

"What do you mean?"

"By the time you start looking for missing girls, Hugo, they're usually in a whole lot of trouble."

CHAPTER THREE

Hugo hung up and wandered into Tom's room, normally Hugo's office, but only when his friend was out of town.

"Change of plans," Hugo said.

"A problem?" Tom asked.

"Could be. I've had some good people work for me but this guy, Bart Denum, was one of the best and is a good friend. You ever meet him?"

"Heard you talk about him, and his daughter, but I don't think we've met."

"Well, his daughter is here, living here in Paris for a few months. Seems to have gone missing."

"He call the cops?" Tom asked. "I hear they handle that kind of thing."

"Funny, but we're not there yet. She's not returning his calls or e-mails, but it's only been a few days. She could be in a jail cell somewhere with a hangover."

"*Touché*."

"Thanks. I need to go check out her place, see if there's any sign of her. I could leave it until later, but I'd rather not."

"Yeah, well, I'm fucking hungry so I'd rather you did."

"So go eat."

"Nah," Tom said. "I'll come with you. Highly trained backup and all that."

"I think I can handle knocking on a door." Hugo tilted his head toward the living room. "Plus, methinks you and Camille have some catching up to do."

"And by that, you mean I have some groveling to do."

"Correct. Let's go." Hugo led Tom back to Lerens. "Sorry, Camille. I have to go check out something for an old friend, which means you'll be enjoying your first pancakes with Tom. His treat."

Lerens looked back and forth between the two men. "They don't serve alcohol there, do they?"

"I don't think so," Hugo said.

"And I'm back on the wagon, I promise," Tom said quickly.

"I wasn't thinking of you," Lerens said. "I could use a shot of something, my face hurts."

Back on Rue Jacob, they started to go their separate ways when Lerens stopped. "Hey, you need help with your little mission?"

"No, thanks for offering, though. A friend needs me to check on his daughter, an aspiring model living in the Marais."

"A model?" Tom said. "You didn't mention that before, you bastard. I'd have insisted on helping."

"I know," Hugo grinned. "Enjoy your pancakes."

♉

Amy lived in a building that sat just off Rue des Rosiers, on the Right Bank, in the Marais district. For some reason, Denum had texted Hugo a photo as well as her address, and in the picture she wore a blue soccer uniform and held a ball. She had brown, curly hair and a bright smile. Definitely a pretty girl, Hugo thought, but he wondered, not for the first time, whether she had the stark beauty required to make it as a model in Paris. Those girls, as far as he could see, tended to be stick thin, almost gaunt, with alienlike eyes and cheek bones like knives. Amy had the kind of athletic beauty that turned heads on the street, but Hugo wondered if that would be enough to match the exotic look required for magazine shoots and fashion runways.

The front door to the building had no lock, which surprised and disappointed Hugo. He pushed open the heavy wooden door and found himself in a foyer lined with mailboxes. A second door led to the ground-floor apartments and a wooden staircase. Amy's place was on the second floor, and from the look of the place, Hugo guessed each floor held three studios, the original large apartments broken into smaller units to exploit tourists and renters like Amy.

He climbed the stairs, noticing how quiet it was in the building despite its proximity to the heart of Paris. Old walls of plaster and brick, not drywall. He turned right down a dark hallway and stopped in front of Amy's door. He listened for a moment but heard no sound. He knocked. Again, silence from inside, so he knocked again, louder this time.

A movement to his left caught his eye, near the top of the stairs, and he glanced over. She was partly in shadow and he couldn't see her face, but it was a young woman, and she was watching him. He started toward her.

"Hi, Amy?"

She turned and ran.

This sudden, unexpected reaction stopped Hugo in his tracks, but only for a second or two. He started after her, calling her name, and followed the sound of her feet clattering down the stairs, wanting to catch her but not scare her further away. *Had she not seen it was him?*

He reached the ground floor as she exited onto the street, and he caught a flash of her terrified face through the glass of both doors as she glanced over her shoulder. It wasn't Amy at all. Hugo slowed for a moment but started after her again, knowing something was wrong. Moments later, he was behind her in the street.

"Hey!" he called out. "Stop, I'm a friend of Amy!"

She didn't hesitate, maybe she didn't hear him, so Hugo took off running again, no more than thirty yards behind her. She jinked right onto a side street, and seconds later Hugo did the same. The girl was lying on the sidewalk, her handbag six feet from her, its contents a trail of debris between her and it.

"It's okay, I'm a friend of Amy's," Hugo said in English. "I'm an American, the head of security at the US Embassy, her dad used to work for me."

"You know Amy?" the girl asked, her voice faltering.

"Yes, ever since she was little." Hugo stooped to offer her a hand. He helped the girl to her feet and caught her when her ankle gave way. "Like I said, her step-dad and I are old friends and colleagues."

Her mouth twitched with a smile. "She calls him her dad, doesn't like people saying 'step-dad.'" She winced again. "I tripped. I think I twisted it." She was trying not to cry.

"Here, rest against this car, give it a moment to recover."

"Thanks. So . . . why were you looking for Amy?"

"Her dad asked me to. You're a friend of hers?"

"Yes. My name's Emily. Emily Edwards."

"Nice to meet you, Emily, I'm Hugo Marston." He bent to pick up the contents of her handbag. He handed them, and the bag itself, to Emily, knowing that their arrangement was beyond his purview. "Do you know where she is?"

"No. That's why I was there." She put her foot on the ground and tested her weight on it. "I think I can make it to that café." She nodded to the spread of tables and chairs at the end of the street.

"Perfect, I could use a top-up."

They walked slowly down the street and took a table outside. She ordered a café crème, and Hugo asked for the same.

"Why did you run away, Emily?" Hugo asked.

"I don't really know. Seems like Amy's been mixing with some weird people lately, then I saw you there with your hat and coat like some gangster, you scared me. Sorry."

"Don't be, it's fine. So how did you meet Amy?" he asked. "Or did you know her in the States?"

"No, we met over here. Two months ago, I guess. I'm a secretary at a modeling agency. She came in to do a shoot there and we got talking. We're both from Florida, know a lot of the same places. Plus, I got the feeling she was a little lonely. Or maybe homesick."

"When did you last see her?"

"Three days ago. We had brunch."

"How was she?"

"Fine. Well, excited. She'd met some guy at a club, and apparently he was interested in having her model for him. I was a little worried that it was just a sleazy come on, but she said it was legit."

"What kind of club?"

"It's called Club Caterina in Pigalle. I'm kind of a homebody, don't do the whole dance and clubbing scene, so I'd never heard of it."

"Was she having any success with her modeling career? You say she had a session at your agency."

"That was something she paid for. For her portfolio. And no, she wasn't having much luck. There are a lot of pretty girls in Paris, and she's one of thousands wanting to be a model. It's funny, a lot of people don't realize that the ones who make it, very often they're kind of odd-looking. Not the usual beautiful face you see walking down the street. There's usually something striking about them, something almost a little off. Those are the ones who make it in high fashion."

"And Amy didn't fit that mold?"

"Like I said, she's a very pretty girl. But she has that cute cheer-leader thing going, you know? Not the haughty model look."

"I know what you mean. So who was the guy, do you know?"

"She may have told me his name, but I don't think so. If she did, I can't remember it. Sorry."

"Did she describe him?"

"No, why would she?" Emily smiled. "I know, you're just doing your job. But no, she didn't."

"And you have no idea where she might be?"

"I don't. She's not really the type to pick up a guy and hide away with him for days at a time. I wondered if she had, you know, and that's why I haven't heard from her."

"Were you expecting to?"

"Yes, we had dinner plans Thursday night. I called and e-mailed during the day to make sure we were still on but never heard back. She didn't show at the restaurant, and didn't respond at all on Friday or Saturday, either. She always has her phone on her, I mean *always*. That's why I stopped by her place, wondered whether she was holed up with someone. I just wanted to make sure she was okay, you know?"

"Yeah," said Hugo. "Me too." *And I'm beginning to wonder.*

CHAPTER FOUR

After he'd given Emily his business card, Hugo put her into a cab and paid the driver in advance. He hesitated for a moment but couldn't see any other option, so he walked back to Amy's building. He began on the bottom floor and started knocking on doors to find someone who'd seen her recently, or someone who might know where she was. Hugo didn't want to call Bart and tell him his daughter was missing, and that's the exact conclusion his friend would draw if Hugo reported not finding any sign of her.

Of the three apartments, or studios, on the lower floor, one person was home. A student at the Sorbonne, he was a wiry, bespectacled young man about an inch taller than Hugo. He said he knew Amy, and it was obvious from the way his eyes lit up that at the very least he had a crush on her.

"*Alors*, I don't know her well, though," he said. "And I think I saw her last Sunday, not since."

"Does she work, have a boyfriend?"

"I don't know. She's never brought anyone here that I've seen, but then I probably wouldn't see if she did. When we talked, she said she was a model, but I don't know anything else about her job."

"Did you two ever go on a date?"

The man looked wistful and shrugged. "She's out of my league."

Hugo smiled. "Women like intelligence, don't underestimate yourself." He handed the man a card. "Call me if you see her. Better yet, have her call me."

"*D'accord*, I will. Is she . . . in danger?"

"Not as far as I know," Hugo said.

He spoke to three other people in the building, one of whom knew Amy by sight but hadn't seen her in weeks. The other two had never even seen her. *City living*, Hugo thought. He'd grown to love Paris, very quickly in fact, but he'd grown up in and around Austin, Texas, where neighbors were people you actually knew, not just shared a building or a street with.

As he passed Amy's apartment, he stopped and listened again, frowning at the silence from behind the closed door. He tried the handle, but that was wishful thinking. He pulled out his phone and dialed Tom.

"You finished breakfast yet?" Hugo asked when his friend answered.

"Yep, just in time for lunch."

"How're things with Camille?"

"Peachy. She's a good sport, but ordered a crapload of food she didn't eat. You know how much orange juice costs at this place?"

"I hope she ordered a large."

"Two. How's your little expedition?"

"Turns out I need your help, if you don't mind. We'll need your lock-picking set. Or mine."

"Sure. Don't want me to mention this to Camille, then?"

Hugo laughed. "Funny. She may be a good sport, but she's still a cop."

"I'll take a cab, be there in thirty minutes. Try not to lurk around looking suspicious in the meantime."

"I'll do my best."

It took Tom forty minutes, which for Hugo was three leisurely walks around the block. As he completed the last one, Tom was climbing out of the cab. "You have any cash, Hugo? I was going to give this guy a credit card, but he got all shouty."

Part of being Tom's friend, Hugo had come to accept, was opening up his own wallet. He didn't mind for taxis, and he no longer had to buy Tom's booze. The problem was the occasional call girl that Hugo would find making coffee in the morning. Even in modern-day Paris, most working girls preferred cash to credit. And unlike booze, Tom hadn't given those up, and his tastes tended toward the high-class, and therefore pricey. Twenty Euros for a cab ride was nothing in comparison.

Outside Amy's door, Hugo wondered for a moment whether he should call Bart and get his permission to enter the apartment. Or track down the building owner and just use a key. The latter was too much hassle, he decided, and the former would cause Denum to worry more.

Four minutes later, Tom had the door open. Hugo took a deep breath and started to walk in.

"Wait up," Tom said. Hugo noticed his friend was wearing a pair of surgical gloves, and he waved another pair at Hugo. "I know you don't want to hear this, but we could be at a crime scene."

"Ah, yes." Hugo took the gloves and snapped them on. "I hope you're wrong, but good thinking."

"And if we are, let's not fuck it up. The French police are already kinda unhappy with me, a contaminated crime scene might make them rethink those assault charges."

"They wouldn't need to," Hugo said. "They'd have a whole new set of charges for both of us. Come on."

They picked their way through the studio apartment methodically. They'd done this together before, many times for the FBI, and they slipped straight back into the routine. Hugo went left, Tom to the right. No words, no chit-chat, not unless one of them found something worth talking about.

It didn't take them long to finish. Hugo ended up in the small kitchenette, noting no dishes in the sink, nor on the little draining board. The fridge was all but empty, some cans of Diet Coke and bottled water, but nothing perishable. The pull-out couch served as Amy's bed, but when he opened it up, the sheets had been stripped off. Maybe she remade the bed every night, but Hugo doubted it.

Tom exited the small bathroom and shrugged. "Think she's cleared out? No feminine products in there at all. Also no toothbrush, toothpaste, or any of those damn face creams pretty girls slather themselves with."

"Kitchen indicates she's gone, too," Hugo said. "Nothing in the fridge to go bad, and all dishes put away."

"We need to check with the landlord to see if she ended the lease. Any idea who it is?"

"No," said Hugo, picturing the downstairs neighbor. "But I know a man who does."

"Good." Tom looked around. "So, you gonna do your thing here?"

"My thing?"

"Yeah, where you point out to dumb old me that it's the things we're not seeing that matter the most."

"If you know that's my thing, why don't you tell me?"

"Makes me all warm and fuzzy to hear you do it. For old time's sake."

Hugo sighed. "Fine. The main thing I'm not seeing is a passport. I'm also not seeing money or bank stuff, though she could be operating here on cash. I'm also not seeing a lot of clothes or any suitcases, which is odd for a model."

"Right. I noticed all that."

Hugo grinned. "Figured you did."

"Now what?"

"Now we figure out if she left the country." Hugo took out his phone and called the embassy, reaching his second-in-command, Ryan Pierce. "Ryan, it's Hugo. Need you to look up a passport number, and check to see if its owner is still in France. If not, where did she go?"

"You're working today, boss?"

"Not officially." *Not officially yet, that is.* Hugo gave Pierce Amy Dreiss's name and date of birth. "Call me back when you know something." He rang off, but before he could put his phone away, it buzzed. An unknown number, but he answered anyway.

"Mr. Marston, this is Emily. Edwards."

"Hi, Emily, please call me Hugo. Have you heard from Amy?"

"No. But I remembered something about that conversation I told you about. Where she was offered a job. I just remembered that she showed me a business card. I can't imagine it's very helpful, but you said call about any little thing."

"Absolutely. What can you tell me about the card?"

"Just that it was white and had a black border around it. Very thin black border, like it was a good-quality card. Expensive, with delicate cursive writing on it."

"Was the writing also black?"

"Yes. I'm really sorry, but that's all I can remember about it because she kind of flashed it, I didn't get to read the name or anything. Just that he was from Spain."

"That's all?"

"That's all, I'm sorry."

"Please don't be, Emily, that's very helpful. If you remember anything else, let me know. Call any time."

"I will."

Hugo rang off and looked at Tom. "The idea that she went traveling may have merit. Our girl now has a vague connection to Spain." Hugo looked around the tiny space and realized that the business card hadn't been in the apartment, either.

"Field trip?" Tom said hopefully.

"We don't know she's there for sure, or where in Spain if she is." He checked his watch. "I'd like to get something to eat. And then we can take a local field trip."

"Where to?"

"The club where Amy met this Spanish dude."

"What kind of club?"

"No idea, but it's in Pigalle."

"I don't know if that's a good idea," Tom said. They both knew that Pigalle had two faces, the saucy, playful one that showed in the day, and the darker, raunchier one that emerged at night. Any club out there was likely to dangle temptations in front of Tom that he didn't need. "You know the name of the place, I assume?" Tom asked.

"Club Caterina. Familiar with it?"

"No. But I can't remember half the places I've gotten wasted in."

"Well then," said Hugo. "We'll just have to behave ourselves and hope they don't remember you."

CHAPTER FIVE

The club was in a post-lunch lull. The tourists who liked naked skin with their *croque-monsieur* sandwiches were off exploring other parts of Paris; the winding streets of nearby Montmartre, perhaps, or back to the hustle and bustle of attractions lining the Seine.

When Hugo and Tom entered, two Barbie-like bartenders looked up but didn't interrupt their conversation. They tended a circular bar that sat in the middle of the club. To the left of the bar were two raised stages, both skewered by brass poles, and to the right sat twenty or so round tables, occupied by a few groups and pairs of men. Beer bottles and carafes of red wine decorated their tables like flower arrangements. The place smelled of stale beer and unemptied ash trays. Smoking was no longer allowed inside Paris bars and restaurants, but clubs like this looked the other way when patrons ready to part with their cash lit up in the corners.

Hugo and Tom took up positions on bar stools and waited for one of the bartenders to pay them attention.

"You have an approach in mind?" Tom asked.

"Not really. Show them the picture of Amy and see if they recognize her. Take it from there."

One of the Barbie twins sashayed up to them. "*Bonjour, je suis Zazie.*" She eyed them for a moment, then switched to English. "You are from America? England?"

"America," Hugo replied. "How did you know?"

She shrugged. "I'm good at my job. Something to drink?" She nodded at the unattended brass poles. "Dancing starts at four."

"Two Diet Cokes," Tom said. "What kind of dancing?"

Zazie looked at him. "Are you serious?"

"*Oui*," Tom said with a straight face. "Oh my, it's not naked girls is it?" He turned to Hugo. "Come on, sweetie, we got this place all wrong."

Hugo tried not to smile, and failed. "Ignore him. We're looking for a missing girl, a friend."

"Also American?" Zazie asked.

"Right," Hugo said. "But she's been living here for a while."

"*D'accord.* You have a picture or a name for this girl?"

Hugo pulled out his phone and found the photo. "Her name is Amy. Amy Dreiss."

"I don't recognize her, but we get a lot of people in here. Also, I'm new and only work fifteen hours a week. You need to ask Alice."

"And who is Alice?" Tom asked.

"She's worked here a long time, knows a lot of the customers," Zazie said, checking her watch. "She'll be here in twenty minutes."

"Well," Tom said. "We better have those Diet Cokes."

"Diet Cokes?" Zazie said. "*Bien sûr.* Anything in them?"

Tom rubbed his hands together. "Well, since you ask . . ."

"Just straws," Hugo said. "*Merci bien.*"

Hugo watched Zazie pour the drinks, just in case. She returned with them and nodded toward a young lady who'd just entered. "She's early. That's Alice."

Zazie called her over and showed the three to a table near the bar. Hugo studied Alice as they sat, curious because she didn't look like she belonged in a questionable Pigalle club like this. She was petite and on the pretty side of mousy, with tiny hands and clear skin that didn't look to be carrying any makeup. She wore a light-beige jacket over a white shirt, and jeans tucked into black boots. In a city full of beautiful women, she probably didn't turn too many heads on the street, but there was something about her ordinariness that appealed to Hugo.

"Can I help you?" she asked, her eyes wary.

"I hope so," Hugo said with a smile. "I gather you know Amy Dreiss."

"Amy . . ." she looked at Hugo and Tom, shaking her head until the realization hit. "*Ah, l'Américaine?*"

"*Oui,*" Hugo said. He showed her the picture. "That her?"

Alice nodded. "And who are you?"

"Friends of her father. When did you last see her?"

"Last week, I think. Maybe five or six days ago."

"She comes in here a lot?" Hugo asked.

"Sure. I mean . . . I don't understand, is she OK?"

"That's why we're asking, we want to make sure she is. Her father hasn't heard from her in a few days and he's worried. I said I'd stop by and check on her, but she wasn't home."

"Oh, I see. Like I said, I haven't seen her in a few days. But when she was here, she was fine."

"Did she come with anyone?"

Alice looked at Hugo like it was a stupid question. "No. Why?"

"Does she have a boyfriend, do you know?" Tom chipped in.

"I don't think so."

"We were told she was offered a job by someone in this club," Hugo said. He figured they'd get further with the full truth. There was no reason this girl had anything to hide and, as a friend, she'd want to help. "A modeling job. Do you know anything about that?"

Alice shrugged. "We have men in here all the time offering jobs like that. Ninety-nine percent of the time it's because they're trying to pick up some girl."

"One thing I don't get," Tom said. "Why would a girl like Amy choose to hang out at this place?"

"Why wouldn't she?" asked Alice.

"Well, it's not near her apartment, for one thing." Tom looked around the bar. "And for a nice, well-educated American girl to hang out at a strip club . . . No offense or anything, but there are a million bars in Paris, most a lot closer to home and less . . . well, strippy."

Alice cocked her head and looked at Hugo, then Tom. A smile

spread slowly across her face, and she began to laugh. She stifled it with one hand, and said, "Oh, I think there's been a misunderstanding here."

"How so?" Hugo asked.

Alice laughed again and looked him in the eye. "Your sweet little American girl doesn't come here to drink or hang out, *mon ami*. She works here."

"Seriously?" Tom said. "Tell me she tends bar."

Alice gestured with her thumb toward the twin brass poles. "You know what French and American men have in common? Both love cheerleaders, especially ones that take their clothes off. And your friend's daughter makes a very sexy little cheerleader."

"You're kidding?" Hugo sat back in his chair and shook his head.

"*Pas du tout.*" Not at all. Alice cupped her small breasts. "And impressive assets. Her stage name is 'Amy D' for good reason."

♉

"Your buddy's not going to like that very much," Tom said, once Alice had retired to the dressing room.

"No, he's not," Hugo agreed.

"The occasion for a real drink, wouldn't you say?"

"I would not," Hugo said emphatically. "Damn, I didn't ask about a Spain connection."

Tom rubbed his hands together and grinned. "Well, if I can't have a drink, at least we can go talk to a stripper while she changes."

"There you go," Hugo said. "Look what being sober can do for you. Sure you don't want to stay and have a drink while I go back there?"

"Fuck you."

They started for the back of the club, Hugo pausing when his phone rang. "Hello?"

"Hey, it's Ryan. Got a hit on your girl's passport."

"That was quick."

"Yeah, I know." Pierce chuckled. "Figured I could cut out early once I got you a result."

"Sounds fair to me. Where did she go?"

"Spain. Specifically, she flew into Madrid."

"Good work, Ryan, thanks. Now go home."

"Ten-four, boss. Call my cell if you need anything else."

Tom pointed at a sign for the office. "Anything useful?" he asked.

"She went to Madrid."

"Do you think she stayed there."

"No idea, but I do know that it's the easiest city to fly into on short notice. It's also very central, and with their rail system she could get pretty much anywhere quickly and easily."

"Spain's a big place to look for one girl. But I assume we're going anyway?"

"Tom," Hugo sighed. "I have a full-time job, remember. An ambassador to report to, people to manage."

"Papers to shuffle, asses to kiss, yeah I get it," Tom said.

"And all we know is she went to Madrid. That's not much of a lead." He took out his phone. "Let me call Bart, though. Let him know that much."

Tom gestured toward the back. "Dude, can we go see the naked girls already?"

"In a moment, be patient." Tom sober was childish, impetuous, hormone-driven, and irritating, but Hugo had gotten used to all that, or maybe looked past it, and had been glad to have his friend sober and healthy. They'd not talked about his binge and maybe they wouldn't, maybe it really had been a one-off. Now, Hugo wondered if Tom acting like this was a way of telling Hugo he was back to his sober, and annoying, self. Bart wasn't answering his phone, so Hugo left a message then went back to Tom, who was waiting impatiently in the back hallway.

"Not there, so let's see if we can find anything else before he calls back."

They followed the faint thump of music to a closed door bearing a "Performers Only" sign. Hugo knocked, and a few seconds later Alice appeared. She wore a micro skirt of black latex and hadn't gotten around to putting her top on yet. She winked at Hugo, who made a point of looking her in the eye, and she said, "Can't wait until four o'clock, eh?"

"I could," Hugo said with a smile, "but it'd be harder to talk to you then, with all that music and wiggling."

"True, but we talked already. Forget something?"

"Yes. Anyone from Spain offer you a modeling job?" Hugo asked. Behind him, Tom maneuvered for a better vantage point.

"Spain? You better come in," she said. Tom all but knocked Hugo over to get into the changing room. One other girl sat at a vanity, wearing a silver dress and white boots. She was in the middle of applying makeup and glanced over as the two men came in, apparently unconcerned at the intrusion. Alice walked to another vanity and opened a drawer. "We get offers all the time. For modeling, pornography, private parties, everything. We all put the business cards in here so anyone can go in and choose something if they want."

Hugo walked over and looked into the drawer, stuffed full of brightly colored business cards, as well as leaflets for health services, adoption and modeling agencies, and adult-film producers. "May I?" he asked.

"Take a look, sure, just put them all back."

Tom wandered over, dragging his eyes away from the still-topless Alice. Hugo piled the cards and brochures on the vanity, and the two men began sorting through them. After two minutes, Hugo pulled a business card from the heap and held it up.

"Looks fancy," Tom said.

"I know. And just like Emily described." It was a thick card, white in color with black edging, and cursive black font. Hugo showed the card to Alice. "You know the guy who hands these out?"

"*Non*," she said. "Maybe I'd recognize him, but a lot of people come through, handing crap out. Sorry. You're welcome to take it."

"Thanks," Hugo said, turning to Tom. "Well, my friend, looks like you're getting your field trip after all."

"Excellent." Tom put down an adult-film brochure. "So where are we going?"

Hugo eyed the card and then smiled at his friend. "Ever been to Barcelona?"

CHAPTER SIX

Back at his apartment, Hugo called his office, then remembered it was the weekend and called Emma, his secretary, on her cell phone. "Sorry to bother you on a Sunday," he said.

"You should be." Emma was, as ever, brusque and to the point. The model of efficiency, Hugo had a hard time imagining what she did on her weekends, and other than the occasional polite inquiry he knew better than to pry. "Not for my sake," she said, "but because you don't need to be working every day of the week."

"That's kind of why I'm calling. Do you know off-hand how much vacation I have left this year?"

"Not exactly, but I'm certain that if you took a two-week walking tour of Turkey, followed by a three weeks in the Seychelles, you'd have plenty of time left over."

"Good. I need to take a trip with Tom."

"Uh-oh, that sounds like trouble. Although he's behaving himself these days, isn't he?"

"Occasionally. We shouldn't be gone long. Can you let the ambassador know tomorrow?"

"He's stateside for another four days—you'll be fine."

Hugo thanked her, promised to check in within a few days, and rang off. He then called Claudia.

"You're breaking our date. I knew it!" Claudia said.

"I'm sorry," Hugo said, "Really, I am, but Amy might be in trouble."

"Amy?"

Hugo spent a few minutes filling Claudia in on his special relationship with Amy, his friendship with Bart, and the concern about her silence and sudden departure.

"Tom and I are off to Barcelona to see if we can find her. It's probably nothing, but I need to check it out," he said.

"Understood. Call me if you need anything, or as soon as you find out what's going on," Claudia said. "And be careful."

They rang off, and Hugo went to his bedroom and pulled a bag from his closet, slowly filling it with clothes and toiletries for the trip. When he was done, Hugo knelt beside his bedside table, a piece of furniture that doubled as a small safe. He opened the front and reached inside, fingertips brushing against the two guns on the top shelf, then to a handheld tape recorder. He looked at the tape though the little plastic window, its faded green paper a clue as to its age. He'd not listened to this for . . . what? *Almost two years*, he thought. Then again, neither had he disposed of it. He looked up as Tom appeared in the doorway.

"What's that for?" Tom asked.

"Oh, nothing."

"Right. That's why you keep it in a safe and are now praying to it, holding it like it's some kind of religious relic."

"Well, it kind of is."

"You're being weird, dude. What is it?"

"It's the tape from an old answering machine. Back when the world had answering machines."

Tom cocked his head. "Oh. Back from when . . ." His voice trailed off.

"Yes."

It was Ellie's voice. Her jaunty, happy voice inviting some unknown caller to leave a message. Hugo wasn't entirely sure why he'd kept the tape, he'd disposed of all her other belongings over the years, in dribs and drabs, as gifts to friends and family, to charity, or just the trash can. But this was different, this was actually *her*. When he listened to the tape, she was there again, for those few seconds, alive and in the room.

"This business with Bart's daughter," Hugo said softly. "Made me think of her."

"Of course," said Tom. "Totally natural. You know, we never really talked about what happened, the accident."

"You know the worst thing about losing someone you love?" Hugo asked.

"No, man, I've been lucky that way."

"It's the moment that you can't remember what they look like. One day something reminds you of them, and yet their face, it doesn't come to you. Makes you feel disloyal, like a traitor."

"Like I said, I've been lucky that way."

"You know, I listened to this a lot when her face started to fade. Somehow it was better than a photo. I guess a picture captures just that moment, but her voice, that brings her back and not just her face. Memories, things we did together."

"We should've talked about this before," Tom said quietly.

Hugo smiled. "You're not the sensitive type, Tom. I don't know how to talk to you about her."

"Yeah, well, I think that says more about you than it does me. You're allowed to have a friend as well as be one, you know."

"Yeah, sorry, Tom. That sounded harsh. It's hard for me to talk about, you know I'm . . ." Hugo cast about for the right word.

"Inhibited? Bottled up?"

"Something like that." Hugo put the recorder back into the safe. "Ready to go?"

"Flight leaves in three hours, and we have a place to stay."

Tom had taken over the travel arrangements, being used to last-minute excursions like this. They were taking a commercial airline, but the apartment belonged to the CIA and Tom had assured Hugo no one minded them using it.

"Three bedrooms, and on the only street in the old quarter with no name," Tom said.

"What do you mean?"

"Seriously. I mean, it has a name when you're there, but look at a map and you'll see this one tiny alleyway with no name. CIA owns the buildings on each side of the alley, which leads from the seafront road into the old quarter. Cool little place, cobble stones and all that old shit. It also has metal gates at each end which get locked at ten p.m. We'll have the code so we can come and go as we please, but it stops nosy people from wandering through at night."

"Nosy people?"

"Yeah, you know. Terrorists, foreign agents, those kinds of nosy people."

Hugo grabbed his bag. "We likely to come across any of those?"

Tom grinned. "Hope springs eternal."

♉

They took a taxi from the Barcelona airport, the driver nipping in and out of the nighttime traffic. As they reached the city center, the car slowed and Hugo lowered his window. The October air was soft and cool, with the faint tang of salt and fish to it.

"I got us here, so I assume you have a plan?" Tom asked.

"We'll go to the address on the business card first thing in the morning."

"Guns blazing?"

"Flash grenades first."

"You're going to be all ingratiating and polite, aren't you?" Tom said.

"Yep. If that doesn't work, you can chopper onto the roof, slip down the chimney, and shoot everyone."

"You've never been to Barcelona, have you?"

"No," said Hugo. "Why?"

"They don't have chimneys."

"Then we'll have to hope my way works. In the meantime, I don't see any reason why we can't scout around a little. Maybe check the place out and find a nice, quiet restaurant nearby."

The taxi let them out by the small Hotel Medinaceli, two blocks from their apartment. They'd given the driver that location partly because of their street-with-no-name but mostly as a security measure, ingrained into Tom's daily habits—should anyone ask the cabbie where they got out, he would point them directly to the hotel, a place that would have no record of them, nor any employee who'd recognize them.

As Tom paid the driver, Hugo looked around to get his bearings. The streets were narrow, the high and wide sidewalks taking precedence over the thin, one-way roads. Buildings four and five stories high surrounded them, old buildings of wood and stone. They walked slowly to their alleyway, which Tom had dubbed "Secret Street." When they reached the entrance, Tom punched in the four-digit code and swung the gate open. No creak, no squeak.

"Hear that?" Tom grinned. "That's the sound of efficiency. Takes a secretary nine weeks to send a fax, but the Company sure knows how to keep a foreign gate oiled."

They walked the thirty yards down the clean, cobbled street until they reached the apartment building. Tom waved a key fob at the iron-grill door and let them into the foyer. Ahead, a new-looking marble staircase wound its way around a glassed elevator shaft. They walked up the stairs to the apartment on the second floor and took a quick tour. Its main living room looked out over the cobbled alleyway, while the three bedrooms sat at the back of the apartment, each with its own small bathroom.

"Pricey real estate," Hugo said, looking at a map. "We're right on the edge of the Old Town."

"And the harbor," said Tom. "And a central highway. And some great restaurants. Shall we?"

"Yeah, I'm starving. Let me leave Bart another message, though." Hugo dialed his number and it went straight to voicemail. "It's Hugo, with an update. We know Amy used her passport to enter Spain via Madrid. And it looks like she was offered a modeling job by a company in Barcelona. I just got into the city with my friend Tom Green. If you're thinking of coming over still, I'm sure you can stay with us." Hugo glanced at Tom and saw him shaking his head vigorously. "On second thought, let me know if you're coming and we'll book you a hotel room in the old part of the city. It's a paperwork thing." Hugo rang off.

"Sorry," Tom said, "but I don't know the guy, and I can't be inviting strangers into Company apartments."

"Yeah, no worries," Hugo said. "I totally forgot what a stickler for the rules you are."

"Screw you. Now let's go eat."

They turned left out of the apartment, walking slowly to the end of the alleyway, where they let themselves out through the iron gates. Two women in green overalls and reflective vests walked toward them, one carrying a broom and the other a long hose that was attached to a beast of a vehicle, squat and growling. The machine inched its way along the street, scrubbing the road as its minions ahead power-washed and swept the sidewalk.

Hugo and Tom crossed the street to avoid being sucked up with the trash, although as far as Hugo could tell the street was already impressively clean. They meandered down the narrow, and therefore amusingly named, Carrer Ample, then cut left through an even smaller connecting street. The smell of cooking meat wafted out to meet them, and both men paused to inspect the menu.

"You know what looks good?" Tom asked, licking his lips. "Frigging everything."

"Smells great, too," Hugo agreed. "But we're supposed to be checking out the address from that card. It's close, so I don't think you'll starve to death."

"Nutrition expert, huh?"

"You've lost weight since you stopped drinking," Hugo said, with a grin. "But you've got a few stores left. Same as I do."

Tom muttered as they moved off, winding their way deeper into the Old Town, drifting past and through the packs of revelers looking for their next watering hole. Hugo kept an ear out for the languages being spoken and was pleased that most people seemed to be speaking Spanish. This was October, several months past the height of the tourist

season, and so far Hugo had heard no English, a little French, and a surprising amount of Russian.

The streets and buildings were fascinating too, the shop fronts
little more than squares, packed in side-by-side along the wriggling
stone streets. Most were closed up for the evening, their metal shutters
spray-painted in bright colors. Hugo couldn't tell if the closed stores
were abandoned or merely shut for the night, but the random squares
of color gave him the impression of an advent calendar; pretty facades
hiding unknown delights, bakeries, flower shops, and toy stores that
would spring open for the residents and tourists in the morning.

They turned a tight corner and found themselves in a large square, a
playground taking up its center, parents chatting and laughing together
as their kids scampered and climbed.

Tom ignored the group, his eyes fixed on a young couple on a
bench thirty yards away. "Smell that?" he said.

Hugo twitched his nose. "Ah, your old friend Mary Jane. You
didn't give that up with alcohol?"

"Maybe I did, maybe I didn't. Sure smells good, though."

Hugo was consulting his phone. "According to my map, it's one
street over. Let's check the place out, then you can come back and ask
for a toke."

"Me? No. I really shouldn't, they say it's a gateway drug. Although
we are on vacation . . ."

"No, Tom, we're not." Hugo started for the far side of the square,
and Tom trotted to catch up with him.

"Can I see the damn business card at least?" he puffed.

Hugo took it out of his wallet as they walked and passed it to Tom.
"Can't pronounce the street name, but what the fuck's 'Estruch Entertainment Enterprises'?"

"I did an online search before we left, obviously, but it didn't tell
me much. They bill themselves as an entertainment company, giving
tours and helping foreigners find work in Europe."

"Employees?"

"No clue, the website doesn't have their profiles. In fact, it had two pages. The home page, which was vague about what they do, and a second one with testimonials from happy clients. First names given only."

"Sounds like a front," Tom said.

"Yeah, and not a very sophisticated one."

"Nice business cards, though."

Around the corner, the street narrowed briefly before flaring out in the middle, like a snake with a full stomach. The buildings around them could have been homes or businesses, Hugo couldn't tell. An ornate water fountain, almost like a sculpture, sat on a stone plinth in the middle of the bulge. Hugo and Tom stood beside it, looking around for street numbers.

"Here you go," Tom said. "Oh look, they want us to come in."

Hugo looked over to see what Tom was talking about. Estruch Entertainment Enterprises took up the ground floor with three apartments stacked above it, judging by the laundry on each balcony. Hugo pressed his nose to the storefront, but the tint of the windows prevented him seeing anything inside. The main door was on his right, a wooden door with glass panels and, like most entrances he'd seen, covered with an iron grill. He couldn't see the invitation Tom meant, so gave him a quizzical look.

Tom grinned, dug into his pocket and stood close to the locked grill. "These metal doors, man, they put all the effort into the ironwork and use sloppy locks that an arthritic granny could open with her middle finger." Metal objects flashed in his hands, and Hugo heard them clinking inside the lock.

"Tom, hang on, no need for that, we just came to scope the place."

"Oh, is that right? You think if we show up tomorrow and ask politely, they'll tell us where Amy is?"

"They may not even know. We're here because this place is our only lead, not because it's a good one."

"If it's our only lead, the sooner we explore it, the better."

"Or, instead of spending the night in jail for burglary, we could check out as many strip joints in the city as we can and hope we find her."

Tom paused. "As much as I like that idea, as an expert on the subject, I can promise you that not only would we fail to cover a hundredth of them, but chances are we'd get delayed at the first and never leave." He turned back to the door. "Sad as I am to admit it, this is a better option."

Hugo looked nervously over his shoulder, knowing that Tom had a point but not wanting to get caught breaking into a building on his first night in Barcelona. He flinched as he heard peals of laughter and the strains of a guitar, but the noise faded quickly away and he breathed a sigh of relief. "Tom, I mean it, we can just—"

"Done." Tom swung the iron door open.

"What about the inside door?" Hugo asked.

"Better locks on that, I'm afraid." Tom winked at Hugo, slipped off a shoe, and used a heel to punch out the window nearest the door handle. "Stealth, dexterity, brute force. I'm the complete package." He reached in and unlocked the door from the inside. "Shall we?"

CHAPTER SEVEN

They stood inside and listened for a moment. No shouts of outrage came from the street, nor were there any startled voices inside the building. Light from the street outside filtered through the window, giving them enough visibility to operate without a flashlight.

Hugo looked around for an alarm panel but didn't see one.

"Could be a silent alarm somewhere," Tom said, reading his mind.

"Yeah, that's what worries me." They were in the reception area, and Hugo started toward a small desk that bore a telephone, a calendar book, and a sleek desktop computer. "Since we've already committed the Spanish version of a felony, how about we make this quick?"

"Fine by me." Tom started down a hallway that looked to run to the back of the building, dividing it into two halves.

Hugo fired up the computer, impatient as it slowly came to life. "Of course," he muttered, when the screen asked for a password. He turned it off and started opening the desk's drawers.

Tom reappeared. "Any luck?"

"Depends," said Hugo, sliding the last drawer shut. "You need any pens, paperclips, or staples?"

"Not right now. Let's try the offices. Two on the left of the hallway, one to the right. A bathroom on the right, too, at the end."

"And another exit?"

Tom grinned. "You're a clever boy, Hugo, I always forget that about you."

"Get started, I want to check their calendar." He picked up the book and flipped through the pages, but the entries were written in an almost-illegible scrawl. That, and the fact that his Spanish wasn't great, made it hard to decipher the words. Some looked like people's names, some could have been businesses. He put it down and started for the hallway, almost tripping on a cardboard box by the wall. He knelt for a closer look, but the box was sealed, looked like it'd been delivered in the mail and not yet opened. He shifted it with his hand, but the weight of it told him nothing of the contents.

He stood and moved to the larger office on the right side of the hallway, hearing Tom rustling through the first one to the left. Inside, and opposite the door, sat a large wooden desk bearing a few stacks of papers and opened pieces of mail, all arranged neatly, as well as a computer and a modern telephone. To his left lay three filing cabinets, a collection of stuffed teddy bears lined up across the top of each one, sitting there quietly, just watching. To his right sat four sleek, brown leather club chairs set up around a coffee table.

Hugo moved to the desk. He reached a hand toward a stack of papers but froze when the phone rang. A second later, Tom's head popped through the doorway.

"Fuck," he said. "You better—"

"I know." Hugo picked up the receiver and held it to his ear, saying nothing. If it was a customer, client, or business partner phoning after hours, they were okay. If not . . . Hugo listened as the man's voice spoke, catching enough of what he was saying to understand who he was and why he was calling. He gently hung up the phone, wiped his prints from it, and started toward Tom. "Security company. We need to leave."

"Dammit."

Hugo took one last look around the room then headed down the hallway. He paused outside the door to the third office, opening it with his hand in his sleeve. He flicked on the light and glanced around. A desk and a computer, a couple of chairs and a filing cabinet. A couple of mass-produced prints on the walls, a sailboat and a landscape. Again, all very neat and tidy, probably just like every other modern, paperless office in Barcelona.

"Hugo, I hear sirens," Tom said.

Hugo listened and heard them too. "You wiped the first office down?"

"No, they don't teach us to do that in the CIA. Are fingerprints really a thing?"

"So I'm told." Hugo brushed past Tom, who followed him to the back door, a solid block of wood that could have been handed down from the Middle Ages. Three large, iron bolts kept it secured. Easy to get out, but impossible to lock behind them. But since the busted window in the front door would give away the break-in, there was no need for subtlety anymore. Hugo slid the bolts and pulled the door open.

Both men recoiled at the stench of garbage that met them in the narrow alleyway.

"Pity the bloodhounds," Tom muttered. "Which way?"

"No clue." Hugo started to his left. Darkness cloaked the path ahead, and the high brick walls all around made him feel claustrophobic. He wasn't in the habit of acting illegally and was annoyed at himself for not reining Tom in, but he was there for a reason, the very best of reasons, and he also knew that breaking a lock or two was a small price to pay to find Amy.

The sirens were louder now, but echoing through the dense, stone passageways, which made it impossible to know which direction they were coming from, or how close they were getting. Hugo swore as they reached an iron gate, heavily chained and padlocked.

"We gotta go back," he said, as Tom stumbled into him.

"I can pick that lock. Probably."

"Quicker to go back," Hugo said, then added, "Probably."

He followed Tom this time, the sturdy figure of his friend striding back toward the overflowing cans and dumpsters that lined the alley. Hugo held his breath as they got near the unlocked but closed wooden door to the business, but they sailed past without anyone seeing them. Hugo breathed a sigh of relief as he spotted the end of the alley, but both men froze as a voice came down at them from above. Hugo instinctively looked up and saw a teenage boy on his balcony, two stories above the street.

The boy called down again, but Hugo couldn't tell what he was saying, nor even decipher the tone. Angry? Curious?

He jerked as Tom grabbed his arm and pulled him away. "Don't look up, you idiot," Tom said. "Now we have to hope he can't describe those boyish good looks."

"Shit, sorry." Hugo knew his friend was right. He should have kept his head down and his feet moving. "Not used to being the bad guy."

In moments they were out in the open, a small plaza with bistros on opposite corners, metal tables and chairs scattered in front of them. People milled about, picking a table, looking at menus while chatting with the waiters, paying Hugo and Tom no heed whatsoever.

"Well, this looks like fate," Tom said, rubbing his hands together. "Bottle of wine? Plate of paella?"

Hugo caught the aromas of the restaurants now, grilled meat and something sweeter he couldn't identify. All of it good. "Sounds tempting, but not tonight, amigo. We're here to keep you dry."

"Weird, I could swear we came here to find Amy."

"No, that's why *I'm* here."

"Then you can monitor my drinking, make sure I don't have too much. A bottle each seems reasonable."

"Again, tempting, but no. After what we just did, I'd feel happier inside the apartment. Let's head back and do a little research into Estruch Entertainment Enterprises."

Tom waved his arms toward the lighted windows of the nearest restaurant. "What about, you know, food and drink?"

"I'm not inhumane, Tom, we'll eat, don't worry. There's a little grocery store on the corner of our street where we can grab something. I'll cook."

"Awesome. I came all the way to Barcelona for some Texas home cooking."

"You're not going to make this babysitting thing easy, are you?" Hugo looked at the map on his phone, then pointed to one of the cobbled streets leading out of the plaza. "This way, I believe."

"We could compromise," Tom said, his voice rising in pitch and desperation as Hugo moved away. "Get something to go, something local."

But Hugo kept walking, knowing that arguing with Tom would only encourage him. A minute later, he could hear his friend's heavy footsteps and disgruntled muttering a few feet behind. Hugo smiled. He was no closer to finding Amy this evening, but keeping himself out of jail and Tom sober was a decent-enough result for their first night in Barcelona.

CHAPTER EIGHT

The next morning, the two men stood in the kitchen, cursing their failure to buy coffee the night before.

"Not that the crap you make would have been drinkable," Tom mumbled. "But still."

Hugo said nothing. It was, in truth, his most recognizable failure—give him the finest beans in the world and the best equipment on the market, and still his coffee would be bad. Better than nothing, perhaps, but not by much.

"Well, put some pants on and let's go find some. I'm pretty sure Barcelona has cafés."

Tom wandered off to his bedroom and reappeared a minute later, tucking his shirt into his pants. "Let's do it."

They let themselves out of the apartment and into the cobbled alleyway. Hugo checked his watch as a seagull wheeled overhead, squawking to his colleagues at the nearby harbor.

"Seven o'clock. Kind of early for you."

"Yep," Tom said. "My body screws with me when I don't fill it with booze. Can't decide if it's rewarding or punishing me."

Hugo smiled, and they set off toward the Old Town. They reached the end of their little street and paused, eyeing the networks of streets, trying to gauge which was the best bet for a café.

"This way," Tom said, pointing straight across the narrow road.

"Based on?"

"Not wanting to stand still any longer."

Hugo shrugged, not having any better directions to give. But they paused as a police car turned the corner and headed down the street toward them. He and Tom watched the car approach.

"Is that a Citroën?" Tom asked.

"A Citroën Picasso, to be precise."

"All the power and prestige of a briefcase on wheels. A small briefcase. A wallet."

"Yeah, but perfect for these little streets. Our cruisers wouldn't fit."

"Maybe," Tom said. "But do they only arrest midgets? You're not fitting in the back of that thing." He patted his stomach. "Me neither."

They waited for the car to pass, but as it got close, the blue light on the roof lit up, and the car stopped. Two officers climbed out and approached them.

The darker of the two spoke in good English. "Would you come with us, please?"

"Why would we do that?" asked Hugo.

The officer smiled, and Hugo couldn't help but notice the sculpted biceps and flat stomach. "I'm asking nicely, Señor Marston. Please, get in."

"You know my name?"

"Yes, sir. I do."

"Interesting. But I always appreciate a friendly police officer," Hugo said, without moving. "And we're happy to oblige local law enforcement, but I'd still kind of like to know why."

"You have no idea?" the cop asked.

"None." Hugo's mind flashed to the previous night's visit to the offices of Estruch Entertainment Enterprises.

"A senior police officer would like to have a brief word with you. He insists, which means you can go voluntarily in the comfort of my car, or we can explore alternatives."

The calmness in his voice told Hugo everything he needed to know: that this cop was used to getting his way, and those muscles weren't just for show. Beside him, Tom cleared his throat. "Well, if it's

Señor Marston you need, I'll be on my way. Haven't had my coffee yet, I'm sure you understand . . ."

"Both of you," the officer said. "And we have coffee at the station. It's really quite good."

"I doubt that," Tom muttered.

Hugo wasn't happy about the surprise interruption to the day, but they could hardly disobey. "So let's test your theory, shall we?"

"My theory?" Tom frowned. "What the hell are you talking about?"

The officers stiffened, as if Hugo was giving a code for resisting. Or running.

Hugo smiled and gestured to the police car. "Let's see if one or both of us can fit into the back of this shopping cart."

The officers held the doors as Hugo and Tom squeezed themselves into the back seat, Hugo folding himself almost in half to make it in, Tom huffing and swearing as he banged his head and got his feet stuck.

"Where exactly are we going?" Hugo asked, raising his voice to make himself heard through the plastic barrier between him and the front of the car.

"Be there in ten minutes," came the reply. All other attempts at conversation were ignored, so Hugo sat back as best he could and watched the city roll past. It took closer to twenty minutes, the morning traffic apparently not bothering their two escorts, but Tom got twitchier and twitchier the longer the drive took.

Hugo tried to calm him down with a joke. "I'm assuming you have unpaid parking tickets or something."

"Hey, it was your name they used, not mine. Plus, you know I don't drive." Tom shifted in his seat and lowered his voice. "You could pull the diplomatic-immunity card, you know."

"They know who we are, Tom. They know we have diplomatic immunity." Hugo grinned. "Well, that I do. God knows what you have. We're going where we're going no matter what card I play. And if this is their version of comfort, I suggest we don't irritate them and find out what the alternative means to them."

"Good point."

A street dotted with police cars told Hugo they were there, and the driver pulled into an empty space. He led them into a building, toward a metal detector.

"Uh, Hugo," Tom said quietly.

Hugo shot him a look. "What?"

"I may have brought a small toy with me. You know, in case the croissants tried to attack us at breakfast."

"This is Spain; they don't have croissants. And seriously, you brought your gun?"

Tom shrugged, sheepish. "Habit."

Hugo took off his boots and belt, passing through the detector without setting it off before turning to watch Tom go down in flames.

"Hey guys," Tom said as he pulled off his belt. "You never patted us down when you picked us up."

"I know," the dark-skinned officer said. "You're not under arrest. And you're not allowed to carry a weapon, so why would I?"

"Well, that's the thing," Tom said. "Hugo, you wanna help me out here?"

"Relax. They know who we are and they're having fun with you. Just set the metal detector off, let them taser you, and we can get on with this."

"Fuck you," Tom said. "Okay guys, I happen to have found a gun in the back seat of your car. I picked it up and put it in my empty holster so that you'd be safe." He opened his jacket. "You wanna take it now? I'm not a big fan of pulling guns in police stations."

The second cop said something to his colleague and stepped forward, snatching the gun from Tom's armpit. Neither man seemed particularly amused, thought Hugo. Nor particularly concerned. *They absolutely know who we are.*

The officers directed them to a stairway, and their footsteps echoed as they traipsed up two flights.

"*Aquí,*" the pale cop said, holding the door open for them. It led into a long corridor lined with doors, an administrative floor, Hugo guessed. He and Tom followed their escorts to an open door halfway down the corridor. An attractive young woman sat behind a desk, and she stood as they entered, gesturing for them to go into the office behind her. Hugo and Tom followed directions to a pair of wooden chairs opposite a large desk.

"Who lives in here, then?" Hugo asked. He looked around but didn't see a nameplate or any photos that might explain who had summoned them here. When the door closed quietly behind them, Hugo turned. "Alone again," he said.

"Any clue what the fuck's going on?" Tom asked.

"Nope. Have you had any dealing in the past that might have, um, rubbed the locals the wrong way?"

"Nope. And like I said, it's your name they used."

"They let you carry your gun, Tom, they know who you are."

"Well, if they did that, they know we're friendly. Which means they'll be friendly."

"And maybe bring coffee," Hugo said.

Behind them, the door opened and both men swung around in their seats to see who'd come in. He was clearly the man in charge, his demeanor told Hugo that, but there was also something familiar about him, tall and slender, with soft gray hair and a tidy mustache. The eyes which held his . . . Hugo took a full second to process the eyes, that face that he'd seen in photographs and once in the flesh on one of the saddest days of his life. Of both their lives.

"Well, well, Señor Marston," the policeman said. "I must say, I am very surprised to see you here and under these circumstances."

Hugo stood and put out his hand. "No matter the circumstances, I am pleased to see you," he said. "And just as surprised, I can assure you."

CHAPTER NINE

Tom rose and looked back and forth between the two men. "Feel like I'm out of the loop here. You guys know each other?"

The tall policeman turned to Tom and extended a hand. "You are Tom Green, Hugo's CIA friend. We didn't get a chance to meet before."

"Before what?" Tom asked.

"This is Bartoli Garcia," Hugo said quietly. "Raul's brother."

"Well, for f . . ." Tom cut himself off and instead reached for Garcia's hand. "It's an honor. Your brother was . . ." Words failed him and he shook his head. "I'm sorry, really. Awesome guy and a good friend."

"*Muchas gracias*," Garcia said. "We weren't as close as we would have liked. I regret that now, very deeply."

An image of Ellie flashed into Hugo's mind, smiling at him, telling him to come home early and spend more time with her. She knew it wasn't always his fault, and she knew he got away whenever he could. It was just her way of letting him know she missed him, looked forward to seeing him. Yes, like most people who'd lost a loved one, Hugo thought, he had his regrets, too.

"At least we got the fucker who shot him," Tom said. "Well, Hugo did."

"And for that I'm very grateful." Garcia gestured for them to sit and then walked behind his desk. He leaned over and pressed a button on his phone. A female voice filtered through. "Micaela, can you bring us some coffee? We may be here a while."

"*Sí, Señor*," she said.

"*Gracias.*" He rang off and looked up at Hugo and Tom. "What are you gentlemen doing here, may I ask?"

"Well," Tom started, "we were heading out for coffee when a cop car pulled up and a couple of burly officers told us to get in."

"I think he means Barcelona," Hugo said. "He sent the car; he knows why we're in his office."

Garcia sat down. "Precisely. I would have sent something more luxurious, but those streets . . . we all have to make do with smaller cars in the Old Town."

"No problem," said Hugo. His mind was working overtime—he'd not planned to contact local law enforcement because he didn't have anything to tell them. Barely a scrap of a clue and, just as important, very little time to investigate that scrap.

"So, Señor Marston, I can only assume you and Señor Green are here on vacation," Garcia said. "If you were here on business, I'm sure you would have notified us."

"Right," Hugo said. "Mostly. A friend's daughter has gone missing and we're looking into it for him."

"Gone missing? That sounds like official business to me."

"It's not. Not yet." Hugo explained. "She's American, been living in Paris. She's an aspiring model and may have been offered a job here. Her father's worried because she's been out of contact and that's not like her. She also missed a meeting with me."

"What makes you think she's in Barcelona?" Garcia asked.

"A guy she met. He offered her a job and was handing out business cards in Paris. The business card led us here."

A knock at the door heralded the pretty young woman, now carrying a tray with three coffee cups.

"Gentleman, this is my assistant Micaela Galaviz." He cleared a space on the desk. "Here is fine, *gracias.*"

She put the tray down and gave the Americans a smile. Hugo couldn't help but notice a light come on behind Tom's eyes, as always happened when a pretty girl smiled at him. Galaviz noticed it too and brushed a friendly hand over Tom's shoulder. When she'd left the room, Tom said, "Nice young lady. How's her coffee?"

"She's a trained lawyer," Garcia said, without smiling. "Her coffee's good, but she does a whole lot more for me than that."

"Beauty *and* brains, eh?"

"And I'd be grateful if you'd show her a little more respect. She's not here for your entertainment." Tom sat back in his chair, and Garcia continued. "Now, while we're on that subject, I believe we were about to discuss Estruch Entertainment Enterprises."

Hugo and Tom exchanged glances. "How did you know that?" Hugo asked.

"Luck. Good or bad, I suppose it depends on your point of view." Garcia eyed both men. "We retrieved video footage from a break-in there last night. It happened to be a quiet night other than that, and I was talking to the officers investigating the crime. I have worked here a long time, and when they said they had film of the burglars, well, I figured maybe it was one of the usual suspects. Someone I'd recognize. Plus, you know, it's always fun to watch those videos, the ones where the bumbling intruders have no idea they were being filmed."

"Ah, yes," Tom started. "About that—"

Garcia cut him off with a wave of the hand. "And so you see my problem. I should be arresting you, not serving you coffee, don't you think?"

"If your coffee is anything like his," Tom jerked a thumb at Hugo, "then feel free."

Garcia raised an eyebrow, clearly surprised at Tom's levity.

"Please ignore him, Chief Inspector." Hugo shot Tom a look. "What do you want us to do to make this right?"

"I'm working on that, but I'm afraid you are not going to like the first step."

"Which is?" Hugo asked.

Garcia took a moment to fill three cups with coffee, then waved a hand over the tray. "Help yourselves to milk and sugar."

When they'd settled with cups in hands, Hugo prompted the chief inspector. "You were saying about the first step."

"Yes. I'm very sorry, but the first step is being arrested."

"Arrested?" Tom said. "You're fucking kidding."

"No, Señor Green, I am not." Garcia sat forward and fixed Tom in a glare. "I am aware of my brother's affection for and admiration of you. I am also aware that he was willing, or at least able, to look the other way when you operated outside the expected procedural boundaries. That might be Paris, but it is not Barcelona. Here we do things according to the law. Policemen do not have the right to break into people's homes or businesses whenever they choose. Even American policemen."

"Do you mean *especially* American policemen?" Tom asked.

"You think I am biased against you? You think I'd allow a German or Japanese police officer to break the law at will?"

"I know that it'd take a crapload more than a quick peek into an empty building for me to slap the cuffs on you," Tom snapped.

Hugo put a hand on his arm. "Easy, Tom."

"Handcuffs? I don't expect to have to do that," Garcia said. "In fact, I will merely ask you to stay in the building until I have decided what we need to do."

"Are we talking hours," Hugo asked, "or much longer?"

Garcia sighed. "I have not told my superiors. If I do, I expect it will be a couple of hours, and then you will be escorted back to the airport."

"Then don't damn well tell them!" Tom said.

"Tom, for crying out loud, will you shut it for long enough to hear him out?" Hugo said.

"I need to check on the progress of the investigation. Specifically, find out whether the owners of the business wish to see the burglars prosecuted. Or, in this case, thrown out of the country. I imagine it would help if there was money to pay for the broken window."

"That won't be a problem," Hugo assured him.

"Yeah, mind if we pop out to an ATM?" Tom asked.

Garcia slammed his hand on the desk. "This is not a joke! If you try to leave here, you will spend the day, maybe several, in a jail cell."

Tom leaned forward, his face reddening. "Look, pal, don't threaten me. We have diplomatic immunity, both of us."

"That does not give you the right to break into businesses here."

"No, but it means we'll get away with it," Tom said. "So how about we skip the chest-pounding and start looking for this missing girl."

"Show me your diplomatic paperwork, and then we can worry about her."

Hugo stood. "Chief Inspector, please. Tom's right in that we have immunity and arresting us will be more paperwork and red tape than you want to handle. He's also right that we're wasting time that should be spent looking for Amy." Garcia opened his mouth, but Hugo continued. "But I agree with you that we have to make this right. We'll pay for any damage and face whatever consequences you want. But not now, not today. We need to work together to find Amy Dreiss first. After that, we're at your mercy."

Garcia considered the two men for a moment, tenting his fingers in front of his face. "Very well, but I expect two things from you. Without reservation."

"Certainly," Hugo said. "What are they?"

"You will inform me before you take any further investigative actions in this case. Which means you do nothing without my permission."

"Absolutely," Hugo said. "What else?"

"You keep an eye on him," Garcia said, pointing at Tom. "I'm beginning to wonder why my brother praised him so generously."

"I grow on you," Tom said.

"Fungus grows on people. As do warts," Garcia allowed his smile to reach his eyes, letting them know they were back on neutral ground. "We shall see about you."

"Trust me," Hugo said. "Fungus and warts are a good comparison."

"Fuck you," Tom muttered.

Garcia scribbled something on a piece of paper. "My cell number, feel free to poke around, but do not enter anyone's property, with or without their permission, without calling me first." He handed the note to Hugo. "Now then. To begin with, are you sure she's missing? And by that I mean missing in a way that requires the police to look for her?"

"That was our hesitation in involving you in the first place," Hugo said. "We can't be sure."

"She's a grown woman," Garcia said. "Maybe she wants a little distance from her father, is that possible?"

"She's not that kind of girl. More to the point, she's not the kind of girl to ignore her father's birthday, miss a meeting with me, and leave the country without telling any of us or her friend in Paris."

"I see."

"At the very least," Hugo went on, "it's worth talking to the people at Estruch to find out whether the guy who was recruiting her works there."

"Can't hurt to ask," Garcia conceded. "Although you could have done that this morning without the nighttime dramatics."

"Seemed like a good idea at the time," Tom chipped in.

"It wasn't." Garcia looked up. "What do you know about that business?"

"Not a lot," Hugo said. "You?"

"From what my officers told me, it's been operating for a number of years, they broker tours and also place foreign workers looking for jobs. Usually in the tourist industry."

"Is that a euphemism?" Hugo asked.

"Euphem . . . ? I don't know that word," Garcia said.

"Maybe I'm being unfair," Hugo said, "but sometimes when people say 'tourist industry' they mean strip clubs."

"Ah. I don't think we know that much about them. I have no reason to suspect they are doing anything illegal, that's for certain. If the police do not get involved, what is your next step?"

"I'd like to talk to the people who work there, at Estruch," Hugo said. "See if they know Amy, or have ever seen her. And I might like to check whether any of them have been to Paris recently."

Garcia picked up his phone and dialed. "Micaela, *Tiene* . . . ? *Bueno.*" He listened for a moment more then hung up. "As ever, Micaela is a step ahead. She has a file for you. Well, she made one for me but has prepared you a copy. A little information on the four people who run and work at that business. You are welcome to take the file with you and talk to them."

"Have they seen the video of us?" Hugo asked. "If so, they may not be too polite."

"No, they gave it straight to the officers on scene, who brought it back here to download, so they've not watched it."

"Glad to hear it," Hugo said. "So we're good to go?"

"There's one more thing . . ." Garcia paused at the sound of a knock on the door. "Ah, that must be her . . ." He turned to Tom and spoke in a quiet voice, the hint of a smile on his lips. "Señor Green, the person you are about to meet. Mess with her at your own peril."

CHAPTER TEN

The woman took three steps into Garcia's office and stopped to look around the room. She threw a quick salute to the chief inspector, her body stiffening for as long as it took, then relaxed. All three men stood, and Hugo couldn't help but admire the confidence in her languid stance as she took them in.

She was a police officer, or department employee of some sort. The light-blue pants and short-sleeved shirt, with small colored patches on the breast, was a uniform; but other than a thin, black belt, she wasn't wearing the accoutrements of most cops—gun, cuffs, baton. She looked fit and strong, an attractive woman with olive skin and hair pulled back into a short pony tail. But there was also something about her that would deter too much familiarity, a sharp edge that differentiated attractive from approachable. She stepped forward and Hugo thought he saw her limp.

"I am Grace Emanuelle Cruz Silva, I was born and raised here." Her voice was clipped, liked she'd learned English in England. "I will be your escort."

Tom opened his mouth to say something, Hugo assumed related to her being an escort, but he closed it again, one witticism kept to himself.

"Nice to meet you. I'm Hugo Marston and this is Tom Green." *Impressive grip*, Hugo thought when she took his hand.

She nodded at Tom and shook his hand, too. "Señor Green?"

"Yes, ma'am, pleased to meet you. For a native Catalan, you speak English very well."

"Thank you. For an American, so do you." No hint of a smile. "Shall we go?"

"Where to first?" Hugo asked.

"I'll take you to your apartment. You can have lunch, siesta, then I'll pick you up at three thirty."

Hugo and Tom swapped glances, unsure if she was serious. "A little early for lunch, isn't it?" Hugo said. "And if Amy is really missing and in trouble, we should get going as soon as possible."

"Don't worry, we won't be losing any time," she said.

"How can you be so sure?" asked Hugo.

A twitch of her lips. "In Barcelona, bad guys take siestas, too."

"You're the boss," Hugo said, starting toward the door. Tom and Grace Silva followed behind but came to a swift halt when Hugo stopped and looked back at Garcia. "It was the teddy bears, wasn't it?" Hugo asked.

For the first time since he'd entered the room, Chief Inspector Bartoli Garcia smiled broadly.

"Yes, Hugo, it was," Garcia said. "And my brother would have been proud of your deduction. Yes indeed, it was the teddy bears."

♉

They were silent in the car, but after a couple of minutes Tom fidgeted and then said, "For fuck's sake, Hugo, stop it."

"Stop what?"

"You're trying to make me ask, aren't you?"

"I have no idea what you're talking about."

"The fucking teddy bears. You're desperate for me to ask what that meant."

"No, actually, I'm not. Not in the slightest." Hugo's tone was mild and designed to irritate his friend. "Makes no difference to me at all."

"Bull. But I'll do you the favor and ask: what's with the lovefest over teddy bears?"

Hugo caught Grace Silva looking in the rear-view mirror, apparently also curious. "Well, since you're asking so nicely," he said. "Teddy bears are what got us busted."

"I don't understand," Tom said through gritted teeth, "as you well know. Fucking explain."

"The surveillance camera was inside one of the teddy bears," Hugo said. "Common for parents to use them to keep an eye on their nannies or babysitters. I wondered at the time why a company like that would have teddy bears, and if there'd been only one, well, maybe I'd have figured it out. But with a whole slew of them, I just assumed it was a collection. A quirk of whoever had that office."

"Really?" Tom said. "A fucking teddy bear?"

"He's right," Silva said. "Very clever, Señor Marston."

"Oh, don't flatter him," Tom said indignantly. "Just wait until he pulls his little Sherlock Holmes trick on you."

"What is that?" Silva asked.

"It's his show-off thing. To impress girls. You wouldn't be interested."

Silva was silent for a moment, negotiating a left turn across the heavy city traffic. "I'm a little interested," she said.

"In?" Tom asked hopefully.

"The trick. Whatever it is."

"Yeah, well, don't be too impressed. Like I said," Tom went on. "It's his show-off thing, like Sherlock used to do to his new clients when they arrived on his doorstep." Hugo cringed as his friend adopted an English accent. "Ah, Lord Porterfield, I see you spent the last six weeks in the Netherlands, training geese to ride bicycles with a one-armed chimpanzee as your chef."

In the front seat, Silva chuckled. "Solve that one, Señor Marston."

Hugo smiled and joined in. "That's easy. You can tell by the mud on Lord Porterfield's shoes that he's been to Holland. It's a distinctive red clay and it's in the soles of his shoes still. Plus, as he moves, he keeps ducking, indicating that he's been around windmills."

"And the geese riding bikes?" Silva asked.

"Elementary. Lord Porterfield is a known activist who opposes the production of foie gras. Additionally, you will notice that his right trouser leg has a band around the ankle where the material has been worn thin. That tells me he was there to rescue geese and has been riding bicycles. Scientific studies have shown that one man can only carry four geese on a moving bicycle, so I deduce that Lord Porterfield has instead been teaching the geese to ride themselves to safety."

Tom grinned. "I told you he was good. Born storyteller."

"Wait," Silva said, "what about the one-armed chimp as the chef?"

"Ah yes," Hugo said, stroking his chin for effect. "The easiest deduction of all. Lord Porterfield smells strongly of bananas and poop. I can only assume his diet stems from a primate's menu selection, one that gets frustrated and flings its feces. However, the poop smell is faint, and so one is left to presume that it was thrown with its weaker arm on account of its stronger arm being missing."

Silva slowed the car to wait at a red light and took the opportunity to clap. "*Fantastico. Muy bien.*"

"Yeah, well," Tom said, "anyone can make stuff up. Not as well as that, though. But he does it for real."

Silva cocked an eye at Hugo in the mirror. "You do? Can you tell anything about me?"

"Oh, it's not as easy as all that," Hugo said.

"Which means 'yes,' just in case you were wondering," Tom said.

"Oh? Then tell me what you know."

"It's guesswork, really, and if I'm wrong, I look like an idiot."

"Everyone looks like an idiot sometime," Silva said. "Go on, tell me what you think, I won't care if you're wrong."

"I'd rather not," Hugo said. "And just so you know, generally people get more upset when I'm right."

"Not me," she said. "Go on."

"Yeah, go on," Tom chipped in. "You've barely met her, so even I'll be impressed."

Hugo rolled his eyes. "I live my life for those moments, Tom."

"I know you do. Now spill it."

"If you're sure," Hugo said.

"I'm sure," Silva said. "Now stop wasting time, we're almost at your street."

"Fine," Hugo began. "But you asked for it. I'd say that you're a former military medic, you're dealing with PTSD, you recently went on a road trip, and you're a fan of the Beatles."

"Impressive," Silva said. "And correct on all counts, so now you have to explain."

"Oh, he won't for a while," Tom said. "He'll make you wait for it, tease you a little."

"Yeah, maybe next time I see you," Hugo said. "I believe that's our road up ahead."

Silva hit the brakes and steered the car to the side of the narrow street. She left the engine running and turned to fix Hugo with a glare. "There's a jail cell back there with your name on it," she said.

Hugo put his hands up in surrender. "Since you're being so persuasive, fine. When you walked into Garcia's office, I noticed that you had a slight limp. But you also had a very erect bearing, very military. Together, those things mean nothing but bear with me because I noticed the decorations on your shirt. They seemed odd because police don't use those and I wondered why someone would wear military decorations on a police uniform. They are military, am I right?"

"Correct," she said.

"Oh, and talking of uniforms, you aren't wearing the usual police utility belt, with a gun and all that good stuff."

"So?" asked Tom. "I noticed that too. Before you, probably."

"Well done, Tom. Now what does it mean?" Hugo asked him.

"No clue."

"Then if you don't mind, I'll carry on."

"Have at it."

"Thanks. Now then, put together I'd say the lack of gun belt means you're off street duty on a semipermanent basis. Normally, someone off street duty would just be fired, although I don't know the intricacies of Barcelona's police policies nor employment law, so I could be off base on that. However, add to that the military decorations, the bearing, and the limp, I'd say you were injured in Afghanistan, physically and emotionally. Which puts you close to the front line and, since Spain doesn't have women as front-line troops, most likely as a medic. The decorations are part of your therapy, I think, and also a way of letting other people know and recognize your service."

"Wow," Silva said. "I am impressed. All of it, it's exactly right."

"Wait, what about the road trip and the Beatles?" Tom asked.

"Both so easy and obvious that I'm embarrassed to tell you," Hugo said.

"Well, I didn't get them, so they're not that fucking obvious," Tom replied.

"The front of your car has more splattered bugs than I'd expect to see if you'd just been tootling around the city. Likewise the windshield, where the wipers don't reach."

"Seriously?" Tom demanded. "Bugs?"

"And you have a Beatles key ring," Hugo said to Silva. "It's old and worn, which tells me you've had it a while, probably because it means something to you. Also, the display on your car stereo, I can see what you've been listening to."

"Great, so you can read," Tom said.

"Not just *can*, but *did*. Anyway," Hugo said cheerily, "that's the Sherlock game. It's funny how Tom asks me to do it, then gets mad when I get it right."

"One day, my friend. One day you'll crash and burn."

"But not today," Silva said with a smile. "Very impressive. And as a reward, I'll pick you up here at three thirty?"

"Sure thing. Thanks for the ride," Hugo said. He and Tom climbed out of the car and shut the doors. Tom took a step, about to walk toward their apartment.

"Hang on a second," Hugo said. They stood and watched as Silva pulled away from the curb and rounded the corner.

"What's up?" Tom asked.

"Just because she needs her siesta doesn't mean we have to have one."

Tom's eyes lit up. "What did you have in mind?"

"A little reconnaissance, a harmless little scouting mission in the neighborhood."

"For real?"

"The young guy in those files, his name is Rubén Castañeda. I saw him in Paris, outside the café where I was supposed to be meeting Amy."

"Are you serious? Why didn't you tell Garcia?"

"I will, but I didn't want to ruin his siesta. Plus, the address in the file is not even a mile from here, well within the parameters of the tourist zone."

Tom grinned. "You're a bad man, Hugo. A sneaky, charming, bad man. And I'm right behind you."

CHAPTER ELEVEN

It was a short walk but so pleasant that Hugo almost forgot what they were doing. The sun cut each little street in half, shade coming from the high stone or brick walls that housed shops, apartments, and small hotels. A gentle breeze wound its way through the old quarter, brushing their faces and rustling the dresses of two young women holding hands and walking in the opposite direction.

"I could get used to this place," Tom said.

It wasn't like Paris, Hugo decided. The narrow streets left no room for the cafés and outdoor tables that made the City of Light so special. No broad boulevards to amble along and watch the people go by. No, this was more of an exploration, like some parts of Paris could be, winding streets free of cars and where scampering children would inevitably run headlong into your legs as you turned a corner.

And around those corners, Hugo was discovering, the streets and buildings would suddenly stretch apart, making room for colorful playgrounds where parents would lounge and smoke in the wooden chairs meant for them. That's where the cafés and restaurants were, the rickety tables being cleared by the owners as the lunch-goers counted their change and headed to wherever their siesta took place.

Hugo spied a small bakery. "You hungry?"

"Fuck, yes."

"Sandwich work?"

"Same again."

They ducked through the low door and, with help from the young man behind the counter, collected crunchy rolls filled with local ham and cheese, glued together with a house-made chutney that the clerk has insisted they try.

"I see what you mean about getting used to the place." Hugo checked his watch. "And we have a couple of hours to find this guy's house and peek in a bedroom window."

"Peeping Tom joke?" Tom asked.

Hugo smiled. "We'll see."

"You know, I think that Silva chick likes you."

"Oh yeah? Or maybe she just doesn't like you, and so is nicer to me in comparison."

"No, she actually smiled at you. Straight face the entire time with me, but smiling at you. Since when were you the funny one?"

"Never," Hugo conceded. "I hope I didn't offend her with my parlor trick."

"She insisted you do it, so if she's offended it's on her."

"Still, we want her on our side as much as possible." Hugo stopped at a cross street and looked left and right. "Just up here, I think."

They turned right onto a pedestrian street, slightly wider than the one they'd come from, wide enough for a line of trees to run up the center of it. It looked to Hugo like this was the back of both buildings—no real entrances, just shuttered windows and paint peeling from the plaster walls. Then he spotted an archway up ahead.

"That must be it," he said.

"Sure is quiet around here."

"Yeah, but that's okay, we're just tourists wandering around, remember."

"Nosy tourists."

"Precisely. Oooh, look, fellow tourist, an archway between these lovely old buildings. Let's explore."

"Do, let's."

Hugo started forward and Tom followed as they passed under the arch into a dead-end space, one door each side of them and another directly opposite. The space was small enough and the walls around them high enough that it was entirely shaded from the sun, whatever dash of heat and light it might receive at midday was long gone, and the cold had settled back in. Hugo felt a chill run up his spine.

"Three doors to choose from," Tom said. "I feel like I'm in a game show."

"It's this one," Hugo said, pointing straight ahead. "And the door's already open."

They exchanged glances. "What do you wanna do?" Tom asked.

"Well, I *want* to go in but—" He silenced himself at a noise from inside the building.

"What are we dealing with here?" Tom whispered. "Is that a house, an apartment? Does he have a wife, roommates, dogs?"

"Most of these are apartments." Hugo shifted to try and see through the crack in the door, but couldn't. "I've got a bad feeling about this, Tom."

"Bad feeling as in we should run away, or . . . ?"

"The second. Let's just take a look."

"I don't know, man. I mean, I'm the first to ignore the rules, you know that, but we're out of our comfort zone and already on thin ice here. Raul's brother has a hard-on for me, and the Ice Queen would love to slap the handcuffs on me. And not in a good way."

"Yeah, I know but . . . Look, if we run into someone's granny in there, I'm just in need of a bathroom, okay?"

"I guess. If we get busted, I'm blaming you."

"I'll tell them I made you do it, how's that?"

"Good enough." Tom gestured toward the door. "After you."

Hugo moved forward silently, ears pricked for sound and his eyes trained on the door. He reached out and felt the old, dry wood under his fingers and hoped it wouldn't creak when he pushed. It didn't, and he and Tom stepped into the small foyer of Rubén Castañeda's apartment.

The living area was immediately in front of them, the ceiling low and the space dark. The floor was a dark-red tile, and the only light came from a floor lamp. They stood still to let their eyes adjust, and to listen. Hugo noticed that the curtains of the window were closed. After a few seconds, they moved cautiously into the living room, immediately separating so that there was six feet between them, two smaller targets instead of one, large one.

They inched forward, but Hugo quickly put out a hand to stop Tom.

"You hear that?" Hugo whispered.

Tom pointed to the small kitchen, a grin on his face.

A cat lay on the stove, watching them, its tailing flicking back and forth with interest. A salt shaker lay on its side, the furry tale swishing across it to make the sound they'd heard.

They moved on, hearing no other sounds in the apartment. Past the kitchen, they went to the right, down a short hallway toward what Hugo assumed was the bathroom and, to the right of it, the closed door of the bedroom. Before they got there, another little room, more of an alcove, appeared on their left, a shelf-lined space that Castañeda used as a storeroom or pantry. Hugo squinted. It was dark back here, but it looked to him like the head-high window was broken. He didn't stop to check it out, not until the bathroom had been cleared. He got there first, and, with a nod from Tom, he pushed the door open. It stopped halfway, jammed against something.

Hugo stopped pushing and leaned inside to see what the obstruction was.

Inside was like a scene from a horror movie. A man lay on the floor, naked and in a pool of blood, with what seemed to be a short spear sticking straight out of his chest. The blood covering the floor looked slick, not yet congealed, telling Hugo this crime scene was fresh. He dragged his eyes from the gore and focused on the man's face, trying to see if it was Castañeda. The bathroom was cramped, and it was hard to tell looking at him upside down, but the dead man looked tall and thin enough. His shiny, bald head distorted the identification, but the face resembled Castañeda's. Something was off with the scene, though, as if there was too much blood. This looked like essentially a single wound, and yet the bathroom was covered in blood, the whole of the floor, the walls, the sink. Someone, presumably his killer, had laid down towels and they, too, were saturated. *All from a stab wound?* Hugo wondered.

Hugo realized he was holding his breath, so he stepped back and exhaled. Tom started forward, to look for himself, but Hugo stopped him with a hand on his chest. "I know you've seen stuff like this before, but it's pretty bad."

"Thanks for the warning." Tom moved to the bathroom door and leaned in. He grimaced and didn't linger. "You weren't kidding, what a fucking mess. Is it him?"

"I don't know, could be except this dude is bald, the guy I saw was running his hands through his hair."

"Wig?"

"We'll have a look for one."

"Or make sure the police do," Tom said, giving Hugo that look, raised eyebrows and a hard stare suggesting that lingering at a murder scene was too reckless even for him.

Hugo knew he had to choose quickly, either stay here and poke about or do as he'd promised Bartoli Garcia—back off and let the Barcelona cops do their thing. Tom shifted from foot to foot, waiting for the decision. Hugo shook his head, gesturing back the way they'd come. "You're right, let's get out of here and call the cops."

"Anonymously, I hope," Tom said. "'Cos remember, we were never here."

"Naturally. Let's go find a pay phone."

"There's one right outside, near the playground."

Hugo started back the way they'd come, then realized something. He stopped and looked for a light switch but, in the dim of the hallway, couldn't find one.

Behind him, Tom swore. "What's the holdup, let's go."

"Footprints. This hall is the only way out of the bathroom, and with all that blood, there will be footprints." Hugo paused to let Tom catch up to what he was thinking.

"Oh, fuck, and we've trampled all over them."

"I'm betting we have. Stay close to the walls and tiptoe."

They moved away from the bathroom, hugging the wall and hoping their feet stayed clear of any prints. They were almost in the main living room when they stopped in unison, frozen by a noise from the bedroom. Hugo silently cursed himself for forgetting to check it. They glanced at each other, but before they could decide whether to keep going or backtrack, a figure appeared in the short passageway, lit from the chest down by a lamp in the bedroom. His shirt was drenched with blood, the front of his pants, too, and Hugo automatically looked to see if he carried a weapon, noticing instead the rolled-up sleeves, the freshly washed hands and arms.

The man stood in the shadows, the doorway a rectangle of black surrounding him, and Hugo couldn't see his face. They stood like that, the three of them, for a moment that seemed to Hugo like an eternity, but that had to be one full second, maybe two. Beside him, Tom shifted and slid forward. With a gun in his hand.

"Keep 'em where I can see 'em," he said. "You speak English?"

"Yes." The man's voice cracked, like he'd not spoken in months. "Of course I speak English. Hugo, it's me."

The man stepped out of the dark room, his arms raised in surrender and his eyes fixed firmly on Hugo's face. Even before the light touched his features, Hugo recognized him, his voice, the way he moved.

"Oh my God," Hugo said. "What are you doing here?"

Tom paused and looked at Hugo. "Don't tell me you know this guy."

"Oh, I know him," Hugo said. "That's Bart Denum."

♉

Tom kept the gun leveled at Denum. "You kill this guy?"

"Jesus, no," Denum said.

"Sure is a lot of blood on you for an innocent man. See me and Hugo? We're innocent men with no blood on us at all."

"Tom," Hugo said, "lower the gun. Bart didn't do this."

"I will, but you better be right about that." Tom tucked his gun away. "How the hell did you know to come here?"

"I was on my way to the airport, going to Paris, when Hugo left the message about Amy coming to Barcelona. I contacted some friends at the TSA. It didn't take long to figure out who she was traveling with, so I flew here instead, came straight here."

Hugo and Tom turned in unison at the sound of footsteps behind them. Seconds later, boots clumped over the tile floor, and Grace Silva and two armed officers came into the room. They stopped at the sight of Bart Denum drenched in blood, and both officers pulled their sidearms, covering the three Americans.

"There's a body in the bathroom," Hugo said. "Make sure your men don't touch anything with their bare hands."

"A body?" Silva's eyes went to Denum.

"He didn't do it," Hugo said.

"You sure about that?" she said. "You saw who did?"

"No."

Silva gave an order in Spanish, and the officers moved forward, past Hugo and Tom. They stopped beside Denum and pulled on latex gloves before patting him down. That done, one of them pulled out a pair of handcuffs. Denum recoiled, and both cops grabbed him, spinning him before pushing him face-first into the wall and holding him there.

"Hugo, what the fuck, are they arresting me?"

"You're being detained, not arrested," Silva said. "Not yet, anyway."

Hugo wanted to protest, but in her position he'd have done the same thing, every good cop would. "Bart, just cooperate, we'll sort this out soon enough."

"I didn't kill him, I found him like that, I swear."

"I know, I don't doubt that. But go with them for now, OK?"

The policemen didn't wait for them to finish their conversation, whisking Denum down the hallway and out of the apartment.

"You two, with me," Silva ordered. She spun on her heel and pulled out her phone, dialing and speaking rapidly in Spanish. To

Chief Inspector Garcia, Hugo assumed. They followed her out like a pair of chastened schoolboys, looking at their feet and saying nothing. Outside the apartment, the two policemen waited, each with a hand on Denum's arm. Silva hung up and turned to Hugo and Tom.

"This is a crime scene, so don't go back in," she said. "The crime-scene unit is on the way. We'll need all of your prints and DNA, now that you've probably contaminated the place."

"No problem," Hugo said. "I'm pretty sure we didn't touch anything, we've done this before."

"What, broken into someone's apartment to find a dead body?"

"Fair enough. But like I said, no problem." Hugo nodded toward Bart Denum. "What are you doing with him?"

"He'll be taken to the station and interviewed, possibly charged with murder. Most definitely with breaking in, unless he can show he had permission."

"I didn't kill that guy," Denum said. "Why the hell would I?"

"I can think of several reasons," Silva said. "You might have believed he'd kidnapped your daughter. Or at least persuaded her to disappear with him. Maybe you killed him out of anger, or maybe you were asking him for information about your daughter, and he died while you were torturing him."

"That's insane."

"No, it's actually perfectly logical. And add to all that," she cut her eyes sideways to Hugo before looking back at Denum. "I can see how the strain of your daughter's disappearance might cause you to act in a way you normally wouldn't. Act desperately, violently."

"No, that's ridiculous. Hugo, tell her."

"It is ridiculous," Hugo said. "There's just no way Bart would have done something like that."

"Please," Denum said. "Take the cuffs off. I'm not going anywhere, not until I find Amy. But we need to be looking for her."

"He's right," Hugo said. "If the dead guy in there is Rubén Castañeda, then we can be pretty sure Amy is in trouble. And the more people we have looking for her, the better. Bart's a good investigator, really good. And for heaven's sake, this is his daughter we're talking about."

"There is no way in the world I'm releasing him," Silva said. "Not now, not today."

"She's right," Tom said.

Hugo looked at him, startled. "Seriously?"

"Look," Tom said, "I'm the first to ignore authority, rules, protocol. The law, even. But we need to work with these guys to find Amy. We're out of our depth here. If he didn't do it, they'll find out soon enough and then he can pitch in. But in the meantime, the entire Barcelona police force is a lot more useful to us than he is."

"Assuming you have any role in the investigation from now on," Silva said. "Which I sincerely doubt."

"Fine," Denum said. "Hugo, I didn't kill that guy but . . . I'm OK." He turned to Silva. "I'll do whatever you want, ask me anything. I'll cooperate, of course. But you have to let Hugo stay on the investigation. Please. He's the best there is, and if anyone can find Amy, it's him. That's my little girl out there, and I'm begging you to do everything you can to find her and bring her home to me."

"It's not my choice," said Silva, "but you'll get your answer soon enough."

"What do you mean?" asked Hugo.

Silva's phone buzzed, and she glanced at it before replying. "Chief Inspector Garcia will decide who gets this case. And whether you play any part in it."

"Then can you please call him?" Hugo said.

"No need," Silva said, showing him a text on her phone. "He's on his way right now. You can ask him yourself."

CHAPTER TWELVE

Hugo and Tom watched as two officers led Bart Denum in handcuffs to a police car and placed him in the backseat. Denum threw a look back at Hugo as he stopped to get in the car, and Hugo was struck by how pale and desolate his friend looked. For all the years he'd known him, Denum had been the jokester, the happy one in any group, using his sense of humor to suffer through the pain of losing his wife. Or maybe just masking his pain. But even in his worst moments, Hugo had never seen him looking so fragile and so vulnerable.

Tom put a hand on Hugo's arm. "Hey, we'll figure this out."

"He didn't do it, Tom. I know you don't know him, but I do. There's just no way in the world."

"Honestly, I wouldn't blame him if he did. A touch of overkill, you might say, but if someone had kidnapped my daughter—assuming Amy was kidnapped, of course—I'd probably do pretty much anything to find out where she was."

"Maybe in theory, but I'm pretty sure even you wouldn't make that much of a mess of another human being." Hugo paused. "Plus, it's not exactly a smart move to kill the one person who might know where she is."

"Fair point. Which leaves us with an interesting question."

"Yeah. If Bart didn't kill that man, who did?"

"Rubén Castañeda has to be the prime suspect, no?"

"I still think that's him in there."

"The guy you saw had hair. The photo in the business profile had hair. That poor fucker was bald as a coot, and not because his killer hacked it off for a laugh."

Hugo grimaced. "True. We'll know soon enough." He straightened as a police car came to a halt in the cobbled street. "All right, Garcia's here. Do us a favor and let me do the talking, okay?"

"I'll try. But if he's a jerk—"

"Come on, Tom, he's got every right to be a jerk. Just because we were friends with his brother doesn't mean we can break every law in his jurisdiction and ignore every instruction he gives us."

"When you put it like that," Tom said. He pointed to a low stone wall in the shade, about fifty yards away. "How about I stand over there while you men hash things out?"

"Good plan."

Tom started to move off, but one of the uniformed officers with Silva trotted over, calling and gesturing for him to stay put. Tom put the back of his hand on his forehead, as if he were faint, and pointed to the wall. Unsure, the officer looked over at Silva, who nodded. Her main concern was her boss, Hugo guessed, currently stalking toward the little gathering. Everyone watched him approach, but Garcia didn't pause as he passed Silva, making straight for Hugo, gesturing for her to follow.

"Spare me any excuses, Hugo," he said. "Just tell me what's going on."

"Officer Silva dropped us off at our apartment and we went for a walk. We knew the address of Rubén Castañeda, thanks to your file, and thought we'd take a peek at the place while we looked for a lunch spot. The door was open so we took more of a peek than we'd intended."

"And found a murder scene."

"Looks like it."

"From what I hear, it doesn't look much like an accident or suicide," Garcia said wryly. "Well, I suppose I could waste some time yelling at you, but most of my annoyance earlier was that I didn't think you had any reason to break into that business. Seems like maybe you did."

"Looks like it," Hugo said. "Unfortunately."

"Not that I approve of or condone your actions," Garcia went on. "My city, not yours. My rules apply, not yours."

"Got it," said Hugo. "And we only went in because of the open door and . . ."

"And what?"

Hugo sighed. "It sounds a little cowboy and your brother made fun of me for it. But sometimes I just get a bad feeling, and when I saw that open door, I got that bad feeling."

"Feeling, eh?" Garcia looked skeptical. "Well, it's not like this guy can insist we prosecute you for burglary, is it?"

"Assuming that's the homeowner, Rubén Castañeda."

"You don't think it is?"

"That guy's bald, I don't know if Castañeda is. When I saw him, he had hair."

"We'll find out," Garcia said. He smoothed his mustache and turned to Silva. "Where are we with the investigation?"

"The crime-scene unit is in there now. One already left with the victim's fingerprints and DNA to try and get a match. We need to find someone who knew him, get them down here for an identification."

Garcia looked over at the police car containing Denum. "And him?"

Hugo said, "That's Bart Denum, it's his daughter who's—"

"I know who he is," Garcia interrupted, "Silva filled me in. What I want to know is whether he killed the man inside."

"Not a chance," Hugo said. "I've known Bart for many years, and he wouldn't do that."

"He's killed before. A simple Internet search gave me that much."

"Yes. But so have I, both of us in the line of duty."

"Debatable in his case. And one could say it's his duty to find his daughter," Garcia said.

"You could, but how does killing that guy help? Whether or not it's Rubén Castañeda?"

"I don't know, but I'll ask him."

"He's not your killer," Hugo said firmly. "But if you act like he is, you're giving the real killer a chance to get away. And maybe take Amy Dreiss with him."

"Maybe, maybe not. Right now he's all I've got."

Hugo shook his head. "Things aren't always what they seem. But fine, take him to HQ and put him somewhere safe. Don't talk to him until I get someone from the embassy down there, a lawyer. Will you do that much, Chief Inspector?"

"Please, call me Bartoli. And don't worry, we'll put him on suicide watch, take his belt and laces and keep eyes on him all the time."

"He's not going to kill himself, not as long as his daughter is missing."

"I expect you're right about that," Garcia said softly. "But what if he believes that she's dead?"

♉

Garcia and Hugo moved away from the crime scene and found a bench in the shade of a plane tree. Someone nearby was cooking, filling the street with aromas of garlic and onion. Tom seemed to have settled into his stone wall, and if he'd been within earshot, Hugo would have made reference to a gargoyle.

"I think we have to assume Amy's been kidnapped, don't you?" Hugo said to Garcia. "There may be something else weird going on, but at this point we have to assume the worst."

"Agreed." Garcia sat and gestured for Hugo to do the same. "Tell me about her."

"About Amy?"

"Of course. I'd like to know something about the young lady I'm looking for."

"Well, physically she's very attractive. Someone recently described her as your typical pretty American cheerleader type, rather than an exotic beauty. I think that's a fair description." Hugo took out his phone and pulled up the photo. "See for yourself."

Garcia studied the picture for a moment. "And you know her because Señor Denum is your friend."

"Yes, but it's more than that." Hugo took a breath. "Bart's wife and my first wife, Ellie, were good friends. Very good friends. We never had kids, so when they went places, Joanna and Ellie would take Amy with them. One day they took a trip to the mall, like they'd done a hundred times before, and some guy decided the light wasn't red enough for him. Ellie and Joanna died immediately. Amy survived, obviously."

"I'm sorry about your wife, Hugo. Raul didn't tell me you'd lost someone."

The mention of Raul Garcia, Hugo's friend and the chief inspector's brother, felt like a bridge to Hugo. Not just a connection to this man, but a way for him to move away from this conversation, because Bartoli Garcia already understood what it was like to lose someone to violence; there was simply no need to explain. No need to try and convey the utter shock he'd felt when the uniformed officer met him outside his home, the disbelief when he'd heard the words, and the numbness that had surrounded him in a black sludge of sadness and inaction. That had been one of the hardest things, the knowledge that there was nothing he could do—to bring Ellie back, to punish her killer, or to alleviate the scorching ache that woke him in the morning and tortured him at night. The white-hot arrows of remembrance that came every day at the slightest suggestion of her: a whiff of perfume, a glimpse of a photo, a song on the radio.

The anger had lessened over the years, and the searing pain of their shared memories had dulled to a glow, an ache that he could bear and even nurse. At a dinner party one night, more than a year after Ellie's death, he'd been talking about ... something or other with a woman who'd said she was some kind of therapist. She'd remarked in rather an off-hand way that when someone dies, our memories of them are the best that we have left, as though everyone should realize that. She'd not been talking about Ellie, she had no idea, but the thought had struck Hugo hard and made him think deeply about his grief. If the woman was right, if it were true that the memories were all Hugo had left of Ellie, he needed to hang on to and cherish them, not hide from or bury them.

So that's what he did. He still didn't talk about her very much, except sometimes to Bart, because he wanted to keep her to himself, and talking seemed to dilute her presence somehow. His memories of her seemed dreamlike now, familiar but hazy, but he was clear of the nightmare he'd lived with for too long. The sadness was still there, but he didn't share that with anyone, either. That was his, and like the memories, he knew that as long as he had that, Ellie would still be with him.

"Anyway, I suppose you could say that Bart and I doted on Amy after all that. Bart especially, of course, but I did when I saw them."

Garcia smiled. "I'm sure."

"She and I developed a few traditions. Habits. Bart was always trying to get her to read, but she didn't have the attention span, or just didn't enjoy it. So I brought over a stack of what today might be called graphic novels. Comic books. She liked Tintin a lot but immediately latched onto Asterix and Obelix, so every time I went over there, I brought her a new one and we talked about the one she'd just read."

"I adore those books!" Garcia said.

"We do, too. And it was such a good way to expand her vocabulary, the funny names of the characters, learning what they meant. At first Bart wasn't too pleased that she was reading comics instead of novels, but I think he came around. We still treated it like it was her and my naughty little secret, like I was sneaking her chocolates or ice cream, but . . ." Hugo shrugged, then looked Garcia in the eye. "We have to find her, Bartoli. She's a precious girl and if anything happened to her, it would destroy Bart. And me, too."

"Hugo, you know that we will do everything in our power to find her."

Hugo raised an eyebrow. "Who exactly is 'we'?"

"The Barcelona police, of course." Garcia said stuffily. Then he winked, adding, "And Hugo Marston. I think it would be best for you to stay on the case."

"Thank you. And Bart?"

"No, first we have to exclude him as a suspect, and then we can cut him loose."

"How do you plan to go about that?" Hugo asked.

"We'll see what he has to say, and also work the crime scene here. The same way we handle every murder."

"How many of those do you have every year?"

"Not as many as you. By quite a margin, and we're thankful for that."

"I'm sure. So what happens now?"

A breeze rustled the branches of the tree above them and a shaft of light painted Garcia's face white. He squinted and looked at Hugo. "What would you do?"

"We need to search Castañeda's place for any signs of her. Not just for evidence of the killer but specifically for signs of Amy."

"*Muy bien*, they should be finished with the murder scene in an hour or two. We can search it then. What about the media?"

"Not yet. I don't imagine she's out where anyone will spot her."

"Then what do you suggest?"

"We need to talk to everyone who works at Estruch. Find out all we can about Castañeda and whether they've seen Amy."

Garcia looked at this watch. "Let's go there now."

Hugo stood and waved Tom over. "Good plan."

The three men started toward Garcia's car but paused when Grace Silva strode out of the house.

"What is it?" Garcia asked.

"We found the entry point. A window into a pantry by the kitchen," she said. "The glass was broken inwards and," here she smiled, "we found some blood."

"The intruder's?" Hugo asked.

"Looks like it." She looked at Garcia. "From where the blood is, it looks like he cut himself on the way out, not the way in."

"Which means Bart Denum isn't your killer," Hugo said. "He was still inside when we showed up and didn't have any cuts on him."

"Maybe," Garcia said. "He could have had an accomplice. Or perhaps he was cut and we didn't see it yet."

"That's absurd," Hugo said.

"Look." Garcia stopped close to Hugo, his face reddening. "He is your friend and you believe him to be innocent, I understand that. And I can assure you that if he is, we will find out and let him go. But at the very least, he was trespassing at a crime scene and almost certainly contaminated it. We will talk to him and find out why he was there, what he did inside, and then, if the evidence indicates he is not responsible, he will be released. In the meantime, I would appreciate it if you would allow us to do our jobs in the way we do them every single day."

Hugo nodded. "I'm sorry. You're right, I just . . . I'll back off and let you do it your way."

"*Gracias*," Garcia said. "At least we have some DNA to collect and analyze. Maybe we'll get lucky and it'll be in the database."

"Yeah," Tom said, "And we'll find out in a week. Can we interrupt this verbal siesta and go grill those nice people at Estruch?"

Garcia threw him a look. "You are here because I need Señor Marston's assistance. I am not convinced I need yours." He turned on his heel and strode toward his car.

"Tom, for crying out loud," Hugo said.

"What? You guys were over there holding each other's peckers like they were made of gold."

"You're very observant for a man who can sleep on a stone wall," Silva said.

"Oh, so you agree with me?" Tom said.

"No, that's not what I was . . . Never mind." Silva huffed and followed Garcia, angling off toward the house.

"I always wondered why they didn't make you a diplomat," Hugo said. "Such a way with people."

"I know, right?" Tom grinned. "Not to worry, though, it's never too late for a career change."

Hugo shook his head and they walked over to where Garcia stood by his open car door, listening intently to his phone. After a few seconds, he said something in Spanish and ended the call.

"We're in luck," he said. "We can go to Estruch now."

"They're all there?" Hugo asked.

"Three of them are." Garcia paused. "And, apparently, Señor Rubén Castañeda has not been seen for a couple of days."

CHAPTER THIRTEEN

Hugo's phone rang as Chief Inspector Garcia was turning the car around in the tight courtyard. Hugo checked the screen, and Tom leaned over and did, too.

"Oh, look who it is," Tom said. "Answer it."

"No. I'll call back."

"Answer it."

"We're busy."

Tom sighed and relaxed into his seat, but his hand whipped up and grabbed the phone. He held it to his ear.

"Hey, Claudia, it's your future boyfriend here. You current one is sitting beside me, hang on." He grinned and passed the phone back to Hugo, who shot him a black look.

"Claudia," Hugo said. "How're you?"

"Good. You busy?"

"On our way to interview some folks."

"Good folks or bad ones?"

"Yet to be determined. What are you doing?"

"I'm actually at a loose end right now," she said. Her voice was tentative, as if she were afraid to ask a question. "And it's been ten years or more since I've been to Spain, so I was wondering if there was any way I could be of use to you. Since, you know, our dates keep getting canceled."

"Yes, they do," Hugo said. "Well, I don't know if there'd be much for you to do."

"Is your friend definitely missing? Do you know anything?"

"It looks like it. The guy she'd met, we went to his place and found ... well, we're not sure who yet. But he was dead."

"Oh, Hugo! That's terrible."

Tom leaned in, obviously listening to their conversation. "Worse for him than us," he said loudly.

"Quiet." Hugo elbowed him. "Sorry, we're in a car, there's no way to escape him. I guess I could shove him out."

Claudia laughed. "That's the other reason I was calling. Tom." She lowered her voice. "How's he doing?"

"He's fine. Annoying. Disrespectful."

"Sober, then."

"For now."

Tom grabbed at the phone, but Hugo held on to it. Tom shouted: "I know you're talking about me, have some fucking decency."

In the driver's seat, Garcia turned his head. "What are you doing back there? It's like having children in my car."

"Sorry," said Hugo, then he spoke into the phone. "I think we're almost there, Claudia, I should go."

"Sure, no problem," she said. "But about me coming over. I'd like to help if I can, I do have newspaper and television contacts over there in case you want to go that route, use publicity to help find her." She paused. "I want to see you, too, of course."

"We could certainly use your help, and I'd like to see you," Hugo said. "Let me talk to Tom. Only because it's ... his company's property and I'm not sure who's allowed in and who isn't."

"I *can* afford a hotel room nearby," she said, with a light dusting of sarcasm. Claudia could afford to buy the hotel nearby. Several of them.

"Good point. Why don't you make a reservation at one in the Old Town, near the harbor." He couldn't think of the one that the taxi driver had dropped them at. "Come on over, and we can take things from there."

When they'd hung up, Tom grumbled. "So much for the boys' trip."

"We're here to find Amy, not go to strip clubs and drink. And

Claudia's smart, an investigative reporter. She said she can hook us up with TV or the newspapers, if necessary."

Garcia bumped the car onto the sidewalk and the three men piled out. "This way," Hugo said, recognizing the café from the night of the burglary. They approached the front of Estruch Entertainment, but before getting there, Garcia paused. "You've read the file on these guys?" he asked.

"Yes," said Hugo. "You?"

"I glanced over it, but that's all. You'd better take the lead."

"They all speak English?"

"Ah, yes." Garcia gave a wry smile. "You take the lead if they speak English."

"But they know the police are coming?"

Garcia nodded. "I told them that we were looking into something related to Castañeda. Silva texted me a photo of the victim's face, for an ID."

The sign on the door let them know the business was open, so they let themselves in, a bell tinkling over their heads. The small reception desk inside was unmanned, but soon a friendly face poked out of the first office on the left. The woman who stepped into the hallway looked Indian, Hugo thought, with coffee skin and very white teeth, which she seemed happy to show off. She wore a tank top and jeans, her only jewelry a diamond stud in her right nostril, a small but unmissable, expensive stone.

"*Hola. Un momento, por favor.*" She disappeared from view, but only for a second or two, then came out to greet them, closing her office door behind her. She spoke quickly in Spanish, focusing her attention on the man in uniform. Hugo's college-level Spanish left him mostly in the dark.

Garcia said something in reply, and Hugo caught the word "American."

"Yes, absolutely," the woman said. She turned to Hugo and Tom. "I wasn't expecting American police, I'm sorry. I am Nisha Bhandari."

Hugo and Tom introduced themselves and shook hands. Her grip was dainty, just the fingertips.

"Are the others here?" Garcia asked. The doors to the other offices were closed, so Bhandari went to each one, tapped, and stuck her head in. Having seen the relative difference in office size, Hugo was interested to see who belonged where.

"Hello, I am Leonardo Barsetti." A man had come from the larger office on the right. His navy blazer, designer jeans, and Ferragamo shoes combined with a portly build and rosy cheeks to hint at that pleasant combination of money and self-indulgence. His hair was dark brown and thick, and there was a lot of life in his eyes. As he pumped Hugo's hand, the American put him at maybe fifty years old. "Please, call me Leo."

Behind him appeared another man, whose singular distinguishing feature was his height. Bespectacled and clutching a handful of files, Hugo thought the man looked like an accountant, tall and slightly stooped, older than his years. He stood meekly to one side, not making eye contact, and gave a half wave when Barsetti introduced him as Todd Finch.

"So you all speak English?" Hugo asked.

"Yes, of course," Barsetti said. "We are in the tourism business, we speak many languages between us."

"Nine," Bhandari smiled. "I speak more, but theirs are more useful. We're very curious why you're here—I hope no one's in trouble."

"That's one way of putting it," said Hugo. "Is there somewhere we can talk uninterrupted?"

"Come," said Leo. "My office has more room, let's go in there."

Hugo lingered as everyone filed into the hallway and Barsetti's office. He was watching for signs of injury, a limp or a wince. As a practical matter, he didn't think Barsetti would have chosen a window as a method of ingress or egress, but as a matter of urgency it wasn't impossible. As far as he could tell, though, everyone was moving fine.

Tom had held back too. "The beanpole," he whispered. "Down the chimney, then out the window. It'd be perfect, if they had chimneys."

Hugo rolled his eyes and moved into the large office, taking one of the four leather chairs around the coffee table. Barsetti opened his arms expansively. "How can we help you, gentlemen?"

Hugo took out a notepad. "First, do you know where Rubén Casta-ñeda is?"

Three heads shook *No*, and Barsetti spoke. "He went to France on company business and none of us have seen him since he left."

"When was he due back?" Hugo asked.

"The weekend." Barsetti shrugged. "But he was in Paris and we sometimes extend our business trips, it's a benefit of living in Europe. I don't think any of us expected to see him, so . . ." He shrugged again.

"Why was he in Paris?" Tom asked. "Maybe you could explain what part of the tourism industry you guys are in."

"Of course. The company was founded by Nisha's brother, Rohit, about four years ago."

"Where is he now?"

"He went to northern Africa to work with some economic-development groups there," Bhandari said. "He started in Tunisia and is now in Libya, the general idea is to achieve social reform by nurturing capitalism and fostering business development."

"Sounds interesting, if a little dangerous," Hugo said. "So you took over when he left?"

"Yes, sort of. I came here for treatment; I had a form of leukemia. The idea was that I would come over here for medical treatment and then, if all went well, to stay and take over." She smiled. "Before you ask, things actually worked out as planned, and now I'm totally healthy."

"Glad to hear it," Hugo said.

"So you guys are from India?" Tom asked.

"Mumbai, yes," she said. "My brother always loved to travel, and my parents gave us each some money to do with as we please. He loved Barcelona, wanted to live and work here. His idea was that we have several eggs in our basket as far as services. So, one thing we do is put together tours for our clients. Not just for Barcelona, but for all of Spain. All of Europe if they want, but of course we specialize here."

"What kind of tours?" Hugo asked.

"Museums, churches, restaurants, sports," Bhandari said. "It depends entirely on what they want, what their interests are. For example,

Leo and I have an interest in antique furniture. We have a lot of tourists who come for that, and we go bargain hunting with them."

"You buy anything for yourselves?"

"Sometimes, but not to keep."

"What do you mean?"

"It's half hobby, half business. We buy and resell, sometimes at auction but usually abroad. We have a guy who ships a lot of furniture, old and new, to eastern Europe and Asia."

"There's a market for European antiques there?"

"Oh my goodness, yes," Bhandari said. "It's a little sad, the poverty those places are enduring, but part of the reason is the incredible wealth of the top echelons of society. And those people, well, they have more money than they know what to do with. They just love antique European furniture, especially the Baroque period. Anyway, that's more of a sideline for me and Leo, Rubén doesn't get involved in that side of the business. Actually, I've been doing a lot more than Leo, lately."

"What else?" Hugo pressed.

"Books," Barsetti said. "Last week I had three people from Japan come in hunting for antique books. People think that Paris is the place to go for those, but there are some incredible bargains to be had here. And it works well because the same guy we use for furniture also helps us crate and ship books."

"Is he a dealer in them or . . . ?"

Bhandari laughed. "We joke with Gregor all the time, he tells people he's in the import-export business. I make fun of him because that's the same cover James Bond uses when he's spying."

Hugo smiled. "Suspicious character, is he?"

"Hardly." Bhandari reached up with one hand over her head, went up on her tiptoes. "He's this tall and just as round. Like a big bear. You couldn't imagine anyone less like a spy."

Hugo thought for a moment. "What's his name? I have a certain interest in antique books, I might pay him a visit."

"Gregor Freed, he's German. Here," Bhandari dug into her purse.

"Take his card, it has his name and address on it. He has a pretty nice store close to the Carrer del Foc, toward the docks."

Hugo took the card. "You said Rubén Castañeda doesn't have anything to do with him, or his business?"

"No, I'm not sure Rubén has ever met him, but maybe he did," Bhandari said. "Not that I can remember, anyway."

"OK," Hugo said. "Anything else we need to know about this Gregor Freed?"

"Well, he's in the flying business," Barsetti said with a shrug.

"Flying?"

"He's got one of those terrifyingly small planes, we're thinking about using him to give air tours of the coast," the Italian said. "I went up with him once, Nisha did too."

"How was it?"

Barsetti laughed. "Nisha liked it enough to start taking lessons from him. I liked it so much I threw up in my lap. Amazing that people would pay to do that. Me, I'll stick to ground level, thank you very much." He paused for a moment. "What's all this about?"

"I'm afraid we have bad news," Hugo said. "A body was discovered at Rubén Castañeda's apartment today. Murdered. We don't have a positive identification yet, but we think it's him. We're hoping you might be able to help with that."

Finch and Barsetti stared at Hugo in surprise, and Bhandari covered her mouth, her eyes wide. Barsetti was the first to speak. "What happened?"

"We're not sure," Hugo said. "Can you tell me if Rubén was bald, if he wore a wig?"

"No," Barsetti began, "I don't think—"

"Yes, he was bald," Bhandari said. "It was a genetic condition. He didn't want anyone to know. His wigs were good ones, expensive."

Hugo put out a hand, and Garcia gave him his phone, the photo pulled up for viewing. "I'm sorry to have to show you this, but it's a photo of the man we found. Is it Rubén Castañeda?"

Barsetti paled as he looked at the picture, but nodded. "That's Rubén. My god, who would kill him?"

"That's what we plan to find out," Hugo said. "I'm sorry, I know this is a shock to you all. Can we ask you a few more questions?"

"Yes, of course," Bhandari said, her voice wobbling. "Whatever we can do to help."

"We'll also need to take DNA samples to match against any found at his apartment, is that OK with you all?"

The three nodded but said nothing.

Tom cleared his throat. "Can you tell me if you do," Tom paused for a second, "adult-themed tour packages?"

"Ah, I see." Bhandari looked up and then away, and Hugo thought there was a flush of embarrassment to her cheeks.

"That was Rubén's idea," Barsetti said. "And from a business standpoint, a very good one. I don't know if you've looked at our website, but we changed it recently based on his plan."

"I did. Seemed sparse," Hugo said.

"Right, and intentionally so," Barsetti replied. "If a group of old ladies from London wants a tour of Barcelona's museums, they won't want to see on our website that we provide also for a tour of the city's more seedy destinations. So, by making the website attractive and enticing, but none too detailed, we give ourselves some room. You will see that we encourage people to e-mail us, and that way they can express their needs and desires, and we can help them, whichever end of the spectrum they are on."

"Great customer service," Tom said.

"It's not as . . . well, most of our clients prefer churches and antiques to massage parlors."

"And probably some like both," Hugo said.

"Actually, you're right," Bhandari said. "And one thing that sets us apart from other companies is the range of things we are willing to help with. That helped us develop a unique customer-service philosophy." She looked back and forth between them, and Hugo got the sense that she was glad to talk about the business, a momentary distraction from the news about her colleague. "I've come to think that in every business you have to have a backup ready. Sometimes people come to us and think they want to do something, see something, and then suddenly they are bored. So you make sure you give the clients what they think they want, but you have something special on standby just in case." She smiled, a little sheepishly, Hugo thought. "Honestly, the backup can be as much for me, for us, as for the client. If they don't have a good time, they tend to blame us, even if they're shown what they ask for. But if we've gone out of our way to have something else on tap, they are more appreciative, that we went above and beyond, and so they speak well of us."

"That makes sense," Hugo said. "You said there's a second part to your business, other than tourism."

"That's true. As with the founder of this firm, a lot of people who come to Barcelona don't want to leave. Because we have so many contacts in the city, it made sense that we also start a service where we help those people who've fallen in love with the city to find work." Barsetti shrugged. "Or anyone else."

"What do you mean 'anyone else'?" Garcia asked.

Bhandari spoke up. "He means you don't have to have been here to want to work here. People go to London or Paris, they work in a pub, then they want to travel and work here. We help them find jobs."

"What do you get out of it?" asked Tom.

"A small finder's fee," she replied. "Everyone benefits, everyone's happy."

"Those jobs," Hugo said, "do they include massage parlors and strip clubs?"

"On occasion," Barsetti said, and he smiled. "What, you think we should be the moral guardians of Barcelona? Of our clients?"

"I didn't say that," said Hugo. "Just trying to—"

"Oh, come now," Barsetti interrupted, "You Americans just love to moralize and tell others what they can and can't do. But how many American strippers have I found jobs for? More American girls than English, French, and German combined."

"Thanks for the lecture," Hugo said. He softened his tone, wanting to get information from these people, not antagonize them. "And my friend Tom here thanks you for providing the city with English-speaking strippers."

"Darn tootin'," said Tom. "Prostitution legal here?"

"Yes and no," said Garcia. "It was decriminalized in nineteen ninety-five. The criminal code does not address it now, but it does make pimping illegal."

"Brothels?" Tom pressed.

"That's where the 'yes and no' comes in. It's not illegal to own a property where prostitution takes place, but one may not hire prostitutes to work there, nor may you gain financially from one who does."

"Murky waters, eh?" Tom said, then he turned to Barsetti. "So, did you or Mr. Castañeda place any Americans in strip clubs lately?"

"Not that I'm aware of," Barsetti said. "Not for several months. Although, I assume because you're here, you're thinking of someone specific. If you tell us who, maybe we can help."

Hugo showed them the photograph of Amy. Barsetti studied it first, then he passed it to Bhandari. Hugo studied their faces, hoping for some sign, some flash of recognition in their eyes, a tightening of the jaw that might give away a connection between them. He thought maybe there was something with Barsetti, a narrowing of the eyes, but it could just have been that the man was thinking. Bhandari's expression never changed, nor did Finch's.

"No," she said. "I'm sorry, I don't think I've ever seen her. What is this about?"

"She's missing," Hugo said. "We know she came to Spain, and we think she was with your colleague in Paris. So you can see why we're here."

"Of course," Barsetti said. "But we don't get to meet each other's clients all the time; we're too busy for that. Perhaps if I could have her name, I can take a look in our database. If Rubén was working with her, she should be in there."

"Thank you," Hugo said. When Barsetti stood, Hugo did, too. "I'll come with you, if you don't mind."

"As you like."

The two men went to the reception area, and Barsetti squeezed himself behind the desk. He tapped at the keyboard with pudgy forefingers, his brow wrinkled in concentration.

"You can't do this from your office?" Hugo asked mildly.

"I could, but this is where Rubén sits. Sometimes he leaves things on his desktop instead of uploading them to the database. I can check both from here." He looked up at Hugo. "You don't trust me, Señor Marston?"

"I have a curious mind," Hugo said, with his most innocent smile. "The young lady in the photo is a friend of mine, so I'm a little more curious than I otherwise might be."

"I see. I'm sorry she's missing. She was a . . . dancer?"

"Not really. She wanted to be a model. She was in Paris for that reason."

Barsetti sucked in his cheeks. "I would think that would be very hard, finding model work in Paris. I'm no expert of course but . . . yes, I imagine that would be difficult."

"I think that's why she came here, after getting promises of work from your Mr. Castañeda. Do you have any modeling agencies as clients?"

"We do not." Barsetti leaned into the screen. "Let me see. What is your young lady's name?"

"Amy Dreiss."

Barsetti was quiet for a moment as he typed, then he shook his head. "Nothing in the database nor anything on his desktop. I'll run a search on the hard drive here but . . ." He shrugged. "I'm sorry."

"Try Amy Denum."

Barsetti ran the search but shook his head again. "No, sorry."

Hugo thought for a moment. "Tell me about Rubén Castañeda. Everything you know, please."

"Yes, of course," Barsetti said. "Although he and I did not get along, I should tell you that right now. My information may be colored by my personal opinion of him, which is not high."

"Why didn't you like him?"

"In my opinion, he was more interested in advancing his own interests, rather than those of our business."

"In what way?"

"His focus was too much on the sordid side of the business. I admit, it brought in more money than arranging tours of the Gaudi buildings, but even so." He frowned. "I just thought maybe he was doing it for his own ends, not financial but because he liked being around that stuff."

"You mean sex."

"*Sí.*" He flapped a hand. "Maybe I'm wrong about that. Nisha and I were not the ones who really had those connections, so perhaps it just made sense for Rubén to handle those clients."

"Maybe. Does he have family in the city?"

"I think his parents are both dead, but I'm not sure. He has a sister, but she's . . . She's in a convent."

"A nun?"

"Correct. At a convent where they're not very fond of outsiders."

"That's OK," said Hugo. "She may not tell me much, but I'm guessing it'll be the truth."

CHAPTER FOURTEEN

They left Garcia's car parked outside the Estruch building and walked in silence, following the chief inspector, who'd promised them an early, very early by Barcelona standards, meal of tapas. They wound their way through the Old Town, heading west, and Hugo continued to admire the architecture, the tight streets that were wide enough to carry cars but narrow enough to deter them, encouraging bicycle and moped traffic, which in turn seemed to defer to the ambling pedestrians without impatience.

Eventually they reached the avenue called La Rambla, and Hugo was curious to see the city's most famous boulevard, the one street featured in every brochure and book about the city. He wasn't disappointed. Tourists and locals jostled with and sidestepped each other as they made their way to the shops and booths that lined the street. At various intervals, performance artists came to life in an instant, dancing to the rattle of coins in their copper pots, costumed and painted to represent any and every creature that the imagination could conjure, aliens and angels, monsters and maidens.

"Hang on to your wallets," Garcia warned. "We're at ground zero for pickpockets."

"I'm not worried," said Tom.

"You should be," Garcia bridled. "You may be CIA, but the devils around here will still steal you blind."

Hugo smiled and shook his head. "I think he's not worried because he doesn't carry a wallet. I'm his personal banker."

"Really?" Garcia looked back and forth between them to see if Hugo was joking. "You don't mind that?"

"He didn't say that at all," Tom said. "It's just that we have this father-son thing going on."

"If we did," Hugo said, "you'd be grounded for life."

They dodged their way across La Rambla and onto a smaller, darker side street. "This is the part of town foreigners probably don't want to wander alone at night," Garcia said. "The thieves here use force rather than stealth. It's not as bad as it used to be, much better in fact, but even so."

Again, Hugo noticed how clean the streets were, and even the graffiti reflected the city's creative reputation. Stick figures in black paint and bold strokes of color flashed on garage doors and pebble-dashed walls, mimicking and celebrating the country's great artists.

They turned a corner and went up two stone steps into a dingy tapas bar, one of about fifty they'd passed since leaving Estruch. Garcia went straight to the bar and shook hands with the proprietor, a tall, skinny man of about sixty, who nodded his mane of white hair as he pumped Garcia's hand.

The man said something in Spanish, and Garcia laughed and spoke in English. "Gentlemen, this is Diego Marquez Medina, and he serves the finest ham in the city. And he used to teach in Florida, so his English is almost as good."

"The best ham in the world!" Medina corrected with a laugh. He wiped his hands on a cloth and then leaned over the bar and shook hands with Hugo and Tom.

They took a table at the back, wooden chairs scraping on the stone floor, and Hugo wondered how many meals had been taken on this worn and scratched-up table. Garcia let them sit and said, "Do you mind if I select some dishes? I don't want you to play it too safe—you should try some of our specialties."

"Sounds great," said Hugo.

"Go for it," said Tom. "What's the local wine like?"

"No," Hugo began, "no wine—"

Garcia waved him off. "We're drinking Rioja tonight, it's on the way."

Hugo knew when he was out-maneuvered, and, despite Tom's jabs at his paternal nature, he also knew it was Tom's responsibility to save himself from the bottle. Hugo could help, and he would, but Tom had to want it.

As if reading his mind, Tom gave Hugo a serious look. "I'll be fine, I promise. Just enough to loosen the little grey cells."

"Ah, *perfecto*, here it is." Garcia sat back so the proprietor could lean over the table and deposit a large carafe of red wine and three glasses. Garcia poured a generous helping for each of them, then raised his glass. "To finding Amy."

"Damn right," said Tom, and they clinked glasses.

Garcia took a sip and then called Medina over, counting off his fingers as he ticked off plates of food that he wanted. That done, he reached for his glass again and looked at his phone when it rang. Reluctantly, he took a sip and put down the glass. "This I need to take, it's the chief medical examiner."

Hugo and Tom sat quietly as Garcia listened. When he hung up, he said, "It's Castañeda all right. The blood by the pantry window, however, wasn't his, so I think we can consider this our first and best break. We're running the DNA now, but it'll take a day or three."

"That long?" said Tom. "I can probably get it done quicker if you don't mind the CIA getting their hands on it."

Garcia smiled. "I don't mind in the slightest. But I can guarantee my superiors will very much. Even if I could persuade them, it'd take four days for the paperwork to find its way to the right desks. And then, if there's a trial, one of your people would have to come testify."

"Ah yes, they wouldn't like that too much," Tom admitted.

"All in all, makes sense to stick with the process," Garcia said. "But I appreciate the offer. I'm sure we'll find a use for your skills at some point. You know, if I need to break into someone's house at night." Garcia winked to show he'd moved past their dispute, to show that the matter was well and truly closed.

"And the autopsy?" Hugo pressed.

"Yes, that's where things get interesting. One moment." Again, Garcia made room for Medina, who carried a large, round tray laden with small plates. He balanced the tray with his left hand and slid the plates onto the table with his right, quick and easy like he was dealing cards.

"What do we have?" Garcia asked him.

Medina tucked the tray under his arm and started pointing. "Iberian ham. Three different types, aged differently. Try each one, you will love them all, but one will be your favorite. There are some apple slices, grapes, and dates to freshen your mouths."

Hugo's mouth started to water, his stomach rumbling at the smell of the food. Not just the meat, but garlic and onion and other spices he was too hungry to parse.

"Also," Medina continued, "the quail you will recognize, but it's stuffed with foie gras. Potatoes fried in garlic, organic tomatoes in olive oil, fresh fish, of course, and several local cheeses." Medina paused and studied the table. "Am I missing anything, Bartoli?"

"If you are, *mi amigo*, we will let you know. Thank you."

Medina nodded in satisfaction and left them alone. The three men spent a minute loading their plates in silence, Hugo licking his fingers when the leathery Iberian ham stained them with grease. "Oh wow, that's good," he said. "Perhaps not so healthy, but very good."

"You can live long, or you can live well," Garcia said, and they all paused, reminded of the Spaniard's brother, a man who'd lived well but who they all wished had lived longer.

Hugo raised his glass. "How about a toast to Raul?"

They chinked glass again and drank in silence. Garcia set his glass down, and said, "We should get to work. The autopsy."

"You used the word 'interesting,'" Hugo said. "And just out of curiosity, how was he identified?"

"Dental records," Garcia replied. "We put in a DNA request, but that's not come back yet. As for the autopsy, and before I tell you the findings, have you heard of Doctor Cecilia Vazquez?"

"Not me," said Tom.

Hugo furrowed his brow, thinking. The name was familiar, but it took a moment to place it. "She's your medical examiner?"

"She is," Garcia nodded.

"How do you know a Spanish ME?" Tom asked.

"She wrote a paper on a few American serial killers, ways to iden-tify times and causes of death in bodies that had been left in the woods or buried in shallow graves. It was partly about maggots, when they eat flesh, how long it takes, that kind of thing. She's very good at what she does. And very nice, too."

"Sounds disgusting," Tom said, feeding a piece stringy ham into his mouth. "And what do you mean, 'nice'?"

"We met when she was in the US. She wanted a tour of Quantico, and I wanted to meet her. I was working a case I thought she could help with."

"Fair enough," Tom said. "So she did the autopsy."

"Yes," Garcia said. "And Hugo's right, she is very good. With Señor Castañeda, however, she was not entirely sure how he died."

"What do you mean?" Tom took a swig of wine, his eyes shifting to Hugo, as if guilty.

"Let's start with the weapon. Turns out it was a *banderilla*. I'm sorry, I don't think there's an English word for it, but it's the short weapon used in bullfighting to weaken the bull and make it angry."

"Delightful," said Tom. "He was killed with one of those?"

"That's where she's not sure," Garcia said. "Because of the force needed, the tightness of the space, and some of the damage to the flesh, she suspects he was stabbed with a smaller weapon and then the *bande-rilla* was stuck into him."

"Gets more and more unpleasant," Hugo said.

"And weird," Garcia said. He pulled up a photo on his phone. "What do you make of this?"

Hugo and Tom studied the picture, which looked to be of a wall beside a bathroom mirror. "Crime-scene pic?" Hugo asked.

"Yes," Garcia replied.

It was a drawing in blood. A hasty drawing, for sure, but definitely not a random pattern from blood spatter or smearing. It was a poorly shaped oval with a diagonal line through it. Two more lines, curved like antennae, appeared above the oval.

"Unless it's a heart with an arrow through it, I can't tell what it's supposed to be," Hugo said.

"Same here," Tom said. "Not exactly Picasso."

"A heart was my guess, too," Garcia agreed. "And believe it or not, that's not the weirdest thing about the crime scene. You told me before that you thought there was a lot of blood for just a stab wound." When Hugo nodded, he went on. "You were right. Whoever killed him also helped themselves to his kidneys."

"Seriously?" Hugo asked.

"Yes."

"Well, that's a little different," Hugo said, exchanging glances with Tom. "And complicates the profile of who we're looking for."

"Now you're confusing me," Garcia said.

"Well, we all assumed this murder had something to do with Amy's disappearance. And that may well be the case, but this information opens up a couple of other possibilities. First, and obviously, is organ trafficking. It could also be a more random murder: a serial killer with a kidney fetish. It wouldn't be the first time. Or it has to do with Amy, and this is misdirection."

"I see," Garcia said. "This may be a big city, but we don't get many serial killers here. At all."

"I know. And your most famous one was a woman," Hugo said.

Garcia's eyes widened in surprise. "You know about her?"

"It's his specialty," Tom said. "He seems very normal, but Hugo does have his creepy side, and it happens to be populated with serial killers."

Hugo smiled. "I'm just interested in the psychology. And catching them, of course." He turned to Garcia. "What did Cecy say about how the kidneys were removed?"

"Well, obviously it wasn't done in the best of circumstances, in terms of reusing them. But she said the poor guy was cut in the places he needed to be, with a few attendant vessels taken, too. There's no way it was someone randomly hacking them out, she's sure of that, so whoever it was probably had medical training."

"How long would that take?" Hugo asked.

"She said in surgery, hours. But if you don't care about the person you're operating on, twenty minutes would do."

"That's not much time," Hugo said. "The problem is, if this person is prepared to kill and steal organs, it's entirely possible he or she is self-trained."

"What do you mean?" asked Garcia.

"Practice. Kill animals and operate on them. Then graduate to humans. Chances are, if this guy's been practicing on people, you'd know about it; bodies would have been found. Then again, maybe he's new to Barcelona."

"I can try and check other jurisdictions, see what comes up," Garcia said.

"Good. In the meantime, we should go talk to Castañeda's sister. We need to learn as much about him as we can."

"That could be a problem," Garcia said. He reached for a garlic potato and wrapped it in a wafer-thin slice of ham. He put the whole thing in his mouth and chewed slowly, his eyes closing. "My God, that's good. So good."

Hugo let him finish his mouthful and helped himself to a lump of Manchego cheese and a slice of apple. He'd lost some of his appetite, though not because of the discussion or even the gruesome scene this morning. He could feel the excitement rising, the thrill of the chase that he always experienced when on the hunt for a killer. The sensation came with guilt, of course—there was no reason he should be enjoying any aspect of a man's demise—but he knew, too, that it was unavoidable, innate. Hugo liked chasing bad guys, and he liked even more when he caught them.

"'Problem,'" Tom prompted when Garcia finished his bite and took a sip of wine. "You were saying?"

"Ah, yes," Garcia nodded. "Castañeda's sister. When we notify family of a death, we send an officer and a grief counselor. We did that this time—they just finished—and ran into a bit of an issue at the convent."

"And that was?" Tom asked.

"It's not one of those open places where tourists wander around, admiring the manicured lawns and stained-glass windows. It's a closed convent. The nuns don't come out, and no one else goes in. The police officer was a man, and she refused to see him, would only talk to the female counselor. And even then, the mother superior or whoever she was sat in and basically ran the discussion."

"So no return visits?" Hugo guessed.

"Apparently not. The news was delivered, and our presence is no longer appreciated there." Garcia leaned over the table and offered a plate of small fish to Hugo. "Try these sardines. I don't know how he does it, but you won't taste better anywhere."

Hugo picked up a strip of the fish meat with his fingertips and popped it into his mouth. A little smoky, a hint of garlic, and maybe lemon? Garcia was right, though, it was fantastic. Hugo helped himself to another sardine strip and sat back, savoring the flavors and thinking about Rubén Castañeda's tucked-away sister.

"Do those nuns come out of the convent to do charity work?" he asked.

"Not that I know of," Garcia said. "The only time they venture out is to go to the market to buy fresh meat and vegetables. Apparently that's Lizeth Castañeda's job."

"How do you know?"

"My officer and the counselor arrived at the convent just as they were getting back. That was part of the problem: they tried talking to her without permission."

"That's how we talk to her, then," Tom said.

Hugo nodded in agreement.

"Did you not hear what I just said?" Garcia looked back and forth between the Americans. "She's not allowed to talk to you, we're not allowed to talk to her, and she'll have someone with her at all times."

"You give up too easily, Chief Inspector," Hugo said with a smile.

"No, but I can't see why we'd want to antagonize a convent when we have no reason to think the woman knows anything. I mean, if she's closeted away from the world, she's probably not even seen her brother for years."

"You might be right, but we need to find out, don't we?" Hugo said.

"I don't know," Garcia frowned. "Look, I'm a policeman first and foremost, which means I want to solve this murder as much as you do. But part of this job is observing the rights of innocents caught up in crime, respecting their wishes. Especially the victims, which she is."

"I've never met the relative of a victim who didn't want their loved one's murderer brought to justice. Unless they did it, of course."

"Hey," Tom laughed, "anything's possible."

"That's true," Hugo said. "But unlikely in this case. My point is that we need to talk to her, and she'd probably like to help us."

"Those nuns wouldn't give you the time of day, assuming you knew how to ask for it in Spanish," Garcia said.

"Yes, not speaking Spanish adds a layer of difficulty over and above us being men," Hugo conceded. A thought struck him, and he pulled out his phone. He called up his list of contacts and pressed one.

"Who are you calling?" Tom asked.

"Yes, who?" Garcia echoed. "Before you take an action, we should talk about this."

Hugo held up a quieting finger as his call went to voicemail. "Hey, it's me. I think we found a way you can help, so give me a call as soon as you get into Barcelona." He put his phone away. "Some outside help is on the way."

"Who?" Garcia asked.

"His girlfriend," Tom said. "Rich Parisian chick who speaks about fifteen languages and is very good at interviewing people. She's way out of his league and I have no idea what she sees in him, but there you have it. Some people are just lucky."

"Yes, some certainly are." Garcia smiled and put his hand on Hugo's shoulder. "However, some are not. She may seem a little distant, but I can assure you that Señorita Silva will be most disappointed to hear you have a lady friend."

CHAPTER FIFTEEN

The plan was simple, if a little crude.

Tom had suggested it, his adaptation of a criminal's scheme he'd learned at the international airport in Cali, Colombia. Learned, he explained sheepishly, because he'd been on the receiving end.

On Tuesday morning, Hugo followed Lizeth Castañeda from the convent, the long walk down to La Rambla via minor streets, two women in habits with their heads down and, it seemed to Hugo, not even talking to each other.

Garcia had briefed Hugo, Tom, and Claudia, but only about the building. He continued to insist that the Barcelona police should not get involved in harassing a nun, when that nun had already made it clear that she did not want to be bothered. Especially when the nun in question was the closest living relative to the murder victim. Bad press every which way, he'd explained, and he was high enough in the food chain to worry about that sort of thing.

Hugo moved closer to the shrouded figures as they neared the Mercat de Sant Josep de la Bosqueria, referred to by most as La Bosqueria. First mentioned in 1217, but officially open and operating on the west edge of La Rambla since the mid-1800s, this market had long been one of the city's major tourist attractions. And its proximity to the always-packed La Rambla meant that Hugo needed to stay close, or risk losing them.

He took out his cell phone while he was still well out of earshot and called Claudia. "Are you in position?"

"This is very exciting, Hugo," she said. "I feel like I'm a spy on a secret operation."

Hugo couldn't help but smile. "If you were a spy on a secret operation, you wouldn't have said that. Can I assume you're where you're supposed to be?"

"In the restroom, yes. And Tom's ready with his hot dog when you are."

"I'll let the phrasing of that statement pass this time," Hugo said. "And a hot dog, really? Why would he choose a hot dog? We're in Spain. They have food here, better food."

"Oh, Hugo, you guys are adorable together."

"Hush. OK, I better disappear, we're headed into the market and I'll need to get close. See you on the other side."

"Ten-four, roger and out." A pause. "Isn't that what spies say?"

"I very much doubt it, my dear."

She laughed and it made his heart skip a beat. "*Bien, mon cheri.* See you soon."

He disconnected and dialed Tom. "Ready?"

"Always, my friend. You here?"

"Yes. A hot dog?"

"That girl's a snitch."

"Don't change the subject."

"Hey, I could be using wine for this. Be glad it's a fucking hot dog."

"Fine," said Hugo. "It's alcohol-free, right?"

"Funny. Where are you?"

"Passing a row of octopuses." The smell rolled up to him like a bank of fog, not entirely unpleasant but not an odor you'd want seeping into your clothes. Movement caught his eye, and he looked at the merchandise on display. "Damn, they're so fresh, some of them are still moving."

"Try a sample."

"Yeah, I would," Hugo said as he hurried past the end of the stall, "but I'm working. OK, now I'm getting close behind them, so I'll hang up. We'll be with you soon."

Hugo kept the nuns directly in front of him, one stall ahead. It was both a great and terrible place to follow someone. As long as they had no idea, it was perfect. The bustle of people, the shouts of the stall owners, the rising flavors of the cheese and smoked-meat vendors, and the bright colors of the food and other wares all combined to assault the senses, create so many distractions that a man strolling casually through the market would never draw anyone's notice. In that way, perfect. If they got suspicious, though, a quick jaunt to the left or right, and they'd be gone. Nuns, Hugo hoped, wouldn't operate under the assumption that they were being tailed. Even so, when they paused, he did too, and when they stopped, he stopped. Every time they moved on, he scanned the crowd over their shoulders looking for Tom, and the rest rooms.

Finally he saw his friend, loitering at a fishmonger's stall right beside the toilets. Lizeth and her companion moved toward him, stuffing cabbages into an already-full bag, and then stopped to inspect the catches of the day. Tom turned toward the two women, a hot dog in one hand, a squeeze bottle of ketchup in the other. Hugo recognized a look he'd seen his friend wear before, the broad grin on a guileless, vacuous face. The dumb American tourist.

Nothing like reinforcing stereotypes while on an operation, Hugo thought.

Hugo himself moved closer and put his hand in his pocket. He caught Tom's eye and nodded. Two things happened at precisely the same moment. First, Hugo stumbled toward the nuns, pulling his hands from his pockets and scattering several hundred Euros on the concrete floor, crying out as he hit the ground to make sure the companion nun, closest to him, couldn't help but notice and felt compelled to help. The second was that Tom broadened his stupid grin and squirted ketchup the length of his hot dog, but not stopping when he got to the end, aiming a steady stream of the sauce at Lizeth Castañeda's pristine habit.

Her squeal was lost in the melee of people trying to help Hugo, and for several seconds she stood stock-still, staring at Tom as if by willing it she could undo the slowly-spreading stain on her clothing. Tom didn't wait; he grabbed a handful of napkins and apologized profusely, pointing straight to the bathrooms behind them.

Sister Lizeth looked toward her companion and gestured over her

shoulder before scurrying into the women's restroom by herself, just as
Tom, Hugo, and Claudia had intended.

♉

As soon as Sister Lizeth stepped through the door, Claudia emerged
from a stall. She drifted past the main door and locked it as subtly as
she could, flinching at the loud clunk. But when she glanced over to
the sinks, the nun was frantically scrubbing away at her habit with wet
napkins, oblivious to anything but the ketchup.

Claudia took a deep breath and moved closer, rehearsing her lines
in Spanish as she had been ever since the plan was devised. She was
all but fluent, just as she was in English, German, and, of course, her
native French, but she was also an experienced journalist, which meant
knowing which questions you needed to ask first. Most interviews
weren't started in order to get answers but to gain trust. And, here,
Claudia knew she had about ten seconds to do that.

"*Hola*," she said, and she got a quick, shy smile in return. "I'm sorry
to bother you, but I need to ask you some quick questions."

"Oh, we have a website, I can give you the address."

"No, Sister Lizeth, it's about your brother. I'm a friend of his." *A
slight stretch*, she thought, *but true in spirit*.

The nun stopped scrubbing at her clothes, and her eyes flicked
toward the door, then back to Claudia. "You're a friend of Rubén?"

"Kind of. I'm working with the people who are trying to solve his
murder."

"The police."

"Yes. And some Americans."

"Really? Why Americans?"

"There is a girl missing. The last time she was seen, she was with
your brother."

"I don't understand. My brother was in America?"

"No," Claudia said. "She and your brother were in Paris. The men
I'm working with are from the embassy there."

"But Rubén wouldn't . . . I mean, they don't think he did anything to her, do they? It's not possible, not Rubén."

"That's why I wanted to talk to you. We need to find the girl and clear his name."

Sister Lizeth glanced at the door again. "But I'm not supposed to talk to anyone."

"I may have accidentally locked it," Claudia said with a smile. "But we only have a few minutes."

"You give me your word you're here to help him?"

"I can promise that I'm here to find the truth. If you believe him innocent, you should talk to me."

Sister Castañeda hesitated for a few seconds. "What do you want to know?"

"When did you last see him?"

"Not for several months. We are allowed to talk on the telephone sometimes, but I haven't seen him since earlier this year." She shifted from foot to foot as she spoke, and her eyes slid away from Claudia's face.

Claudia wished Hugo were here. He would have spotted the attempt at deception, of course, but he would have known how best to handle this woman. His way with people, the honesty he exuded, always put people at ease. Even this timid nun, Claudia was sure, would tell him what she knew in a heartbeat. But he wasn't here, and instead he'd trusted her with getting at the truth. She felt a sudden rush of affection for the man who'd waited patiently for her, the handsome American she'd kept at arm's length for . . . too long?

She put him out of her mind and forged on. "Lizeth, please. You're not a good liar, which is a good thing, given your chosen way of life. I promise you, if Rubén did nothing wrong, we will clear his name. If that girl is found dead, he'll be called a murderer. Maybe he is one, I don't know, but if not we can't help him unless you tell me whatever it is you're trying to hide."

Sister Lizeth's head dropped. "I saw him a week ago. I could only talk to him for a minute or so. He came to the convent, and they wouldn't let us be together long. But he gave me an envelope."

"What was in it?"

"A plastic card and a small key."

"The card, was it like a credit card?"

"No, I think it's a key card. Like to get into a hotel room."

"Do you know which hotel?"

"No."

"And the key? Do you know what that's for?"

"I don't. I'm sorry. But he said he wrote an address on the inside of the envelope."

"What were you supposed to do with it?"

She shrugged. "He said that if anything happened to him, I should go to the address, or if I couldn't go myself, I should call the police. That was all he said, all he had time to say. And he passed me the envelope when no one was watching."

"How was he acting, his demeanor?"

"He seemed fine. The things I'm saying make it sound like he was being sneaky or desperate, but he wasn't at all. It was like we were kids again and this was our fun little secret."

"What did he think might happen to him?"

"I don't know, but the way he said it, it wasn't like he was in any danger. More like, 'If I get hit by lightning or kidnapped by aliens.' Like the idea of something *actually* happening was silly, but this was just in case. He was smiling, happy."

"He didn't say anything about a girl called Amy?"

"Like I told you, we didn't really get a chance to talk."

"Did you go to the address in the envelope?"

"No. I mean, I didn't know anything had happened to him until yesterday, and I got scared, so I didn't even tell the police. I didn't know about this missing girl. Do you think it has something to do with that?"

"I don't know, but I think we should find out."

They both turned as the handle to the restroom door rattled. They stayed quiet, but a confident fist knocked on the door.

"I should go," Sister Lizeth said.

"Wait—the envelope. Do you have it?"

"Not with me, no. It's in my room at the convent."

"The police will need it."

"Of course, but . . . if my people know I had it, I will get in trouble."

Claudia stepped forward and put a hand on her arm. "When do you come back here?"

A second knock, this time louder.

"I can say I forgot something and come back this afternoon. I won't be alone, but we could meet here. I could give you the envelope the way Rubén gave it to me."

"Good idea. Four o'clock right here?"

Sister Lizeth nodded, and Claudia gave her arm a reassuring squeeze. "Then I better unlock that door and let your watchdog in."

"Don't say that." Sister Lizeth was trying not to smile. "She's really very nice."

Claudia went to the door and flicked the lock, then pulled the door open. She smiled at the nun on the other side and said with a smile, "Oh, sorry, I didn't realize I'd locked it." She breezed past the anxious woman and headed back into the busy market. She found Tom and Hugo at a juice stand.

"Buy me a drink," she said to Tom with a wink.

"They say there's a first time for everything," Hugo said. "You never know, but it doesn't seem likely."

"How is it you'll pay for a woman but not buy her a drink?" Claudia asked. She loved this about her two American friends, the way she could team up with one to poke fun at the other.

"First of all," Tom began pompously, "I will point out that I've not hired a lady of the night in months. That you can prove. Second, please note that whenever possible, I stick you or Hugo with the bill, so it's not like I'm thrilled at paying for anything."

"You do have a talent for sticking me with all manner of bills," Hugo agreed.

"I'm not finished. Third of all, paying directly for services seems far more honest than paying for drinks when the outcome is uncertain. One is an honest trade, the other a risky gamble." He gave his friends a grin. "Think of it as a matter of principle, that I don't like to gamble."

"Right. Principle," Hugo said. He turned to Claudia. "How did you get on?"

"Very well; I think you'll be proud of your little spy."

Hugo laughed, "I told you, it's not spying when you talk about it like that."

"Anyway," Claudia continued. "It worked perfectly and she was willing to talk to me. I mean, she doesn't seem to know much, but about a week ago her brother went to see her. He gave her an envelope."

"A letter?" Hugo asked.

"No, she said it had a key card and a regular key in it. She doesn't know what the keys are for exactly, but he wrote an address on the inside of the envelope."

"Why would he do that?" Tom asked.

"He told her to go to the address or give it to the police if something happened to him."

"Then why didn't she?" Tom pressed.

"Partly because she's not had much time to do anything, but mostly because she was scared. She seems pretty timid by nature."

"Where is the envelope now?" Hugo asked.

"At the convent, but she's bringing it back here this afternoon. I'm meeting her in the restroom at four, and she'll give it to me then."

"Why can't we just swing by the convent and get it?" said Tom. "I mean, it's potentially evidence in a murder case, and so I'm pretty sure the police can bust their way in there and take it if they want to."

"She thinks she'll be in trouble for having it, for accepting it from her brother and then not turning it over immediately."

"I think we can cut her some slack," Hugo said. "By the time the Barcelona police get a search warrant and get organized, it won't be much before four." He turned to Claudia. "Good job for getting her to tell you about it. I'm impressed."

"Don't be, it's what I do for a living." She gave him a wink. "Natural-born spy is what I am."

CHAPTER SIXTEEN

Hugo looked at his watch and said, "I need to check in with Bartoli; we're supposed to go through Castañeda's apartment this morning. Tom, you coming?"

Tom shook his head and mumbled about needing to "check in at the office," which Hugo took to mean either his friend needed a nap, wanted a drink, or had to account for his use of the CIA's apartment. He hoped it was the first or third option, and he was uneasy about letting Tom disappear on his own for any length of time. But he had work to do Time was ticking away too fast in the search for Amy, and babysitting Tom couldn't be a priority right now.

The three of them agreed to meet back at the market at three thirty and, when he took his leave, Hugo bent to kiss Claudia on the cheek. She was staying there to meet a local reporter for lunch because, even though they'd agreed not to go public about Amy's disappearance yet, they needed to be ready in case that plan changed. He was surprised when Claudia turned her face and met his lips with hers, a kiss that lingered and let him know that she was there to do more than just help him find his missing friend.

Tom, of course, couldn't let that go unnoticed. "Oh, for fuck's sake," he said. "Get a room."

"I have one," Claudia said sweetly. "It's just a matter of using it."

"Yeah, well," Tom said. "Be careful, you're on foreign soil and there's more competition here."

She cocked an eyebrow at Hugo. "Competition? You didn't mention that."

"A slinky cop called Grace Silva. Keep an eye on her," Tom said. "Or maybe on him."

"Is that right?" Claudia asked with a smile.

Hugo shrugged. "I disagree about Officer Silva, I got no sense of anything from her but professionalism."

"That's your insensitivity, not her lack of signaling," Tom said.

"Whatever it is," Hugo said. "I don't have time for it. I'll fill you guys in when we meet later. And Tom. Stay out of trouble in the meantime."

♉

Chief Inspector Garcia was waiting for Hugo in his police car, the engine running and the radio on. He switched both off and climbed out when he saw Hugo approaching.

"How did it go this morning?" Garcia asked.

"A nun got covered in tomato sauce, just as planned." Hugo filled him in about the meeting between Claudia and Sister Lizeth. Garcia listened intently, grunting occasionally, and raising both eyebrows when he heard about the envelope.

"She did very well, your friend," Garcia said when he'd finished.

"Smart woman," Hugo agreed, letting his mind linger, just for a second, on some of her other talents.

"*Bueno*, the crime-scene people have given us the go-ahead to go through the place."

"Who supervised them when they were here?"

"I put my best officer on it."

Hugo smiled. "Officer Grace Emanuelle Cruz Silva?"

"Precisely. Oh, and she gave me a sketch of the layout—thought we might find it useful."

He gave Hugo a sheet of paper from a file on the dashboard. Thin black lines showed the rectangular shape of the apartment, the entryway that led into the main living space, and the kitchen at the back. "That space between the kitchen and the bathroom, that's the pantry?"

"Where our killer escaped, yes."

"It's possible he hid in there when Bart came in, cut himself breaking the window and getting out, maybe when Bart was in the bathroom with the body."

"Your friend doesn't remember hearing glass break. I think it more likely the killer, assuming not your friend, left a car or motorcycle in the alleyway behind the apartment. He couldn't risk coming out the front door, covered in blood."

"How is Bart?"

"Cooperating, amid the angry outbursts. He's not making this easy, for himself or us."

"He's terrified for his daughter, Bartoli, surely you understand that."

"I know. But there's something you must understand. Him too. Nobody likes to admit it, but we have to consider the likelihood that we're now looking for another body, not a missing girl. Whether it's a serial killer or someone selling human organs, it doesn't look very hopeful."

"All the more reason to get on with the search," Hugo said.

They pulled on surgical gloves, and Bartoli pulled off the police tape that was stretched across the front door and let them in with a key.

They searched methodically, Hugo aware he was going behind Garcia, making sure he'd not missed anything. When he worked with Tom, he didn't have to, didn't feel the need; but with any other cop in the world, Hugo had to be sure. He started with a desk that sat opposite the door, looking at each paper and receipt, hoping something would leap out at him. Around him, the apartment smelled musty, the damp that comes with old buildings made of stone and plaster, but light filtered in from the front window, and the place seemed tidy, well-kept. When he got to the fridge, he wrinkled his nose; old milk and something else that had soured.

Hugo paused at the door to the bathroom, the crime scene itself. The door was shut, and he pushed it open gently, as if showing respect to a room that had itself been violated. He stood in the doorway, looking in, with Garcia right behind him.

Two thick swirls of red stretched across the tiled floor, with spatter on the underside of the sink and on one wall but, considering the butchery that had taken place in the room, it was relatively clean. Even so, the smell of dried blood rose up and hit Hugo like a wave, and he almost retched. He felt a tap on his shoulder. Garcia wore a blue, cloth mask over his nose and mouth, and he offered one to Hugo, who nodded gratefully and quickly put it on. The thick cloth was scented with peppermint, a heavenly escape from the stench of decaying matter.

He raised his voice and spoke slowly. "What did the crime-scene people take from here, do you know?"

Garcia pulled out his phone and tapped on it. "We keep our files electronically. I can access the police and forensic reports from anywhere. You have to love technology. Ah, here. Three towels, the shower curtain, razor, nail scissors, open box of condoms, and lots of fingerprints, which I'm sure they're working on right now."

"So everything else is untouched, unmoved?"

"Of course. They would take what they thought might be evidence, or lead to evidence, and leave everything else as it was."

Hugo stepped carefully into the bathroom and looked at the tub, to his left. It, too, looked relatively clean. He stepped in and inspected the shower nozzle, then looked down. "Did your crime-scene people take samples from the drain?" he asked.

"There was nothing like that on the list, no."

"Then they need to get back here and do that. Whoever killed him may have washed off in the shower. There could be trace evidence in there. Hair, in particular."

"You mean, the killer showered while standing over a dead, skewered, body?"

"Yes. Have your forensics people check the sink for evidence, too. Otherwise, I think we're done here."

Garcia stepped out of the bathroom and pulled off his mask. He dialed a number on his phone and spoke in Spanish. Hugo gleaned that his instructions were being relayed to the crime-scene unit.

"They'll be here within the hour. Nothing else for them to do?"

"No. Can I look at the list of evidence they collected from the rest of the apartment?"

"*Sí*, no problem." Garcia pulled up the list on his phone and handed it to Hugo, who studied it intently.

"Interesting," Hugo said. "Did he own a car?"

"Yes, it's been towed to our impound lot. Scroll down, you'll see what we took from it, which will be everything that was in the vehicle."

"Why everything?"

"Standard procedure. Not just for evidence but for inventory, to make sure all possessions are catalogued, stored, and returned. The cars we seize sometimes go from place to place, so we like to take everything out to ensure nothing goes missing while it's in our custody."

"Ah, yes, here it is." Hugo read through the list of Castañeda's possessions, but he didn't see what he was looking for. "What about his office, at Estruch, did someone go through that?"

"He was working from the little desk in the reception area. He was the new guy and so didn't get his own office. There should be a document in the file with whatever was taken from there, too."

"Got it. Basically nothing."

"Yes? I don't recall. You used the word 'interesting,' a moment ago," Garcia said. "What were you referring to?"

"Some things that I would have expected us to find, but didn't. Most notably, a cell phone. It's not on any of the lists of evidence collected by your people."

"If they found a phone, they would always collect it. Always. These days there's all kinds of data on there we can use, people run their lives on them."

"Yes they do, and that's why I'd really like to know why no one's found one."

"I'll call Estruch right now and get the number. We can get the phone company to ping it, or triangulate, or whatever they do."

"Get it and we'll just try calling it first." Hugo winked. "Sometimes, the old ways are the quickest."

Two minutes later, Garcia had the number and was dialing it.

"Should I leave a message?" he asked.

"Just a brief one, saying who you are and to please call back. On the off-chance some innocent has it, we don't want to scare them away."

Garcia nodded and put it on speaker so they could both listen in. Hugo kept one ear open for the sound of a phone ringing in the apartment, just in case they'd missed it. But the place remained silent and, wherever it was, Castañeda's phone rang but went to voicemail. Garcia spoke slowly, in Spanish.

"*Habla Bertoli García, inspector en jefe de la policía de Barcelona. Regréseme la llamada en cuanto podáis, por favor.*" Then he hung up the phone and looked at Hugo.

"You told whoever it is to call you back?"

"Yes."

"Time to get your people working on tracking it," Hugo said.

"Agreed." Garcia called his office and spoke rapidly in Spanish, reading off the phone number. When he hung up, he said, "A few minutes ago, you said there were 'things' you expected to find here. What else?"

"If Rubén gave a key and a key card to his sister for safekeeping, in case something happened to him, you'd think he would have kept copies for himself."

"So someone took his phone and those keys?"

"Looks like it."

Garcia looked down as his phone buzzed. "A text," he said.

"The crime-scene people?" Hugo asked.

"No. And I don't understand what it means." Garcia looked up. "All I can tell is, it came from Rubén Castañeda's phone."

CHAPTER SEVENTEEN

"Show me." Hugo took the phone out of Chief Inspector Garcia's hand and read the words on the screen.

** huevos y bacon unhygienic

"I don't get it," Garcia said.

"Nor do I." Hugo frowned. "*Huevos* are eggs, right?"

"Yes. But what does it mean—eggs and bacon are dirty, unsafe? Some sort of code?"

"I guess so." Hugo studied the words, remembering his training from Quantico, the way he'd been taught to look at not only the literal meanings of the words but also the meaning behind them, the way they were strung together, even the punctuation. Something about the words tugged at him, tempting him to guess and get it right, but he couldn't.

"Kidnappers?"

"I don't know. It may not even have been meant for us. Dammit, where's that track or ping, or whatever it is?"

"It'll take a while, Hugo. We have a process we have to go through, and it's only quick if the phone company feels like cooperating. If not, we have to get a search warrant, so it will be an hour at the earliest, three or four if we get resistance."

Hugo shook his head, frustrated. They couldn't just sit and wait; even if the phone company took a while, they could still be working. "Let's go visit our friends at Estruch in the meantime."

"Very well. Any particular reason?"

"I'd rather talk to each one alone. Last time they were in a group, but if any of them knew anything, they might have been unwilling to say so in front of the others."

"Good. Who do we start with? They closed their office this morning, after my men produced the warrant and searched Castañeda's desk, but I have their home addresses."

"Who's closest?"

"Leonardo Barsetti. Not even ten minutes."

They set out on foot, and as they walked Garcia talked about the city, as if his secondary role was as a proud tour guide.

"The Old Town where we are, and where most tourists come to see, has four districts: the Ribera, the Gothic Quarter, Barceloneta, and the Raval. We are going to an area known as the Born, which is part of the Ribera. You should see how it's changed in just the last ten or fifteen years."

"For the better?"

"Depends on how much money you have. If a lot, then yes. Shops, restaurants, and a lot of rich foreigners have moved in."

"Meaning our Señor Barsetti has money?"

Garcia smiled. "There are still a few hovels left, we shall have to wait and see where he lives."

It was no hovel. The two men stood on the steps of a building that looked as if it were made of marble, four stories high and tended by a doorman in a gray suit who watched them as they craned their necks upward toward the penthouse, where, according to Garcia's notes, Leonardo Barsetti lived.

"Must be one helluva good tour guide," Hugo said.

"I was thinking the same thing. Let's ask how he does it."

Garcia showed his credentials to the doorman, who instantly became less suspicious and more curious. He watched them all the way to the elevator, and Hugo had the impression that as soon as the doors curtained shut, the man would be on the house phone to Barsetti, to let him know and maybe hope for a crumb of information about why the police were in his building.

The elevator opened into a foyer opposite two large wooden doors. Garcia knocked, and a moment later they swung inward, but not all the way open. They were being held by a striking woman who was, Hugo guessed, in her late sixties. She had silver hair and wore a light-blue cardigan over a cream blouse and a slightly formal gray skirt. Barsetti had looked to be around fifty, and Hugo wondered if he lived with his mother.

She spoke in Spanish, and Hugo caught only the word "*policía,*" which indicated that the doorman had indeed called ahead. Garcia replied, showing his credentials again and gesturing once to Hugo.

"American?" she said in English. "How charming. Come in, please."

She shook hands with both men and led them into a large sitting room, gesturing for Hugo and Chief Inspector Garcia to share the sofa. As he sat, Hugo admired the apartment, its parquet floor crisscrossed with worn but expensive-looking rugs, the mix of heavy and delicate furnishings. There was something warm, too, about the wood paneling of the walls that kept the place a certain shade of gloomy, and yet this was counterbalanced by the large windows that looked out over the street below, welcoming in the bright Barcelona light. She sat delicately on the edge of a chaise lounge, knees together and hands clasped on her lap, as if she were trained to listen politely to anyone who came in. Hugo noticed now that she was wearing makeup, a touch of lipstick and some rouge on her cheeks.

"I'm sorry," he said, "I didn't catch your name."

"Rosario Figueroa," she said. She held Hugo's eye as if expecting a reaction to her next words. "I am Leonardo's wife."

"I'm Hugo Marston, working with the chief inspector on this case," Hugo said. "Thank you for seeing us."

She smiled, just a little. "You thought I was his mother, perhaps?"

"I didn't think anything," Hugo lied, with his most disarming smile. "That's why I asked."

"Most people assume wrongly." She switched her gaze to Garcia. "If our ages were switched, no one would ask if he was my father."

"I agree, there is a double standard," Hugo said. "May I ask, how long have you been married?"

"Eighteen years. We met in Paris and got married a week later. No one thought it would last, of course, but here we are. I suppose there are a few cracks that we paper over, but that's true of most marriages. Do you know of any perfect ones, Señor Marston?"

An image of Ellie flashed into Hugo's mind. He didn't know if their marriage was perfect, he thought maybe it was, but then again, maybe it simply hadn't had time to develop cracks. Hugo's second marriage had been far from perfect. "No, I can't say that I do."

"As long as marriage is limited to human beings, no such thing will exist," she said. "Ah, but you're not here to ask me about that, are you?"

"No, not really," Hugo said. "Is your husband here?"

"No. Leonardo travels a lot and when he's not traveling, he works a lot at his office. I suspect he has a mistress, too, but I am not sure about that." She smiled. "He would be the rare specimen not to, wouldn't you think?"

"Well, I've never had one," Hugo said with a smile, trying to lighten the mood. "Perhaps things are different in America."

"You came all the way here from America, on a case?"

"No, I live in Paris."

"How very nice. Why do you need to speak to my husband?"

Hugo glanced at Garcia, not sure how much he wanted to give away. This was, after all, his investigation. She picked up on the look and cocked her head at the chief inspector.

"Really just for background information. Did you know Rubén Castañeda?"

"*Did* I know him?"

"Yes," Garcia said. "You didn't . . . your husband didn't tell you? I'm afraid he'd dead."

"Oh, no, how awful. And no, he didn't tell me." She slumped in her seat, her mouth tight. "But I did know him, of course, he works . . . worked with Leonardo. I met him a few times, that's all. He seemed like a nice young man, very handsome and charming. Please, how did he die?"

"I'm afraid he was murdered," Garcia said.

Figueroa sat up straight and opened her mouth, but for a moment no words came out. When she spoke, it was in a whisper. "What happened?"

Garcia's tone was soft. "It's probably better if we keep the details under wraps for now, if you don't mind."

"No, of course. I'm sorry, I didn't mean to . . . I just . . ."

"It's natural to ask," Garcia said. "Please, no need to apologize."

Hugo watched her closely as she fought to control her emotions. He couldn't tell, though, whether the battle was being fought because she was an upper-class Spaniard who wasn't supposed to show distress or because she was trying to hide something. Like how well she knew Castañeda.

"Is my husband . . . do you think he knows something about this?"

"It's just routine," Garcia assured her. "We have to talk to everyone who knew him or worked with him. We had a chance to meet with everyone at his business yesterday, but we also like to talk to people a second time, in case there's anything new they remember."

Well played, thought Hugo.

"Yes, of course," Figueroa said. "I'm afraid I don't know when he'll be back. Sometimes he calls and sometimes not, we give each other a lot of freedom." She sighed and looked down. "He takes advantage of that more than I do, but then he is younger. And a man."

Hugo and Garcia exchanged glances, not knowing how to respond to that. Figueroa seemed to sense their discomfort and smiled. "I'm sorry, that sounded self-indulgent. As I said before, our marriage is unconventional. I won't tolerate my husband paying for his extracurricular habits, but otherwise, as long as he's discreet, I am quite forgiving. Like I said, as long as he doesn't pay for it." She shuddered, the idea of that clearly repugnant.

"That's really none of our business," Garcia said, "I hope you don't feel we were intruding."

"You weren't," she said, "but I was explaining. And when I speak to him, I will tell him you were here."

She rose to her feet, signaling an end to the conversation. Hugo and Garcia stood, too, and followed her out to the elevator. She smiled, but said nothing, as she closed the large doors. In the elevator, Garcia said, "There's a café next door. Are you hungry?"

"Now that you mention it," Hugo said, "I am. Good idea."

The lunch crowd had thinned, and they managed to find a table by the window, away from nearby ears. A waiter in jeans and a black waistcoat took their order, both men opting for the seafood paella.

"I'm thinking we need to expand our search," Garcia said when the waiter had left. "Can your friend Tom help? He has connections, right?"

"He would have suggested it if there was more he could do. I'll talk to him, but he's pretty proactive when it comes to catching bad guys."

"Where is he now?" Garcia asked.

"I'm not sure. Being proactive, I hope."

"Interesting man, he is."

Hugo smiled. "What do you mean by 'interesting'?"

"I think what I don't quite understand is why he's your friend. I don't mean to insult you, or him, but you seem like an odd pair."

"Yes," Hugo agreed. "I suppose we do. We were roommates at Quantico, during our FBI training. Fate put us together and never got around to separating us."

"No, you two are friends. He just seems a little . . . wild for you, for your personality."

"He is, on the surface."

"But you look beyond the surface."

"That's the best way to find a friend," Hugo said. "How boring to spend your time with someone just like you, why not just be alone?"

"Good answer."

"It's more than that, though. He's a genuinely good person. Troubled, as you can probably tell. But a lot of his problems stem from his work, stuff he's done on behalf of his country. And don't underestimate his intelligence, Bartoli, he's a very smart man. The bumbling drunkard act is," Hugo stopped himself and couldn't help smiling. "Well, only half of it is an act. And the other half he's working on."

"He drinks too much?"

"Most of us do, Tom's just an expert. But like I said, he's getting things under control."

"With a little help from his friend."

"He needs the occasional reminder, yes."

The waiter returned with their food, steam rising from the little clay pots in which the rice and seafood was served. Garcia pulled out his phone and laid it on the table. He stared down at the screen as he picked up a fork and poked at his food. Steam puffed from the little holes he made in the rice as he prodded it. "Those punctuation marks then '*huevos y bacon*' and '*unhygienic*,'" he read.

"Any new ideas?" Hugo asked. He balanced a mussel and some rice on his own fork and blew gently on it.

"Well, we did some training recently, all about social media and the Internet. I'm no expert, but at first I thought it was one of those Twitter things, like you can use punctuation to mark key words or topics."

"Not a Twitter user, sorry."

"It's just something people can click on to see more posts on that subject." Garcia paused and stared down at his meal. "Wait, I got that wrong. For that you use the other symbol." He took out his phone and showed it to Hugo.

"The pound sign, or hash?"

"*Sí*, except this is asterisks, sorry. It's not that after all."

Hugo's head snapped up. "Wait, did you say . . . can I look at that message again?"

"Sure, help yourself."

Hugo picked up the phone and reread the text. He forgot about the sum of the message, opaque as it was, and instead looked at each word and character as if it had its own, stand-alone meaning. The close focus paid off, and like a kaleidoscope coming up with a beautiful picture, Hugo saw the meaning behind the text.

"It's her. It's Amy," he said. He sank back in his chair and stared at Garcia's blank face.

"How do you know?"

"But I'm an idiot, I should have seen it before." He thumped the table in frustration, the elation fading as he realized they'd wasted precious time. "Dammit, I really should have seen it before."

"Seen what?" Garcia said, impatient.

"The asterisks. You were absolutely right, they should have been pound signs, but they weren't." Hugo shook his head. "She's a genius, that girl. An absolute genius. She knew her dad would worry and that she'd missed her meeting with me. She knew I'd come looking for her."

"Hugo," Garcia growled, "if you don't tell me what you're talking about..."

"You asked me about her, remember? How I knew her, what she was like. I told you that I used to read to her, that she loved mystery stories and picture books like Tintin?"

"Yes, I remember."

"What did I tell you was her absolute favorite?"

"You said..." Garcia frowned as he thought. "You said Asterix the Gaul. Aha! Asterix and asterisk!"

"Right, and the last word is a character in the series, Unhygienix, the fishmonger. The phone would have changed it automatically to *unhygienic*. She knew I'd either be here looking for her myself, or eventually have access to this message. Clever, clever girl."

"Most definitely. What about the eggs and bacon thing? That sounds English or American."

"Yeah, it does." Hugo thought for a moment. "She and I were supposed to meet at a café in Paris. That's where I saw the man who turned out to be Castañeda. Anyway, it's an American café, serves American-style breakfasts."

"Like eggs and bacon."

"It makes sense but..."

"But what? It fits."

"Not completely. Look, there's two ways to read a message. You can look at the overall communication and get meaning that way. Or, in this case, you can look at the specific words that are used and decipher the meaning that way."

"So?"

"Even when you look at individual words," Hugo said, "there's still an overall continuity, a theme to the way the message is being expressed."

"I don't understand, I'm sorry."

"I mean that if the first and last parts are from the Asterix series, the middle part will be, too." Hugo snapped his fingers. "All the other references were characters, so maybe this one was, too."

"Eggs and bacon?"

"Sure, she knew the books inside and out. Way better than I did."

"Then we need to look at the books."

Hugo smiled. "I thought you'd just had Internet training. Can you run a search on your phone?"

"Ah, of course. What exactly should we say?"

"Type 'eggs and bacon' as one word, no spaces. Then 'asterix,' a space, and 'character.'"

"OK, done. Let's see." Garcia squinted at his phone. "Not seeing . . . ah, *bueno*, here it is."

"Which book?" Hugo felt his heart hammering in his chest.

Garcia was smiling. "The character's actual name was Huevos Y Bacon. The book is Asterix in Spain, which means she's here, she's still in Spain."

Hugo let out a genuine sigh of relief. "Thank heavens for that."

"Is there something else in the message?" Garcia asked.

"I don't know, not that I can see. Why do you ask?"

"Well, there's something I don't really understand," Garcia said. "Why didn't she just say that it was her? And tell us where she is?"

"She might if I'd phoned." Hugo leaned forward as he explained. "I can't be sure, but she wasn't just into fictional mysteries, she was fascinated by true crime, which meant she'd grill me for details of cases when I saw her. One that I remember talking about was the kidnap of a twelve-year-old girl. This girl was a twin, and after she'd been kidnapped, she sent her twin a message, a letter, and told her to come get her, but come alone without telling a soul. A mall is where she was supposed to go. Anyway, the twin didn't tell the police or parents, just like her sister had said. She showed up at the mall, right time right place. And she disappeared, too."

"Kidnapped?"

"Right. The note hadn't come from the sister, but the kidnapper."

"It was a trap."

"The code was Amy's way of telling me what she needed to tell me, and letting me know it was really her."

"Why do you think she didn't call? Maybe her kidnapper is within earshot?"

"Yes. And I bet whoever it is doesn't even know she has that phone. I have to think, too, if she's not saying where she is or who has her, it's because she doesn't know."

"We should try calling it, talking to her."

"No. It could put her in danger, if it rings or buzzes. She'll call if she can, and in the meantime there's no need to risk her safety again. The good news is that if we can ping it, either we'll find her or she'll be close by."

Garcia looked at his phone. "No word on that yet. What can we do while we wait?"

"We need to talk to those Estruch people." Hugo checked his watch. "But before that, let's head to the market and catch up with Claudia and Tom. We can get those keys and find out what Rubén Castañeda was hiding from the world."

They paid their bill and headed out into the street. They started walking in silence, but after a minute Garcia turned to Hugo and asked: "By the way, what happened to those girls, the twins who were kidnapped?"

"We found the second one. Got a fingerprint off the letter he'd sent, which took us straight to him."

"And the first girl? Her twin?"

"She was dead by the time her sister read that letter."

CHAPTER EIGHTEEN

They stopped at a small grocery store to buy water, and Hugo stood aside to let a young woman exit the shop. She had long, dark hair and was pale but pretty. She carried her groceries on her back in a worn, army-green backpack and, as she stepped out onto the narrow sidewalk, she reached up and plucked a half-smoked cigarette from behind a drainpipe, taking an immediate puff to bring it back to life. She shot Hugo a smile as she swung her leg over her bicycle and peddled away down the street.

As they walked toward the market, Hugo turned to Bartoli Garcia and asked, "What did you make of Barsetti's wife?"

"Like you, I was a little surprised when she opened the door. But, like she said, a young woman marrying an older man wouldn't raise the same eyebrows."

"Very true. This seemed a little different, though, like she'd come to the conclusion he'd married her for her money a little late."

"What do you mean?"

"I just think that when a rich man marries a beautiful girl twenty years younger than him, he's not surprised that she's attracted to his bank account as much as his personality. Rosario Figueroa, on the other hand, seems a little bitter about the whole thing."

"If he's sleeping with other women, the bitterness is justified."

"Let me ask you, how is infidelity seen over here? I know in France that it's not exactly the norm but it happens, and it isn't seen the same way it is in America. Instant recriminations and divorce."

"I think it is the same here as in most of Europe. Neither spouse goes into a marriage expecting their partner to have sex elsewhere, but on the other hand the reality is that you can love someone and have sex with someone else. Your Disney view of marriage is not reality, and in Europe we prefer to live in the real world, not a pretend fairy tale."

"So why take the vows and promise fidelity?"

"We promise things all the time we cannot possibly control. Have you ever told a woman you'd love her forever and then you didn't?"

Again, Ellie flashed through Hugo's mind, the one woman he *had* expected to love forever, a woman taken away from him before he'd had a chance to test his promise. "Actually, no."

Garcia laughed. "You Americans. If that's true, it's because you haven't told enough women you love them." He put a hand on Hugo's shoulder. "You should do it more, they like it."

"What if they hold me to it?"

"Then I suggest you don't say it to any American girls."

It was Hugo's turn to laugh. "I'll think about it. In the meantime, explain Rosario Figueroa's attitude. According to you, she should be a little more realistic about what her husband might get up to. And yet, as I've said, she seems bitter."

"There are few rules in love or marriage, Hugo, especially once you get it up and running. But I can tell you there are a couple of things that will upset an otherwise open-minded partner. First, if you sleep with the wrong person."

"Meaning?"

"Your friend's wife, your ex-wife, or perhaps a colleague or superior at work."

"Makes sense. And it sounds like he'd be in trouble if he slept with a prostitute."

"Yes," agreed Garcia. "Although that felt different. Like, if he did that, it'd be the end."

"I got that sense, too. I'm not sure I understand the reasoning behind it, why the difference."

"Me neither, but every couple lives within the boundaries of its own peculiarities. Other people's oddities don't have to make sense to us, we just have to recognize them, I suppose." Garcia stroked his mustache in thought. "Anyway, the other *faux pas* I was going to mention is being indiscreet. Having a lover should never be an inconvenience or embarrassment to your spouse. You don't take her to the restaurants you frequent with your wife, and you don't parade your mistress in the street where friends and family can observe."

"You should write a book on this," Hugo said.

"Ha! My wife would kill me."

"So it may not be prostitutes, but you think Señor Barsetti is perhaps being indiscreet, either with his choice of partner or in where he's taking her."

"That's another thing," Garcia said. "If it's not a *her*, Señora Figueroa might not like it. That's a different type of deception."

"All the more reason to talk to him, and the people he works with." *And maybe have Tom do a little covert surveillance.*

☿

The address written on the inside of the envelope didn't take them to a hotel. Instead it led them into an industrial pocket southwest of Barcelona, near the busy port. Hugo looked out of the passenger window as the stone buildings and residential streets flattened out into the bland boulevards and grimy square units that were the nuts and bolts of the city, the gritty but necessary connectors that kept the shops full and the tourists fed.

Garcia piloted the car, with only Hugo for company. Behind them, two more police cars ferried eight police officers for backup, and the farther away from the city they got, the happier Hugo was they were there. Tom had protested mightily at being excluded from the expedition, but Garcia had insisted that until they knew what was awaiting them, the Barcelona police would go alone, with Hugo as the only exception.

Claudia had pouted a little, too. The journalist in her felt aggrieved that she'd taken risks for the investigation and been rewarded with a seat on the bench, far from the action. Hugo had felt worse about leaving her behind than he did about Tom's relegation. After all, she wasn't the one likely to pull some stunt to land them all in hot water. She really would, if asked, have trailed behind the armed police and kept her role to a watching one only.

As it was, Hugo had sold Tom on his replacement mission, unashamedly tapping into his friend's more lascivious side.

"We think he's having an affair," Hugo said. "We'd like to know who with."

"You want me to follow the guy around until he meets his dame. I'm not some scrubby private eye, you know."

"True, but you might get to photograph him with a beautiful lady in some compromising positions."

"Well, since you put it that way," Tom mused.

"Claudia, you want to go with him?" Hugo knew Tom had a crush on her, and an assignment like this would be irresistible to him. And the pair of them, Hugo knew, loved to flirt with each other when he was around, as if the competition was not for his affections but for his jealousy.

She shrugged. "Sure. He's more fun than you anyway."

"I don't doubt it," said Hugo. But they both knew she wasn't there just to watch for Barsetti, but to keep an eye on Tom himself.

The three police cars pulled up to the curb beside a chain-link fence, which separated them from an acre of storage units, rows of little white garages all sporting wide, blue roll-up doors.

"This is the address," Garcia said. He picked up the radio handset and said something in Spanish.

"Makes sense," Hugo said. He pointed ahead. "There's the entrance, I'd bet the key card is to get onto the property, and the key is for a padlock on a specific unit."

"The number written in the envelope was one seventeen, so we'll look for that one. Also, I think we should go in on foot," Garcia said. "Could be little alleys and walkways in there, we can be stealthier and more thorough without the vehicles."

"Agreed."

They walked forty yards to the entrance, and Garcia swiped the card. The front gate clanked and rattled its way open, and the men slipped inside one by one, each scanning the facility. The shuttered doors of the storage units were like closed eyes, giving nothing away, and for a moment everyone stood silent, watching and listening. No people, no signs of movement or life whatsoever.

"Let's get on with it," Garcia muttered.

"Agreed," Hugo said. "This way."

Garcia put a hand on his arm. "Let us go first. Remember, we were talking about traps earlier."

Hugo nodded. "I don't think this is one, but point taken."

"*Bueno.*" Garcia spoke to two officers, gesturing at Hugo. The men moved closer to the American.

"Babysitters?" Hugo asked.

"You're the brains of this operation," Garcia said with a smile. "We don't want to see them splattered on the concrete."

"Nicely put." The truth, Hugo suspected, also had a little to do with not letting an American command Spanish police or be seen by junior officers to be leading an important and potentially dangerous operation.

"Thank you." Garcia waved an arm and took lead on the squad as it moved along the front of the storage units. Hugo saw that the numbers were written along the side of each one, the first being 001. The squad of men moved fast but quietly, Hugo swept along in the middle of them in a way that told him they were very good at their job. The two men behind him, making up the tail end of the group, scuttled sideways, their eyes glued on where they'd come from, in case danger rose up from behind.

They rounded the last unit and started down the row behind it, Hugo's heart beating faster as they moved past the numbers, 109 . . . 110 . . . 111 . . . 112 . . . When they reached unit 115, Garcia raised an arm and the officers stopped as one. He pointed at two men, and they trotted ahead, past 117, putting two units between them and the target.

From thirty feet away, Hugo studied the padlock that clamped the roll-up door to a metal hook in the concrete. It looked normal enough, but he couldn't be sure until he was in front of it. He fished in his pocket for the key.

"I should take that," Garcia said, his hand out. Hugo gave it to him, and Garcia immediately moved to the unit's door, knelt, and tried the key in the lock. He looked over and nodded, then removed the padlock entirely. The police officers closed in on the storage unit, and Garcia stood back as two of them knelt and pointed their semiautomatic weapons at the metal door. One other grabbed the handle that would roll the door up, and he counted down from three, silently, using only the fingers on his left hand.

When he hit "1," the officer stood and flung the door up. With a screech of metal, the unit's eye blinked open. Hugo couldn't see inside, but he knew immediately something was wrong: none of the police officers had moved. At least two of them should have darted into the space to clear it, but instead they all just stood there, staring. Even Garcia just stood there, and after a few seconds, the gun he'd leveled at the entrance dropped down to his side, as if any desire for self-protection had wilted away.

Hugo started toward them. His movement caught Garcia's attention, and the chief inspector seemed to drag his eyes away from the space to look at Hugo. His face was white and his eyes entirely blank, as if unable to process what he'd seen. When Hugo got to the unit, he looked inside and felt his stomach lurch. His first reaction was to run in there, to see if it was her, if it was Amy. It took every ounce of professionalism and self-control to hold his ground, but he knew he'd potentially screwed up the Castañeda crime scene and he simply couldn't do that again, no matter what. He slowed his breathing until he felt he could speak, then turned to Garcia.

"No one goes in here. Call a crime-scene unit. Have them process the place as soon as possible."

Garcia waved an arm toward the open space. "Shouldn't we ... I mean, maybe she's not ..."

"She's dead, Bartoli. She's dead." Hugo stood in front of Garcia, wanting to block out the image so the policeman could concentrate on his job. "We need to get who did this, so get the crime-scene people here. And have your men scour this place for surveillance cameras and tell them to seize all of the footage, no matter how far back it goes."

"*Sí, sí.*" His voice was a whisper. "Is it her? Is it your friend's daughter?"

Hugo felt the bile rise in his throat and again took a few breaths to calm himself. "I don't know. I can't be sure without seeing her face. But even if it's not Amy, we need to do this right, because someone lost a daughter today."

CHAPTER NINETEEN

Hugo paced outside the yellow crime-scene tape. The girl's face had been covered, so he didn't know who she was, but a sickness weighed heavy in his stomach at the fear that the naked body on the concrete floor was that of Amy Dreiss.

Whoever she was, she'd died horribly. Her killer, or killers, looked to have laid her out on plastic sheeting and butchered her in a gruesome reprise of the murder of Rubén Castañeda. The girl lay face down, and her head had been wrapped in the plastic sheeting, possibly to suffocate her or perhaps to disguise her for a little while or maybe just to keep her quiet during the cutting. A spear jutted out of her back, a short *banderilla*, just like before.

The on-call medical examiner was old and crotchety, barking instructions to the patrol officers and his assistant from the moment he arrived. Garcia had warned Hugo that Tomás Miguel Chavez was the short straw when it came to medical examiners—he was thorough enough but agonizingly slow and unpleasant to deal with. He looked ridiculous, too, Hugo thought, with a short, stocky body, a large bald head, and a bushy beard that he contained in a sterile blue beard cover. He took an age to put on his scrubs, seeming to relish the frustration of the officers watching and waiting for him, like a prima donna preening on stage. When he finally entered the crime scene, he insisted everyone, police included, stay outside the tape. He then spent almost a good twenty minutes in the storage unit, Hugo chaffing at the delay, the theatrics. When Chavez came out to talk to Chief Inspector Garcia, Hugo's temper was primed, and he couldn't help but to walk over and join them.

"*¿Y quién es él?*" snapped Chavez.

"*Es un colega estadounidense*, Hugo Marston."

"*Yo no le rindo informes a los estadounidenses, dígale que se retire.*"

"I'm not asking you to report to him," Garcia said in English. "You are reporting to me, Doctor Chavez, and you and I both know that you speak English fluently, so doing so will be no hardship." Garcia wagged a finger. "Please remember that in your offices you are in charge, but out here I decide who's involved in the investigation, not you."

The ME drew himself up to his full height, which was roughly Hugo's shoulder, and glared at both men. "I do not appreciate interference from outsiders, particularly Americans."

"What's your problem with Americans?" Hugo asked.

"You know best. Always. About everything. I have been doing this job for thirty years and have no intention of suddenly changing the way I package evidence or determine the cause of death of a murder victim because you are here."

Hugo shook his head in bewilderment. "No one's asking you to do any of that."

"Then why are you here?"

Hugo put his face close to the doctor's. "Because the young lady in there might be a friend of mine. Because even if that's not her, she's still missing and I'm trying to find her before . . . before that does happen to her. And yeah, she's an American too, so if that means you have to wear an extra pair of gloves or chin strap so you don't get infected, then I suggest you fucking do just that. In the meantime, I have no interest in your petty dislike of me or anyone else, so how about you act like a professional and do your goddam job."

Garcia tugged on Hugo's sleeve, pulling him away. "Enough, that's not helping."

"I don't like pettiness and I don't like bullies," Hugo said. "That jackass is both."

"I'm not saying you're wrong," Garcia said. "But I'm not refereeing a boxing match between two stubborn men, even if one is a . . . whatever you said. Understood?"

"Tell him the same thing."

"*Bueno*, I will. Now, take a deep breath and let me do the talking."

"In English, if you don't mind."

"Oh, I don't mind at all," Garcia said with a tight smile. "But he might."

Hugo lingered behind Garcia, and even though Doctor Chavez deigned to speak in English, he pretended that Hugo wasn't there.

"She was naked and I didn't see any clothes in there. No indication of her name, and obviously I can't tell her nationality. I also can't tell you how she died. Possibly suffocated. As you may have noticed, her body was cut up by someone with a little medical knowledge." Chavez shrugged. "Or someone with a lot of medical knowledge, trying to hide that fact. Anyway, whoever it was took her kidneys."

"Before or after death?"

"Possibly during. There was a lot of blood in there, so I am certain it was as she died, or immediately after."

"If it's not our missing kidnap victim, do you think you will be able to identify her?" Garcia asked.

"I have sent my assistant back to headquarters. He has her fingerprints and will run them first thing, if she has any sort of criminal record, we will identify her."

"And if not?" Hugo said.

"Then we will think of something else," Chavez snapped. "We have done this before, you know."

"Always with such charm and professionalism?" Hugo growled.

"And time of death?" Garcia said hurriedly.

"I am not sure yet. I would estimate twenty-four hours, but I cannot be precise right now."

"Thank you, Doctor," Garcia said. "We appreciate the information."

Chavez didn't reply, just turned and walked to his van.

Hugo turned to Garcia. "Let me see her face. That's all I ask."

"When the photographer and crime-scene team is finished," Garcia said.

Hugo ground his hands in his pockets as he waited. Several times he started to do a lap of the storage units to keep himself busy, but each time he turned back, not wanting to be too far away when the crime-scene team finished. It was only ten minutes, but it felt like an hour.

"You can go in," Garcia said. "You have gloves?"

"Yes."

"Please touch only the plastic sheeting. My colleague here will record your entry on video, and the identification, to ensure no allegation of contamination can be made."

Hugo nodded and, after a moment's hesitation to steel himself, walked into the storage unit. The woman's body lay on her plastic shroud still. Her blood pooled in the wrinkles of the material, mini trenches and lakes of dark liquid, darker than the thin streaks that crisscrossed the rest of the sheeting like tendrils. He stood at her head and pulled on his surgical gloves, the familiar clamminess somehow a comfort in the moment.

He knelt and took a steadying breath, ignoring the video camera catching his every move. Dr. Chavez had unwrapped her head to examine her, but he draped the plastic back over her to leave the crime scene as close as he could to how he'd found it. With trembling fingers, Hugo pulled at the sheeting, but it caught and didn't come off. He realized he was holding his breath and exhaled slowly. When he inhaled again, the smell of her blood reached his nostrils, another flashback to the body of Rubén Castañeda, and a hundred other murders in his past. He breathed through his mouth and lifted the girl's head to uncover it, fighting against the stiffness in her neck, death's grip resisting his deferential touch.

He adjusted his position and tugged at a corner of the plastic sheet that had caught under her face. Wisps of brown hair, matching Amy's, showed through the thin material, poking out from under it. Whoever did this had wrapped the plastic tight on purpose, not merely to cover her up. That itself told Hugo it was no act of remorse, that the monster who'd killed and opened up his victim had no regrets at all, and quite possibly no soul.

With a final tug, the plastic mask slid from her head and Hugo pulled it away, at the same time turning her head to see her face. His heart lurched at the sight of the girl's pale features, drained of blood and life, her waxen lips, and the half-closed eyes that stared at him, dull and empty. He felt the sob before it hit him, and he sat back on his haunches, unable to control the tears that flowed, tears of sorrow, of disgust, and wretched tears of relief that the poor dead girl in front of him wasn't their beloved Amy.

CHAPTER TWENTY

As gently as he could, Hugo loosely placed the plastic over the dead woman's head. He stood slowly, more aware now of the smell of her body that had been lying open to the elements, to the flies that had started to collect in the unit, buzzing over her.

"*Señor*," the videographer spoke, his English slow and painful. "*El jefe*, my boss, he said you have to see that." He was pointing to the wall, but with the light pouring in, with his eyes still blurred from tears, all Hugo could see were shadows.

"That, there." The man was pointing again. "I have pictures, but he wants you to see it."

Hugo squinted, and slowly the drawing on the wall came into focus. It was a picture in blood, the same mean streaks they'd seen at Castañeda's apartment, but this time the picture was complete, fully formed. The top two lines were curved this time, not straight, twin crescents that descended into what he'd previously thought was a heart. Except it wasn't, he'd been wrong, because beneath those curved lines was the face of an animal.

"A bull's head," Hugo whispered to himself. "Those were horns." He looked back at the body, the *banderilla* projecting from it, and wondered if that's what the line was. *Or maybe . . . ?* He turned to the videographer. "That line through the head. Does it look like anything to you?"

The man just shrugged, the flickering of his eyes telling Hugo he probably didn't even understand the question. Hugo took out his phone and took several pictures of the mural, then backed out of the unit, stealing one more glance at the still form of the dead girl.

Outside, he found Garcia. "It's not Amy, but that picture in there..."

"A bull." Garcia shrugged. "I don't know what it means, do you?"

"No, but look at this." Hugo pulled out his phone and both men looked at the photos he'd taken. "The line through its head."

"A protest against bullfighting?"

"Yeah, I was thinking the same thing. We need to see if either Castañeda or this woman, when we figure out who she is, have anything to do with bullfighting. Whether they're supporters, fans, or protesters, whatever. Where and how often do they have it here?"

"Here?" Garcia blinked in surprise. "Oh, you didn't know?"

"Know what?"

"Bullfighting is popular in Spain, Mexico, and Colombia... other places, too." He shook his head. "But not here. It has been banned in Catalonia since the beginning of two thousand twelve."

"Really?"

"It's very popular in the south, and of course Pamplona has the bull running," Garcia said. "I think most foreigners have no idea it's banned here unless they try to go to a fight. Then they get a surprise."

"Interesting," said Hugo. "But I'm glad to hear that, it always seemed barbaric to me."

"And to me. Speaking of barbaric, what do you suggest we do next?"

"I think you need to have a team working specifically on the issue of organ trafficking. I don't know if it's a distraction, but it seems like a lot of work to go to, and risk, just for that."

"I have people who can start looking at that, I'll call now."

"Great. In the meantime, I have a phone call to make myself, but I think I'll need your help with it."

♉

Hugo sat in the front seat of Garcia's car and dialed the number the chief inspector had given him.

"This is Hugo Marston, do you speak English?"

"*Sí, señor*," said the woman's voice. "Sorry, I mean, yes sir. We were told to expect your call. You wish to speak with Bart Denum?"

"Yes, please."

"*Un momento*, I will put him on. It will take a minute or two."

"I'll wait."

Outside, Grace Silva watched him through the car's windshield. He'd not seen her arrive, and she was looking at him in a way that made Hugo uncomfortable. Perhaps, he thought, because he watched people the same way, although he tried to do it when they wouldn't notice. Perhaps she'd been here earlier, seen his response to seeing the victim's face, and wasn't used to displays of emotion from her colleagues. In truth, Hugo had surprised himself. Not at the relief he'd felt, but that he'd not been able to mask it, keep it to himself. A straight face was as essential in the FBI as a gun and a badge; anything else was a sign of weakness and would be pounced on by colleagues, if not one's superiors. Maybe he'd been out of the action for a long time, but Hugo knew it wasn't weakness. It was coming to this place, coming to Barcelona to find a friend. To save a friend. And all the while, the memory of Ellie hovered close to the surface. A horror story of its own, and one he'd shelved and ignored, waiting for the feelings of loss and sadness to melt away when in reality they'd sat there like a virus, all too ready to attack when he least expected it, was least able to fight back.

"Hugo, is that you?" Bart's voice was frantic. "They said they found a body, a girl, Jesus please tell me—"

"It's not her," Hugo interrupted. "Bart, it wasn't Amy." A silence on the line. "Did you hear me? It's someone else, not Amy."

A sob from Bart. "Oh my God, thank you, thank you."

Hugo listened to Bart's ragged breathing, his mumbles of gratitude, let him gather himself. "Are you doing OK?" Hugo asked.

Bart's voice was quiet. "I'm locked up, Hugo, so no. But they'll have to let me go now, right?"

"Yeah, it looks like the same thing."

"Then they know it wasn't me—I've been here, locked up."

"Look, I know it wasn't you. They probably do, too. But they don't have a solid time of death yet, so it's still theoretically possible that . . . well, you know."

"No, I don't fucking know!" Denum exploded. "Hugo, for fuck's sake, I have to be out there looking for her, I *have* to be."

Hugo kept his voice calm. "I know. I really do. But like every police force they have their procedures, stupid and unnecessary delays that hurt innocent people, but we have to be patient. *You* have to be patient, and know that I'm out here doing everything in my power to find her. You know I am, Bart, I'm doing everything I can, and the cop I'm working with is good. Very good."

"He better be, Hugo. Because I'm going nuts over here. And if someone hurts my baby while I'm locked up, there's gonna be hell to pay. I mean that."

Hugo didn't doubt it. "Fair enough. Look, I need to get back to finding her. I'll talk to Chief Inspector Garcia about your situation, do what I can. And I'm going to find Amy, if you believe anything, believe that."

"Thanks, Hugo. Please do. And soon."

Hugo heard voices in the background as someone took the phone from Denum and rang off.

When he climbed out of the car, Grace Silva was waiting for him. "We have an ID on the body."

"That was quick," Hugo said.

"Yeah, well, we don't get many of these, so they tend to be fast-tracked. Anyway, her name is Delia Treviño. Twenty-five years old, from Madrid. Been in Barcelona two years, it looks like. Minor criminal history, a lot of drug-related crimes."

"Like what?"

"Possessing and selling marijuana and cocaine, prostitution, several theft charges."

"Nothing violent?"

"No. But when we checked for police involvement, she came up as the victim of several assaults." Silva frowned. "Always the victim, never the perpetrator."

"In that line of work, I can't say I'm surprised."

"It's sad."

"Not as sad as the way she ended up. Do you guys have any leads on a black market for human organs in the city? This is the second person whose kidneys were taken."

"Chief Inspector Garcia is working on that, but I talked to a few people at the station. There are always rumors about this sort of thing, but so far we don't have anything solid, no ongoing investigations or specific suspicions of it happening here. We'll canvass all our detectives, tell them to talk to all their informants, but as of right now, nothing. Maybe it's a new ring here."

"It could be, but I'm not yet buying it as the motive for these murders."

"Why not?"

"It's a tough way to make a living, killing people for their body parts," Hugo said. "It's messy at the front end, and unless you're very practiced at killing people, it's easy to damage the goods you're trying to steal. Apart from the fact that, you know, you're killing a human being. And even if you don't mind that, there's a fine line in the way you have to do it. Not damaging the organs is a priority, but if you're too careful about it, the victim fights back and you wind up dead, injured, or arrested."

"Not if you catch your victims by surprise or just shoot them in the head."

"Maybe. We don't know how our victims died, but they weren't shot in the head. Anyway, even if you kill them, you then have to remove the organs, which takes skill. You yourself have medical training, from the military. Do you think you could remove someone's kidneys in a way that would leave them transportable and transplantable?"

"I doubt it." She shrugged. "Then again, maybe ... I really don't know what condition they need to be in."

"And that's the other problem. There's no shortage of people waiting, and presumably willing to pay, but even if you know how to cut them out of someone, you're going to make a mess, and who's willing to pay for a kidney sliced out in a storage unit?"

"You're assuming the recipient knows that. How would they? These people are desperate and I doubt ask too many questions. Even if they knew, I bet most of them would be willing to scrape one off the floor and sew it into themselves if it meant they have a chance to live."

"I suppose so."

"And why just the kidneys?" Hugo asked. "Why not the liver as well, or even the heart?"

"I'm pretty sure the liver and heart are much harder to take out, carry, and store," Silva said. "And not worth as much."

"You say that like you know how much people are willing to pay."

"That's what the Internet is for; I looked it up online. I'm not saying it was a definitive price list, but these figures come from Human Rights Watch, so they won't be too far off. Anyway, you can sell a liver for around one hundred thousand Euros. Just one kidney sells for twice that." She smiled. "You have to admit, if someone can collect half a million Euros for a few body parts, ones you can take out in twenty minutes and fit in a sandwich bag, well . . ."

"People have killed for a lot less," Hugo agreed.

"So it's still a possibility. But we need to explore that link between Castañeda and Treviño, don't you think? Find out why he wanted his sister to know about this place. That's the most important thing."

"Definitely. And I think I know who we should start with."

♉

They divided the search. Chief Inspector Garcia went back to Castañeda's apartment, and Hugo intended to question Leo Barsetti. First, he returned to the CIA pad to look for Tom. The apartment was dark when he got there, and a loud snoring emanated from Tom's bedroom, giving Hugo mixed feelings of relief that he was safe, and worry that he was drunk. Hugo stepped quietly to the bedroom door, which was half open. He was about to poke his head inside when he heard a voice behind him.

"Well, hello stranger."

Hugo wheeled around to see Tom grinning at him. "Tom. Then who . . . ?" He jerked a thumb at the bedroom. "That's a man snoring."

Tom scooted past Hugo, opened the bedroom door wide, and flicked on the light. He walked over to the bed and picked up his iPod from the side table, poking at the screen and shutting off the snoring.

"You're a strange man," Hugo said.

"Not at all. It's the first place you went when you broke in here."

"I didn't break in, I let myself in."

"Whatever. You and anyone else would've headed straight in there and I would've snuck up behind them."

"Expecting intruders, are we?"

"Always." Tom pushed past him again and started down the hallway to the lounge. "And if you must know, I find the sound of snoring to be quite relaxing."

"Like I said, you're a strange man." They settled into armchairs. "Apart from setting snoring traps and meditating to the sound, what have you been doing? Anything useful?"

"Yes and no. You and your Spanish friends seemed to have everything under control, so I went for a couple glasses of wine, and then did what you suggested: I started following our man Barsetti." Tom grinned. "Turns out you were right, he is a dirty old man, but it's not a girlfriend. He has a penchant for strip clubs."

"That so? Nice work."

"I'm one helluva cop."

"Of course you are. And let me guess, once you followed him into one, you couldn't possibly leave, am I right?"

"Exactly! This undercover gig isn't as easy as it looks on TV."

"When did you last see him?"

"About an hour ago, and three blocks away. He was trying to coax a young lady into a private room. Believe it or not, I'd had enough by then. All those boobs and jiggling asses were beginning to lose their glamor." Tom ran a hand across his face. "Sometimes I think I'm growing up, and it scares me."

"We live in hope. Address?"

"It's called Casablanca, walking distance from here." Tom drew a map on a piece of paper and handed it to Hugo, who stood.

"Not coming with?" Hugo asked.

"Nap time. And like I said before, all those jiggling parts ... I'm afraid if I overdo it today, I'll never be able to set foot inside a place like that again."

"Horror of horrors."

"No fucking kidding. Next thing you know, I'll be campaigning to make prostitution illegal."

"One step at a time, my friend," Hugo said. "One step at a time."

CHAPTER TWENTY-ONE

Night had begun to settle over the city when Hugo stepped out of the apartment, into the cobbled alley. He checked the piece of paper Tom had given him, the rough drawing now settled in his mind. He crumpled the paper and dropped it into the next trash can he saw.

A block away, Hugo wrinkled his nose. He'd noticed this several times before, the occasional patches of sewer-smell telling of an ancient system that struggled with modern demands. But he didn't mind such olfactory intrusions, as they were reminders he was in a place with real history; and for someone born and raised in a more prefab nation, that was just fine. As long as one didn't linger.

The club sat off a side street of the busy Carrer Nou de la Rambla, a stringy and often shady north-to-south artery leading out of the center of Barcelona. The club itself sat between a juice bar and a store selling anything and everything to do with the Barcelona soccer team, the strip club's discreet and anonymous entryway watched over by two large gentlemen in black pants, tight white dress shirts, and red bow ties. If it wasn't for them, Hugo thought, an unsuspecting tourist might just wander under the white-on-black Casablanca sign, looking for a tall glass of champagne and a piano player named Sam, and stagger out traumatized.

Hugo lingered outside, gambling on Barsetti leaving the club soon, if he hadn't already. Hardly a regular at these places himself, Hugo knew that they got expensive quickly and, from what she'd said before, he was pretty sure the Italian's wife would be less than happy at him spending her family money on women grinding themselves on his lap. Hugo looked over his shoulder at the two men in the doorway, but they were lost in conversation, paying no mind to anyone, so he stayed there for a moment, watching the exit. After a couple of minutes, he strolled slowly down the narrow street, pausing to look into shop windows like a tourist who had all the time in the world.

Hugo checked his watch and turned toward the club. As he got close, one of the security guys tugged the door open, and the Italian appeared, looking slightly startled and none too steady on his feet, his naturally rosy cheeks positively glowing. Hugo approached him.

"Mr. Barsetti, do you have a moment?"

Barsetti squinted, as if having a hard time recognizing Hugo. When he did, suspicion took over. "What are you doing here?"

"Looking for you."

"Why? How did you know I was here?" His words were slow and a little slurred.

"Lucky guess. There's a café up the street, can I buy you a coffee?"

Barsetti drew himself up. "I don't have time." He looked at his wrist but wore no watch, and the moment seemed to deflate him. "Fine. Coffee would be good."

They walked along the sidewalk in silence, Barsetti a little unsteady on his feet, and then settled into a quiet corner of the café. "You should know that we spoke to your wife earlier today."

"My wife? What does she have to do with anything?"

"Nothing, we were looking for you."

"I have been busy today." His eyes shifted left then right. That was a tell as far as Hugo was concerned, a sure sign that whatever information Barsetti gave about his day would be either a lie or incomplete.

"No problem. We've not had a chance to talk about Rubén Castañeda. I'm curious about what you thought of him."

"I told you yesterday."

"You told me *some* stuff yesterday," Hugo said. "I was hoping there was more, or that you'd forgotten to mention something."

"Like what?"

"I don't know." He gave Barsetti a friendly smile. "If I did, I wouldn't be here, I guess." The Italian didn't respond, so Hugo changed tack. "Does Estruch keep a storage unit?"

"I don't know. Why?"

They stopped talking as a waiter arrived at the table. Barsetti ordered an espresso, Hugo the same. When the waiter left, Hugo said, "A storage unit. Rubén had the keys to one, gave them to his sister for safekeeping."

"It must have been his, then. What was in it?"

Hugo ignored the question. "How did you come to work for Estruch?"

"I worked in tourism in Italy. Rome and Florence. I met my wife that way, did you know that?"

"I didn't, no."

"She was beautiful. She still is," he added. *A little too hurriedly*, Hugo thought. "And, I won't lie, the fact that she was very wealthy was appealing. Not because I wanted her money; I was young and stupid enough to think I was going to make my own fortune."

"Is that right?"

Barsetti waved a disparaging hand. "That's true for every young person. You know anyone in their teens or twenties who plans to grow up to be an office worker, bored out of their mind and waiting for the day they can retire?"

"Point taken. There was money in tourism when you started?"

"I thought there was." The waiter flitted past, dropping off their little cups as he went. Barsetti stirred a cube of sugar into his and took a sip. Hugo could see the man's mind turning over, ticking backward a decade or two. "Maybe there would have been anyway, but I suppose you could say there was money in tourism for me."

"Your wife."

"Yes, my wife. Are you married?"

"No."

"Smart man." Barsetti gazed around the café. "People come to places like this to meet people, get to know members of the opposite sex. Fall in love with them. But love doesn't last." He looked down at his coffee cup. "I think perhaps Rubén was right about that."

"About what exactly?"

"He didn't do ... He was something of a philosopher, did you know that?"

"No one has said so, but tell me what you mean."

"Not in an intellectual way, he wasn't a great mind or anything. Not by a long way. But he had these views that aren't mainstream, and he lived by them."

"Like what?"

"Like he didn't believe in love or marriage. We had our first argument about that. I thought he was looking down on me, judging me. He thought sex was good, clean fun and not something that should be hidden in dark clubs, certainly not be illegal." Barsetti's watery eyes studied Hugo's face. "I'm saying that his work for us in the sex industry, it didn't seem seedy to him like it probably does to you. He was selling a product to people who wanted to buy, and putting them in touch with people who wanted to sell. From his point of view, it could have been anything, it just happened to be sex. Or companionship."

"Is that your word or his?"

"His, and he was right." Barsetti leaned forward. "But the point I'm trying to make is that you probably think his murder had something to do with his work with clients in the sex trade here. I'm telling you, you're wrong. It was no different to him than showing someone to a church or the Picasso museum."

"Maybe," Hugo said. "It may have seemed like that to him, but not everyone is so ... *naïve* about the trade. Whatever his take on it, Mr. Barsetti, there are a lot of unpleasant people in that business."

Barsetti sat in silence, so Hugo pushed on, not sure what he should be asking but not willing to let the Italian go just yet.

"Do you know anyone in the import-export business, by any chance?" Hugo asked.

"What kind of imports and exports? Like Gregor Freed?"

"I suppose. Who else do you know?"

Barsetti shrugged. "Lots of people, I'm sure. I bet some of our clients do that kind of work."

"But you don't know for sure?"

"No, not really."

"And you're still not willing to share your client lists with us?"

"We do that and we might as well shut down the business. It's hard enough keeping..." His voice tailed off.

"Keeping what?" Hugo asked. "Keeping Rubén Castañeda's death a secret?"

"You expect us to call his clients and tell them, 'Hey, Rubén was murdered, but don't worry, you're in safe hands'?"

"What have you told them?"

"Nothing. If someone asks, we'll say he left the business."

"His death will be public knowledge soon; his name will be in the press. His clients will just have to run a quick search on him and they'll find out what happened."

"Possibly, but that's our approach. You should talk to Nisha, she makes those decisions."

"That OK with you?"

"That she decides? Of course, it's her business."

"But if it goes down the tubes, it's your livelihood."

"Ha!" Barsetti looked up and gave Hugo a tired smile. "You forget who I'm married to. I'll be just fine."

"Your wife doesn't mind you visiting Casablanca?"

Barsetti stared at Hugo for a moment. "It's not what you think."

"What do I think?"

"Don't play games with me. I had my reason to go in there and it has nothing to do with you."

"Since Rubén Castañeda was killed, pretty much everything has something to do with me. Especially when you're hiding information from the police."

"I'm not hiding anything."

"Then tell me what you were doing in there, if not getting drunk and . . . finding a little companionship."

Barsetti drained his coffee cup. "Like I said, nothing to do with you."

"Fine." Hugo took out his phone and pulled up Delia Treviño's picture, the mugshot Garcia had sent to him earlier. He placed the phone in front of Barsetti and watched his face. "You know who that is?"

"No."

"I don't believe you."

Barsetti dragged his eyes from the phone. "Why not? I don't know her."

"Aren't you curious why I'm asking about her?"

"So tell me."

"That storage locker that doesn't belong to Estruch. Rubén Castañeda's storage unit."

"What about it?"

Hugo tapped the picture on the phone. "We found this young lady in it today."

"What do you mean . . . 'found'?"

"She was dead, Leo. And her insides had been scooped out. What do you make of that?"

Hugo watched as Barsetti's red face drained to white, and his lips trembled. He put both hands on the table and, unsteadily, pushed himself up. His voice was a whisper. "I told you. I don't know her. I don't know her."

Barsetti turned and staggered to the door of the café, pausing to look over his shoulder at Hugo for a moment. He opened his mouth as if to say something. Hugo waited, but the Italian seemed to change his mind, and instead shoved the door open and stepped outside into the street.

CHAPTER TWENTY-TWO

Chief Inspector Garcia sent a car for Hugo and Tom early the next morning, wanting a meeting at police headquarters to discuss where they were and where they needed to head with the investigation. He'd laid out coffee and croissants, the latter piled high on a large plate on the conference table in his office. Tom sniffed the air as they walked in.

"Now that's what I call hospitality."

"French style, to make you feel at home," said Grace Silva. "And you're welcome." She was perched on the edge of the table with a cup of coffee next to her. "For once I didn't have to pay out of my own pocket."

Bartoli Garcia was sitting behind his desk and looked up. "You are already overpaid, Silva, so either stop your complaining or I'll get someone else to fetch breakfast."

Silva winked at Hugo. "That a promise, *jefe*?"

Garcia chuckled and shook his head in mock exasperation. He stood and walked around his desk to the conference table, taking a seat in front of the croissants. He helped himself to one, and a napkin. "Sit, everyone."

A shuffle of chairs later and they were in work mode, all except one of them, who was more intent on choosing the biggest pastry and topping off his coffee cup.

"When you're ready, Tom," Hugo said.

"Sorry, just prepping. Fire away."

"*Gracias*," said Garcia, clearly not meaning it. "I wanted to update you on our latest victim and coordinate what happens next. A lot of moving elements, and a missing girl, so let's not waste time." He took a sip of coffee. "Now then. Delia Treviño was twenty-five years old. Bad childhood, worse teenage years, and her adulthood is bottom of the barrel, as you say. We've had uniformed officers and some detectives try to talk to her associates, I'm not sure she had friends, and so far no one knows anything."

"Family?" Hugo asked.

"Father is dead, brother has been in prison for the last three years, and her mother hasn't seen her in nearly a decade."

"Where does she live?" Tom asked.

"Her last known address, the one in our records, is an apartment building in the north of the city. She's been gone a long time—the current resident doesn't know her, and the property manager doesn't remember her. The associates we talked to said she went from friend to friend, staying a few nights all over the city. Oddly, no one had seen her for the past two weeks, which may be nothing more than some questionable people trying to distance themselves from her murder. The bottom line is that we have no good address for her."

"People like that make good victims," Hugo said. His head was beginning to hurt, a dull throb that seemed to echo and amplify the voice of Bart Denum, as if his friend were sitting there whispering in Hugo's ear for him to get on with it, to find his little girl. "No connection at all to Castañeda or Estruch or . . . *anything* useful?"

"One thing, though it seems a stretch," Garcia said. "She has ties to a couple of gangs in Barcelona. It's not a huge problem here and they tend to stick to their own turf, but our young lady is documented by the city police's task force as associating with members of several gangs."

"That unusual?" Hugo asked. "You'd think most people would stick to just one."

"Depends," Silva said. "I've done a lot of work with them, mostly prevention and trying to rehabilitate people wanting out, mostly girls. Anyway, people who are on the fringes of society also operate on the edges of the gangs. The people who sell their daily helping of marijuana, as opposed to dealable amounts of drugs, the people who sell them guns and sex. No one much cares what their affiliations are, as long as they don't flaunt another gang's colors."

"Why do we care about gang stuff in this case?" Tom chipped in.

"Because," Silva said, "one of the gangs she was affiliated with is a prison gang out of southern Spain. Los Matadores."

Hugo sat up straight. "The Matadors?"

"Right," Silva said. "To be honest, I don't really get the connection because Los Matadores are a prison-only gang. In other words, unlike your American Bloods and Crips, once you're out of prison, you don't really have anything to do with them. You just join when locked up, defend each other, and then," she shrugged, "that's it."

"Like the Tango Blast gang in Texas," Hugo said. "Same deal."

"It may just be a coincidence," Silva said. "But with those drawings on the wall, it's an interesting one. That reminds me, we did identify the person who leased the storage unit a month ago. It was paid for in cash, which isn't helpful, but the owner did require identification, which he took a photocopy of."

"Fake ID?" Hugo guessed.

"Actually, no." Silva said. "But it might as well have been."

Hugo sank back in his chair. "Rubén Castañeda."

"Right," Silva said. "The surveillance cameras are mostly fake ones, by the way. The two that work are by the entrance and the office. I have men looking at the video from the last couple of weeks to see if anyone else we know went in or out, but that's a slow process. Another dead-end for now, I'm afraid."

Hugo shook his head and looked at Bartoli Garcia, hoping for a glimmer of news, the thinnest of new threads for them to follow. As insistent as Bart's voice was, urging him on, Hugo was even more unsettled by the silence that was Amy, a black hole that was expanding inside him, a growing pain in an already-fragile heart.

As if reading his mind, Garcia shook his head. "Not much good news regarding Señor Castañeda, either. We've looked at him as closely as we can but see no connection to either the Treviño girl, or bull-fighting. Nothing at all."

"Dammit, we've got to come up with something," Hugo said. "Time's running short, and we can't keep running into dead-ends."

"What do you suggest?" Garcia asked gently.

"I've talked to Barsetti, and he's hiding something," Hugo said. "It may only have to do with his marriage, but I showed him a picture of Delia Treviño and he went weak at the knees. Can you send some people out to talk to her associates again, but this time show them a picture of Barsetti?"

"*Sí*, of course. What else?"

"Look into the gang connection. Maybe Los Matadores are sticking together out of prison. Maybe they're making money through selling human organs, or maybe they don't like it when members try and leave them. I don't know, but can you look into both angles?"

"Today."

Tom spoke up. "What do you think about going public? Seems to me we're a little mired here and could use whatever information we can get."

"I agree," said Silva.

"You may be right," Hugo said. "But if we go that route, there's no turning back from it."

"What do you mean?" asked Garcia.

"He means be prepared for a shit-storm," Tom said. "Every loon with a conspiracy theory will call in and tell you why the government has her. Every delusional wacko will call to tell you they've just spotted her hang gliding over the Old Town. And if it's a slow week in the US, be prepared for half a dozen irritating media types to start following and reporting on your every move. Also, just being practical, remember that a pretty girl missing in a foreign city is a great news story, but a shitty tourist logo."

All eyes turned to Chief Inspector Garcia. He was a policeman, Hugo knew, not a politician, but if his job was anything like that of his counterparts in the States, the people he reported to would look at this with one eye on the businesses and restaurants that would suffer from negative publicity. And if they were concerned about that, Garcia would be, too.

"I think," Garcia said finally, "that I will let other people worry about the image of Barcelona. I will focus on catching the criminals." He looked around the table. "I will need to make a few calls first, of course, let some people know this is coming." He fixed his eyes on Hugo. "Your friend, Claudia, perhaps she can contact me this afternoon and we can arrange a statement. Get it on the news this evening."

"Sounds good, I'll have her call you," Hugo said. "In the meantime, I'll talk to Nisha Bhandari, and maybe one of you can pay a visit to Todd Finch." He stood. "Let's not sit around and wait for this press conference, folks. We've got to get a move on because Amy's out there on her own somewhere, and so far this investigation simply hasn't been good enough."

They all turned as the door to Garcia's office swung open and his secretary, Micaela Galaviz entered. She looked around the room, as if sensing the tension in the air.

"Sorry to interrupt," she said. "But there's been an incident you should know about."

"An incident?" Hugo asked. "Not another murder, please."

"No, *señor*, not that," Galaviz said. "It's your friend Bart Denum. He tried to escape."

♉

Hugo stood by Denum's hospital bed, looking down at his friend. A swathe of bandages circled his head, and his right wrist was shackled to the railing of the bed. A machine in the corner of the room beeped softly, keeping tabs on Denum's heart rate, while a policeman stood outside his room, keeping tabs on visitors.

Chief Inspector Garcia stood behind him, silent, waiting.

"You know," Hugo said, "in Switzerland it's not illegal to try to escape custody. They recognize that being held prisoner runs counter to every instinct a person has, that the desire for freedom is innate and so powerful that people cannot help but act upon it. So if you try to escape from prison, they don't add time to your sentence."

"I'm guessing you didn't tell that story to every murderer and psychopath you ever captured."

Hugo turned and smiled sadly. "I didn't capture any in Switzerland."

"And you know we're not there, *sí*?" Garcia held up a finger to silence Hugo's response. "I would also bet money that even if the Swiss don't punish you for escaping, they will hold you accountable for injuring someone during your attempt."

"Yes, true," Hugo admitted.

"Then you'll understand that any plan to release him is now impossible."

Hugo couldn't argue, knew it would be futile. "Are your men seriously injured?"

"No, thankfully—for them and for your friend."

The story, as Hugo understood it, was that Bart had lain on his bunk not responding to guards when they brought him food. They'd ignored him and tried again an hour later, but seeing that he'd not moved and was still not responding, two of them entered his cell. Bart leapt up and attacked them, shouting that he was leaving, that he needed to find Amy, and all three had fought in the cell for two minutes until one of the guards had swept Bart's feet from under him, bringing him crashing to the floor. According to the policemen, the American's head hit the edge of the metal bunk on the way down, rendering him bloody and unconscious. Hugo had no reason to doubt their story but, from the marks on his body and the fact that he was still unconscious, he wondered if the two burly guards hadn't spent a few extra seconds administering their version of justice to the oblivious Bart as he lay on the floor.

"So what happens now?" Hugo asked.

"He lies here until he wakes up, and then he goes back to his jail cell."

Hugo shook his head. "This is all so wrong."

Garcia's tone softened. "*Bueno*, I understand why he did what he did. That he has emotional problems and that he wants to find his daughter. But it is out of our hands now. We must focus on finding Amy so that when he wakes up we have some good news."

He was right, of course, Hugo knew that. He bent and took his friend's limp hand and gave it a squeeze. "I keep telling you this, Bart, and I promise it's true. I'll find Amy for you. One way or another, I'll find her, no matter what it takes."

CHAPTER TWENTY-THREE

The chief inspector left Hugo at the hospital when he was summoned by his superiors to explain why an American was attacking Barcelona police officers in their own jails. Ever the pragmatist, Hugo thought, Garcia had said, "Well, this'll give me a chance to talk to them about the media appearance we're planning."

On the sidewalk, Hugo watched for a moment the procession of people coming and going from the hospital, the sick, the worried, and the newly recovered. The occasional blare of a siren announced newcomers as ambulances nosed through the crowded pedestrian crossings, but those lost in their own world of pain and sickness paid no heed to the arrival of others, barely looking up at the whoop of the siren and the flash of angry lights.

A taxi dropped off a man with a worried look on his face, and Hugo made a snap decision, hailing it before it could melt into traffic. He dug into his wallet and pulled out the card Nisha Bhandari had given him. Gregor Freed seemed tangential to the investigation, but Hugo had a few minutes, and the direct path hadn't given them any answers. Why not try a side street?

The cabbie headed south toward the docks, and Hugo reached for his phone to dial Claudia. She answered immediately. "Hey," he said, "I need to see a friendly face. What're you up to?"

"Not much," she said. "I worked on a press release, just a very rough draft for you guys if you ever want to take a look. Killing time as much as anything, though."

"Thanks. Turns out we will be needing that today."

"What's going on?"

"Looks like we're going to go to the media for some help."

"Does that mean things aren't going well?"

"Correct. And I may have irritated a few people just now."

"You? I find that hard to believe."

"I'm just frustrated," Hugo said. "Not much progress, not any at all really, and all the news we get seems to be bad. Amy's out there on her own, Bart's not helping himself, and we were just sitting there eating croissants and drinking coffee."

"Everyone needs to eat, including cops. And you."

"You know what I mean."

"What did Bart do?"

"I'll tell you later. I'm assuming you heard about the girl we found?"

"Tom told me," she said. "So awful."

"We're all relieved it's not Amy but you're right, it was pretty horrific. Anyway, I'm calling about the media thing but also to see if you can get away for lunch. Like you said, I need to eat. Just a quick sandwich, I don't really care where or what, it'd just be nice to see you."

"It would," Claudia said. "Come to the hotel, we can get a bite in the restaurant here, and in the meantime I'll polish up that press release."

"Great. I have one thing I need to do first." He looked at his watch. "It's ten thirty; I'll be there around noon."

♉

Inside the store, a burly man stood over a large, walnut table, a rag in one hand and a spray can of polish in the other. He smiled and said, "*A sus ordenes.*"

Hugo gave an apologetic smile. "*Habla Ingles?*"

"Yes, I speak English, of course. You're on vacation here?"

"I wish." Hugo said with a smile. "This is your store?"

"Yes, sir, it is. I am Gregor Freed."

"Nice to meet you, I'm Hugo Marston. Tell me, do you sell books?"

"No, I used to, but they turned out to be too much of a distraction."

"How so?"

"They are heavy, dusty, easy to damage. And, to be honest, I like people to use what I sell them. I found that when people buy old books, it's to put them on a shelf, or to impress their neighbors, so I'm not so interested in dealing with them."

"I suppose that can be true."

Freed chuckled. "You are a collector? I hope I didn't insult you. Sometimes I can be a little blunt. If you like, I can refer you to some good stores not far from here."

"You didn't insult me at all," Hugo said. "And I'm not really a collector. I mean, in a very amateur way, perhaps, for my own satisfaction and pleasure."

"That's the best reason of all."

"And I read every book I buy."

Freed clapped his big hands together. "Now that I approve of. And a great way to broaden your horizons."

"You're right about that." Hugo thought about the Arthur Rimbaud book he bought a couple of years previously, a nine-part poem soaked with the author's absinthe and opium use, and fueled in part by Rimbaud's affair with a married man. Not the regular reading fare for a former FBI profiler.

Freed gestured to his shop floor. "No books, but maybe I can sell you a chair instead."

"Tough to get into my carry-on luggage."

Freed smiled. "Maybe I can find you a letter-opener, I believe we have some carved in Namibia."

"No, thanks. Actually, Nisha Bhandari gave me your name."

"Nisha?" Freed's eyes opened wide with surprise. Hugo thought he saw in them a moment of calculation, too, one impossible to decipher so soon. A business opportunity, a shared secret, even a flash of jealousy over a beautiful woman. Eyes could be the window to the soul, Hugo knew, but people weren't above dressing their windows in a way to fool the outside world. "Oh, well then," Freed said, "tell me how I can help."

"Is there somewhere we can talk?"

"Of course, my office. Follow me."

Freed led Hugo toward the back of the store, a winding route between tables, book cases, and glass cabinets full of medals and other rusty-looking trinkets. In a clear space in front of the wall that separated the office from the shop floor, lay a pile of lumber and what looked like foam padding. The German paused at the doorway and bade Hugo enter.

"We're planning to remodel a little," Freed said. "Unfortunately, my office isn't as big as it looks. Partly because I do a poor job of keeping it organized, and for that my apologies."

"No problem." Hugo picked his way past several cardboard boxes and lowered himself into a collapsible director's chair, hoping it would bear his weight.

Freed saw his hesitation and laughed. "Don't worry, if that thing can hold me, and it can, you'll be fine." He sank into a swivel chair behind his desk. "Now then, what can I do for you?"

"Well, I was wondering if you knew a couple of Nisha's colleagues. Leo Barsetti?"

"Yes, of course. I haven't seen much of him lately, but he helps Nisha and me with the business."

"How about Rubén Castañeda?"

"I know him a little, too," Freed said. "I think we've met once or twice. Maybe three times, I couldn't be sure. Is he in trouble?"

"A little worse than that. He's dead."

Freed stiffened. "Dead? What happened?"

"I'm working with the Barcelona police, just to be clear about my involvement," Hugo said. "I can't go into too many details, I'm sure you'll understand, but it's an odd situation."

"So you are more than just an amateur book collector."

"I work at the US Embassy in Paris," Hugo said. "There may be a connection to something that happened there."

"Rubén was murdered?"

"It sure looks that way."

Freed shook his head slowly. "Ach, that's unbelievable."

"Was he involved with your and Nisha's business in any way?"

Freed opened his mouth to answer but stopped when the bell at the front door rang. "I should probably . . ."

"Go ahead," said Hugo. "Take care of business, I don't mind waiting."

"Thank you, things have been a little slow. We do a lot on the Internet and not in person these days, so it's nice to see a real customer now and again."

Freed squeezed his bulk through the door, and Hugo listened as he greeted the customer, a woman, in Spanish. He listened for a moment to see if he could understand any of what they were saying, but the words flowed too quickly, washing away any meaning he might otherwise have gleaned from picking out the odd word here and there. Instead he focused on the room around him, poking open the cardboard boxes to find what looked like Christmas baubles wrapped in tissue paper. He leaned forward to inspect the desktop, picking up a sheaf of green papers stacked neatly on the corner of the desk nearest him. They looked to be shipping invoices, listing items of furniture to be packed up and delivered abroad. Nothing suspicious, which disappointed him, but his natural curiosity kicked in. International shipping was something he knew nothing about, and he'd always been impressed at the way goods, even perishable ones, could be shuttled around the globe with both haste and precision. The invoices showed that Freed and Bhandari used forty-foot containers, sent by rail within continental Europe and shipped out of the docks for destinations further afield. After a couple of minutes, Hugo looked up as the bell jingled again. He could hear the customer and Freed saying their good-byes, so he put the papers back feeling slightly guilty at his nosiness.

"Sorry about that," Freed said, sitting. "She'll be back with her husband tomorrow, likes a couple of dining tables I have in stock."

"Glad to hear it."

Freed's face fell as he remembered why Hugo was there. "Ah, Rubén. Poor Rubén. Can you tell me what happened?"

"Not really," Hugo said. "So you and he didn't really know each other?"

"That's right, only through Nisha and only a little."

"And how do you know Nisha?"

Freed smiled, and Hugo thought he could now interpret the shift in the man's attitude earlier. Maybe jealousy, maybe protectiveness, but now his eyes glowed with mention of Nisha Bhandari's name.

"It was more than a year ago, almost two. It was a meeting of local businesspeople, small businesses run by foreigners. There were a series of presentations about the law, accounting, that kind of thing. Social media was one of them. Anyway, we were the only ones who attended all of the presentations, and we got to talking because of our shared interest in antiques. We'd also both wanted to get into the exporting business, recognizing the opening of markets elsewhere."

Hugo watched Freed as he talked. He wasn't just remembering, he was reminiscing, picturing his early meetings with Nisha Bhandari the way a love-struck boyfriend might. Hugo was tempted to ask outright, but he'd seen no evidence that the feelings were mutual and didn't want to alienate Freed.

"And so you went into business together?" Hugo asked.

"We did. It's strange; it didn't feel like a business venture, really. It was more us trying something, just giving it a shot."

"And how's it now?"

"It's tailed off a little. The economy is not what we'd like, locally and globally. I'd say we're at about half what we were doing this time last year." He shrugged. "But it's OK, I'm sure it'll pick up again, and neither of us rely on the furniture export as our primary source of income."

"Glad to hear that. Are you married, Mr. Freed?"

"Ach, call me Gregor, please. No, I'm not married but I do, how do you say, hold a candle for a certain lady." He looked down, as if embarrassed. "I think you know who."

Hugo smiled, his impression confirmed. "I've been there; it's nothing to be ashamed of."

"I'm not ashamed, just a little . . . well, a man can only wait so long, don't you think?"

"I know exactly what you mean." Hugo pictured Claudia and felt an impatience to see her. "The question is figuring out how long that is."

"We have one other shared interest. I've managed that at least."

Hugo furrowed his brow, then remembered. "Ah yes, flying."

"I took her up the first time just to show off, to impress her." He grinned. "You can imagine how pleased I was that she took to it, wanted lessons. She's a natural, that one." He sighed wistfully. "Ah well, I suppose I'm in no hurry." He gestured toward his store. "It's not like women are banging down the door to get to me."

Hugo put his hands on the arm of the chair and pushed himself up. "Well, if I see any lingering on the sidewalk out there, I'll send them your way."

"Or," Freed said quietly, "you could put in a good word for me."

Hugo put out his hand. "Sure thing."

℧

Hugo climbed out of the back of a taxi and went into the lobby of the Hotel Alfonso. *A boutique hotel*, he thought, looking around. Rich wood paneling made up for the lack of windows, and the plush but miniature rooms would no doubt, and legitimately, be called "cozy." Where he stood in the lobby, it smelled faintly and pleasantly of polish, and the flowers on the table beside him were real, and fresh. He noted the expensive carpets, too, his boots sinking into the thick pile as he made his way through the lobby toward the sound of clinking dishes and gentle conversation.

Claudia was already at a table, her fingers tracing patterns on a glass of water. When she saw him, she leapt up, surprising herself as well as Hugo with her display of excitement, and they both laughed. He held her for a moment, breathing in the scent he could never name, but that reminded him of her, no matter where or when he smelled it.

"It's good to see you," she said. "We leave it too long."

"Yes," said Hugo as he sat. "You sure do."

"Oh, hush. You're only a little better."

"But the intent is always there."

She looked down at her glass, as if acknowledging the distance she'd put between them. "You know, I always think that it's easier when you're younger. Finding someone is easier; wanting to be part of a couple is more natural. No, that's not the right word."

"I know what you mean, Claudia, and it's OK. You have your life the way you want it, you like your life the way it is. There's nothing wrong with that."

"You think that means there's no room for you?"

Hugo smiled. "A little room, occasionally, perhaps."

"*Oui, c'est vrai.*" Yes, that's been true. "It's strange, you know, it's like I've hit my stride since papa died, and recently things have gotten so much better. With work, with my friends . . ." Her voice tailed off and she gave him a sad smile. "I sound very selfish, don't I?"

"Not at all. Look, I have no intention of upsetting the nice balance you have in your life. I'm not the kind of guy who'd stop you from seeing your friends or complain if you work late. Come on, surely you know that about me."

The waiter arrived and Claudia ordered a mixed-grill platter and a double serving of garlic bread, all to share. When they'd first met she'd done that, ordered their food, and it had become part joke, part tradition and, as always, she did it with one eye on Hugo in case he objected to her selection. When the waiter left, she said, "I know, Hugo. It's hard to explain, I'm just worried about making a commitment I can't keep."

"I'm not asking for any commitment at all." He smiled. "Just the mixed grill."

"Just that?" She returned his smile. "A little more, I hope."

"We'll see."

While they waited for their food, Hugo told her about Bart Denum and his ideas for how they should use the media to help find Amy. She nodded along, listening and asking the occasional question, reaching across the table to give Hugo's arm a squeeze now and again, and he welcomed the support and understanding. He finished updating her just as the waiter returned, pushing a cart with its own griddle. Their food—chicken, lamb, and beef—sizzled and spat, the rich aroma taking over Hugo's senses as the waiter carefully transferred the meat to a plate that sat in the middle of the table. He also put down the garlic bread and a trio of clay pots, explaining in broken English that they contained mustard, salsa, and a garlic mayonnaise.

As they ate, Hugo steered the conversation away from the case, even though Amy's disappearance was an ever-present whisper in his mind, an ache in his heart. He wanted a moment of normalcy, a break from the unrelenting pressure of the investigation and a moment's respite from the fear that he might not find Amy, not in time. Just a moment's respite, that was all. And so they talked about everything else, some new restaurants in Paris Claudia had discovered, her chauffeur Jean's newfound love (a basset hound named Clint, after Clint Eastwood), and the odds that global warming would destroy New York City. Neither of them knew, of course, but it got them imagining and laughing about the art they'd save, and the people they might not. After an hour, Claudia swiped the check from his hand and reminded him, "She who orders, pays."

They lingered on the sidewalk in front of the hotel. "You have plans for this afternoon?" Hugo asked.

"I'm seeing an old friend of my father's, he used to supply papa with Spanish wine. You?"

"I need to find Nisha Bhandari and have a chat."

"About?"

"She runs that company. Seems to me that if we're missing some piece of inside information, she's the one to share it."

"You already talked to them all, though."

"In a group setting. I always go back to my main players in an investigation, talk to them a second or third time."

She smiled. "One of those psychological things?"

"Something like that. The first time I talk to someone, usually they're caught off guard, even if just a little. That element of surprise can result in one of three things. They forget to tell me something, they intentionally hide information, or they make snap decisions about what they think I need to know."

"Makes sense," Claudia said.

"Now, if someone's truly wanting to help, the second time I see them, they try extra hard to come up with new information, which addresses the first and third of those problems."

"And if they're hiding something?"

"Then I have to hope I'm good enough to spot it."

Claudia put a hand on his arm and looked up at him. "I really admire you, Hugo. You're a good man, and you work so hard to help those people who need it. You are very selfless, and I want you to know how much I admire you for that."

He smiled. "Is there a 'but' coming?"

She let go of his arm and laughed. She stood, looking at him for a moment, still smiling, then she started to walk back into the hotel. On the second step, she looked over her shoulder. "There is one, Señor Marston, most definitely." She patted her behind. "And I'm free tonight, all night, if you can get away to discuss it." Not waiting for an answer, she blew him a kiss and disappeared into the hotel.

"Not exactly what I meant," Hugo said to himself. "But an answer I can live with."

He turned and saw two street sweepers leaning on their brushes, grinning at him. One gave him the thumbs-up and, for the first time in months, Hugo felt a lightness swirling in the center of his chest, a weightlessness that flowed all the way through him and put a bounce in his step as he headed away from the hotel.

♉

Nisha Bhandari, according to her colleague Todd Finch, was most likely at her yoga class. "She comes to work early and stays late," Finch said. "And when everyone else takes lunch or a siesta, she has her yoga class."

"Every day?" Hugo didn't want to walk two miles not to find her.

"Every weekday, maybe even weekends. Has done since she got here, so I'm sure you'll find her there." Finch hesitated. "Can I ask why you need to talk to her? Is there some news about Rubén?"

Curiosity? Hugo wondered, *or concern?* "No real news," he said. "Just a few follow-up questions, that's all. Thanks for your time."

"Sure, I was just wondering," Finch said quickly. "It's just that someone said you were FBI, and I didn't understand why the American FBI would be involved in a murder here in Barcelona. You know, if there's something bigger going on, maybe we should be told about it."

"Something bigger?"

"Yeah, like terrorism. You guys fly abroad and help local police when there's terrorist attacks, I've seen that on the news."

"Ah, I see. I can promise you, Mr. Finch, there are no concerns of terrorism here. I'm helping out a local investigation, that's all there is to it, and like I said, this has nothing to do with terrorism."

"You can't tell me why exactly?"

"I don't work for the FBI anymore, Mr. Finch. I work for the State Department in Paris, and all I can say is that a girl missing somewhere in Barcelona should be enjoying her day in Paris right now."

Finch nodded. "OK then. Thanks. And good luck."

Hugo shook hands with the man and left, heading deeper into the Old Town, toward the yoga studio. He felt a need to hurry, yet he also couldn't help but take in his surroundings, wander almost randomly in the general direction he was headed. He wanted to explore this place, take in the side streets that twisted like the branches of an old oak tree—worn smooth with time, beautiful and ancient, impractically narrow at the tips only to open up into wide squares that blossomed with shops, cafés, and restaurants.

Turning the corner out of Carrer d'Avinyo, Hugo paused outside a stone building to make sure he had the right place, checking the small notice on the brick wall. He pushed open the door and walked up the stairs to the second floor, where he found a small waiting room. Half a dozen women and one man stood there, some stretching, others chatting, all with rolled-up mats and towels tucked under their arms.

A receptionist, willowy and tanned, said something to Hugo in Spanish that he took to mean, "Can I help you?"

He gave her his best smile. "*Hola. Habla Ingles?*"

"*Sí*," she said, looking him up and down without subtlety. She smiled, as if she liked what she saw. "I mean, yes. You are American?"

"That's right," said Hugo. "I'm looking for a friend of mine, Nisha Bhandari."

The woman pointed toward a closed door. "Finish in two minutes."

"*Gracias.* OK for me to wait here?"

"Of course." She pursed her lips. "You practice yoga?"

Hugo patted his stomach. "Think I should?"

"Everyone should." She stepped back from the desk and swung her right leg up to her ear, holding it there with one hand on her ankle. "Two years ago, I cannot touch my toes. Now, this."

"Impressive," Hugo said. "I think it'd take me more than two years to do that, though."

"Maybe, maybe not." She dropped her leg and snatched a brochure from the desk in front of her. "Come see us, we find out, yes?"

"Very tempting, thank you," Hugo said. He took the brochure and studied the front for a moment just to satisfy her. He folded it carefully into a square, tucked it into his front pocket, and gave her a smile. The door to their left opened, and they both looked over as Bhandari's class began to file out of the studio. Nisha was the fifth one out, coming through the door while chatting to an older woman with bleached-blond hair. Hugo caught the Indian woman's eye. "Excuse me, do you have a few minutes?"

She hesitated for a moment, clearly surprised to see him there, then turned to her companion and said something in Spanish. The older woman smiled at Hugo and moved away.

"I suppose so," she said in a low voice. "Let's talk outside."

"Of course." He followed her down the steps into the street.

"I don't mean to be rude, Mr. Marston, but I do yoga for two reasons. One is to remain fit and limber, which is becoming less and less easy as I age. The other is for my mental and emotional health."

"And being bugged the minute you step out of the studio about a grisly murder doesn't do much for your sense of inner balance?"

She cocked her head. "Are you making fun of me?"

"Not at all, I'm apologizing. I know I'm bothering you at a bad time, but I don't really have a choice. The police don't have a lot to go on here, and a young girl is missing."

"Ah, yes, the police. I meant to ask you this when we met, but why exactly are you involved?"

The question of the day, Hugo thought. "Amy, the girl who's missing, is a friend of mine. I'm hoping my experience with the FBI will be useful to the police."

"Oh, I don't think you told me that." Bhandari wiped a towel over her face. "Look, I usually walk to a health-food store, get myself a protein shake. I'm happy to talk to you on the way."

"Maybe I'll get one of those, too," Hugo said. "Been eating a lot of meat lately, something green sounds good."

"Yes, the food does take some getting used to. Most of it is very good, but they tend to go light on the vegetables and fruit." She started to walk, and Hugo went with her. "Or, they coat the vegetables in oil and garlic."

"And mayonnaise."

"Right." She cast a glance sideways. "You seem to stay fit, though. You said you live in Paris?"

"Thanks, yes. I do a lot of walking there, and occasionally run."

"When you have to chase someone?"

Hugo laughed. "Oh, I don't do much of that anymore. I call in the reinforcements if that type of running is called for. I meant that I jog once a week or so."

"I have to exercise a lot because I have a weakness for food." She smiled, almost shyly Hugo thought. "Well, for many self-indulgences, really. Hence the yoga, it keeps me focused."

"On your work?"

"Yes, for one thing. But this city is full of distractions, temptations."

"Your colleague Leonardo, does he succumb to those?"

"Oh, I see. Is that why you're here, to quiz me about my friends?"

"Maybe that's a good place to start. Are they friends or colleagues?"

She seemed to think for a moment. "I suppose they began as colleagues but are now friends. When you work so closely to people, as long as you get on well, you can't help but become friends."

"True. Do you all get on well?"

Again the pause. "Yes. I think Leo has been under some stress lately, but that's with his marriage. Work is something of a relief for him, or so it seems to me. He's very good with clients, charming and knowledgeable."

"That reminds me," Hugo said. "It struck me as odd that a Barcelona tourist business would be operated by four people, only one of whom is from Barcelona. From Spain, even."

Bhandari laughed and looked up at Hugo. "It's stranger than you think, because Rubén was from the south, Cadiz or somewhere. Anyway, I said the same thing when I arrived. And then Leo and Todd challenged me. I spent an entire afternoon quizzing them about the city, its tourist destinations and its restaurants. Everything, really. They were very excited about showing it off to me, too, which I thought was a good sign." She shrugged. "Plus, Leo is Italian. A lot of foreigners can't tell the difference when they speak to him or see him. They think he's Spanish."

"And as long as he does a good job, why should they even care?" Hugo added.

"Precisely. He does have a tendency to exaggerate a little, I will say that. But this job, it is partly advertising, no? So maybe exaggeration is to be expected, maybe it's a plus not a minus."

"And Rubén?"

"He was more straightforward." She pointed down a side street, and they turned onto it. "And yes, he had his issues, the ones I told you about before."

"The sex trade."

"You make it sound very dirty. Here, it is not. And to him it was not. I think he actually had a strong moral sense about him, and I am certain, absolutely certain, he would never have engaged in anything illegal."

"When we in America think of the sex trade, we think of dirty old men going to foreign countries to have sex with underage boys and girls."

She bridled. "You know that's not what we do, what we provide. And, anyway, I get the sense that Americans generally view sex quite differently. More prudish."

"I'm not so sure it's that way as much as it used to be." Hugo said. "Although we'll never tolerate adults having sex with children, at least I damn well hope not."

"And Rubén felt the same way. His clients were here for the sex clubs, the strip clubs, the gay bars, but not that . . . not children." She shook her head. "He would not have done that."

But Hugo wondered. Something had gotten Castañeda killed, and if he'd ventured too far from the world of adult sex into the underground world of child sex . . . Hugo knew from experience that the kinds of people who operated in dark alleys and cheap motels, who hid their activities and their profits from the law, those people weren't always picky about their friends, which meant that if Rubén Castañeda had upset the wrong people, there was always the possibility he'd been served up to the ruthless dealers in human organs. Served up alive maybe, and possibly even made an example of. And if Amy had been there, at the wrong place at the wrong time . . . Speculation for now, Hugo reminded himself, a possibility to keep in the back of his mind but not to obsess over.

He changed tack. "Do you know someone by the name of Delia Treviño?"

"Here we are." She paused with one hand on the door and frowned in thought. "Delia Treviño? I don't think so. That name doesn't seem familiar."

"Do you mind taking a look at a photo?" Hugo said.

"Of course not." She gestured inside with a nod of her head. "Mind if I get my smoothie first?"

"Sure, let's go in. Sorry." Hugo let her go to the counter, and he sat at a small table by the front window. He took out his phone to pull up Delia Treviño's mugshot, and he noticed that he had a message from Claudia. He looked up to see Nisha Bhandari weaving between the tables toward him, and he left Claudia's message for later.

The Indian was, he thought, an attractive woman. Despite her claim to the contrary, she looked very fit, her yoga pants attracting the attention of several customers as her hips sashayed past them. She wore her hair in a ponytail, and that somehow accentuated the wideness, and enormity, of her eyes. She slid into the seat opposite him and offered her drink.

"Spinach, kale, blueberry, some whey, and a few other things. Try it?"

"I'll get my own on the way out, maybe," Hugo said. He leaned back, smiling but suddenly aware that she smelled good, too.

"You should." She took a sip and wrinkled her nose. "But I'd skip the kale, if I were you. A little bitter."

"Thanks for the advice." He turned his phone toward her, displaying the mugshot. "Do you happen to recognize her?"

"Let me see." Bhandari leaned forward, her fingertips brushing against Hugo's as she reached for the phone. She squinted. "I don't think so. No, I'm pretty sure I don't. Whoever she is, looks a little pale or sick in this photo."

"We think she was a drug user."

"Is she a suspect or something?"

"No. She was killed, in the same way as Rubén Castañeda."

"Oh, no, I'm sorry to hear that." She tilted her head. "No one ever told us how he died. I mean, murdered, yes. But not . . . any details."

"The police never give details. No point in upsetting his friends, for one thing. And from their perspective, the fewer people outside the investigation who know, the better."

"I guess that makes sense." Her phone rang, and she picked it up. "Excuse me, it's work. Hello? Is Leo not there? Well, leave him another message. I'll be there in about ten minutes." She rang off and looked at Hugo. "A group of Rubén's clients from Japan, he was supposed to take them around the city tonight. Leo has been filling in where possible, just because I have no interest in that kind of thing, spending the evening with a bunch of increasingly drunk and horny Japanese businessmen."

"I can imagine."

"Apparently Leo's missing right now, so I need to head into the office to handle this."

"He do that a lot, go missing?"

"Not really, no. He's been a rock since Rubén died. I don't know what I'd do without him."

"Todd Finch, too?"

She smiled. "Todd's a little strange, I know. He's not the best with the clients, but he's amazing with numbers, is great setting up our technology in the office, and helps us all stay organized." She stood. "I'm sorry to cut this short, though. Do you have more questions?"

"Yes. Maybe once you figure this crisis out you can call me?" Something about the way she stood so close to him made Hugo want to squirm. He couldn't tell if she was doing so on purpose, he couldn't even tell *what* she was doing, but he felt like a freshman in high school being approached by the football team's head cheerleader.

"It'll make life easier for me if I can tell these clients that I have dinner plans," she said.

"I guess we can do that. Where and when?"

"Depends on when I get done putting out fires. How about you give me your number, I'll text you?"

She typed his name and number into her phone, then picked up her mat and towel and walked out of the juice shop, leaving Hugo to watch her bobbing pony tail, and try very hard not to lower his gaze to the tightness of her yoga pants. As he stood to leave, he felt the brochure in his pocket poking at him. He pulled it out and looked around for a recycling or trash can. He took one last look at the folded paper, letting it fall open, and his eye caught on one face in a crowded photograph of the studio's instructors. He looked again and, sure he was right, his heart quickened.

He strode out of the juice bar, but Bhandari was nowhere in sight. He thought for a moment, then headed the short distance back to the yoga studio, taking the stairs two at a time. He was out of breath when he reached the reception desk, where the same young lady looked at him with surprise.

"That was quick," she said. "Nisha tell you to come back so soon?"

"No." Hugo laid the open brochure on the desk, his mind working. He could go with the truth but didn't want to alert this girl, or anyone else, to what he was asking about, or why. He pointed to the face. "Who is that?"

"Oh, she worked here, but not for a few months. That picture is old."

"I'm asking because she looks familiar. What's her name?"

"That's Delia. Delia Treviño."

CHAPTER TWENTY-FOUR

Hugo called Chief Inspector Garcia the moment his boots hit the sidewalk.

"We have our first connection," Hugo said. "Delia Treviño was an instructor at Nisha Bhandari's yoga studio."

"Is that so? Interesting, because it's not just her studio."

"I don't understand."

"Leo Barsetti's wife, Rosario Figueroa. She goes there, too. Grace Silva went back for a second interview with her this morning, showed her Treviño's mugshot. She didn't say anything about Nisha Bhandari going there, but she recognized Treviño."

"Interesting, because Bhandari didn't. Or said she didn't."

"Well, it might depend on how long each had been going, whether she was actually their instructor or not. I'll send Silva over there now to talk to the management, get as much of that information as possible."

"Good idea."

A pause on the phone, and when Garcia spoke, Hugo heard a smile in the man's voice. "You should wait there, take my young colleague to dinner after. To discuss the case, of course."

"Of course." Hugo didn't feel like revealing that he already had two women lined up for the evening. He couldn't even remember the last time he had that problem, let alone adding another into the mix. "I plan to head back to Estruch. I had a quick chat with Todd Finch earlier but I cut it short to find Bhandari. Couple of things I want to ask him."

"Help yourself. I tried before, and he's not been evasive, exactly, but a little hard to find or pin down. I'd meet you there but we're working on this media thing."

"No problem, I can handle it." Hugo rang off and checked his phone to see how far away he was from Estruch, then set off at a brisk walk. According to Garcia's files, Finch was from New Zealand. Hugo had been there twice, both times to help out local law enforcement in murder cases, and he hoped to use those visits as a bridge to Finch's trust. When he got to the building, he let himself in. The place was quiet.

"Hello?" he called, stepping into the reception area. He looked down the hallway. The door to the front office, to his left, was cracked, and he thought he saw movement. The quiet had put Hugo on edge, and the lack of response didn't help. He touched his hip where his gun would normally lie but noticed the lack of weight even before his hand felt the gun's absence.

"Anyone home?" he called out. Movement in the office again, but still no response. Hugo set his feet so that he could either lunge forward or head back out the door, trying to control his breathing.

The door to the office swung open, and Hugo froze. He found himself staring at an equally startled Todd Finch, who put both hands up when he saw Hugo.

"Bloody hell, mate, you scared the living crap out of me!"

"Sorry," Hugo said. "I called out a couple of times when I came in but . . ."

"Ah, right." Finch opened his left hand, where a set of head phones nestled. "Sorry. Don't get much peace and quiet around here, so when I need to concentrate I put these in."

"Makes sense."

"Find Nisha?"

"Yes, thanks. I had more questions for you, too, if you don't mind, probably should have chatted when I was here earlier, but I did need to catch Nisha first."

Finch shifted from foot to foot. "Err, OK, what do you want to know?"

"Well, maybe you told me, but what is it you do for Estruch?"

"I do the accounting and the tech stuff."

"The website?"

"The website's not much, been planning to work on it. But yeah, that and the Internet connections, social media, basic PowerPoint stuff. We're not high-tech, but there's always things to be done. I suppose mostly I work on the accounting side of things, and most of that seems to be chasing down people for money."

"What about Leo and Nisha's side business, the antiques."

"That's more of a hobby than a business, best I can tell. But no, I don't have much to do with that at all. I think Leo keeps all the documents, bills, and shipping info in his office." He shrugged. "I offered to do it for them, but Nisha said she didn't want to make extra work for me when I wasn't benefiting from it."

"Nice of her."

"Yeah, but I'm not always that busy, so I wouldn't have minded."

"Do you enjoy your job?" Hugo asked.

Finch thought for a moment. "Have you been to New Zealand?"

"Twice, actually. One of the most beautiful places I've ever been."

"Isn't it?" Finch smiled. "Thing is, it's not good to be different there, like I am."

"Different?"

"Yes. It's kind of an outdoorsy, trendy . . ." He sought for the right words but ended up just shrugging. "Well, everything New Zealand is, I'm not. I'm tall and skinny, don't like people all that much, keep to myself. I stuck out over there, and that's not good. Over here," he chuckled, "well, people don't seem to care about the differences."

"Maybe that's just because you're in a city." Hugo said.

"Could be. Either way, the answer is that I like living in Barcelona. The job itself is OK, sometimes I feel like a bit of a dogsbody, not really one of the principals, you know?"

"They treat you that way?"

"Not really but, as I said before, I'm not great with people. I mean, I get on fine, but I'm not the type to spend the day leading a bunch of old hags around the city, pointing out its finest features."

"More the realm of people like Leo Barsetti and Rubén Castañeda?"

"Yeah. Leo's good with the older folks, a real charmer." He paused. "Rubén was too, I suppose."

"You suppose?"

"He was. I never quite figured him out, to be honest."

"What do you mean by that?"

"Well, have you ever seen those cop shows, where they have profilers and stuff on them?"

Hugo smiled. "I don't watch those much, no."

"Well, I love them. Watch all of them I can. I'm not a people person, Mr. Marston, which is to say I'm not interested *in* people, but I am interested *by* them. Does that make any sense?"

"Actually, yes."

"I think I know what makes Nisha and Leo tick, but I never figured out Rubén. He was more . . . secretive, or something."

Hugo gestured to the chairs near them. "Mind if we sit while we talk? I feel like I've walked all over Barcelona today." It was the truth, his feet did ache, but Hugo also knew that if Finch was sitting, he'd be more invested in their discussion, less likely to suddenly leave. A simple matter of physics that played on the mind: it's easier to walk away from a conversation while you're standing up than it is while sitting.

"Yeah, sure." They sat, Finch folding himself into place with a slight wince. "Getting old," he said. "Used to play rugby and squash, ten years ago, but both buggered my knees pretty badly. We don't get much of a winter here, but I can tell when it's coming."

Hugo smiled. "Where in New Zealand are you from?"

"Town called Hamilton. North Island."

"And what brought you to Europe?"

"A long story. I was studying to be a vet. Figured since I wasn't wanting to work with people, I'd try working with animals, but the more into it I got, the more I realized I didn't much care for them, either. It's a great way to make a living, pays well, and if you focus on large animals, you don't have fussy old women with their punt dogs to—"

"I'm sorry," Hugo interrupted, "'punt dogs'?"

"Yeah, little dogs. Small enough you can punt them if you want to. Anyway, I realized that I'd been drawn to the job for the wrong reasons."

"Which were?"

Finch shrugged. "The pay, the lifestyle, the idea of a quiet country cottage somewhere near Hamilton."

"Doesn't sound bad."

"I'm sure it's great, but not if you don't like dealing with animals. I just didn't have the patience. Like I said, I think it was the theory of the job more than the reality that appealed to me."

"So you changed course and came to Spain?"

"Pretty much. I'd already studied accounting, was good with figures." He smiled, as if to himself. "And figures don't kick you in the balls when you're not looking."

"How did you end up here?"

"Pure luck. I was staying with a cousin who has a place here, she knew Nisha's brother, Rohit, somehow, and since I have the accounting background and speak English, French, Spanish, and German, she thought I'd be a good fit."

"Are you?"

"That'd be for Rohit and now Nisha to say, not me."

Not for the first time, Hugo got the sense that, much like Gregor Freed, Finch held Nisha Bhandari in high regard. But he didn't want to press that point; not yet, anyway.

"So you were saying, you couldn't 'profile' Rubén, as it were."

"Well, you know. Not really. I mean, it's not like I'm an expert or anything. I just couldn't get a read on him, like what motivated him, what his real interests were."

"Some think they were a little sordid."

Finch hesitated. "Look, if they've not told you this, someone probably will. I didn't get on well with him. He could charm the birds out of the trees when he wanted, but something about him rubbed me wrong."

"Can you be more specific?"

"Not really, no. Maybe it was the way he took the business, or his part of it, toward all the strip clubs. But I don't really care about that, I'm not a prude or anything." He shrugged his bony shoulders again. "I can't really explain it, just didn't like the guy that much."

"What about Leo, you said he's a charmer, too."

"Yeah, but in an old-fashioned way." He waved a hand. "I'm doing a crappy job of describing them. Then again, I don't really know why you need to know this stuff."

Hugo sensed the beginnings of the end of the conversation, so he changed his tactics. He took out his phone and pulled up the mugshot of Delia Treviño. "Have you seen this woman before?" he asked.

Finch held the phone at arm's length and squinted. "No, I don't think so. Who is she?"

"Unfortunately she was killed recently too. We're wondering if there's a connection."

"Sorry, I can't help with that."

"That's OK. Do you know if Estruch has a storage facility here in Barcelona?"

Finch shook his head. "Why would we?"

"I don't know," Hugo said. "Maybe for old business papers, tax records, something like that."

"No, Nisha's way too careful with the company finances for that. And if she wasn't, I wouldn't let her stick sensitive financial information in a storage unit. We get people's credit-card numbers, home addresses, all kinds of information we need to protect. And with us helping people get jobs here, we even get copies of their passports and whatever other personal details we need."

"Makes perfect sense," Hugo said. "Who here has access to all that information?"

Finch cocked his head, suddenly wary. "We all do. Why?"

"No idea," Hugo smiled. "Just seemed like the right follow-up question."

Finch nodded and put his hands on his knees. "Well, I should get back to work."

"Sure, can I ask just a couple more questions?"

"I suppose, if they're quick. I mean, I want to be helpful but . . ."

"I understand," Hugo said. "And I really appreciate how cooperative you've all been. I was just wondering, was there anyone else who didn't really like Rubén?"

"Here?"

"Anywhere."

"I mean, no. I don't think so. He and Nisha . . . got on fine. Same with Leo, but then Leo gets on with everyone, except maybe his wife."

"Yes," Hugo said, with a conspiratorial smile, "we did pick up some tension there."

"I certainly don't know of anyone who'd want to kill him, I mean, jeez, that's . . . that's just nuts."

"The whole thing's a little nuts. Murder usually is," Hugo said. "Well, thanks again, Mr. Finch, I'll let you get back to work." He handed Finch a business card. "My mobile is on there, if anything else springs to mind."

"Including the small stuff, anything can be helpful, eh?"

Hugo wasn't sure whether Finch was being sarcastic or referencing one of his television shows, so he just nodded his agreement.

He let himself out of the front office, turning to watch Finch walk back down the hallway, his long legs and slight stoop giving the impression of a man much older than forty. *Squash and rugby?* Hugo thought. *How very hard to imagine.*

CHAPTER TWENTY-FIVE

They arranged to meet at a small restaurant/hotel that, according to the reviews Hugo looked at online, was famous for its desserts and discretion. On the walk over there, Hugo called to let Chief Inspector Garcia know about his plan to talk to Nisha Bhandari over dinner, but Grace Silva came on the line, so he told her, instead.

"Oh, *really*?" she said when he named the restaurant.

"Yeah. Something I should know?" Hugo had asked.

"Not the usual place for a police interrogation."

"That would be the police station," Hugo replied.

"Or any other restaurant, perhaps one not known for rich chocolate cake and secret love affairs."

"Cake, eh?" said Hugo. "Sounds delicious."

"I'm sure it is. Enjoy it, and I'll be sure to pass the message on to Chief Inspector Garcia."

There was an odd tone to her voice, and Hugo thought about what her boss had said before. He put it out of his mind and called Tom.

"Can you do something for me?" Hugo asked him.

"Depends."

"Funny. So listen up, I'm having dinner with Nisha Bhandari tonight."

"You serious?"

"Yeah, of course."

"Do your other girlfriends know?"

"Again, funny. You want to help me or not?"

"Didn't realize it was that kind of dinner."

"For fuck's sake, Tom. This investigation isn't moving fast enough, we're all chasing down rabbit trails, interviewing people like it's a damn cold case. I need to scratch some people off my list of suspects, and if I can't do it by asking nicely, I'll do it another way."

Hugo heard the note of desperation in his own voice, and clearly Tom did, too.

"Sure, man, sorry. I didn't mean . . . whatever you need, you know that." There was a hint of amusement in what Tom said next. "And if you're starting to play dirty, well now, you know very well I'm up for some of that. Like I said, whatever you need."

"Thanks. Here's the deal." Hugo explained his plan, surprised that Tom held his tongue, and at the end he told his friend his role.

Tom chuckled. "Man, you are getting sneaky, I fucking love it. And don't worry, I'll do my part. One question, though."

"Shoot."

"Are you gonna . . . you know?"

♉

Hugo arrived fifteen minutes early and took his seat at a table for two near the back of the restaurant. He watched the other couples and small groups as they filed in and sat down, but he was skeptical that the place was all that illicit. A reputation garnered, he knew, was tough to shake, and maybe the management liked it that way—every business needed an angle. Bhandari hadn't mentioned its reputation, but she had told him to wear a jacket, no tie. And no jeans, although the boots, she'd laughed, could stay. As was his custom, he'd dressed up to play it safe, and he was glad he'd done so. When he'd glanced at the menu on the way in, the food looked wonderful. Also to play it safe, he pulled out his phone to check his bank balance.

Nisha Bhandari arrived on time, clad in a cream silk dress that hugged her petite body, the perfect complement to her dark skin. A diamond necklace sparkled as she stood at the entrance to the dining room, turning her head, looking for him. She spotted him and gave a little wave, and Hugo noticed that pretty much every eye in the room followed her progress to his table.

As she approached, Hugo stood and held her chair, finding himself at a loss for words. "I hope you don't mind me saying this, but you look stunning."

She gave him a coy smile and sat. "Girls just hate it when handsome men say things like that."

"Well, that may be true, but this is more of an official dinner." They both sat. "I'm less sure of the protocol for those," he said with a smile.

"I'm all in favor of mixing business and pleasure," she said. "As long as they don't interfere with each other, what's the harm?"

"Sounds like you and Rubén Castañeda share a philosophy."

"Wow, straight to business, I see."

"Sometimes I can't help myself, sorry. Something to drink?"

Hugo caught the waiter's eye, and he scurried over. "*Señor?*"

"Do you drink champagne?" Bhandari asked.

"Doesn't everyone?" Hugo said.

She spoke to the waiter in Spanish, Hugo picking up on the words "bottle" and "Nicolas Feuillatte." The waiter left, and Bhandari smiled at Hugo. "Don't mind if I order do you?"

He thought of Claudia. "Nope, happens all the time."

"I'll let you choose your own food, don't worry."

"Feel free, I have no idea what's good here."

"Everything."

"Then maybe I'll choose your food, as well."

She laughed, and Hugo noticed the whiteness of her teeth and the way she half covered her mouth with her hand, which he found appealing. He was uncomfortable flirting with her because he was here to work and because of his feelings for Claudia, but he could tell they were attracted to each other, and he reminded himself what he'd told Tom: the investigation needed to move on, suspects needed to be ruled out, and his discomfort was irrelevant. *Isn't this just another form of interrogation?* No reason to feel guilty.

And no reason not to enjoy himself, just a little. It wasn't a date, sure, but other than the occasional meal with Claudia, when had he sat across from an attractive woman and enjoyed himself? *Too long*, he thought, *way too long*.

When the waiter returned with their drinks, Bhandari winked and said, "Go ahead, I'm not even slightly picky," so Hugo ordered mussels in a tandoori sauce for them to share, a goat-cheese salad, and a platter billed as "the catches of the day," which he also suggested they split.

Bhandari raised her glass, and Hugo clinked it with his own. "Cheers," she said.

"Cheers indeed."

She hesitated, then said, "You know, you started off all business, but now I'm not so sure."

"All the sharing?" Hugo said. "Good point. Although, since this is an investigation, I'm also hoping to share information."

"Oh, you have information to give me? Or by 'share' did you mean I just tell you things?"

From the tilt of her head, he knew she was teasing, and he couldn't help but smile. "The latter. Although I promise that I'll tell you what I can."

"Sure you will. But don't worry, I watch television, I know how this works and don't expect you to say too much, really." Her face became serious. "But tell me this, are you any closer to finding that girl?"

"I wish we were," Hugo said. "We're doing all we can, but we're running out of leads."

They were silent for a moment, then Bhandari sighed and gave Hugo a sad smile. "OK, how can I help?" she asked.

"I don't know. I feel like I don't know enough about any of you."

"By that you mean . . . ?"

"Well, the people who work for you. You yourself."

"You think we have something to do with it?"

"I know for a fact you do," Hugo said gently. "If only tangentially, through Amy's connection to Rubén. I'm pretty sure he was using the contacts that he built working for you somehow."

"To do what?"

"That's the part I don't know. I'm guessing establish contacts with people in other countries, and maybe with people on the lower end of the socioeconomic spectrum here."

"For what purpose?"

"For now, I'll just call it illegal importing and exporting."

"Drugs?" she looked shocked, and the couple at the table nearest them turned to stare.

"No, no," Hugo said. He nodded at the older couple and whispered. "Let's change the subject for a minute, go back to date mode." He cleared his throat. "So tell me more about you."

"You sure that's date talk?" she whispered back. "Because that could be an investigator's question, too."

"Perhaps." Hugo took a sip of champagne. "But we're mixing business and pleasure, remember?"

"Ah, yes, how silly of me. So what do you want to know? You already know where I was born and raised."

"And that you have a brother."

"I had a sister, too, actually."

"You did? She's deceased?"

"Yes, she died during birth. I didn't know anything about it, but I was told that the umbilical cord got wrapped around her neck. My mother once confessed to me how relieved she was, because my brother was only a couple of years older and she didn't want three toddlers running around the house."

"Quite a handful, I'm sure."

"Oh, I was an angel," Bhandari laughed. "Most of the time, anyway."

She talked about her childhood and her brother, Hugo paying attention because he was interested but also keeping the shadows of their conversations under scrutiny, listening for tone and context in case something important tried to slip past unseen. He did this almost without thought, and absolutely without guile, because looking behind words, and indeed actions, had long ago become second nature to him. It wasn't that he intentionally mixed work into his leisure time, it was more a case of the two becoming utterly inseparable, at least in this regard.

But for once, when she was done, Hugo talked about himself. She was a good listener, and somehow the way she asked him questions made it easy for him to share. He was, he also knew, at a time in his life when he wanted to talk about Ellie, release some of the pain he'd built up in the years since she died. But also share her in the way a child boasts of his dad's job as a policeman or doctor, because he was proud to have known her and wanted her remembered. For her part, Bhandari smiled at his recollections and encouraged his stories. On the few non-Claudia dates he'd been on over the years, women had seemed to tense up at any mention of Ellie, as if inevitably in competition with the dead woman. Nisha Bhandari didn't do that, just refilled their glasses, laughed at his jokes, and shimmered in that cream dress as her eyes and smile broke down Hugo's barriers. He'd mentally put aside the investigation, telling himself that after three glasses of champagne, his judgment was not to be trusted, and so he let himself enjoy the evening as a civilian, where a man sitting across from a beautiful and flirtatious woman was allowed a sliver of poor judgment, especially in a place like this.

At the end of the meal, the waiter piled their plates along the length of his left arm and spoke in English. "May I suggest a dessert? Perhaps one more dish for you to share?"

"I'm pretty full," Hugo said. "You?"

"We'll have a large slice of your famous chocolate cake," Bhandari said. "But please, send it up to my suite."

"Yes, *señora*, of course. And the bill?"

"That, too. *Gracias*." She looked at Hugo and giggled, her hand over her mouth again. "Don't look so shocked. We keep a suite here, on a part-time basis. When the hotel's not full, they let us use it for business meetings, or comp it for a night or two for important clients."

"I had no idea."

"It's not as impressive as it sounds. Most of the time this place is full." She drained her glass and smiled. "But occasionally, I get lucky."

Hugo opened his mouth but didn't know what to say, and when she saw his face, Bhandari laughed again.

"Oh, goodness, I need to be more careful about what I say, I'm sorry."

"It's quite alright," said Hugo. "I'm just not used to..." He shrugged. "To mixing business and pleasure, I suppose you could say."

She reached across the table and put a hand on his arm. "You are a little too easy to tease, Hugo. I really think we can talk better in private, I mean it." She withdrew her hand and dropped her napkin on the table. "And there's no way we can leave this place without trying some of that chocolate cake—that would be a sin."

Hugo stood when she did. "If you say so. Lead the way."

♉

He sat on the small sofa as she thanked and tipped the waiter at the door. Once the young man left, she locked the door and walked over to the side table, where two small plates and a slab of chocolate cake sat—a bowl of strawberries and a fresh bottle of champagne arriving with their order.

She turned to Hugo, and their eyes locked. "Hungry yet?" she said, her voice barely a whisper.

"No, not really." His own voice was thick, from the champagne but also from an evening of flirting, being teased, and feeling a raw desire that had been away from him for a long time. Her dress clung to her body, moved with her, and in the low lighting of the hotel room, the contrast with her dark skin exaggerated every curve and dip of her figure. She perched on the little table behind her, still holding his eye, and Hugo knew that there was no longer any pretense at business, that only one thing filled their thoughts. She moved first, reaching up to her shoulders, fingers sliding under the straps that held up her dress. She slid them sideways, and her dress slipped down her body in slow motion, rippling as it fell and holding Hugo mesmerized, as if he were watching the unveiling of a perfect statue. The silk pooled around her ankles, and she stepped out of it, naked, and moved toward Hugo. His breath caught in his throat, and something in his mind was telling him to stop this, pleading with him that this was wrong, a mistake he would regret. But he stood and went to her, cupping her face with his hands, stopping to kiss her hungrily as she circled his waist with her arms and held him tightly.

"Come with me," she said, taking his hand. He watched her body as she led him into the bedroom, the muscles of her legs, her back, her bottom, admiring her beauty and confidence, her skin absolutely flawless. She knelt on the bed and turned off one of the lamps, throwing Hugo a look of pure devilment, her lips curled in a smile and her eyes open and hungry.

"Give me two seconds." Hugo took out his phone and tapped out one quick text to Tom, the number 2. Then he threw off his jacket, letting it fall to the floor beside the bed as she pulled him down on top of her. They kissed for a full minute, and then her hands began working at the buttons on his shirt, flicking them open like they were snaps. Beside them, Hugo was dimly aware of his phone ringing, an insistent reminder of the real world, the place he ought to be instead of here. The phone stopped, and Hugo rolled onto his side to allow her to undo his belt, hearing her sigh with pleasure at the sound of it slipping free of its loops. Again his phone rang, but it went quiet after three rings, the silence not the ringing finally bringing Hugo back to earth. If he was right, it would ring again in five . . . four . . . three . . .

"Wait, hold on," he panted as his phone sang once more. "I'm sorry, I have to get this."

He swung his legs over the side of the bed, his fingers scrabbling for his jacket and then dipping into its inside pocket.

"What is it?" he snapped. "This better be good." Nisha Bhandari curled her naked form around his body, the warmth of her making him dizzy with desire.

"Dude, it's me."

"Tom," he said, for Bhandari's benefit. "What do you want?"

"This is your wake-up call. And while you've been wining and dining one of our suspects, another one has gone off the deep end."

"What are you talking about?"

"The cops located Delia Treviño's most recent place of habitation, such as it is. They went through her stuff, didn't find much until they sent the crime-scene tech in. He pulled some interesting finger prints."

"Whose?"

"Our very own Leonardo Barsetti."

"Are you serious?"

"Aren't I always?"

"We need to find him, and now." Hugo didn't want to say Barsetti's name, invite questions from the man's boss, who now lay on the bed, her head propped in one hand, watching him intently.

"Way ahead of you, that's why I'm calling. Well, one of the reasons. Your buddy Garcia thinks your particular brand of sweet-talking might come in handy."

"What are you talking about?"

"The dumb fuck Italian is sitting on the roof of a parking garage, six floors up. I think he's admiring the skyline, but the chief inspector thinks he's deciding whether to spill his guts to us or take a swan dive and spill them on the plaza below."

"Oh, no."

"Oh, yes. I'm with Garcia now, you wanna head over here? I'll be taking bets any minute, so be thinking about which way your Euros are going."

CHAPTER TWENTY-SIX

The Barcelona police had surrounded the parking garage and emptied the plaza below, and then turned off the flashing lights of their cars and the two ambulances that waited, so as not to cut deeper into Leo Barsetti's knife-edge condition.

By the time Hugo arrived on the top floor, Barsetti had been there almost an hour. Chief Inspector Garcia and half a dozen cops stood at the back of the roof, giving Barsetti all the room he wanted, all the space he'd asked for.

Hugo spoke to Garcia in hushed tones. "How did this happen?"

"We ran the prints from Treviño's place, made some specific comparisons to the people in the case. He was an easy match."

"He told me he didn't know her, but if you remember," Hugo said, "when I showed him her photo, he got weird, more or less ran out of the café we were in."

"Now we know why."

"Yeah, but this is a little extreme. How'd he end up here?"

"We went to his house to talk to him, didn't Silva leave you a message?"

"I didn't notice, honestly."

"Anyway, he was leaving as we were arriving. When we tried to pull him over, he took off, led us on a kind of low-speed chase to here."

"That's not good," Hugo said.

"What do you mean?"

"In high-speed chases, the bad guy hopes to get away. Hence the high speed." He shook his head. "The low-speed ones, they don't. They're buying time, nothing more."

"They expect to get caught?"

"Right."

"Which means they're guilty."

Hugo shrugged. "Of something, yeah, usually."

"Of lying to us, at the very least."

"Maybe, but people lie to the police all the time, and they don't threaten to jump off a building when caught."

"Good point."

"What about his wife, does she know?"

"Not yet," Garcia said. "The cars that went to his house all followed him here. I've just sent someone over there to bring her here."

"OK, but make sure she doesn't see any of this, take her to a lower floor or something. She could be one of the reasons he's up here, and if that's the case, them seeing each other isn't going to help matters."

"We'll be careful with her." Garcia sighed. "I'll be honest, Hugo, I should probably call in one of our hostage-rescue experts, they're the ones we use for talking down people like this."

"I know, but they don't know the case, they don't know what's going on. I do."

"Exactly my thinking." Garcia grimaced and, in the flat light of the parking garage, his face looked tired and gray. "Go do your thing, and don't make me regret sending you over there."

Hugo took a deep breath to clear his mind. Flashes of the evening circled his consciousness, the dinner, Nisha's dress, her soft skin. He willed them away and moved slowly toward the low concrete wall where Leonardo Barsetti sat, his legs dangling six floors above certain death, his shoulders slumped forward as if he'd already made up his mind and was just waiting for the right moment. A cold wind had picked up, and Hugo pulled his jacket around himself for warmth.

"Leo," Hugo called out, when he was thirty yards away. He kept his voice soft so as not to startle the man.

Leo Barsetti turned his head slowly, his eyes blank as they settled on Hugo, then flickering with recognition. "What do you want?" he said.

"Can we talk? Just for a moment, just talk."

"No."

"Why are we here, Leo?"

Barsetti turned his head away, staring once more at the open space beneath his feet. "Why are *you* here?"

"Well, I guess the main reason is because I don't want you to jump off that ledge." When Barsetti didn't respond, Hugo moved in a wide arc toward the roof edge. When he got there, he leaned on it, about twenty feet from the Italian, who sat to his right as if he didn't know Hugo was there. "Leo, talk to me."

Barsetti snorted. "Because you care so much?"

"Yes, I do. I don't want you to jump, Leo, because whatever has you up here isn't as bad as you jumping. Whatever it is, it's fixable. But if you let go now, that isn't."

"Fixable?" Barsetti looked at him, and Hugo wasn't sure whether he didn't understand the word, or thought Hugo was insane.

"Whatever the problem is, we can get past it. I'll help you figure a way out, I promise."

"How can you do that when you don't know what the problem is?"

"Then tell me," Hugo insisted gently. "That's all I'm asking."

"Why?" Barsetti turned his head to look at Hugo. "Why did they send you to talk to me?"

"The truth? Because I'm good at it. I've been trained to talk to people who are in this situation."

"Just that?"

Hugo smiled softly. "You'd have to ask them. But I'm glad they did, Leo, because what I said before is true. I don't want you to jump, and I very much want to help you. No matter what."

Barsetti stared at him for a moment. "There's nothing you can do. Even if I get down and we go for a nice drink, there's nothing you or anyone can do." He sighed. "I would like a drink right now."

"So let's go have one. I'll buy."

"I don't think so." Barsetti looked away again. "If I come down, I'll be straight in handcuffs and taken to a jail cell. If you want to be honest with me, tell me that."

"Not if I can help it."

"You're not in charge, Señor Marston. Anyway, it doesn't matter."

"Why do you think you'll be going to jail?" Hugo asked. His first priority right now was to save Leo Barsetti's life, but the fact that this man was threatening to kill himself meant that something had changed in the investigation, and Hugo could only imagine that change meant that either Amy was in more danger than before, or they were getting closer to finding her. Either way, this was no time to put the brakes on. And the truth was, if Barsetti had something to do with her disappearance, he was welcome to take a nose dive off this parking garage. But before he did, Hugo wanted to find out why the man was up here, get whatever information he could about Amy's whereabouts.

"Oh, I'm not going to jail."

"Leo, do you know what happened to Amy Dreiss? I promise you, if you help me find her, I will do everything in my power to help you, no matter what you've seen or done."

"Give it up, Señor Marston. Let her go and get out before they lure you in, too."

"Lure me into what?"

Barsetti's head snapped around, and his face reddened with anger. "You think I'm here because I want to be? You think this is how I planned my life to end?"

"No, I just don't—"

"I didn't claim to be perfect. I'm weak like . . . like everyone else."

"Leo, what did you do?"

"They tricked me, oh my God, they tricked me and I made it so easy for them." His voice calmed. "That's the thing about being weak, I suppose. It doesn't harm anyone but you, not until someone finds out. Then it's not weakness anymore, it's a wound and they can dig into it, make you scream and cry, make you do whatever they want. Even be silent."

"Be silent about what? Is that why you're up here, Leo, because someone is trying to keep you quiet?"

Barsetti looked ahead, out over the city, and his tone was almost wistful. "This place, it's so beautiful. But you don't know, do you, what goes on in the streets, in the houses, in people's heads? You don't know what they're planning. And when you do, it's too late. Too late for you, too late to help the people you should help, and too late to see this city as anything but ugly and broken."

"We can protect you, Leo, you must know that."

"Do you know who the matadors are?" he asked.

"Sure, they're the guys who kill bulls. What do they—?"

"'Kill bulls,' that's almost funny. Those matadors are extinct, they can't harm anyone."

"Then who?"

"They are people who kill. What is the American word, a gang?"

"Right," Hugo said. "A gang. You're involved with them?"

Barsetti shook his head sadly. "I didn't know it."

"Leo, we can protect you. Take you back to Italy, or go to America. Wherever you want, just tell me what's going on."

"There are some things you can't be protected from. The things you have done, the things you have seen. The things you have allowed to happen." He slammed his fist against the wall but didn't seem to feel it. "They tricked me and I let them do it."

Hugo stood slowly and moved a step closer. "All I want to—"

"Stay away from me!"

"Fine, OK, I'll stand here." Hugo leaned his hip against the low wall and faced Barsetti. He shot a look over to Tom and Chief Inspector Garcia. They stared back at him, unmoving, like they were carved out of stone. There was nothing they could do, Hugo knew, it was all up to him. He stood quietly for a moment, gathering his thoughts. "Leo, do you want to talk to your wife?"

"She's gone."

A cold chill ran through Hugo. "Gone where?"

"Away."

"Leo, did you do something to her?"

"She was good to me, you know. I mean, it was an odd marriage and we both knew why we were in it. She held up her end of it all better than I did, I know that, but don't think I didn't try."

Hugo pulled his phone from his pocket and surreptitiously sent Tom a text that read, *His wife?* "Leo, what did you mean by 'she's gone'?"

"Do me a favor, Señor Marston. Stop. Please, just stop."

"I can't do that, Leo. I need to find my friend Amy, she's just a girl, and wherever she is, I'm going to find her and bring her home." *Please, just let her be alive when I do.*

Hugo's stomach lurched when Barsetti waved a hand in front of him, but he was gesturing to the skyline. "It's funny how I've spent the last couple of years leading people around this city, showing them the things that make it great, making it bright and open for them. All that time, I didn't see that there was another world operating here, people trading in the shadows while everyone around them wanders through looking at the light, seeing nothing of the blackness around them."

Hugo's phone buzzed, but Barsetti didn't seem to notice. Hugo checked the screen. *Wife not home. Unable to locate.* Another blank to infuriate Hugo, so he decided to change tactics. "That's very poetic, Leo, but I don't have time for poetry. Nor do you, especially if you've done something to your wife."

"It's not poetry, it's life. And death." He turned and looked at Hugo. "I hope you find your missing girl, Señor Marston. If you believe anything about me, believe that."

"I need your help to do that, Leo. Come down from there and help me."

"I'm done with helping people. Except myself." He shifted forward a few inches. "You may think you're the good guy here, but I know what would happen. You'd use me and then send me to prison."

"No, Leo, that's not true, we just—"

"It *is* true, and you're not using me and then throwing me away, I won't let you." Barsetti blinked and then sighed. "And they won't be able to use me, either, ever again." He put his hands on the ledge beside him and, before Hugo could take a step toward him, the solid figure of Leonardo Barsetti slid forward over the ledge and dropped from view. Hugo felt a rip of horror as he leaned over the edge to see the Italian's body fall silently to the plaza below. Police and paramedics ran toward the motionless form, but Hugo knew that their efforts would be in vain, that Leo Barsetti had put himself beyond the reach of those who wanted him alive, and even those who wanted him dead.

The police officers on the roof raced toward the ledge, leaning over and staring down at the motionless form of Leo Barsetti, and the commotion unfolding below. Hugo took one more look and moved away, his jaw clenched with frustration and anger—both directed at himself for failing to save a man's life. Grace Silva beckoned to him, so he angled toward where she stood with her phone in her hand.

"Has something happened?" He grimaced. "Something else, I mean."

"What he did, that wasn't your fault, Hugo."

"I'm trying to tell myself that."

"Well, it's true. And yes, something else happened—we got some DNA results back."

"The blood from the window?"

"A positive hit."

Hugo's mind went to Leo Barsetti. Was his fall from the ledge a final, grand exit, knowing he was caught? He looked back to where the Italian had jumped. "Was it him?" Hugo asked.

"Actually, no."

Hugo looked back at Silva. "It wasn't? Someone else from Estruch?"

"No. We have a new player, one who has a criminal record, so we're looking for him now." She checked her watch. "Chief Inspector Garcia doesn't think we'll do anything tonight, either way. He wants you there for the interview tomorrow morning, though. He's setting up an interpreter for you. How about I give you a ride home now and pick you up at eight tomorrow morning?"

A wave of tiredness swept over Hugo and, although he didn't try too hard, he couldn't think of much else he could do tonight. "Yeah, I guess that's fine, thanks. So tell me about the DNA match."

"I don't know a lot right now," she said. "But I do know that he works at a hospital in the city, as a nurse." She paused to let that sink in. "So as well as a criminal record, he probably has the medical knowledge we're looking for."

CHAPTER TWENTY-SEVEN

C hief Inspector Garcia and Grace Silva sat on one side of the table, across from a stocky man who looked to be in his early forties. He was handsome in a rugged way and had the look of a working man, not a nurse, with features that were heavy and dark. The man ran his fingers through his thick black hair every minute or so, as if it gave him comfort.

Hugo settled into a chair behind the one-way glass and put on headphones proffered by the interpreter, Cristina Sanchez. She was a chirpy, smiling lady in her early fifties, with blue eyes that sparkled at Hugo, as if they were about to embark on an adventure together. She put on her own headphones, winked, and held a microphone close to her mouth, waiting.

Through the window, Hugo watched Garcia flip pages in his notebook, then pick up a pen. The policeman stared at the man across from him and then started speaking.

"*Esta entrevista está siendo videograbada y necesito que empiece usted por decirme su nombre.*" Sanchez murmured her translation in a voice that was low, but clear: *This interview is being videotaped, and I need you to start by telling me your name.*

"*Mi nombre es José Paniagua. Y no entiendo por qué estoy aquí.*" *My name is José Paniagua. And I don't understand why I'm here.*

"*Para allá vamos en un momento. La manera en que esto funciona es que usted me contesta todas las preguntas que yo le haga antes de que usted pueda hacerme cualquier pregunta a mí, ¿está claro?*" *We'll get to that in a moment. And the way this works, you answer all my questions before you get to ask yours. Clear?*

The man nodded, and his eyes flicked up to the big window. Hugo leaned forward, listening intently to Garcia's questions and Paniagua's answers as they came through Cristina Sanchez, his eyes looking for any telltale giveaways on the man's face.

"Where do you work?" Garcia asked.

"The Hospital Clínic de Barcelona."

"How long have you worked there?"

"Eight years."

"And what exactly do you do there?"

"I'm a nurse. I have worked in different departments; right now I'm in the intensive-care unit."

"And previously?"

The man shrugged. "In eight years, you get to work everywhere."

"Give me some examples."

"The emergency department, that's where I started. I've been in the children's wards, oncology, general surgery, post-op."

"How old are you, Señor Paniagua?"

"Forty-one."

"Ever worked with the anesthesiology doctors?"

The man's eyes narrowed. "No. Is this about drugs?"

"Why would you ask that?"

Paniagua looked back and forth between Garcia and Silva. "They're the ones who have access to drugs. I mean, all doctors do but . . ." He shrugged again. "I guess they have a reputation for becoming addicted."

"Do you know any who are?"

"No, not at all."

"This isn't about drugs, Señor Paniagua, it's about murder."

Paniagua sat bolt upright in his chair. "Murder? I don't . . . what do you mean?"

The panic on his face seemed real enough, Hugo thought. But then again, if he was guilty, he'd have known the question was coming and acted accordingly.

"Your DNA was found at the scene of a murder here in Barcelona."

"That's . . . that's not possible."

"There's no mistake, *señor*, so not only is it possible, it's a fact."

The man slumped back in his seat. "I don't understand how . . ."

"Do you know the name Rubén Castañeda?"

"No, I don't think so."

"It's yes or no," Grace Silva said. "Either you do or you don't."

"I don't recognize the name, no."

Silva flipped open a folder and slid a photograph of Castañeda across the table. "You know this man?"

"No."

She took back the photo and glanced at Garcia, who nodded. She put a second photo in front of Paniagua, the booking photo of Delia Treviño. "How about her?"

"No, I don't know her, either. Who are they? What did they do?"

"They got murdered," Silva said. "You're sure you don't know them."

"Yes, I've never seen either of them before, I promise."

"OK," Silva said. She looked down at the file and read off Rubén Castañeda's address. "Do you know where that is?"

"No, I don't."

"It's in the Old Town, that help remind you?"

"No." Paniagua's voice rose, insistent. "I don't know about any of this!"

"You're seriously telling us that you've never been there. You're sticking to that story."

"Yes, never!"

Chief Inspector Garcia spoke up, "How about Estruch Enterprises. Ever had dealings with them?"

Paniagua thought for a moment. "The name is familiar, but I can't place it."

"Tourism company," Garcia said. "That help?"

"I don't know. All I can say is, the name's familiar. I'm not sure why, though."

"Ever heard of Nisha Bhandari or Todd Finch?" Silva asked.

"No."

"Leonardo Barsetti?"

"No," he insisted again. "I don't know any of these people, these places. This is some kind of mistake, it has to be."

Garcia put out his hand, and Silva passed him another photo, this one of Amy Dreiss. "You know who that is?"

"Is she dead, too?"

"She better not be," Garcia growled. "Her name is Amy Dreiss."

"I don't know her," Paniagua insisted, "by face or name. I'm sorry."

Garcia leaned forward. "What I'm wondering, Señor Paniagua, is how it is that you don't know a single person involved in this case, and yet your DNA was found at the crime scene. That tells me one of two things. Either the DNA is lying, or you are."

"I'm not lying!"

"Well then." Garcia stood, and Silva followed suit. "In that case, I shall have the DNA retested to confirm that we've made a mistake. Now, this being a murder inquiry, we'll need to put you in our own special accommodation for a few days while that happens. Perhaps it'll give you a chance to reflect on some of the names we've given you; maybe time will bring a little clarity to your memory."

José Paniagua looked up at the two detectives, his face white with fear. "But I haven't done anything wrong, why are you keeping me here? I don't know any of those people and I don't understand how my DNA can be where you said. Look, I'm a nurse, I help people, I don't hurt them. I bring people food and medicine; I take care of them when they need help. I even donate blood every month. I don't have any reason to kill anyone."

Garcia put his hands on the table and leaned over him. "You know how we matched your DNA, right? Why we have your profile in our database?"

Paniagua's head dropped. "Yes, I think so."

"Right. So don't act like you're some angel of mercy, a pure heart filled with love and affection for your fellow man."

"You don't understand, it wasn't like that. I was just a kid."

"Twenty. You were twenty." Garcia straightened. "Wait here."

Hugo watched as Garcia and Silva left the interview room, and moments later they entered the viewing room. Hugo slipped off his headphones and stood.

"Well," Garcia said. "What do you think?"

"He's either innocent or a good actor," Hugo said. "And trust me, I've seen a lot of convincing performances by guilty people, good enough to fool me and everyone else."

"There's no arguing with DNA. We can have it retested, but right now it places him at the scene."

"And no links between him and anyone in the case?"

"Actually, yes," Garcia said, "but they're pretty minor and could all be coincidences. I wanted to see if he'd admit to any of them, and then talk to you, see if we should put them in front of him."

"Tell me."

Garcia checked off his fingers. "First, Nisha Bhandari received some of her cancer treatment at his hospital. We'll confirm whether he worked directly with her or not."

"We should do that right away. If he's acting innocent, the best way to make the facade crumble is to catch him in a lie. We need something positive to challenge him with, to find an inconsistency in what he's telling us."

"I can do that now," Silva said. "Do you want me to show his picture to Nisha Bhandari, see if she recognizes him?"

"No," Hugo said. "If you agree, Bartoli, I think that's a bad idea. If she's involved somehow, this would tip her off."

"You really think she might be?"

"I don't like to rule anyone out until I have to," Hugo said. An image of her played in his mind, clothed and then naked, the softness of her skin and the brightness of her eyes. "I thought maybe initially, but now I don't see how."

"But you're keeping an open mind?" Garcia asked. There was something in his eye, as if he had a question for Hugo he didn't want to ask right there and then.

"Of course. Everyone's in until they are conclusively out."

"*Bueno*," Garcia nodded.

"You were telling me about some other connections?"

Garcia smiled and glanced at Silva, who was hovering by the door. "Ah, yes. Grace here let me know she's also a monthly blood donor at the hospital."

"Oh, OK," Hugo said. "But I wasn't aware she was a suspect."

"Just making sure everything's out in the open," Silva said. "As for donating, I feel like I have to. After seeing so many people die in Afghanistan, some of them bleeding out because we didn't have the supplies." She shook her head sadly, then looked at Hugo with a gentle smile. "Something you should consider, Señor Marston. Painless, self-less, and they give you cookies afterward."

"I should," Hugo said. "You're absolutely right. And let us know what the hospital tells you about our friend's work schedule. You know, while you're on the phone with them check to make sure no one's stolen from or misplaced any of their blood supply."

"Will do. Shouldn't be more than a quick phone call." Silva nodded to them and left the room.

Hugo turned to Garcia. "So, how did you have this guy's DNA profile?"

"When he was twenty, he got caught peeping into a few windows. I haven't read all the reports, but it seems like he was originally charged with a sexual offense but was convicted of something much more minor. As part of the plea deal, though, he agreed to give his DNA."

"When was this?"

"In nineteen ninety-three. We were a few years behind you Americans in collecting and testing DNA, but just in time for Señor Paniagua."

"Lucky for us."

"Right. Two more connections, before I forget, and they're about as weak as the first ones. Leo Barsetti and his wife are on the board of the hospital, do a lot of work with getting healthcare there for poor children."

"Anything Paniagua was involved with?"

"Not that we know. I'll have Silva check into that, as well."

"The last connection?"

"The weakest of them all, and it's to do with our Mr. Finch. Not a connection at all, it's just that he lives two streets from the hospital, so it's possible they've crossed paths in the neighborhood."

"Bit of a stretch," Hugo said. "But worth looking into. We should also get the medical records of everyone involved, see if Paniagua's name comes up on their charts or treatment papers."

"We'll need their permission. I don't think we could persuade a judge to order those."

"Then let's ask," said Hugo. "Be interesting to see who doesn't mind and who does."

Both men looked as the door flew open and Silva stepped back in. "I was on my way to my office to call the hospital, but I got interrupted. One of the guys manning the phones after the press conference said it might be something."

"Something good, I hope." Hugo said.

"Well, we get a lot of weirdos whenever we make public appeals, but sounds like this one should be checked out. If she's telling the truth, the woman who called actually laid eyes on our killer."

CHAPTER TWENTY-EIGHT

They sat in her cramped living room, Hugo and the chief inspector perched on the edge of a worn couch, their knees pressed against a battered coffee table that had been cleared off, except for Garcia's tape recorder. In a small kitchen to their right, Esmeralda Quintana bustled about, making herself coffee. The two men had declined a cup for themselves, eager to hear what she had to say. A little eager to leave, too, because the smell of boiled cabbage filled the small apartment, such that Hugo was relieved when the competing aroma of coffee drifted through to them. When Quintana finally collapsed into her armchair opposite them, Garcia leaned forward and switched on the recorder. He spoke in Spanish, repeating her name, giving his own and Hugo's. He asked her a couple of questions, and when she shook her head, he turned to Hugo.

"She doesn't speak any English, I'm sorry."

"That's alright, I didn't expect her to. If you don't mind, translate as we go along, as best you can."

Garcia nodded and turned back to their witness. He spoke in a gentle voice, coaxing the story out of her, and it came in short, worried sentences. Unable to understand what she was saying, Hugo concentrated on her body language. Her clipped manner and the way she looked at them told Hugo that she was worried for her own safety, worried that by seeing a killer she might have put herself in harm's way. Garcia reassured her, though, and she spoke more calmly, though he could tell she was apologizing a great deal. After a few minutes, the chief inspector thanked her and turned to Hugo. Esmeralda Quintana twisted her hands in her lap, then opened a drawer in the table beside her and pulled out a packet of cigarettes and a lighter.

"She works for the city as a street cleaner," Garcia said. "She's in a crew of three responsible for part of the neighborhood where Castañeda's apartment is. That night, she'd finished her shift and was walking back home. She took the alley behind his building as a shortcut and had just entered it when she heard breaking glass. She looked up and saw someone appear in the street suddenly."

"What does that mean, 'appear in the street'?"

"I asked pretty much the same thing. But that's what she said, this person suddenly appeared. No one there one moment, then a dark figure."

"Did she see the person climb out the window?"

"No, she said she didn't. But she also said there's no door there, so he must have; there was no other way for him to appear like that."

"And the description?"

Garcia shook his head. "That's where she started apologizing."

"I was afraid of that."

"Yeah, the person had startled her, so she hid in the shadow of a doorway farther down the alley. The best she can say is that he was about average height and build, maybe a little taller than average."

"Man or woman?"

"She didn't know, couldn't say."

"Was the person carrying anything?"

"Oh, I didn't ask." He turned to Quintana and spoke in Spanish. The woman hesitated for a moment, then spoke for a full thirty seconds. When she'd finished, Garcia sat back and looked at Hugo. "She says she can't be sure. The light wasn't great and there were a lot of shadows, and of course she was trying not to be seen herself. But she is pretty sure the person was carrying something."

"Description? Any idea if it was a plastic bag, a handbag, a small cooler?"

Garcia put the questions to Quintana, who just looked at them both and shrugged. "*No se, lo siento.*" I don't know, I'm sorry.

Hugo had no more questions, so the two men thanked Quintana, and Garcia handed her his card, urging her to call him if she thought of anything else. They let themselves out of the ground-floor apartment, and Hugo gulped in the fresh air, filling his lungs and feeling the breeze wash over his face.

"I know how you feel," Garcia said with a smile. "I never liked cabbage much."

"I was surviving until she started to smoke," Hugo said. "Don't know how she does it."

"We all have our vices," Garcia said. "Don't you?"

"Probably. But they don't involve cabbage or cigarettes, I can promise you that."

Garcia chuckled, then became serious. "I have to say, I was hoping for more from her. The best thing we can say is that the person she saw was of average height or maybe a little taller, and was carrying something. You thinking Castañeda's organs?"

"Could be. I'm still not sold on that theory, though."

"Wasn't it yours in the first place?"

"Yes." Hugo gave him a small smile. "That's the investigator's prerogative, though, to come up with ideas and then abandon them. Although I'm not ready to abandon it, either."

"Maybe whoever it was stole something else, something we don't know about. Maybe all this is about a robbery."

They started walking toward Garcia's police car, parked a block away, both men deep in thought. Hugo spoke first. "You know, we forgot to ask whether the person she saw was limping or otherwise seemed injured."

"I didn't think of that, but clearly they were, otherwise there'd be no blood."

"True, but if they were limping, it'd be an indication of where they were injured. A leg as opposed to an arm. Might be helpful if we find someone with a recent cut on their leg."

"Or arm," Garcia said with a rueful smile. "Should we go back?"

"No, we can call her later if we need to. I'm not sure I can face that gas chamber again today."

"Then a wasted visit, don't you think?"

"Not entirely." They reached Garcia's car, and Hugo looked at him across the roof. "We did learn one thing pretty valuable."

"What's that?" Garcia asked, brow furrowed with uncertainty.

"We know there was only one killer."

♉

On the ride back to the police station, Garcia's phone rang. He answered the call and listened quietly, muttering a few words in Spanish before hanging up.

"I don't know what to make of it," he said. "You remember we sent people back to Castañeda's apartment to check the drains."

"Yeah, they find something?"

"No, that's the point. Nothing. Traces of bleach or some bleaching agent. No hair, skin, soap, bubble bath . . . nothing."

"Someone cleaned up," Hugo said. "That's good to know."

"Only if we figure out *who* cleaned up."

"Well, yes, fair point."

Garcia's phone rang again, Grace Silva's name appearing on the screen. Garcia hit the speaker button. "Hugo is with me, what's up?"

"I heard from one of the detectives we'd sent to talk to Delia Treviño's friends, such as they are."

"Bunch of prostitutes and drug users, aren't they?"

"Mostly, yes. But a couple of them recognized the photo the detective showed them."

"Whose photo?" Garcia asked.

"Leo Barsetti. Turns out his wife was right about the affair, if you can call having sex with a prostitute an affair."

"He was . . . with Delia Treviño?" Garcia repeated.

"Yes, very much so. For about the last two months, though the two statements from her friends indicate they'd not seen him around her for the last couple of weeks."

"*Gracias*, Grace. Can you leave copies of those statements on my desk? We're headed back there right now, and I'd like to see them for myself." He glanced at Hugo and smiled. "And, I guess, I'll translate them for our guest."

"One more thing," Silva said. "The hospital confirmed that no blood has been stolen or is missing from their supplies. Which means that the blood at Castañeda's house came out of a vein."

When Garcia hung up, Hugo said, "That explains why he turned white as a sheet when I showed him Treviño's photo," Hugo said. "He knew her, and intimately. Although . . ."

"Although what?"

"His reaction seemed very real to me, he was truly surprised."

"Which means?"

"Which means he's not the one who killed her."

Garcia sighed. "Unless we find out who did, we'll never know." He slapped the steering wheel. "What a coward's way out."

"Killing himself?"

"Yes, of course. If he's innocent, why would he? If he's guilty, he's a coward."

"I think suicide is a little more complicated than that." Hugo held up a placating hand. "You're right in that if he was innocent, it seems unnecessary. But it wasn't like we were about to pin this on him. Something else was going on, and I'm sure it has a lot to do with Delia Treviño and her death."

"Guilt?"

"Maybe, but a man can feel guilty without committing suicide, or murder."

"What then?"

"I don't know, Bartoli. Right now, I really don't know. Let's go see what those statements say, and maybe we can come up with some new ideas on the way." He looked at his watch, then stared out of the window. The colorful flashes of the storefronts blurred, and the people on the sidewalks now looked solitary, individuals making their way in the world alone, rather than sharing the city together, neighbors in a community. Hugo knew that this altered image was a fiction of his own making, a reflection of his own sense of inadequacy, but he couldn't shake it. Still gazing out of the window, he spoke in a quiet voice. "You know, I keep checking the time, looking at my watch as if I can slow it down. Every tick feels like Amy is farther away from us, more in danger. Anything you can think of, Bartoli, I'll try absolutely anything you can think of, but we have to find that girl. Time is going by too fast, it's running out. For us and for her. We have to find her, and soon."

CHAPTER TWENTY-NINE

They executed the search warrants that afternoon. Grace Silva took Hugo to Estruch, and Chief Inspector Garcia went with two detectives Hugo didn't know to Leo Barsetti's home. The Italian's wife still hadn't shown up, and a judge deemed that fact, and Barsetti's final words to Hugo about her being "gone" as sufficient legal cause to allow a complete search of each premises.

Silva had picked up her phone to let Bhandari and Finch know they were coming, a courtesy call, but Hugo put a hand on her arm and shook his head.

"No reason to think they're involved," he said. "But since we don't know who is and who isn't, it's not good to give people a chance to hide or destroy evidence."

"I should have thought of that," Silva said.

She parked the police car out of sight of Estruch, and when they entered the front of the business, they caught Finch and Bhandari at the computer where Castañeda used to sit.

"Hugo, what are you doing here?" Bhandari asked. She wore a light-blue T-shirt and jeans, and smiled up at him, pleased at the surprise. Her eyes, though, were puffy. As if she'd been crying or had not slept.

Hugo felt a pang of compassion, and also desire, but suppressed both. "Nisha, the police have a search warrant. Since Leo's wife is still missing and, well, Leo said some things to me before he jumped last night."

"Oh, yes, of course. You know where his office is."

"Actually Ms. Bhandari," Silva said, "the warrant is for the entire premises."

"But . . . why?"

"Leo had access to every room here, didn't he?" Hugo asked.

"Of course, yes."

"That's why," Hugo said gently. "You guys can stay and watch us if you like, but you can't interfere or move anything, OK?"

"Of course." She glanced at Todd Finch. "We should let them do their thing. Can you work from home this afternoon?"

"No problem." Finch had taken the warrant from Silva and was reading it carefully. His face was blank as he handed it back to the policewoman. "I'm no lawyer, but it looks fine. Should we get an attorney to look this over, Nisha?"

"What for?" she said gently. "We have nothing to hide." She gave Hugo a tired smile. "Please try not to make a mess."

"We'll be careful," Hugo promised. "Can you tell me if Leo was working on anything in particular, anything urgent or especially important?"

"Nothing out of the ordinary," Finch said. "That antiques guy called this morning, wanting to talk to him, but other than that, I can't think of anything."

"Gregor?" Nisha asked. "Did you tell him what happened?"

"No, he left a message, I didn't talk to him."

"OK, good." She turned to Hugo. "Gregor and Leo were friends, I should tell him myself." She stood and gave Hugo and Silva a sad smile. "I was trying to do some work but . . . I can't believe this has happened. I can't believe this is all happening. I should go talk to Gregor, tell him."

Hugo and Silva waited while Bhandari and Finch collected their coats and bags.

Bhandari lingered at the door. "Hugo, can I talk to you outside for a moment?"

"Of course." Hugo looked at Grace Silva, who gave him a quizzical look. "Be right back."

They stood in front of the main window, Hugo conscious that Silva was watching them as much as she was rifling through Castañeda's work area. Over Bhandari's shoulder, Todd Finch stalked off toward his home, throwing a glance over his shoulder, a look that made Hugo wonder, not for the first time, whether there was something between him and Nisha Bhandari, or whether the New Zealander perhaps just wished there was.

"About last night," Bhandari said. "I'm not sure why I behaved that way. I wanted to apologize and also ask you something."

"Please, no need to apologize, we're both adults here. What did you want to ask me?"

"You seemed a little . . . hesitant last night. Like you didn't really want to be there with me." She looked down. "Usually I'm pretty good at reading people, but you seemed a little torn, unsure or something. I wanted to ask if everything was all right?"

"Yes," Hugo assured her. "I just . . . I shouldn't have been there like that, dinner, fine, but not . . . you know. You're a potential witness in at least two murders and a disappearance. Not to mention Leo's demise."

"I didn't think of that, I suppose."

"That's OK, Nisha, it's my job to think of it, not yours. I'm just glad nothing happened between us."

"Saved by the bell, eh?" she laughed.

"I suppose so. It's not often my friend Tom saves me, usually the other way around." He gave a gentle laugh. "Anyway, I should get back to work."

"Wait." She put a hand on his arm. "There's something else. I should have told you before but," she looked down, "I was embarrassed. I'm embarrassed to tell you now, but I think I have to."

"Embarrassed?" Hugo looked up at the retreating figure of Todd Finch. "Do you mean you and . . ."

She glanced over her shoulder and then looked back at Hugo. "Todd? Oh good heavens, no. I mean, it's been obvious for a while that he's interested and all, but no. I'm not."

"Then what did you want to tell me?"

"About me and Rubén."

Hugo blinked in surprise. "That's kind of a big deal to not tell me until now."

"Because of last night?"

"No, Nisha, because of what happened to him."

"Does that make me a suspect now?" She grimaced, knowing that the joke was in poor taste.

"It means a lot of things." Hugo ran his fingers through his hair as he thought. "OK, I need to let Chief Inspector Garcia know, and he'll want another statement from you. A complete one this time—no omissions, OK?"

"What about last night?"

"We had dinner last night. If anyone asks, tell them the truth, but really, Nisha, all we did was have dinner."

"Sure thing. I'll wait to hear from your policeman, I'll tell him about Rubén."

"Thanks. How long were you guys seeing each other?"

"Not long. I don't usually think it's a good idea to date colleagues at work, but there was something between us and we both wanted to explore it. Not love or anything like that. As you put it, we were both adults."

"Nisha, you should have told us."

"I know. But I really didn't think it could have anything to do with his death." She looked up at Hugo. "You probably think I've been very cold about that, too."

"People respond to tragedy in different ways. I know that better than most people."

"It's just so unreal. I mean, we didn't even know each other that well; it was like we were just starting to. And now, I keep thinking he's away on vacation or something."

"OK. Look, I'm sorry, but I have to ask something else."

"The answer is no."

"You know what the question is?"

"Whether I was sleeping with Leo." She looked away. "God, what must you think of me?"

"Adults, remember."

"Well, I wasn't, I promise you that."

"I believe you, and I'm sorry for asking. How about Rubén? It may have a bearing on the forensics. Was he seeing anyone else?"

"No. We talked about that, I said I didn't mind, but he didn't want to see anyone else. He was sort of insistent I didn't, either."

"When did you guys spend time together?"

"The Spanish have this wonderful thing called siesta." She looked down again, this time blushing gently.

"Your place or his?"

"Oh, mine, always. I went to his apartment once and, well, let's just say my standards of cleanliness were a little higher than his."

Hugo smiled, thinking about the change in tidiness of his own apartment when Tom was staying there, as opposed to when his friend was away. And the comments Claudia had made to that effect. "I know what you mean, absolutely. Well, thanks for being honest with me. I'll have Chief Inspector Garcia get those details down in a statement, probably this afternoon."

"Still OK for me to go see Gregor Freed?"

"Yes, of course."

They parted with awkward smiles, but there was something about what she'd said that nagged at Hugo. He couldn't be sure if it was a personal feeling, though, or something related to the case. He watched her walk away, and once she was out of sight, he called Tom.

"Interesting development," Hugo said.

"Let's start with last night's interesting developments."

"Funny."

"Not like you, Hugo, to play games with someone like that. You get what you needed?"

"Yeah. You check Barsetti's body today?"

"Sure did. Not a scratch on him. Well, lots of crushed and mushy bits, but as far as a three-day-old scar, nothing."

Tom was right. The idea that Hugo would essentially seduce a witness for an investigation was as far from his comfort zone as he'd ever been. In other cases, he'd pretended to get angry, got in people's faces to intimidate them in order to get results. He'd lied and cajoled, even flirted. But the fact that Amy Dreiss was relying on him to save her life, in Hugo's mind, that changed the rules. Obliterated them. As necessity is the mother of invention, Hugo had told Tom grimly, urgency spawned desperation. As it was, his close but brief encounter with the naked Nisha Bhandari had convinced him that, like Leo Barsetti, she too was unmarked by broken glass. He'd found it surprisingly difficult to focus on the task, to switch off the human emotions and feelings, but as hard as it had been to concentrate, he was confident that if she'd gashed herself on Castañeda's pantry window, he'd have seen the scar from it. But her body, he'd had to admit, was flawless.

"Nothing on her, either," Hugo told Tom.

"Including clothes?"

"Stop it, how the hell else was I supposed to do this?"

"Oh, relax. No one's judging you, Hugo. I'm certainly not in any place to do so."

"True enough."

"She's off the list of suspects then?" Tom asked.

"You'd think so, wouldn't you?"

"What's that supposed to mean?"

"Look, my inspection wasn't exactly done with a magnifying glass under surgical lights, and I just found out she withheld information from us."

"Like what?"

"Like she and Rubén had struck up a relationship just before he died."

"That's kind of a big deal."

"I told her that, and I'm not sure why she'd withheld it."

"People always lie about sex. Thing is, we know there was only one person in there, and we know neither she nor Barsetti had cuts. That list is getting shorter."

Grace Silva stuck her head out of the doorway. "Are you coming to help? I'm not sure what we're looking for."

Hugo nodded and spoke into the phone. "Gotta go. I'll call if we find anything." He followed Silva inside and, once the door had closed behind them, Hugo locked it. "Last time you searched here," he said, "where did you look?"

"Just Castañeda's area. That was all we were allowed to do."

"And you found basically nothing, right?"

"Right. What are we looking for this time?"

"Any tie between Leo and Delia Treviño. Between anyone and Delia Treviño." Hugo shook his head. "Shoot, anything out of the ordinary, anything at all."

Silva gave him a tight smile. "Whatever that may be."

"Yeah, sorry. But that's the best we can do right now. Why don't you go over Castañeda's work area again, see if anything's different. I'll start with Barsetti's office."

They spent two hours poking through desk drawers and digging through files. An hour into their work, a technology expert showed up to access the Estruch computers to scan them for evidence. The man joined Hugo in Barsetti's office, but the sharp tapping on the keyboard somehow irritated Hugo, making it hard for him to concentrate. He was looking at a folder containing shipping documents from Gregor Freed, the same bright-green papers he'd seen at the man's store. He couldn't help himself but look over the names of the pieces of furniture listed, looking for styles he recognized or even book titles he might know. But it looked like a couple of armoires and storage chests, no books or smaller pieces at all. Curious, he looked to see where the various shipments were sent to, and how often. He pulled out a pen and notepad and scratched down the dates and destinations.

He sat back to think but was interrupted when his cell phone rang. Camille Lerens's name popped onto the screen.

"*Salut*, Camille, how're you?"

"*Bien, mon ami.* And you?"

"Not good, still can't find my friend's daughter, but turned up a couple of bodies in the search."

"*Merde*, I'm sorry. I'm not having much more luck here. You know I'm working on the case of that girl you found."

"You are? Good, I hope you figure out what happened."

"Well, it wasn't suicide. We have an eyewitness, saw a man punch her and throw her off a bridge a few miles upstream from where you found her. Haven't been able to find out who he is yet, or why he wanted her dead."

"Husband? Boyfriend?"

"Not that we can discover. In fact, she's from Bulgaria, only been here a couple of weeks, so unless she came here with someone, probably didn't have either one of those. Although . . ."

"Although what?"

"Well, looks like she was a *cocotte*."

"A prostitute? How do you know?"

"We did a rape kit on her body. Multiple profiles."

"Sounds like you're probably right." *That poor girl.*

"We're rounding up the usual pimps. That's our best guess for the guy on the bridge, but so far no luck."

"You'll get him. Anything you need from me?"

"Not really, I was just checking in to see how you were doing. We will need a statement when you get back into Paris, but you didn't see anything the other witnesses didn't, so there's no hurry. Although I might also use your help if I don't have the *salaud* in handcuffs by the time you get back."

"Happy to lend a hand, though it's looking like I've lost my touch."

Lerens paused, then spoke gently but firmly. "You're the best in the business, Hugo. You'll find your friend, I know you will."

They rang off, and Hugo looked down at the shipping folder, a thought drifting through his mind, more like a whisper he couldn't quite hear. He put the folder back and went into Bhandari's office and started searching through the filing cabinets. When he didn't find what he was looking for, he pulled out his phone and dialed Tom.

"Hey, it's Hugo."

"I knew you'd need me sooner or later. Unless you're calling for a fucking sandwich, in which case, fuck you."

"Calm down, Tom, I do need you. I'm afraid we're going to have to pull a little extrajudicial move here, but we can't get busted, OK?"

"Sure. Who's the target?"

"I'll tell you, but one other thing." Hugo grinned down the phone. "I'm working with the cops closely enough that if things do go sideways and we're caught, any evidence will be inadmissible. I'm basically an agent of the Barcelona police, so assuming they have the same kinds of evidence rules we do, that's not good."

"Call a lawyer and ask. And then tell me what you're talking about."

"No time, we need to do this today, now."

Silence for a second, then Tom caught on. "Ah, I get it. What you're telling me, unless I'm much mistaken, is that when you say 'we' are about to do something illegal, you actually mean 'me.' As in, not you at all."

"Smart man, Tom."

"Which means this conversation never happened either."

"What conversation?" Hugo asked.

"That's cool, no worries. You're the one who got us busted last time, anyway. And by a fucking teddy bear. What do you need?"

♉

Hugo took a taxi to Gregor Freed's shop down near the docks, the sky just starting to dim. The traffic made the journey slow and frustrating, but it gave Hugo time to think. He checked his watch and hoped that Nisha would have had time to get out there and break the news about Leo. Hugo didn't like to play with people's emotions, but sometimes people were at their most talkative when they'd had a shock. Not that the guy wasn't talkative last time, he just didn't say a whole lot.

Hugo had the money ready to go when the cab pulled up in front of the store. A light burned orange in the window, a relief that the place was still open. Hugo pushed the front door and went into an empty showroom. It smelled of wood polish and dust, like a library for furniture. He wandered between the pieces, his fingers trailing on the smooth, old wood of desks and tables, feeling the cracked leather on the top of an old couch.

"Hello?" he called out. He listened but heard no reply. *Maybe talking to Nisha in the office?*

He kept walking, a gentle meander through the large room, his eye resting on the old clocks and statuettes that adorned the plainer pieces of furniture. One in particular seemed familiar. It was bronze and had the head of a lion, its lithe body in a crouch, a goat's head protruding from the beast's back and with a writhing serpent for a tale. He'd seen it in . . . Florence? He searched his memory for the name of the piece and it came to him quickly, the *Chimera of Arezzo*, one of the best-known examples of Estruscan art. This was a copy, of course, but a good one and it carried some of the emotion he'd seen in the original. The open mouth of the lion seemed to roar in anguish, not anger, the beast's sleek body crouching as if to pounce while its own tail writhed and snapped, and the goat's head stretched and contorted itself as it tried to escape its own bizarre body.

He stopped when his phone rang. It was Tom.

"Mission aborted," Tom said.

"How come?"

"She's here."

That's what I was afraid of, Hugo thought. "Anyone with her? What's she doing?"

"I have no idea. I showed up, peeked through a window, and saw her. Want me to knock on the door and ask to borrow some sugar?"

"Probably not."

"What are you doing?"

"Trying to find this Freed guy, at his store. Hoped Nisha Bhandari would be here, too. It's where she said she was headed."

"So who's there?"

"Not sure yet, but the place is unlocked, like it's open for business."

"Likely in the crapper. Or getting a sandwich. Oh, hold on. Your little lady is leaving. Want me poke around inside?"

"If you can get in."

"The Pope's still Catholic, right?"

"As far as I know. But don't get caught, and call me when you're done."

"Ten-four, little buddy."

Hugo rang off and moved toward the back of the large store but stopped when he heard a noise. He kept moving toward the sound, which he thought must be coming from the office. It sounded like someone crumpling paper, breaking wood, but as he got closer, Hugo picked up the distinctive smell of smoke. He moved quicker as the noises became louder, the sound of paper and wood burning. He reached the closed door to the office, smoke streaming under and over it, gray tendrils seeping into the main area of the store.

Hugo reached the door and dabbed at the handle to test its heat, pulling away when it burned his fingertips. He moved backward and looked around for a fire extinguisher but didn't see one, then pulled out his phone. He realized he didn't know the number for emergency services, so dialed Chief Inspector Garcia, pacing impatiently as he waited for the policeman to pick up.

"Bartoli, it's Hugo."

"Hugo, what—"

"I'm at Gregor Freed's antiques place. It's going up in flames and I don't know the number for emergency services."

"Hold a moment." The line went quiet, and Hugo stepped away from the office, the heat coming off the door in waves to scorch his forehead and hands, the roar of the flames getting louder by the second. Garcia returned. "Fire trucks on their way—get out of there, Hugo."

A thought struck him. "The door to the office is closed and the fire just started," he said.

"So?"

"So there's a good chance someone is in there, I need to check."

"Hugo, no! That's probably an old building, no telling whether it's structurally sound. The fire might bring it down on top of you, so just get out and let the firemen do their job. They'll be there in minutes."

"Thanks." Hugo slipped off his coat and used the material as a glove between his hand and the door handle. He gave it a turn and shoved it open, stepping back as smoke billowed out over him. He held his breath, covering his mouth and nose anyway, and tried to get into the little office, but the heat was too intense, the smoke too thick. In seconds, his eyes were stinging and he was blinded with his own tears. He backed away, moving quickly into the main showroom, where the smoke was thickening into a choking fog.

He ran to the front door and staggered into the street, coughing his lungs clear and taking deep breaths of fresh, cool air. He wiped a sleeve over his eyes and blinked until he could see straight.

Sirens echoed to him through the streets, and he knew it was a matter of minutes before the whole building would be cordoned off. He broke into a jog, passing the front of the store, looking for a way around to the back. An alley cut to his right, and he headed straight into it. From here, there was no sign that the building was on fire, and Hugo hoped the building wouldn't go up in flames just yet. His mind worked as he ran, wondering whether the fire was intentional, and if so, who'd started it. And, most important of all, why?

Behind him, the sirens grew louder, and he tried to picture the layout of the store in his mind, figure out where the office might be in relation to where he was. He stepped past a dumpster, narrowly avoiding a puddle of brown water that had pooled over a blocked drain.

He reached a crossroads in the alley, the one he was in split by another that ran left and right. He turned right. *Leads right behind the building, my best bet.* Thirty yards later, he found the door. He stopped, breathing hard, and held the flat of his hand toward it, recoiling with the heat. The door itself was metal, with no handle or apparent way to open it from the outside. *A fire escape*, he thought. *How ironic.*

He moved back the way he'd come, unable to access the building and unsure he wanted to, anyway. The line between bravery and reck-lessness could be fine, but running into a burning and empty building seemed to be pretty clearly on the reckless side of things.

He made his way to the front of the store at a brisk walk. As he rounded the corner out of the alley, two fire trucks screeched to a halt, their sirens dying as men poured from the flung-open doors, the flashing lights bouncing off the surrounding buildings, where curious faces peered out of windows and half-opened doors. He crossed the

MARK PRYOR 241

street to put some distance between himself and the glass windows in case they splintered, and he kept his eye on the firemen, with their axes and fireproof suits, connecting flat hoses and unhitching equipment like it was a military drill.

He looked down when his phone buzzed. "Hey, Tom, find anything?"

"Nice pad. Ground-floor apartment, chic and modern."

"Great. Find anything else?"

"Yes and no. Which is to say, she's gone."

"I know, you told me she left."

"I'm not talking about her popping out to the grocery store or getting a manicure. She's gone."

"How do you know?" Hugo looked back at the store and saw half a dozen firemen carrying pieces of art from the building, a public service he wasn't sure firemen would provide everywhere. In his experience, they focused on the fire itself, and if property got damaged in the fighting of it, so be it. He was pleased to see, too, that the contorted lion sculpture, the *Chimera of Arezzo*, was being cradled to safety. *A fireman with an appreciation for art*, Hugo thought.

"I found the room she uses as an office. She left a fucking note, man."

"Tell me it's not a suicide note."

"I didn't touch it, but I took a picture. I think you need to get Garcia and his troops over here."

"What did it say, Tom? For crying out loud."

"Well, I'm going from memory here, so don't quote me. She said she was going to disappear, that if she didn't, they'd find her and kill her the way they found and killed Rubén Castañeda and Delia Treviño."

"Who's 'they,' did she say?"

"She sure did, not that it means anything to me. She said the people after her, and please excuse my Spanish here, are Los Matadores. Did I say that right?"

CHAPTER THIRTY

As night fell on the city of Barcelona, the city's lights came on like sprinkles of snow, sharp flecks of white pricking the dark, a growing flurry until the night itself seemed to recede. Hugo watched from the front seat of the police car speeding him toward Nisha Bhandari's apartment, the young driver swerving them in and out of traffic, mumbling his apologies to Hugo, who just gave him the thumbs-up. The blue light over their heads flashed off the license plates of the cars in front of them, off the home and store windows, and even the road signs as they cut their way into the Old Town.

Chief Inspector Garcia was waiting for him outside the ground-floor apartment, an electronic tablet tucked under his arm.

"Thanks for coming so quickly," Garcia said. "We got an anonymous call from a pay phone nearby that there was someone screaming for help in the apartment."

"Oh yes?" Hugo feigned surprise.

"*Sí*, the emergency operator thought perhaps the caller was English or Australian." Garcia held Hugo's eye. "Or American."

"I was fifteen miles away, you know that."

"And your trouble-making friend?"

"Tom?" Hugo looked around, relieved to see that his friend had obviously anticipated this sort of inquiry and made himself scarce. "Haven't seen him in hours, no idea where he is."

"Any reason he'd be here?"

"Can't think of one." Hugo gave him a weak smile. "When I see him, I'll ask."

"Maybe give him a call. I'll need him to tell me himself he didn't break into her apartment." Garcia sighed. "Hugo, look, I know every police force does things differently, but I try to do things by the book here, I've told you that. If I find out either of you were in that house for some reason, this investigation will be seriously compromised."

"And I appreciate that. My only interest, though, is getting Amy back, I've told *you* that. As for Tom, I'll have him come by and talk with you." Hugo looked over at Bhandari's apartment. "Did you find anything in there?"

"We're working on it. So far, just the note I told you about on the phone. As for her, I have people watching the train stations and the airport. Bus stations, too, but no sign of her. You really think she's in danger?"

"Did your people find anything on Los Matadores?"

"It's strange," Garcia said. "We have good gang intelligence officers, and they have no file on this group, no people in custody claiming to be gang members. The inspector in that unit said they're barely active outside the prisons, and when they are, it's down south. He had no idea why they'd be up here." He shrugged. "Maybe expanding territory, but he didn't know anything about it. He even wondered if it was a foreign gang setting up, using a Spanish name."

"Yeah, that could happen. We had something like that in Paris a couple of years ago, although it was an old gang coming back to life. These open borders help with all kinds of trade, good and bad."

"Except we've not heard about anything like that here. No increase in drug arrests, overdoses, and our confidential informants aren't reporting anything new. Like I said, it's bizarre."

"What about in the house, just the note?"

"As a matter of fact." He pulled the tablet out and tapped the screen a few times. "Watch this, but it isn't pretty."

Hugo leaned forward and squinted at the screen. "That's Barsetti," Hugo said.

"In all his glory," Garcia said with a grimace.

"Not something I need to be seeing," Hugo agreed.

"Actually it is. Someone else enters the room any min—"

"There's someone, a woman." Hugo studied the moving images. "Holy cow, is that Delia Treviño?"

"Her glory is a little more . . . palatable, wouldn't you say?"

Hugo looked up. "Do I need to watch the whole thing, or is it what it looks like?"

"It's most definitely what it looks like. Leo Barsetti having sex with Delia Treviño."

"Which we knew about," Hugo said. "So the question is, why does Nisha Bhandari have a video of it?"

"No idea."

"Where did you find it exactly?"

"On a thumb drive in a box of papers from Estruch." Garcia shrugged. "Maybe she didn't even know it was in there, could have taken Castañeda or Barsetti's stuff from the office to go through and it was already there."

"Possibly." Hugo saw activity inside Bhandari's house. A thought tickled at him, a gentle cascade of things he'd seen in this case that didn't quite add up. "Any news about the fire?"

"The lead investigator called me while you were on the way here. They managed to put it out pretty quickly, though the back of the building is gutted inside. Anyway, the fire department wants to know whether their investigation is separate or part of ours."

"I guess that depends on what they find, to some extent. If you want my opinion, though, we should work with them for now, act like it's part of our investigation until we're sure it's not. He have anything useful to tell you?"

"No, not really. He told me about the interior offices being destroyed, but that's about all. Most of the furniture and antiques were saved, not even water damage."

"Yeah, I saw them carrying a bunch of stuff out. Glad they did." Hugo pictured the scene in his mind, the quiet chaos being managed with professionalism and speed by the Barcelona firemen, at least one of whom had an eye for a good piece of art.

A particular piece of art.

Hugo felt his stomach drop, and he stared at Chief Inspector Garcia as a few of the pieces fell into place. "I was right, it was no accident," he said.

"The fire? I think that's pretty obvious, but—"

"Not the fire." Hugo pointed to Garcia's phone. "I need to make another call to the jail, and right now. Can you set that up?"

"Sure, I'll have them bring Señor Denum to an interview room. We need to record all these calls."

"It's not Bart Denum I need to speak to," Hugo said. "It's José Paniagua."

"Paniagua. Are you serious?"

"Seemed like a nice guy, don't you think?" said Hugo. "But you'll have to ask him about it, I don't think he speaks English."

"Ask him about what? What does he know?"

"I'm curious if he was nice enough to donate more than just his blood."

♉

Hugo paced back and forth while Chief Inspector Garcia phoned the police station and arranged for José Paniagua to be taken to an interview room. Hugo had declined to explain to Garcia what it was about, excusing himself to the other side of the street to think. And to call Tom.

"Are you nearby?" Hugo asked.

"Depends who's asking," Tom chuckled.

"They know you called."

"Bullshit. They *think* I called, but no one's proving anything. Anyway, I thought you said that the important thing is getting Amy back, not shoring up some future criminal case."

"Yeah," Hugo conceded. "I think I did say something like that."

"Well then, you're welcome. What's going on there?"

"They're going through her place, trying to figure out if she's really in danger."

"And no doubt you have an opinion on that."

"I do."

"You gonna share that with them?"

"Sooner rather than later," Hugo said. "I just need to check one thing. You know how it is, I don't like to release the hounds until I'm positive they'll chase the right rabbit."

"You think Nisha Bhandari is the rabbit? Makes her sound all cute and fluffy."

"If I'm right, she's far from that." Hugo heard a note in his own voice, of frustration, impatience, and Tom clearly heard it too.

"Speak up, man, what's the problem?"

"The problem isn't just proving Bhandari is behind all this, but finding Amy. And finding her before it's too late."

Tom was quiet for a moment. "Hugo, look. I know you're close to her, and to her dad. But, you have to know the reality of this. If the situation were reversed, you know what you'd be telling me, right?"

"Tom, seriously?"

"Yeah, man, seriously. I don't know what's going on in your head, I never fucking do. Shit, we've had that fucking discussion a few times, Mr. Buttoned-up. But you have to know that if Amy was mixed up with these people, there's a very small chance of finding her alive, especially if Bhandari has bolted. I'm sorry, Hugo, but you'd be saying the same thing to me."

"I know the reality, Tom. I just need to do everything in case she's the exception. I don't have a choice, and if the situation were reversed, you'd do the same."

"Yeah, OK. I just . . . you know."

"Thanks, Tom. You don't have to worry about me."

"I'll damn well worry about you if I want to. And you know what, you may be right, I heard about your clever little deduction on that message Amy sent."

Hugo paused. "Dammit, Tom. I'm an idiot. Can you do something for me?"

"Whatever you need. Especially if it helps prove you're an idiot."

"Can you dig up whatever you can on Gregor Freed, and then get down to his store? I need a plan of it, blueprints or something, but I also need to see if the place has been altered. Officially or unofficially, I have no idea how planning permission works around here."

"Am I looking for anything in particular?"

"Garcia just said the 'offices' were burned. I only saw one there, so I need to know if there's an extra room at the back, next to the office."

"Yeah, sure. On my way, I'll call you if I find anything."

"Great, I gotta run." He rang off as Garcia gestured him over. Hugo trotted across the street. "Well?"

"He's donated blood, plasma, and marrow. The latter only once, two years ago."

Hugo grinned. "No good deed goes unpunished."

"You mind explaining now?"

"I'll apologize, too, I knew this was a theoretical possibility, but I've never seen it, never come across it, so it just didn't occur to me until I saw, or remembered that sculpture."

"What sculpture?"

"The *Chimera of Arezzo*."

"I don't know what that is," Garcia said.

"You don't need to. All that matters is that Nisha Bhandari has chimerism, it explains why her DNA wasn't found at the crime scene." Hugo saw confusion on Garcia's face. "It can happen when one twin dies in the womb—the other somehow absorbs the DNA of the one who died, so that if he's tested later in life, he can have two different profiles."

"But she wasn't a twin."

"I know. The other way it can happen is with a bone-marrow transplant and blood transfusion. Your body keeps its original DNA, but because you have someone else's marrow, it will continue to produce the donor's blood. Nisha Bhandari had cancer, which included a bone-marrow transplant. I'm certain that the dates will match up with the time that José Paniagua donated."

"Wait, are you saying the blood at the Castañeda crime scene was hers?"

Hugo smiled. "I guess technically it was both of theirs. But she's the one who left it there."

"She'll have some cut on her, then. Assuming we find her."

"No, she won't." Hugo looked sheepish. "Don't ask me how I know, but she doesn't have any cuts. I think she went to Castañeda's place to kill him. She took a syringe and simply pulled a little of her blood and left it behind. She knew it would clear her and that, if the donor had no criminal history, we'd never identify him."

"Unlucky for her."

"Very," said Hugo. "But I'm betting she tried to cover her tracks. Contact the hospital, see if she's been in touch about donating blood."

"You think she was going to try and find out who donated to her, either to scare him off, or worse."

"Yes."

"So she killed Castañeda. You're sure of that?"

"And she's working with Freed. She went to see him, said she needed to tell him about Leo's death in person because the two men were friends. But neither of them was there." Hugo thought back to the crime scene, something that hadn't registered with him at the time, but one of those snippets of information he tended to log away in the hope it would matter later. He saw the bathroom, the blood everywhere, the shower. He snapped his fingers. "Has anyone been into the apartment recently? Is it still closed off?"

"I think so, it should be."

"The shower. Nisha was a foot shorter than Rubén Castañeda, wasn't she? And he was only a little shorter than me."

"So?"

"I stood in the shower, and the head was pointed at my chest. Get someone down there to take photos and measure. If someone rinsed off in there, they'd have adjusted it to their height. The fact that it was the right height for Bhandari, and the fact that there was no hair in the drain, tells me she was there, and cleaned it out. She claimed his place was too dirty for her, and if that's true, it seems unlikely he'd clean the drain and nothing else."

"So where is she now? And where's Amy Dreiss?"

"I can't tell you for sure," Hugo said. He nodded toward Bhandari's apartment. "But I have an idea. Can I go help with the search? There are a couple of pieces of paper I need to find."

CHAPTER THIRTY-ONE

Hugo walked into the modern apartment, three members of the crime-scene unit glancing up as he entered, then turning back to their work, the painstaking examination, assessment, and cataloguing of Bhandari's property. Garcia had let them know she was now the prime suspect, shading their approach away from the urgency of finding her and toward the extra diligence required to catch her. Hugo walked through the main room, clean and furnished with modern white pieces, no mess or clutter anywhere. The kitchen lay to his left; to his right, he saw three open doors. *Two bedrooms and a bathroom?*

He poked his head into the room on the left, obviously her bedroom, then checked the other two without touching anything. He was right, except that she'd been using one of the bedrooms as an office.

Hugo turned to the crime-scene men. "Any of you guys speak English?" he asked hopefully.

The men looked at each other, and one held up a hand. "Yes, a little."

Hugo spoke slowly. "I just want to know, have you finished in these rooms?"

"*El baño y la cama, sí.*" The man gave an apologetic smile. "Sorry, we are finished in the bathroom and bedroom. Chief Inspector Garcia wanted us to wait before doing the study."

"Wait for what?"

"You, I think." The man stepped forward and handed Hugo a pair of surgical gloves. "*Por favor*, do not sneeze on anything."

Hugo smiled. "Thanks, I won't."

He started with the filing cabinet, his eyes skimming over the tabs labeled, *Taxes, Investments, Employees, Prospects*. He was looking for documents relating to her business with Gregor Freed, and he found them in the bottom drawer of her sleek desk. He pulled out a folder and saw three green sales sheets that matched those in Leo Barsetti's desk.

"Finding anything?" Grace Silva stood in the doorway.

Sitting behind Bhandari's desk, Hugo looked up. "I think so. I have a theory, anyway."

"If it helps, we heard from the fire investigators. It was arson, for sure. Started in the office with some kind of liquid. No bodies or anything like that, though."

A shudder of relief passed through Hugo. "Good, that's good."

"So let me guess," Silva said with a smile. "Your theory is that Bhandari, Barsetti, and Freed were losing money, and the fire was set to hide that, and get an insurance payout."

"Actually, no."

She raised an eyebrow. "Then what?"

"That theory doesn't account for everything we know. What about Delia Treviño and this new gang, Los Matadores?"

"Barsetti killed Treviño to stop his wife from finding out about them and leaving him. Maybe Treviño was blackmailing him and, given her criminal background, I'm betting she had friends in this gang, maybe used them to intimidate him. Maybe they even killed his wife for some reason."

"I didn't take Barsetti for a killer, did you?"

She held his gaze. "Did you take Nisha Bhandari for one?"

"Not for a while, I'll give you that."

"Chief Inspector Garcia told me that Bhandari had no marks on her body from the broken window. Apparently he got that information from you."

"That's right." Hugo didn't look away, kept his voice and his expression neutral.

"Curious how you'd know that," she said with a slight smile.

"I asked nicely."

"And you took her word for it?"

"No." He held up the three sheets of paper. "But if you want to check for yourself, we need to decipher these."

"Decipher?" she stepped into the room, a puzzled look on her face.

"The sales and shipping records I saw in Barsetti's office indicated only a slight downturn in business. Freed himself told me about that, which is why I don't think the fire was for insurance money."

"Maybe they had debt we don't know about."

"I don't think so. I realized pretty late that the message from Casta-ñeda's phone was from Amy. When I did, I was so busy being relieved she was alive, so preoccupied with finding her, that I didn't stop to think *why* she was alive. More specifically, why she was alive when other people weren't."

"And now you know?"

"These sales and shipping records indicate just a few pieces of large furniture."

Silva threw up her hand in exasperation. "So business *wasn't* as good. We're back to insurance fraud."

"No, this was intentional. The selection of these pieces was done to complement the other things they were shipping."

"Other things, like drugs?" Her eyes widened as the truth hit her. "People. Amy Dreiss."

Hugo nodded. "They were using the same forty-foot containers for less but larger furniture. What do you think the larger pieces were for? The extra room in the containers?"

Silva shook her head in amazement. "Nisha Bhandari was involved in human trafficking?"

"That's what I think. I suspect she was relatively new to it and was using the furniture business as a cover."

"But if they were already making money, why take the risk?"

"Same reason as always, I imagine. Money."

"And a live person is much less messy, and I suppose requires less care even, than a human organ."

"Especially if she's drugged. I mean, look, they take them from a place where no one will miss them, stash them away for a few days with a bottle of water, and then straight into a shipping container and gone."

"So where is Amy now?"

Hugo sat up straight and stared at Silva. "The same place Nisha Bhandari is. And probably Gregor Freed."

"Where?"

Hugo stared at the sales sheets again, then pointed to a line at the bottom. "What does this mean?"

Silva leaned over and looked. "Last week they reserved a, what did you call it? A shipping container, in the name of whoever that signature is. Looks like Gregor Freed."

"That's where they are, all three of them." Hugo stood and moved quickly around the desk. "We need to get men down to the docks, as many as possible and as soon as possible. If we don't, Bhandari and Freed will be gone. Does the form say where the container is headed?"

"Let me see." Silva studied the shipping log.

"At the very least," Hugo said, "we can set up at the other end, be waiting for them if we don't get them in time here."

Silva looked up from the page. "No, we can't. Not where they're going."

♉

Ten minutes later, Chief Inspector Garcia was on the phone to the port authority. His frustration was evident as he was put on hold several times, then transferred a few more. Eventually he found someone to talk to, and Hugo could only listen as the conversation passed him by, his own frustration growing as the minutes ticked away. Eventually, Garcia thanked the person he'd been speaking to and rang off. He walked over to where Hugo and Silva stood, waiting.

"*Bueno*," he said. "Not much we can do tonight." He held up a hand. "Relax, Hugo. He said there is one container ship on its way out of the port now, and it was loaded this morning, so they're not on it. One more was scheduled to leave tonight, but it's having engine trouble, so it won't go until the morning. Other than that, the first ship due out is at ten tomorrow morning."

"Where to?"

"All over. Almost all of the ships make multiple stops."

"Any of them going to Libya?"

"Yes, all three stop in Tripoli."

"We need to get down there, find the container those bastards are hiding in," said Hugo. "How long is the trip?"

"He said it was about fifteen hundred kilometers, which is eight days at sea. Not much fun in a shipping container."

"They aren't in it for fun," said Hugo. "Back home, people are buying those things and converting them into homes, so I'm guessing with a few creature comforts, it's a pretty decent way to escape a life sentence."

Garcia gave him a wry smile. "Assuming they escape. You think Freed is with her?"

"Yes, I'm guessing she knew we were onto her, or suspected, and this was their escape plan. I just hope they have Amy with them."

"If Freed was prepared to burn his business down . . ."

"Yeah, I know. Let's just hope they see Amy as an asset, not a hindrance. How are we going to do this?"

"I'm sending an incident commander to work with the port authorities. They'll try to identify the precise container, work through the night if they have to. Hopefully we can narrow it down to the right one, I'll need whatever paperwork you have for that, the sales log, there should be an identifying number on there."

"Then what?"

"If we can find the container tonight, we'll clear the area as discreetly as we can and then set up around it. If we can get a look inside, we'll do that, too. Either way, at first light we'll make contact and try to talk them out of there."

"Talk them out?"

Garcia nodded. "Of course. If that doesn't work, we'll use a giant can opener and pry them out, maybe with the help of some tear gas."

"Good plan. You're going to let me do the talking, right?"

"I figured you'd ask that. And I don't know the answer right now. I'll have to run it by my superiors. I'm guessing they won't be wild about the idea, but I can try."

"At the very least, I want to be there to advise."

"That might be a good compromise. In the meantime, I suggest you go get some rest. I'll send a car for you at four tomorrow morning."

"I'll be waiting. What about you?"

Garcia looked at his watch. "I'll grab some sleep in a couple of hours, but I have a few things to do first. You should go now, though. One of us needs to be fresh in the morning."

CHAPTER THIRTY-TWO

At ten minutes before four o'clock, Hugo stepped out of the apartment. The city was quiet around him, light falling onto the street in yellow patches from the lamps along the sidewalk. The previous night, he'd dissuaded Tom from coming along, worried that his friend's special brand of recklessness might be especially dangerous to the mission at this juncture. When Hugo mentioned the time he was being picked up, Tom went back to his bottle of Rioja and didn't put up much of an argument.

Somewhere in a neighboring street, a moped puttered along. The sound of its engine echoed against the stone walls of the winding, narrow streets, the only sign of life. The storefronts that he could see where shuttered, the apartment windows were dark, and even the bars along this street had shoveled out the last of the night owls hoping for one more drink, their doors now locked and gated.

Hugo leaned against a crumbling wall between two grilled windows, his imagination spinning with tiredness and nerves. He imagined himself like a World War II spy in his hat and coat, waiting for his nighttime rendezvous with an attractive contact. His imagination didn't deceive, at least in part, because it was Grace Silva who showed up at four a.m. in her pint-sized police car. Any mystique or romance vanished, though, when Hugo slid into the front seat and looked over at her. Her eyes were heavy, and she barely nodded, just checked the rearview mirror and started the car forward.

"Thanks for coming to get me," Hugo said. "Do you know if they found the container?"

"They did. It's at the top of a stack of five, so we've not been able to get very close yet."

"Yet?"

"We're assuming that Bhandari's inside and knows how the port works. She probably doesn't, but we're playing it safe."

"Which means?"

"That we didn't want to move the container too early. She might be expecting the next movement to be the loading, so we didn't want to move it just a few feet and then leave it for a few hours. If she can see out and realizes it's not on the boat, well, that wouldn't be good."

Hugo nodded. "So when we get there, it's moved to somewhere we can access it, isolate it."

"Right."

"Makes sense to me," Hugo said. "Was I right about where the container is headed?"

"Yes, you were. Tripoli."

"Into the waiting arms of her brother. Nice family business they have." He looked at her. "You get any sleep?"

"A few hours. I'll sleep tonight when this is over."

"You and me both." It was a loose double entendre at most, but they both smiled anyway.

Silva pulled out of a side street and turned onto the B-10, heading south. They started to see more cars, their headlights like sparks of light whipping past.

"I memorized some information about the port for you," Silva said.

"You did?"

"It has two international terminals, TCB and TerCat, and I think is the third busiest port in the whole of Europe. And the trip they are planning is one-and-a-half thousand kilometers, which usually takes eight days."

"So Chief Inspector Garcia was telling me. What else?"

"Well, containers come in different sizes, usually twenty and forty feet in length. The largest ships can carry ten thousand containers and, in fact, a ship lost between six and seven hundred containers in the Bay of Biscay recently, and that was a small percentage of its load."

"Wouldn't want to be in one of those when it goes overboard."

"No, and it's definitely a risk they're taking. Anyway, Barcelona's port handles about two thousand forty-foot containers a day. When a ship arrives, the yard unloads them all and has the same number of containers ready to load. Turnaround can be as little as twenty-four hours in some ports, with ships coming and going at all times of day and night."

"Well now, you have been studying."

"That's just background. Each container has a unique number, which was marked on the paperwork you gave us, and which is also matched to a bar code that can be scanned wherever the container goes. That's how they are tracked, how they know where to place them on the ship, and which ones to unload at the destination port."

"And how you found their container at the dock."

"Exactly."

As they grew closer, Hugo felt the tiredness leave his body, washed away by the adrenaline that was starting to make him fidget. Silva glanced over. "We have a good team out there, it'll be fine."

"I know." Hugo looked out of the side window, quiet for a moment as the lights of the city blinked at him. When he spoke, he heard the anxiety in his own voice. "But if Amy's in there, she's shut in a metal box with one, possibly two murderous lunatics. If we rattle that cage the wrong way, if things go bad and we're not quick enough, they'll kill her."

And if she's not in there . . .

Soon they left the highway and sped along the arrow-straight Carrer de la Lletra A, sweeping left out of a traffic circle into the port itself. Silva announced their arrival over the radio, and Hugo saw that their path had been cleared. He shivered involuntarily as they drove between two rows of shipping containers, neat stacks of yellow, blue, white, and red, like Lego bricks pressed into place by a giant. Hugo lowered his window, and the cold morning air rushed in, filling the car with the smell of diesel oil and the sea. He looked up at the sky, more gray than black now, and saw the long, dark arms of the dock-yard cranes stretching over them. They reached the end of the row, and Silva slowed.

"It's here somewhere, can you see—?"

"There." Hugo pointed, and Silva directed the car past a shorter stack of containers, pulling up behind a longer row where the Barce-lona police had staged. Hugo counted twelve police cars sitting in a square of light created by portable lamps. Most were the small patrol cars like the one he'd arrived in, but he also saw four SUVs and a mil-itary-style combat vehicle. Twenty or so police officers stood in small groups, about half in green fatigues, and the other half in the blue of the city police.

Garcia was in the closest group, and he turned as Silva parked the car. He strode over and opened Hugo's door for him.

"*Hola*, Hugo. You didn't bring coffee?"

"I'll buy you one after," Hugo said. "Are we ready to go?"

"Pretty much. There's an open area on the other side of these con-tainers, and on the other side of that is where theirs is located, the top of a stack. We'll drop it gently into the open area, surround it, and then start talking."

"I'm ready to advise, if that's still allowed."

"Ah, yes, I've managed a special treat for you." Garcia's skin was gray with tiredness, but for a moment his eyes sparkled.

"What's that?"

"You're in business." He handed Hugo a bullet-proof vest. "Put this on. I told my superiors that the one thing the people have inside is that they all speak English."

"Wait, do we know who's inside?"

"No, but we're operating under the assumption that all three are: Bhandari, Freed, and young Amy. Anyway, I told them that if Amy hears your voice, can understand what you're saying, that might be helpful somehow." He shrugged. "They weren't buying it initially, but then I told them you were trained in this stuff by the FBI, and I think they got a little," he hesitated, "how do you say? Like when you see a famous person?"

"Starstruck?" Hugo offered.

"*Sí, exactamente.* So, they agree to let you lead the negotiation."

Hugo took off his coat, slipped into the vest, and then pulled his coat back on. He put a hand on Garcia's shoulder. "Thank you, Bartoli, I'm very grateful and I'll do my best." He looked around. "Are you the senior officer here?"

"Yes, but I have a colleague who will lead the assault on the container, if it comes to that. I'll introduce you."

Garcia led Hugo toward a group of four men in dark-green fatigues and combat boots, and when they were close, he called out to them. "Miguel."

The largest in the group, and the only one wearing epaulettes, turned and looked Hugo up and down. He thrust out a hand. "Miguel Luna." The man's serious face melted into a wry smile. "I'm sorry, my English is not good."

"Nice to meet you." Hugo shook his hand and returned the smile. "*Lo siento tambien, porque mi Español es peor.*" He'd hoped to say, *I'm also sorry, because my Spanish is worse*, and since the two policemen chuckled, Hugo assumed he was at least close to getting it right.

"No problem," Luna said, his voice a deep rumble. In America, he'd have been a shoe-in for a linebacker, with the wide shoulders and narrow waist of a bodybuilder. He thumbed at Garcia. "He will, err . . ."

"Translate," Garcia finished for him. He turned to Hugo. "Why don't you tell us what you think, how we should approach this. We don't have much time for planning."

"Agreed. Are we going to be able to see inside the container?"

"Probably not," Garcia said. "We have a special camera, a small one, but I don't know what you call it in English."

"Fiber-optic? Like on the end of a wire?"

"Yes, that. Perhaps there is an opening, but on most of these," he waved a hand at the stacks of containers, "there is not. That also means they can't see us, which is a benefit."

"But they're not soundproof?"

"No. We have a loud speaker—that will work."

"How will they communicate with us?" Hugo frowned, not happy with the practicalities. "We might not be able to hear them respond."

Garcia grinned. "We have mics we can put on the container, don't worry. Also, they're at the top of a stack right now, so we flew a helicopter over the top to see if our thermal camera could tell us anything."

"And did it?"

"Only that there are people inside. It's not like the movies, where we can see outlines, but there was heat detected, so we can be sure someone's in there."

"But we can't tell how many?"

"No, but in about twenty minutes, you can just ask them."

♉

Hugo's plan, like all his best plans, was simple.

As dawn broke, a crane growled into place beside the stack of containers topped by Bhandari's. Its arm stretched up over the metal box, and Miguel Luna barked a command at his men, the armed response team. They snapped into action, burly men with grim faces and more than enough firepower for this job shuffled in their gear to form a circle around the empty patch of dock where the container was to be lowered.

As soon as they were in place, Garcia gave orders to his men to take their positions, a secondary ring out of the immediate line of fire, there in case someone fled from the container and made it past Luna's men. *Unlikely in the extreme*, Hugo thought, *but best to be prepared*. They moved a little more slowly than Luna's men, several of them dropping cigarettes onto the dock and grinding them out before heading to their assigned places.

The last piece of preparation trundled around a stack of containers, then backed into the clearing. Six policemen hopped out of the bed of the truck and went to work, unloading and stacking sandbags to shoulder height, about a dozen feet from where the mouth of the container would be sitting. They'd scrambled to get the bags after a conversation Hugo had with Garcia and Luna when he first arrived.

"Do we know if these containers are bulletproof?" Hugo had asked.

Garcia had looked surprised. "You think they have guns with them?"

"No idea." Hugo said. "But I don't want us to be standing there unprotected if we find out they do."

Garcia turned to Luna and spoke rapidly in Spanish. Luna replied, an answer that began with "No," and when he'd finished speaking, Garcia said, "He doesn't think so. He said the metal walls might stop a .22 caliber, but not much more than that."

"I agree," said Hugo.

The sandbag wall in place, they waited and watched as the crane picked up the container, a light-blue cube that had seen better days. Metal groaned as it cleared the container below it, and all eyes followed its progress as it swung into the open air and began its slow descent.

Hugo, Garcia, and Luna started forward and took their places behind the sandbags as the container neared the ground. With them came a police technician whose name Hugo hadn't caught. The man carried a shoe-box-sized speaker that was connected by a twenty-foot loop of wire to a magnetic, cuplike device. This would be their set of ears.

All four men instinctively stepped back as the container reached eye level, giving the heavy metal box some respect. The technician waited a moment longer, then left their refuge and approached it. He pressed the cup to the side wall, then knelt and flipped a switch on the speaker. He stood and gave Hugo the thumbs-up just as the container settled onto the dock, giving a tired groan and throwing out a skirt of dust. The tech walked backward to the sandbags, spooling the wire as he went.

The crane operator had done well; Hugo was no more than eighteen feet from the end of the container, and he inspected the heavy padlock that kept it shut. It was encased in a white plastic skin, a thin seal designed to break when the lock opened, a measure to prevent anyone from tampering with the contents, and a way to know if they had.

Miguel Luna handed Hugo a small bullhorn and gave him a nod. "Good luck."

Hugo nodded back and turned the megaphone on. He walked past the sandbags to the container and banged his fist on the cold metal. He waited a moment, then banged again before returning to his position. He held the mouthpiece to his lips.

"Nisha Bhandari, Gregor Freed, this is Hugo Marston. I'm with the Barcelona police, and your container is surrounded. I'm very much hoping we can resolve this without anyone getting hurt."

They waited for a reply, and when none came, Hugo looked at the police technician. The man knelt by the speaker and checked the wire running into it, then put his ear to the speaker. He nodded to let them know it was all working fine. Hugo tried again.

"Nisha, this is Hugo. Can you let me know that you and Gregor are OK. And Amy, too." He felt his throat catch when he said her name, hoping desperately that he was right and that she was there, with them. Alive.

A sound came from the speaker, not words, more of a rustling and a gentle *clink* as though someone was moving inside. Hugo looked over at Miguel Luna, who was inspecting the container through a pair of binoculars, looking for a crack, a sight-line into the metal box.

"Nisha, this container isn't going anywhere. It's over." It suddenly struck Hugo that if Amy was in the container, other girls might be, too. "We have food and water for you and for anyone with you."

The silence persisted and Hugo lowered the bullhorn.

"What are they doing?" Garcia asked.

"Considering their options. And we need to make sure they know that surrendering is the best one." He raised the megaphone. "We have a couple dozen armed men here, Nisha. You need to talk to us, let us know you're OK, and who's in there with you."

The men froze as the speaker came to life, a muffled grunting sound and the shuffling of feet, or . . . something.

"We don't have a lot of time," Hugo said into the megaphone. "We can't wait forever, so if you want to talk to us, now would be the time."

The movement inside the container stopped, and the four men all stared at the silent speaker, willing it to come to life, hoping for the sound of a human voice.

Hugo wasn't ready to give up. "Nisha and Gregor, one of you needs to speak up, say something. I don't want my friends in uniform pumping gas in there—you'll spend the rest of the week throwing up in a concrete cell. Talk to me and we can make sure that doesn't happen."

Beside Hugo, Miguel Luna shifted from foot to foot. He'd been the one to pull the plug on smoking the container out. It had been a close call, but several factors weighed against. First, they didn't know if Amy would be in there, injured or unable to move. If she was already in poor condition, subjecting her to a few minutes of smoke could be fatal. Second, the tightness of the container and the fact that it had just one point of entry rendered the gas as much a hazard to the police as to the occupants. Finally, Luna had pointed out that the only way to get smoke in was to open the container doors, and if they'd done that, they might as well go straight in.

The speaker remained silent.

"We can't talk at them forever," Garcia said.

"Agreed." Hugo frowned, unhappy. "I don't think we have much choice. Tell Miguel to do his thing. When his men are moving in, I'll keep talking, keep them focused on me." Hugo hoped that would work, but he wasn't entirely convinced that whoever was inside couldn't see through a crack somewhere.

Garcia turned to Luna and spoke quickly and quietly. In turn, Luna raised his radio and gave instructions. Eight of the armed men jogged forward, their boots scuffing the concrete, their equipment jangling softly as they ran.

Hugo spoke into the bullhorn. "I can give you another ten minutes, maybe fifteen, Nisha. But the port authority wants its dock back. If you have something you want, something we can realistically do for you, you need to say so, and say it now." The eight men had reached the container, and they split into two lines of four at the doors, crouched and ready. "There's nowhere to hide, Gregor. We're still at the point where we can help you, rescue something from this mess."

Hugo had rehearsed these words in his mind. In a different situation, he might have tried to cause a split between Bhandari and Freed, but since there was no way for just one of them to come out, and since he had no idea what weapons they had, creating tension between the two would likely do more harm than good. Especially since Nisha Bhandari had shown little compunction about killing those who crossed her.

Hugo lowered the megaphone again. He shook his head in frustration, then looked over at Miguel Luna, who stood with the bolt cutter in his hand. Hugo nodded and gave him a wry smile. "*Buena suerte.*" Good luck.

Miguel Luna stepped between the two lines of his men and stood in front of the container. He took the bolt cutter and set its blades around the steel loop of the padlock. He widened his stance, looked at his men, and squeezed the arms of the cutter. Hugo could see Luna's muscles flexing and shaking as he pressed metal on metal, fought against the tempered steel of the lock. Twenty seconds into it, Hugo thought Luna had lost, but the policeman gave a final cry of triumph when the steel of the solid lock snapped and it clattered to the ground. Luna kicked it aside and threw the bolt cutter after it, then pulled on the lever mechanism of the door. Both doors swung open at once, and Luna stepped aside as his squad leader led the short charge into the box.

The sun was alive on the horizon to Hugo's right, casting long fingers of light between the stacks of containers around them but leaving patches of the dock in murky darkness. Unsure what visibility would be like in the container, the armed unit had affixed flashlights to their rifles. Now, arrows of light flickered inside the container like some crazy light show, a performance made all the more hectic by the shouts of the policemen announcing themselves, yelling warnings not to move. In thirty seconds, the shouting stopped, signaling to Hugo that the container had been made safe. He stepped out from behind the sandbags, and Garcia followed him.

They waited, peering inside, seeing the dark shapes of the policemen and the still outlines of furniture. As Hugo's eyes adjusted, he looked to see who else was inside but couldn't make out anyone in civilian clothes.

And then, as he watched, two policemen pulled Gregor Freed out from under a desk on the left side of the container. With apparent ease, they hauled him to his feet and dragged him outside, holding his arms and planting him in front of Hugo, Garcia, and Luna. The big man was pale and shaking, his eyes squinting at the light.

"Who else is in there, Gregor?" Hugo demanded.

"No one. Just me. She locked me in there and left."

"Bullshit," Hugo said, his temper flaring. "Tell me who else is in there, or I'll have one of these men shoot you in the goddam foot."

"No, just me!" Freed insisted. "She made me, she locked me in."

"How the hell is a five-foot woman going to force a big oaf like you into a container?" Hugo snapped. He turned to Garcia. "Get him out of my sight, Bartoli, I swear I'll punch him in the mouth if he keeps lying to me."

Garcia spoke to the two men holding him, and they both nodded. One took out handcuffs and secured Freed's hands, then they both marched him away from the container to a waiting police van.

Hugo looked at Garcia. "Can we go in?"

Both men looked at Luna, who nodded. "*Sí*, no problem."

Hugo stepped onto the metal floor of the container, and the smell of human waste swept over him, almost forcing him back out. His eyes watered, and he looked where the smell seemed to be coming from. Pieces of furniture lined the container. He could see the dim outline of two armoires at the back, and next to them on either side, matching wooden trunks. Closer to him, a few tables were stacked on top of each other and secured with heavy straps. One of the armed policemen had lifted the lid of one of the old trunks, and as Hugo watched, the man dropped the lid shut and turned away, a gloved hand covering his own nose and mouth.

Another officer was kneeling beside a second trunk, on the opposite wall of the container. Hugo walked over and looked inside. It was half filled with food, tubes of meat paste, packets of bread and chocolate, and at least twenty water bottles. Supplies for the journey.

He could see the two side-by-side armoires clearly now. Their doors had been broken open by the armed officers, and his heart sank when he realized they were empty.

And yet . . . he slowly approached them, something not quite right dragging him closer.

They'd been wedged in so tight, there was no gap between them—an impressive stroke of luck for the space conscious. But the shipping container wasn't close to being full, so space wasn't at a premium. And there was something about the doors. They reached the top of each armoire, about a foot over Hugo's head, but they came down only to his knees. He looked inside the one on the right, rapped his knuckles on the wood interior, and kicked its base with his toe.

Something moved inside.

"Hey," he shouted over his shoulder. "In here." His tone translated the message, and he pointed to the base of the armoire. "*Aquí*," he repeated. *Here*. Two men aimed their weapons into the armoire as Hugo's fingers scrabbled for purchase inside, looking for a way to release the false bottom. He found a gap at the back left corner and worked his finger in. He looked at the two men beside him, nodding to let them know he was about to pull it up. He took a breath to steady himself, then tore the base of the armoire upward, stepping back and out of the line of fire of whoever might be inside.

The two policemen stiffened and snapped commands at someone in the hidden compartment, but their tones rapidly softened. They knew whom they were looking for, they'd seen pictures of Nisha Bhandari, Gregor Freed, and Amy Dreiss.

The officers let their weapons fall to their sides, their voices soft now, almost cooing with sympathy.

Hugo's heart leapt, days of fear and anxiety evaporating into pure joy. Tears pricked his eyes as he stepped forward knowing that they'd done it, they'd found Amy, and they'd found her alive.

CHAPTER THIRTY-THREE

Hugo stopped the stretcher just as they were about to load it into the ambulance. He'd caught a glimpse of Amy as they'd taken her out of the armoire, but he had been shooed back by the paramedics trying to treat her, and then shuffled out of the container entirely by the crime-scene techs there to collect evidence and photograph its interior.

Now, Amy lay on her back, with a red blanket covering her body and only her head visible. Her skin was like alabaster, stretched tight over her chin and cheek bones, giving her a fragility that made Hugo shake with sadness and anger. But when her eyes focused on his, there was still that spark in them, the glint of mischief that a little girl had carried with her into womanhood. He took her hand, a frail little bird that fluttered in his when he touched it.

"Hugo," she said. Her voice cracked but she managed a weak smile. "I knew you'd find me. I just knew it."

"I had a lot of help," Hugo said, swallowing a lump in his throat. "From a strong girl and her old friend, Asterix the Gaul. Now you rest, and I'll come see you at the hospital a little later."

"Is my dad here?"

"Yes. I'll bring him with me, he's been worried."

"Is he OK?"

"He will be," Hugo smiled. The truth was that Denum had not been doing well. After receiving treatment in the hospital, he'd been returned to his jail cell a broken man. No arguing, no pleading, just a pale, withdrawn shadow of himself. Hugo gave her hand the tiniest of squeezes. "You better believe he will be now."

"I'm sorry. This is all my—"

"Hush," said Hugo. "None of this is your fault. Not one bit of it."

"Did you catch her?"

"Not yet. Do you know where she might be?"

"No." Tears filled Amy's eyes, and she squeezed his hand. "She's evil, Hugo. I don't think I was the only one, so you have to find her."

"I know, sweet girl. I know. And I promise, I will."

"Yes. Of course." She held his eye for a moment, then relaxed her grip, settling into the thin mattress. Heavy eyes blinked with exhaustion, and she let out a long breath.

"*Gracias*," Hugo said to the paramedics, stepping back so they could load her into the ambulance. Two of the armed response team climbed in with her, as much for Hugo's comfort as for necessity but, as Hugo had learned over the years, you can never be too careful.

He stood there and watched as the ambulance left, its lights flickering on and its siren beginning a slow wail as it headed toward the main exit. Hugo turned and walked over to Chief Inspector Garcia. He sat in the passenger seat of a police van, his legs dangling out sideways as he talked on his phone. In the back of the van, Gregor Freed sat chained to a bench, his broad shoulders sagging, his head down.

Garcia nodded to Hugo, said a few more words, and hung up. "She's going to be fine, *sí*?" he said.

"*Sí*," Hugo said. "She's a tough one."

"Ay, she had to be." He held up his phone. "I was just talking to the prosecutor. They won't be filing any charges against Bart Denum."

"Thank you, he'll appreciate that very much. As do I."

"He did it for the girl, not you two," Garcia said. "No need to further traumatize her." He hesitated. "And, as you said before, I couldn't promise that I wouldn't have lost my head too, in the same circumstances."

"Well, whatever the reason, we all appreciate it." Hugo nodded toward the back of the van. "Is he talking?"

"No, won't say a word."

"We need to find Nisha Bhandari," Hugo said. "Amy was our first priority, but now she's safe, we have to do everything we can to find that woman. I'm sure there were other girls; Amy wasn't the first. If we get Bhandari, maybe we can trace them and bring them home."

"I told Freed that, said he could help himself if we're able to recover anyone else." Garcia shook his head in frustration. "He didn't seem to care."

"Doesn't surprise me, any help he gives us essentially confirms his guilt."

"We have the airports and train stations locked on alert for her, as best we can. Her car is being watched, and I don't think she can rent one without us knowing."

"She may have already left." Hugo eyed the docks. "A lot of boats coming and going. Once she's on the dock it can't be too hard to stow-away on one."

"Good thinking, I'll contact the port authority and have them start a search."

Hugo frowned. "Although . . ."

"What?"

"That's a little unplanned for her, isn't it?"

"Not if she had the boat already picked out."

"In which case it'd be the same one the container was going on, because she'd know about it, know where it was going, how long it'd take, and have someone on the other end to meet her."

"Her brother."

"Precisely. And if we found the container, we'd start looking every-where else but the docks for her—train stations, airports."

"She's very smart, that one," Garcia said. "Suggestions?"

"Have the ship searched, top to bottom. Use dogs, thermal imaging, whatever it takes."

"*Bueno.*" He punched numbers into his phone and gave rapid com-mands in Spanish. When he hung up, he said to Hugo, "What do we do in the meantime?"

Hugo looked at the ground, frowning. "Give them what they want, but have a backup just in case."

"What?"

"She was talking about her business, what made it successful. She said you give the clients what they think they want, but you have to have something special on stand-by just in case." Hugo looked up at Garcia. "She said the backup was as much for her as for the client, to save her neck when things were looking bad."

Garcia raised his arms by his sides. "I don't understand."

Hugo pointed to Freed. "Is the van locked?"

"He can't get out, don't worry."

"Oh, I'm not worried about that," Hugo said. "I want to know if I can get in."

♉

Hugo stepped into the rear of the van and pulled the door closed behind him. Chief Inspector Garcia's face peered in at them through one of the two square windows, brow knitted with worry. The stench of sweat and urine filled the small space, but the man shackled to the bench didn't seem to notice and seemed barely to care that Hugo was there. Gregor Freed sat with his elbows on his knees, his head drooped, his eyes fixed on the dirty floor.

"Mind if I sit down?" Hugo asked.

Freed grunted but didn't move.

"Thanks. I have one question for you," Hugo said mildly. "And don't worry, it's not about you or your little business. I'll leave the cops to handle that." He paused, but Freed gave no acknowledgement that he'd heard. "I'm interested in your friend, Nisha Bhandari. Nice scheme, to leave you stuffed in a can like so much tuna while she makes her getaway."

Freed's head shifted, just an inch, but enough to let Hugo know he was listening. And interested. Hugo continued as if he'd not noticed. "I mean, I know she's coldhearted, but leaving you as the decoy, as bait even. What are you, Gregor, some goat tethered to a stake for us to find and chew up?"

Freed turned his head and threw a hard stare at Hugo, but something in the man's eyes wavered, an uncertainty settling in, a seed of doubt nestling into soft earth. Hugo gave him a sympathetic smile and kept talking. "The police have locked down the airport, are watching the train stations, and patrols will be all over the main roads. If I were you, I'd be pretty mad at being duped like that, sucking up all our time and attention so that she can fly away into the sunset."

Freed snorted and shook his head.

"That's it, isn't it?" said Hugo. "She's literally flying away and leaving you to rot in a tin can on the ocean. And now, Gregor, you get to move from that tin can to another one, a jail cell. Could be there for the rest of your life, too."

Freed shuffled his feet. "In that case, why should I tell you anything?"

"Because I can help you. I don't want much, just one little thing, and in exchange you have my word I'll tell the chief inspector that you cooperated." Freed gave a deep sigh but said nothing. "Not much time here, Gregor."

Freed turned and looked at Hugo. "I used to be a footballer, did you know that?"

"No, and right now I'm not very interested in your life story."

"I was good, quick feet. They used to say I was like that guy on the Flintstones when I ran. But I wasn't quite good enough, and I liked to eat. Got to be, some of the time I would dance past the defenders and some of the time I'd fall flat on my face. Ach, I think I fell flat on my face again."

"Listen to me." Hugo leaned closer, his teeth clenched. "This isn't about you. It's about me getting my hands on the woman who kidnapped one of the most precious people in my life. Which means that either you help me, and help yourself in the process, or you can sit there feeling sorry for yourself, stinking of piss, and telling me stories that waste my time. You do the former, I will do what I can for you; but if you don't, I will do everything in my power to make sure that you spend every single day of the rest of your life in prison."

Freed stared at the floor again. "Fine. You said you had one question? You might as well ask. I will help if I can."

"Which airport is she flying out of?"

"I don't understand. You said you had the airport covered."

"You taught her to fly, and right now I'm guessing she's very grateful."

"Wait, you think . . . she's taken my plane?"

"That's exactly what I think. Where do you keep it?" Freed stared at Hugo as his cohort's plan sank in, but Hugo didn't have time to waste. "There are dozens of airfields and airports within a hundred miles of Barcelona. If you keep stalling, she'll be up and away—we may never catch her. She'll sell your plane for a few thousand in cash and you'll be here, with us."

"Saucedo Airport, it's about sixty kilometers away."

"Thank you." Hugo pulled out his phone and opened the Notes application. "When did you last fly it?"

"Me? About two weeks ago. Why?"

"Just wondered. What kind of plane is it? What markings?"

"It's a Piper PA-44-180 Seminole. Registration is EC-FLP."

Hugo tapped in the information as Freed spoke. When he'd finished, Hugo opened the van doors and stepped out to a waiting Garcia.

"You need to get on to the Saucedo Airport right now. Have them ground a Piper PA-44-180 Seminole, registration EC-FLP."

Garcia stepped away and made the call, pacing as he moved up the chain of command. After a moment, he barked a question and strode over to Hugo as he listened to the reply.

"*Gracias*," he said. He covered the phone's mouthpiece and spoke to Hugo. "The plane's there, but they don't have security, there's not much they can do except deny permission to take off."

"Dammit. Tell them to stall as best they can, make any excuse, weather-related, contaminated fuel, whatever."

"Will do." Garcia relayed the instructions and hung up. "I told them we're on the way. We should call local police and have them head that way."

Hugo was already moving toward the gaggle of police cars. "And risk them using lights and sirens to scare her into the air?"

"We can tell them not to." Garcia trotted beside him.

"Will they listen?"

"Probably. But the manager thinks he can delay her for thirty minutes."

"Good, because *probably* doesn't cut it. We need to get there as fast as we can."

"We'll take mine," Garcia said, pointing, "the large one." He called to Luna, who was talking to a group of his men. Garcia shouted instructions in Spanish, and Luna responded immediately, directing his men into three of the SUVs. Grace Silva tumbled into the back seat of Garcia's car a heartbeat before the chief inspector gunned the engine.

"Not leaving without me," she said, panting and strapping herself in. "Where are we going?"

Hugo turned in his seat and grinned at her. "Hold on tight, we're headed to a small airport to try and stop Bhandari from getting away."

"She flies a plane?" Silva asked.

"Gregor Freed was nice enough to teach her."

"Why didn't they go together?"

"Because she's not interested in saving anyone but herself, and he made a very nice distraction for us."

"Clever *puta*," Silva said. "Any idea where she's going?"

"None," Hugo said. "Which is why we need to stop her."

CHAPTER THIRTY-FOUR

The airfield lay north of Barcelona, which meant cutting a path through the city's morning traffic. The four police vehicles stuck close together, lights and sirens scaring the cars in front of them out of their way, the little convoy writhing and snapping like a snake as it swung through the lanes, occasionally onto the hard shoulder, then back onto the road proper.

When they were clear of the airport, Garcia's phone rang. He'd put in a call to the police department's air unit, requesting help in case Bhandari took off. They'd finally called him back, and Hugo suffered through a rapid-fire Spanish conversation.

"They will help, but not quickly enough. We have two planes and three helicopters. One of the helicopters is available and has a pilot, but he won't get there before we do. And I'm not sure what he can do on his own, anyway."

"Follow her if she takes off."

"Of course, and as best he can, but she'll be flying faster."

"How about the military?"

"I asked about that. They won't get involved unless there's a known threat to the public or a violation of airspace. Like when she doesn't follow her flight plan or tries to fly into another country."

"She's probably going to do both of those things, Bartoli, so they need to scramble."

Garcia snorted. "I said the same thing, but they are a reactive force.

I mean, they won't stop a plane before it commits some act like that, only after."

"By which time she'll be in Romania or Libya."

Garcia waved a hand in frustration. "I told them that, too. They didn't listen."

"One helicopter? I guess we'll have to do this ourselves, then."

Hugo held on tight as they rocketed along the highway, his eyes shifting between the sea of red tail lights ahead and the clock on the car's dash. When the cars ahead parted and the road opened up, he felt flashes of hope, but inevitably the morning free-for-all closed around them again, causing both Hugo and Bartoli Garcia to mutter their curses as if they were prayers to a mischievous god of transportation.

Garcia swerved into the middle lane and accelerated between two eighteen-wheelers, cursing at the one in the passing lane. He checked his mirror to make sure the other cars had followed, then grunted in satisfaction. "The storage unit, I meant to ask you. Did Bhandari also kill Delia Treviño?"

"She or one of her people, yes. And before you ask me why, I can only guess for now. Drive a little quicker and you can ask her yourself."

"Doing what I can," Garcia said. "In the meantime, take a guess."

"A guess? OK. I'd say Treviño was involved pretty heavily. Male pimps usually have an enforcer who's a woman, someone to befriend and then basically bully the new girls into behaving. She certainly has the history for that role. Anyway, I'd guess that Treviño pissed her boss off, either threatened to go to the cops or wanted a larger slice of the pie."

"A business dispute," Garcia said drily.

"Or maybe an attempted takeover, who knows?" Hugo said. "Either way, a bad idea. And Leo's jump makes more sense now, too. If he didn't do it himself, he knew Bhandari would. He simply had no way out."

Garcia suddenly slammed on the brakes to avoid rear-ending the car in front, which eventually responded to the lights and sirens and edged out of his way. "These damn people," he said. "They should take the train, or bus."

Hugo smiled and decided to distract himself by calling Claudia.

"Hey, handsome," she said. "I texted you a while back, ignoring me?"

"Not intentionally, sorry."

"Busy right now?" she asked.

"Stuck in traffic, as it happens."

"I hear sirens, is there an accident?"

"Those are ours. We're trying to get to a small airport, but apparently sirens here are an invitation to drive slowly in front of us." Beside Hugo, Garcia chuckled. "Anyway, I'm calling to let you know we found Amy, she was in a shipping container. She's alive."

"Oh, thank God, Hugo. Will she be OK?"

"Yes, poor baby is in bad shape, but physically she'll be fine. I called Bart straight away, he's beside himself with relief."

"So you were right about the trafficking thing."

"Well, we also found Gregor Freed in the container. He's not talking, but yeah, I think it's pretty clear now what they were up to."

"Do you think there were other girls?"

"I do. I just hope we can get one of them to talk, maybe track down other victims and get them back." Hugo sighed, tried to block out the image of other girls stuffed into those containers. "Where are you?"

"Distracting Tom."

"From what?"

"Pretty much everything, but mostly coming to find you."

"If we make it to the airport in time, he's gonna be mad about missing the catch."

"Is that where Bhandari is?"

"Yes." The car surged forward as the traffic in front of them parted. "I should go. I'll call once we find her." He stated it as an absolute, as if there was no doubt this would happen, but the trip was taking too long and Bhandari would get suspicious if there were too many delays at the airfield.

"Please do," she said. "In the meantime, I'll forget to tell Tom where you're going, and why."

"I'd appreciate that." When he'd hung up, Hugo looked automatically at the clock. "How much farther?"

"Twenty kilometers, maybe a little more. The roads should be emptier as we head north; I think we'll be there in less than fifteen minutes." Garcia's phone rang, and he pushed the speaker button. Hugo listened, understanding enough to know it was the airport manager but not getting the gist of the message. He did hear the stress in the man's voice, though. When he hung up, Garcia glanced across at Hugo. "Sounds like we need to make that ten minutes, not fifteen."

"What happened?"

"He sold her the line about possibly contaminated fuel, which had her waiting at the hanger. But then another plane took off, one that she'd seen fueling up."

"Dammit, how did that happen?"

"Yeah, not smart, but he's not a law-enforcement officer and he feels bad."

"She's ready to go?"

"Pretty much. He's going to send out two planes ahead of her and ask one to stall, but the other planes are small and she could always go around."

Hugo looked out of the window. "Ten minutes it is, then. How do you want to do this?"

"Without hesitating." He smiled grimly. "Shock and awe, as you might say."

"As best we can, anyway," Hugo agreed.

"*Bueno.* I'll tell the men behind us that we'll be going in hot, straight to the runway."

Garcia radioed the other cars, giving them information and instructions. When he put down the handset, he said, "I told them we'd try and get in front of the plane, along with Miguel's car. The other two will flank her, keep her in a nice straight line."

"Good. I saw a sign for our exit, one kilometer."

"Already? *Bueno.*" Garcia guided his vehicle to the right lane, the traffic in front of them gliding left to give him and the three SUVs behind a clear run off the highway. "It's not even five kilometers from here."

"Time to kill the bells and whistles, then."

"The what?" Garcia asked.

"I'm sorry, lights and sirens."

"Ah yes." He reached to the panel on the car's ceiling and snuffed out the siren, then the lights.

Hugo turned in his seat and saw that the cars behind had done the same thing. He could hear the car's engine now, an angry roar that took them down the exit ramp and onto a narrower road, one that had probably been the main path into and out of Barcelona before the highway had been built. The traffic was lighter here, especially going north, and Hugo felt the tension rising in himself, but also coming off Garcia, who gripped the wheel with both hands and stared at the road ahead. It was as if the quelling of the siren signaled the start of the action, the way a gun started a sprint or a whistle kicked off a big game. Silence like this meant they were heading into enemy territory, hoping to see their prey before they were seen. Hoping, at this point, just to be there in time.

A road sign told them they were close, three kilometers from the airport, and Garcia barely slowed to make the hard right turn onto the small road that would get them there. Hugo pulled out his phone and tapped on the map function. He zoomed in to where they were, trailing his finger on the screen to bring up the airfield. He studied it for a moment.

"OK, this should be pretty straightforward," Hugo said. "The main gate will be open, right?"

"The manager said it is, yes."

"Good. This road dead-ends into the airfield. When we go through the gate, the main office building will be to our left, that's where your manager is. Also on the left is the fueling station."

"The runway?"

"That'll be straight ahead of us. This scale put it at about a thousand meters long. On the right are three hangars, and looks like maybe a repair shop or something. Planes access the runway via a paved section, it connects with the center of the runway so they have to taxi north or south, turn around, and then accelerate to take off."

It was Garcia's turn to glance at the clock. "We're about two minutes away, time for one last check-in with the manager." He hit the redial button on his phone, and the manager's voice came on the line almost immediately. "*¿Dónde está?*" Garcia asked, and Hugo understood that much. *Where is she*?

He missed the reply, though, garbled out by the man who seemed at panic's edge. Garcia's voice was calm in reply, almost soothing. But when he hung up, Hugo could see the tension in his body. "She's done waiting. He was watching her out of the window; she's moving to the access ramp to the runway. There's one plane ahead of her trying to go slow, but at some point it'll need to accelerate, either to stop her passing it on the tarmac or to make sure it takes off safely."

"Remind me to hand those guys medals when this is over."

"If we catch her."

"Whether we catch her or not, they've gone above and beyond to help us."

"That's true," Garcia said. "If she's on the runway when we get there, are we going to shoot at it?"

"At the plane?" Hugo shook his head. "I don't think so, not if we can help it. We don't need a hundred gallons of airplane fuel exploding all over us."

"The airfield!" Garcia exclaimed. The trees on either side of them fell away, and the road opened up to reveal the chain-link fencing of the small airfield. Garcia touched the brakes as they flew through the main gate, giving Hugo a second to scan the office buildings to his left and the hangars to his right before turning his attention to the runway, directly ahead of them.

"There she is," Hugo said, pointing. A small plane was at the junction where the approach met the runway, at its midpoint. To its right, and Hugo's, a Cessna sat at the head of the runway, and Hugo could hear the rev of its engines. But Bhandari's Piper edged forward, like a car in traffic, and Hugo guessed she'd been waiting for the Cessna to take off for several minutes and was running out of patience.

The Cessna revved louder, as if recognizing the police presence, welcoming it. But Bhandari had seen them, too. Her plane shifted forward, making the runway proper and turning right toward the Cessna. Bhandari steered the plane down the middle of the tarmac as if she knew the Cessna would just sit and wait.

"How much room does she need to take off?" Garcia asked.

"I'd guess most of it, it's not very long," Hugo said, "but—"

He cut himself off as Bhandari answered for him. They were a hundred yards from the runway, and Hugo watched as her plane turned, swiveling in place to point south into the wind. She'd seen them, known they would cut her off if she used the whole runway, and she must have known she didn't need to.

Her twin engines growled and snapped in anger, and the little plane lurched forward, picking up speed as Garcia and the three SUVs behind hurtled toward the runway, trying to get ahead of her. It was a crazy game of chicken, Hugo thought, and Bhandari had nothing to gain by losing.

"We're not going to make it," Garcia said.

"Cut left—go at the runway in a diagonal. You won't have to slow down."

Forty yards from the intersection with the runway, Garcia angled to the left, and the car bumped from the tarmac onto the grass, its tail sliding out before the wheels gripped the dry earth and propelled them forward. Hugo looked out of his window and saw the tiny figure of Nisha Bhandari in the cockpit, alone at the controls. They were closing in on her, and she on them, and Hugo had the sensation that the spinning propellers were sucking the car into them, intent on its destruction.

The car took one more bounce as it left the grass for the runway, a hundred yards or less from the end of it, and behind him, Grace Silva swore as her head hit the roof of the car. Garcia jinked to the right, trying to stay ahead of the plane, but it was almost on them, bearing down on Hugo's side, the spinning blades of the nearest propeller ripping the air just feet away and the nose of the plane like a cannonball headed straight for him. Hugo gripped the handle by his head and willed the plane to slow, to change direction, even to crash off the runway, but it was there, its engines screaming with fury, and he opened his mouth to shout at Garcia—tell him to slow, to stop, that it was too late.

And in a flash the plane was gone.

The wheels lifted from the tarmac and disappeared above them, the plane's shadow flickering over the windshield as it fought to gain height. The police cars screeched to a halt in a line across the runway, all eyes on the little white plane. Hugo opened his door and stepped out onto the tarmac, and several other policemen, including Garcia and Silva, did the same. Hugo's eyes flicked back and forth between the plane and the tree line in front of it.

"She's not high enough," he said to Garcia. "She's not going to make it."

Garcia hesitated, then picked up his radio handset and rattled off a command, and Hugo heard the word *ambulancia*. For the next few seconds, time seemed suspended. The Piper's engines howled with the effort of taking the plane higher, and its climb was in slow motion, the trees looming over it, surrounding it. For a moment, Hugo thought he'd been wrong because the nose of the plane crested the first line of trees like a drowning man surfacing, and the plane seemed to shudder with relief. But the climb had been too steep and the plane was laden with fuel and, no doubt, Bhandari's escape provisions. It seemed to pause in the air for a fraction of a second, like it wanted to float on the morning breeze, and then the nose dipped and the rest of the plane followed, a graceless flop into a forest of pine trees, and the airfield echoed with the eerie cracking and snapping of wood as the plane crashed through the branches below it.

The sound of the plane hitting the ground reached them as a muffled *whump*, and Hugo braced himself for an explosion. When it didn't come, he turned to Garcia. "Come on, we have to find a way in there."

A wire fence ran between the end of the runway and the trees, with no gate or way through from where they were. Luna snapped out instructions to the occupants of one of the SUVs, and Hugo presumed it was to have them wait at the airfield, lock it down, and ensure no witnesses to either the escape or the crash left. The other two cars took off for the airfield entrance with a squeal of tires. They turned right out of the gate onto a grass verge, and followed it along the boundary of the fence. The vehicles bounced and jumped, but the track was wide enough to take them to the tree line where the runway ended. The officers leapt from the cars, Hugo, Silva, and Garcia leading the way.

"There!" Silva spotted a path into the trees, not much more than an animal track, and they took it single file. A low boom reached them, and moments later a plume of dark smoke appeared over their heads, tinging the air with the acrid smell of burning rubber and plastic.

"She hit the first line of trees," Hugo shouted over his shoulder. "She can't be far." But the trees grew thick and tall here, and the brush between them made the going slow. They shuffled and swore and ducked their way along the trail, and after five minutes, one of the men behind Hugo spotted the chimney of smoke to their right. They all turned and walked side by side through the trees, stopping as one when the white of the plane appeared. Luna drew his pistol, and several of his men did the same. It was a precaution, of course, but Hugo wasn't concerned about being unarmed or being in danger—he was sure Bhandari was no longer a threat, and he trusted Luna's men would make sure of that if he was wrong.

They closed in on the wreckage, and Hugo said to Garcia, "Tell them to keep an eye out for flames. There's a hundred gallons of gas in that thing, we don't need anyone else killed."

Garcia relayed Hugo's instructions, and one of the men said something in reply. Garcia translated for Hugo. "He's a pilot. He said the fuel tanks are in their own compartments with fire walls. He says one already went up, and unless the fire wall on the other tank is broken, we should be safe."

Hugo gave him a wry smile. "'Should be,' eh? I suppose that's good enough."

They pressed forward, circling the plane. Both wings had broken off, the left was black and burned, and it stuck upright as if pretending it were a tree. Two of the plane's propellers were twisted, and the others were missing, snapped off and lying on the forest floor somewhere. As they closed in, Hugo saw Nisha Bhandari. She was little more than a shadow, a silhouette that looked to be strapped into the pilot's seat, motionless. He couldn't tell if she was bleeding; he wasn't that close. He kept his eyes on her and stepped past the nose of the plane, which had been sheared off and lay twenty feet from the rest of the wreckage. The door to the cabin was partially open, but the tilt of the plane had it wedged into the earth. Miguel Luna gestured to two of his men, who moved to the front of the cockpit with their pistols trained on the unmoving figure inside. He and another officer worked to open the door, pushing and pulling, rocking the fuselage and finally wrenching open the door wide enough to clamber in.

Miguel Luna went in first and by himself. He headed straight to Bhandari, and Hugo could see him moving around, but not much more. In less than a minute, he was outside again.

"*Está muerta*," he said. *She's dead.*

"You're sure?" Hugo asked.

Luna spoke in Spanish and Garcia translated. "He said she has no pulse and it looks like her neck is broken. Her legs are pretty messed up, too, a lot of blood."

"I need to see for myself," Hugo said. Without waiting for a reply, or permission, he moved to the door and climbed into the plane. Broken glass littered the cramped passenger compartment, crunching under his feet, and the acrid smell of burned plastic wrinkled his nose as he moved to the front of the plane, his eyes fixed on Nisha Bhandari.

Even before he reached her, Hugo knew she was dead. Her head lay at an impossible angle, the back of her skull resting on her left shoulder, lifeless eyes staring blankly up at the ceiling. Luna had gone above and beyond in feeling for a pulse, but Hugo did the same thing, as much out of habit as necessity. He almost recoiled at the warmth of her skin, as if it were harboring her life still, but Hugo reminded himself that most of the bodies he'd touched were long dead. Feeling no pulse, he withdrew his hand and perched for a moment on one of the passenger seats.

He looked out through the window at the forest, at the police officers stepping over debris from the plane and the broken limbs of pine trees, a couple of the men on their phones, the others just looking around at the crash scene. A sadness swept over him, and a powerful sense of frustration that made him ball his fists and want to punch the remaining glass out of the plane. But he took several calming breaths, telling himself he'd done all he could to bring her in alive. He took one last look at the waxen, unreal head of Nisha Bhandari and eased himself out of the plane. Garcia stood there, waiting for him.

"She's definitely dead," Hugo said.

"Forgive me if I don't shed a tear," Garcia said.

"Don't worry, I won't either. Not for her."

They stood in silence for a moment, then Garcia said quietly, "There's never justice in death, is there?"

"I've never seen any," Hugo said quietly, remembering the conversation they had before. "And when the bad ones die, they might stop hurting people but they leave us with too many questions that we can't answer."

They stood side by side in silence, staring at the wreckage. Two men who knew everything about losing the good to the bad, who already lived with unanswered questions and the shared belief that even though Nisha Bhandari had lost her life, she'd escaped justice.

CHAPTER THIRTY-FIVE

The next afternoon, Hugo went to the hospital, pleased to see a police presence, one Chief Inspector Garcia had offered before Hugo could ask for it. Until they knew the full extent of the human-trafficking ring, Hugo wasn't about to leave Amy dangling out there as a loose end for some unknown trafficker to tie off. The two guards outside Amy's door recognized Hugo immediately—they'd been part of the expedition to the airfield—and they both saluted, backing the gesture up with friendly smiles. Hugo shook hands with both of them and pushed open the door to Amy's room.

Bart Denum looked up, and Amy turned her head, their eyes drifting from Hugo's face to the large bouquet of flowers in his left hand. He set them on a table at the end of her bed.

"Flowers," Denum said, shaking his head and smiling. "Hugo, you saved her life. You didn't have to bring flowers." He stood and walked over to Hugo, wrapping him in a giant bear hug. When he spoke, his voice was a whisper. "I don't know how to thank you, my friend. I owe everything to you."

"No, you don't," Hugo said. "You guys are family. What the heck was I supposed to do?"

Denum released him and went back to Amy's side. Hugo moved to the bed, and she held up a hand.

"He's right, Hugo. Thank you." Her eyes were glistening with tears, but the smile was there, too.

"You have some color in your cheeks already," Hugo said, taking her hand and sitting beside her.

"I'm OK," she said. "Lost a little weight and I have this urge for pancakes."

Hugo laughed. "I'll take you back to Paris, then. I believe I know where we can find some."

"Can't wait," she said. "Although Dad says he's moving back there with me, to keep an eye on me."

"Just for a while," Denum said, his tone serious. "A year or two, that's all."

Amy rolled her eyes, but they all laughed. "I think I learned my lesson, Dad, but thanks."

"And I'll be there," Hugo said.

"Then that's good enough for me," Denum smiled.

"So, did you give a statement yet?" Hugo asked Amy.

"This morning, but we didn't get through everything. That nice chief inspector said he'd be back this afternoon."

"Bartoli Garcia?" Hugo asked.

"Yes, I think so."

"I knew his brother, in Paris."

"He told me," Amy said. "He's pretty high on you, Hugo."

"Thanks, he's not so bad himself." He hesitated, then asked, "Do you mind if I ask a couple of things? Just for my own knowledge. I won't hold you to anything or cross-examine you, I promise."

"Sure."

"Thanks. I think I have a handle on most of what happened, but I'm not completely clear on Rubén Castañeda's role in all this."

Amy gave him a weak smile. "That's funny you should say that. For a while, he didn't know his role, either."

Hugo looked at her quizzically. "What do you mean?"

"Rubén was vain, charming, and probably a sex addict." She turned to her father. "Sorry, Daddy, you may not want to hear some of this."

Denum squeezed her hand. "I think you might be right. I'll go find some coffee, leave you guys to talk. You want anything, either of you?"

They both shook their heads and waited until he'd left the room. "You were saying," Hugo prompted.

"Yes. He was very involved in adult entertainment. It paid well, and it satisfied something in him." She flashed Hugo a look. "Just to be clear, he and I never . . ."

Hugo held up his hands in surrender. "You're a grown-up, Amy. What you do or don't do isn't my business."

"Well, I just felt like I should say that. You may know I ended up dancing in Paris, which wasn't the best. That's why I went with Rubén, when he said there was better work in Barcelona."

"But why did you skip out like that? Without telling anyone."

"Partly because I knew everyone would try to change my mind, to stop me. It sounds crazy, suddenly going to a new city with a guy I just met, so I knew you and Dad, him especially, would try and talk me out of it. But I couldn't exactly explain, tell him I was stripping in a bar to make money, so how could I explain this was going to be a step up?"

"You could have canceled our breakfast plans by e-mail, you know."

"But Rubén was supposed to talk to you, explain it all. That way you'd know, without being able to talk me out of it." She sighed. "It made sense at the time, I promise."

A lot of crazy things do at your age, Hugo thought. He said, "The important thing is, you're safe."

"So what do you think now, about him being involved?" Amy asked.

"It sounds to me like he was bringing girls to work at sex clubs, maybe as waitresses, that kind of thing. Then Bhandari was essentially taking them. I'm betting he got suspicious, maybe went to some of the places where his clients were supposed to have been working and they weren't there. More to the point, if he'd asked, no one would have known where they'd gone."

"As sex slaves. My God, how awful."

"So what happened when you got here?"

"I heard him argue with her, on the phone. We were at his apartment, and she said she was coming over to talk, and that was the last time I saw him."

"You didn't see what happened to him?"

"No, after that phone call, he told me to go explore, and when I got back, she was waiting for me in the street. She said she wanted to talk, so we went for coffee. At the time, it didn't seem strange because she was so nice to me, asked about where I thought I'd be working, that kind of thing. Said she and Rubén had a miscommunication, but all was fine. Another guy showed up, big guy, she left me there at the café with him."

"Who was it?"

She wrinkled her brow in thought. "Thing is, I don't know. I don't know who it was or why he was there. The next few hours are a blank, so like I told that Inspector Garcia, I think she or he drugged me. When I woke up, I was in a small room."

"The storage unit?" *Or Freed's office?*

"It was dark, I don't know. I had no idea what was going on, didn't even really click that she was behind it. Honestly, it sounds crazy, but I had no clue what was going on."

"Perfectly understandable, actually," Hugo said. "Rubén didn't share his fears with you, but I'm betting he was trying to protect you."

"Yes, he must have been. He gave me his phone when I went out that day, and they didn't search me, not after they took my own phone. Not at first, anyway." She gave a gentle laugh. "I knew you'd be looking, that my dad would make you look."

Hugo smiled. "Of course. On both counts. And I don't want to tire you out now, I can read your statement later and maybe fill in any blanks over those pancakes. I just wanted to know whether Rubén Castañeda was one of the good guys or the bad guys."

"He was slow to understand, I guess. But he wasn't part of that gang, Los Matadores, that the inspector mentioned."

"I'm not even sure there was a gang," Hugo said. "If so, we'll find them. Poor Rubén, serving girls up to be trafficked, and he had no idea. The reluctant matador."

He turned as the door opened. Chief Inspector Garcia and Grace Silva walked in and shook hands with Hugo, the latter holding on to Hugo's hand a shade longer than was necessary, he thought.

"How's the patient?" Garcia asked.

"I'm tired," Amy said. "But happy to be here. You have more questions?"

"Of course," Garcia said. "But we'll take it slow, just answer as many as you can handle." He shot Hugo a stern look. "You've not been inter-rogating her, have you?"

Hugo looked sheepish. "I wasn't planning to, but I may have been a little curious."

"Well, get out of here so we can do our thing and not tire poor Amy out more than we have to. I'll brief you later, and if I've forgotten to ask anything, I'm sure you'll let me know."

Hugo stood. "No doubt, it'd be my pleasure."

He leaned over and kissed Amy's forehead, and she squeezed his hand. "Thank you, Hugo. Not just for finding me, but for being there for my dad. I don't know how he would have coped without you, without knowing you were there."

"You're welcome. Now tell these nice people everything you know, and I'll come see you tomorrow morning."

♉

He took a cab back into the Old Town, to a café off Carrer d'Allada Vermell, where Claudia had agreed to meet him. On the way, he dialed Tom.

"You bastard," Tom said. "You cut me out of the action!"

"Yeah, see, I was thinking this was all about finding Amy and stop-ping a human-trafficking ring."

"Boy Scout."

"Thanks."

"You know what, Hugo. Just this once I'll forgive you." Tom's tone softened. "You did well, man, especially the pressure you were under. Being her friend, and all. You did really well."

"Thanks. And you know I appreciate your help."

"Such as it was. Next time I get to sleep with the beautiful but evil mastermind, deal?"

"She's all yours," Hugo said. "But let's be real clear, I didn't sleep with her."

"Right, sure. Whatever."

"What are you up to?"

"I gotta head back. The Company has a little job for me to do in Romania, of all places. Courier job, which could mean illegal currency, documents, holding the hand of a new spy, or some bad guy's head in a container."

"Delightful."

"I was kidding about the last one. I'm hoping for a fresh, young spy, a beautiful rookie who needs guidance."

"Whatever it is, I wish you luck," Hugo said. "Unless it's the fresh, young spy. Unless it's a dude."

"You could be more supportive of my career goals, you know."

Hugo laughed. "I'm on my way to see Claudia, I'll check in with you later."

"Give her my love. And I need to clear the apartment by tomorrow lunch, so factor that into your little chat with her, will you?"

The taxi pulled to the curb. "I'll be sure to do that." He hung up, handed some bills to the driver, and walked into the café. Claudia had found them a table by the window, and she rose to greet him with a kiss.

"How's Amy?" she asked.

"She'll be great. Talking to the police right now."

"You don't want to be there for that?"

"Yes and no," Hugo said. "All I wanted to do was find her, I can guess most of the details, and the ones I can't guess, I can get from her or Bartoli later."

A waiter arrived, and Hugo ordered coffee for them both. When he'd gone, Claudia said, "Well, I can't guess them. Honestly, I've got no idea how this all happened, so would you mind explaining a couple of things?"

"Sure, what do you want to know?"

"Tell me about Nisha Bhandari."

"Nice girl," Hugo said with a wry smile. "A little misguided, perhaps."

"Was she a psychopath?"

"That term is overused, if you ask me. Most people who do bad things aren't psychopaths, they're just greedy or stupid or find themselves in a place where they think it's OK to act badly because no one's watching. Or so they assume."

"Which of those applied to her?"

"Honestly," Hugo said. "I think she might have been one of the few psychopaths I've come across."

"Why do you say that?"

Images of Nisha Bhandari flashed through his mind. The sleek body in the cream dress, the bristling woman annoyed at her yoga being interrupted, the clever businesswoman happy to show churches to old women and provide strippers to old men. And then there was the stuff he'd not seen, because she'd been able to hide it. The ability to kill and feel nothing, to stage a crime scene, and seduce most of the people around her.

"One of the chief attributes of psychopaths is charm. That and the ability to manipulate people around them. She slept with Rubén Castañeda to get control over him, and for access."

"Access?"

"To what he was thinking. Men are known to be closed emotionally, but most guys open up at the start of a relationship."

"I need to remember that," Claudia smiled.

"Yeah, you should. Anyway, I'm betting as soon as she saw he was suspicious of her, she hopped into bed with him. She used sex to snare Leo Barsetti, too. I'm betting she met Delia Treviño at the yoga studio and somehow found out about her past. Maybe blackmailed her or paid her to sleep with Leo, and filmed it to have leverage over him."

"That's cold."

"It is. And that's the other chief attribute of the psychopath. Zero empathy. She didn't care, wasn't capable of caring, that by blackmailing him into silence—"

"Wait, Leo Barsetti knew about the trafficking?"

"I'm guessing he found out; it's the only thing that makes sense to me." Once again, Hugo felt the frustration of the grave, the silence of those who could have enlightened the living, completed the stories that were now left unfinished. "Only, he couldn't live with it. That's why he jumped, he was scared of going to prison for being complicit, and he felt horrible about not standing up to Bhandari."

"He could have gone to the police. At least told them what he knew."

"But that would have damned him, too. His wife would have found out he'd been sleeping with a prostitute, and, as she told us, that was the one thing she wouldn't tolerate."

"Do you know what happened to her?"

"There's an irony," Hugo said. "He sent her away. He wanted her gone from the city so she'd be safe. Bhandari had said something about Leo being less involved in the furniture business. I think that was on purpose, her design. Even so, he found out about the trafficking but couldn't say anything because by then she had that video of him. And I'd bet a million dollars she also convinced him that Los Matadores was real. That he couldn't escape them, and that his wife might also be in danger. He didn't even dare tell us."

"No wonder she was successful in business; she was quite the sales-woman." Claudia stirred her coffee. "So, tell me this is none of my business if you want, but Tom said something about you and her . . ."

Hugo leaned over and took her hand. "Yeah, for a moment there, it was close. She was . . . alluring, and knew how to use her charms." Hugo grinned. "Plus, a man has his needs, and when the girl he's really inter-ested in isn't available . . ."

"Oh, Hugo, tell me you didn't sleep with that psychopath!"

"I'm teasing you, of course I didn't." *Of course?* Hugo thought. *It was much closer than that.* "I was trying to rule her out. I needed to see if she'd been injured climbing out of Castañeda's window."

"Looking for cuts, eh?" Claudia said, a skeptical look on her face.

"Honestly," Hugo said. "That's all it was."

"I believe you. I think." She took a sip of coffee. "So what about the storage unit?"

"I'm not sure yet. I think probably Rubén rented it as a sort of safe house, in case he was right. A place to hide that was cheap and wouldn't require dealing with a landlord. Pretty good idea, to be honest. Anyway, that's why he gave the keys to his sister, just in case."

"But Bhandari found out?"

"Seemed she was good at that."

"And you're sure that matador stuff was made up?"

"The police here couldn't find any evidence of a gang so, yes, I'm betting it was the same as the kidney removal. Pure manipulation and distraction. Clever, too."

"You think?" She grimaced. "To me, it's just sick."

"It is that, for sure. But if she'd been arrested and taken to trial, it would have given her lawyers something else to point at. Several somethings, like gang wars and organ trafficking." He held up a hand. "I know, it sounds crazy, but I've been in courtrooms, I've seen jurors buy dumber theories than that."

They sat in silence for a moment. "It just doesn't make sense," Claudia said eventually. "How one person can decide that another human being is just an object. A piece of meat to be bought and sold. And not care about the misery they put that person through, their families."

"You remember what I said about psychopaths having no empathy? It's almost like it's not their fault. I mean, of course they can help their actions, control those, but they don't know the pain of losing someone. They don't feel fear the way we do, nor anxiety or stress. So for you and me, it'd be impossible to treat a person like that, but for someone like Nisha Bhandari, it really was the same as shipping furniture."

"Just more lucrative."

"A lot more lucrative. And slavery has been going on since the dawn of time. It's not like she was doing something that had never been done before. As horrible as it is, human slavery, in particular sex slavery like this, has been alive and well for thousands and thousands of years."

"What about Gregor Freed?"

"Ah, see, that's more interesting to me. I don't think he was a psy-

chopath, just very greedy and somewhat delusional. Maybe in love
with Nisha Bhandari, maybe he deluded himself about what they were
doing. I'll try and ask him." He took a sip of coffee. "She had him build
a little room at his shop, next to the office. I'm guessing it was to hold
people like Amy until they shipped them out. A slaver's mini prison."

Claudia shuddered. "Well, you put a stop to a couple of slavers,
whether he was delusional or psycho."

"Yep, with a lot of help from my friends." Hugo thought for a
moment, then pulled out his phone. "I need to call Camille Lerens. Do
you mind?"

"Only if I can eavesdrop."

"Sure thing." Hugo dialed and waited for the French policewoman
to pick up. "Camille, it's Hugo."

"*Salut.* What's up, is Tom in jail again, need bail money?"

"Maybe, I have no idea where he is."

"That's a bad sign." Her voice softened. "I heard you found your
friend Amy. I knew you would, Hugo, I'm so happy for you."

"Thanks, I appreciate that. And it's kind of why I'm calling."

"Oh yes? What can I do for you?"

"Other way around," Hugo said. "Did you solve that murder yet,
the girl in the river?"

"No, we're still looking for a boyfriend. We know she wasn't
married."

"While you're looking, keep your eyes open for a human-trafficking ring."

"Oh, *merde*, you think that's what happened to her?"

"I do. The marks on her body—they weren't cigarette burns, it was
someone's way of branding her—and her physical condition. I'd say
you're having trouble finding her boyfriend because she doesn't have one."

"Just a pimp."

"Or two, but yes. If your people are anything like the evil woman
down here, they're targeting foreign women, either bringing them in or
picking them up in Paris. That way, fewer people notice when they go
missing."

"That's pretty devious. But thanks, Hugo. We'll start looking in that direction, work with the gang people. When are you coming home?"

"A couple of days," Hugo said. He held Claudia's eye. "I'm hanging out with a pretty girl, might try and take some time off and see what develops."

Claudia covered her mouth, her eyes wide as if scandalized.

After a few more words, Hugo rang off and sat back in his chair. All around them, the café was filling up, and Hugo felt a moment of great happiness. He was in a beautiful city just waiting to be explored, he was with Claudia and, now that Amy was safe and Tom was leaving, he could enjoy her company without distraction. If, of course, that's what she wanted.

They enjoyed the silence for a minute, watching people come and go. After a while, Hugo asked, "So, what do we do now?"

"I was thinking about that." Claudia played with her spoon. "I'm in no hurry to get back to Paris, are you?"

"Not really."

"Then, if you'd like, we can go to your bachelor pad, pack your things, and head to my hotel. Spend a few days in Barcelona together."

"Now that's what I call a great plan." Hugo said with a smile. He dropped some money on the table and stood. They stepped out of the café and started walking hand in hand.

"This is more like it," Hugo said. "Some peace and quiet, a pretty girl, and nothing on my schedule."

"Well, I'm no psycho," Claudia said, nudging him with an elbow. "But I'll try and keep you entertained."

Hugo laughed. "One psycho per trip for me. It's a very firm limit."

"Well then, if that's the case, we'll be just fine."

"Yes," Hugo said. "That's exactly what I was thinking."

ACKNOWLEDGMENTS

I'd like to thank the usual suspects, and some new ones. First, my wife, Sarah, and the kids for making my research trip to Barcelona the most wonderful family vacation. Er, research trip. My thanks, also, to the people who willingly loaned me their names to be characters—what a fun game that has been, and long may it continue. Especially when I bump you off in future books.

Sincere thanks, also, to Craig Carlson, owner of the Breakfast in America restaurants in Paris, for giving Hugo a place to satisfy his pancake cravings. And to George Farris, of Above and Beyond Aviation here in Austin for your advice on how to crash a plane in the right way. Thank you, too, Bill Hensel, for the information about ports and containers, which was invaluable. Thanks to my Spanish translator, the real Rosario Figueroa, not just for your quick responses but also for the time and thought you put into the help you gave me. And on the gory side of things, thank you, Dr. Satish Chundru, for advising on organ removal and other such delights. And also for acting like my questions weren't weird. And for not notifying the authorities about them. . . .

To my friends at Seventh Street Books who continue to work hard to make my journey as an author so wonderful, and to the thousands of dedicated book sellers across America, nay, throughout the world, who provide shelves for authors and new delights for readers. I could name dozens, but let me pick out Scott and Raul at BookPeople here in Austin; Brenda, John, Dean, and McKenna at Murder by the Book in Houston; Barbara at the Poisoned Pen in Arizona; and Pete at McIntyre's in North Carolina. To my agent, Ann Collette, my thanks always. Sorry for the dearth of chocolate last year; that will be remedied.

ABOUT THE AUTHOR

Mark Pryor is the author of *The Bookseller, The Crypt Thief, The Blood Promise,* and *The Button Man,* the first four Hugo Marston novels, and of the true-crime book *As She Lay Sleeping.* An assistant district attorney with the Travis County District Attorney's Office, in Austin, Texas, he is the creator of the true-crime blog *D.A. Confidential.* He has appeared on CBS News's *48 Hours* and Discovery Channel's *Discovery ID: Cold Blood.*

Visit him online at www.markpryorbooks.com, www.facebook .com/pages/Mark-Pryor-Author, and http://DAConfidential.com.

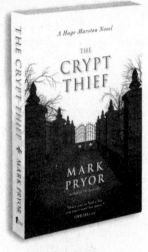
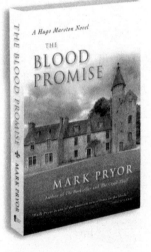